I0586553

YONKERS
Yonkers!

a story of race and redemption

by Patricia Vaccarino

Modus Operandi Books

Modus Operandi Books • New York

Published 2018 by Modus Operandi Books
www.modusoperandibooks.com

ISBN: 978-0-9963494-1-3
Library of Congress Control Number: 2017916029
Printed in the U.S.

Praise for Patricia Vaccarino's YONKERS Yonkers!

YONKERS Yonkers! reminds me of classics like "A Tree Grows in Brooklyn" and "To Kill a Mockingbird." This great story is about race and ethnicity in America during the 1960s and early 1970s. It was so detailed and intriguing that I felt like I was being drawn into someone's life. I felt for Herman Lynch. He faced a true struggle. He wasn't the best looking kid and he was black. He had many obstacles to confront, but because of his friendship with Cookie Colangelo, he is forced to straddle between two worlds: black and white. Today, the color lines are looser and it's cool to be a person of color. The Millennials don't see the world the way their parents or grandparents saw the world. And yet, there is a great history lesson here of what has changed and also of what has not changed...It's the notion... the more things change, the more things stay the same. The characters capture the collective Yonkers mindset of how people thought back then, and, in many ways, still think the same way about the world today.

—Wali Collins, Comedian, Actor, Author

YONKERS Yonkers! is a story of coming of age during the time of heavy drug use, Woodstock, Vietnam and the beginning of the civil rights movement as experienced by Cookie, a talented Italian girl in Yonkers, a town bordering New York City but culturally miles apart. Cookie, whose mother is mentally ill and whose father doesn't know how to cope with his two daughters, fends for herself. She recognizes prejudice and with her we learn the quirks of the close knit Italian population, the blacks in the projects who have to live carefully to stay alive, the negligently run Catholic schools, and here and there a teacher who does make a difference. This is a terrific book. I have never read a book that crawls so into the innards of ethnic groups showing their prejudices and fears. It is a great book for adults and young readers.

—Edith Lynn Hornik-Beer, Author/Journalist

As if by literary magic, Patricia Vaccarino's *YONKERS Yonkers!* acts as a time machine to give a keen view of people, place and period. The people are primarily the working class Italians of the place. The place is Yonkers, NY, a city in Westchester County just north, and in the shadow, of New York City. The period is the time of Woodstock, as the 1960s came to a close, and it takes the reader through the very early 1970s. Gum popping adolescent girls, their counterpart teenage schoolboys, the local suspected mob guy, the town gossip, and the ways that neighborhoods and even blocks functioned in those days are all depicted with crystal clarity.

Vaccarino's lyrical writing and flawless dialogue capture the essence of the life of these Yonkers girls in their early teens. There is humor, pathos, heartbreak, and great insight into how social morés and psychological and psychiatric advances have been made in the generation-plus since those years.

—Dean Landsman, Author, Digital Strategist

Here's an invitation to take a walk on the wild side—of hard-scrabble Yonkers, New York, in the late 1960s. The sharply defined characters who inhabit Yonkers play out their lives against a backdrop of Vietnam protesters marching in the streets, Richard Nixon and his Enemies List inhabiting the White House, and the music of Woodstock blaring from car radios. Think you know New York? Pick up a copy of this book; you'll be transported right to the heart of Yonkers.

—Linda Jay, Copyeditor/Copywriter

"I really enjoyed the book, so much of the dialogue sounded as if I was hearing my teenaged self speaking—it brought back a lot of memories and sort of transported me back to that time and to myself at that age."
—Deb Bowers Citrone, Educator, former Yonkers resident

YONKERS Yonkers! is a great book! Having grown up in Yonkers, I can attest to the fact that Patricia Vaccarino has managed to capture the essence of that city in the late 60's and early 70's, including the racial strife of the times. I knew people like Cookie Colangelo and her father Johnny, as well as guys like Herman Lynch. Whether it's describing the legendary Untermeyer Park or attending the Woodstock Festival, through her talented writing Patricia has a way of making you feel you were there. This book is a treasure!
—Jeffrey Gurian, Comedian/Radio Personality/Author

For Joseph M. Puggelli

and

In memory of my family and friends

with love

WHY ITALIAN GIRLS CRACK THEIR GUM

(An old man's symphony)

On the street the boys play bocci ball
Then the girls come
Wearing their midriff blouses
Close to their skin
Showing off their bellybuttons
Above skinny leathery pants
Too tight to take friction
from the ground
from clattering sparks
from Papagallo stiletto heels
Strutting down the pavement in Cha Cha steps
Pop, snap, crack, crack, sizzle-crack
The sound of those girls cracking their gum
Will drive you wild
Those girls call all the shots
And soon those boys see them coming
They get a funny look that comes over their faces
like they can't see nothing except those girls
And they can't see nothing because
Even though I'm an old man and I can't see nothing except
those girls
Nobody can see nothing except those girls
They are Italian Girls
And in the whole world there's nothing like them
Nothing.

—Concetta *"Cookie"* Colangelo, 1970

"You can't scare me. I was born in Yonkers."
—Derkquon Battle Aka Rapper *DQ the Don*

Welcome to the hood! I'm glad you decided to visit Yonkers. I've been wanting you to come by to say hello. Allow me to introduce myself. My name is Concetta Mary Bernadette Colangelo, but everyone calls me "Cookie." I'm scrappy enough to remove your left eyeball, your right lung, your trail of entrails (your guts) and your whole heart, as if only a small part of this organ could ever satisfy me. Aside from being a gangster, I am a hippie too. I'm going to Woodstock and no one's going to stop me.

One

Saturday, August 16, 1969

On the day that Woodstock erupted from being an ordinary rock concert to become a twentieth century hippie phenomenon, Cookie Colangelo was twelve years old. She learned about Woodstock from a news bulletin on TV. A special *CBS Evening News* report with Walter Cronkite broadcasted an update about a rock concert that was changing the world. And more than anything, Cookie wanted to change the world. As soon as she learned the news, Cookie put on her bellbottom jeans that had seventeen patches, including an upside down American flag plastered on her seat, and a white bubble tufted see-through peasant blouse over a tiny hot pink mesh bra. She was packing up her magenta tie-dyed cloth shoulder sack with snacks for the road, a pack of *Marlboros* in the red box, two books of matches, and a full pack of *Juicy Fruit* gum. As an afterthought, she added a pot of *Yardley* lip gloss in the shade *emphatic pink* to make her lips soft and kissable. Although wearing lip-gloss was not a hippie girl beauty trick, Cookie Colangelo wasn't an ordinary girl. She was an Italian girl, and all Italian girls know you always have to be at your best because you never know when you might meet an incredible boy.

More than anything, Cookie wanted to meet the *Blind Owl* Alan Wilson, the lead guitarist for the blues-rock band *Canned Heat*. He wore glasses and looked a lot like Cookie believed she looked. He had a round, owlish face, chubby cheeks, and mischief flickered in his eyes. Intelligent-looking was one way to describe the *Blind Owl*. In Cookie's estimation, he was wise and knew it was best to stay away from most people in this world because they weren't looking out for you.

I'm on the road again! Cookie hummed the *Blind Owl*'s most popular song.

Cookie was hell-bent on going to Woodstock and no one was going to stop her. Then an unexpected complication happened. Cookie's father, Johnny Colangelo, locked her inside of her bedroom. The door had been fitted with a bronze Dutch bolt that slid into place and locked the door without a key—from the outside. Cookie's father put a lock on the door so she would not join the mass exodus of hippies and wannabes jamming the New York State Thruway on the way to the rock festival in Bethel, New York. Cookie's father could be that way. He was Italian and his mission was to ensure that his daughter would forever remain a virgin. No small undertaking; Italian girls are not destined to be virgins for very long. Doomed from the onset, the nature of the Italian girl is to invite attention and advances, unwanted or otherwise, from the entire human species regardless of sex, age, religion, ethnicity, or national origin.

Although Cookie Colangelo was twelve and looked twelve, she fancied herself older, almost thirteen. She also had a propensity to brood about the nightmarish possibilities of spending the rest of her life in Yonkers. She sprawled across her bed and looked up at her brass headboard that resembled the bars of a prison cell. She was imprisoned in this room and looked around for the slimmest chance of escape. Her bedroom was painted a shade of faded rose with an off-white trim and her walls were decorated with posters. The largest poster was of a neon green peace symbol painted on a black background.

The green peace symbol was designed to glow in the dark, especially in a room illuminated by a blacklight.

One poster of the blues rock band *Canned Heat* had a profile shot of Alan Wilson looking baby-faced and innocent. Musicians called him the *Blind Owl,* presumably because he was smart and wore gigantic black-framed, coke-bottle eyeglasses. Another poster featured a fierce-looking Mick Jagger, larger and more prominent than the rest of the Rolling Stones. Brian Jones was shoved to the side. He had a soft bowl haircut and the fringe of his bangs turned under, covering his eyebrows, almost touching his eyes. Brian Jones' face looked puffy and his eyes looked tired, but it didn't matter; he was dead. The month before, Brian Jones had drowned in his own swimming pool. Drugs and foul play were suspected, but the exact circumstance leading to his death was never conclusive. Her gaze drifted to the poster of the *Blind Owl* where she wished he had the secret power to release her from captivity, like a bird poised for flight, so she could get on the road to Woodstock.

Cookie reached under her mattress and felt around until she found her tiny brass hash pipe, a spare that had never been used. She stuck it in her cloth shoulder sack. Her father had taken her primary hash pipe that had been lying out in the open, defiantly and triumphantly, on her plain brown walnut dresser. He had bent the hash pipe in half. He was too dumb to know she could still use it in a pinch.

She kept her most prized possessions under the mattress. There was a copy of the *Yonkers Herald Statesman* newspaper, dated July 20, 1969, the day the Apollo 11 became the first spaceflight to land human beings on the Moon. The entire front page of the newspaper was consumed by a grainy black & white photo showing astronaut Neil Armstrong planting an American flag on the face of the moon like he owned it. Under the mattress, a pair of Roman Catholic scapulars, a small card with a prayer to baby Jesus, and a hunk of rose quartz that Cookie had found in the backyard and considered to be a lucky talisman, and a 14-carat gold heart-shaped locket were shoved together in a loose collection. There was also a small vial of Quaaludes that Cookie called her *ludes* after she had stolen them from her Mother, who was too crazy to know the pills were missing. Cookie's most prized possession was her black & white notebook. She had several black & white notebooks. This one was the latest edition. Cookie had swirled Elmer's glue into the image of a peace sign and let it harden on the cover.

She had a modern-looking, wrought iron, low-to-the-ground, square-block-shaped bookcase full of classics, including Dostoevsky's *Crime and Punishment*, Einstein's *Theory of Relativity*, and A.S. Neill's *Summerhill School* that were far too sophisticated for a normal twelve-year old girl to read, especially an Italian girl from Yonkers. Cookie had checked out some of the books from the Yonkers Carnegie Library in Getty Square. She loved the old library and spent many hours walking in a circle around the second floor in the children's section of the rotund building. Truth be told, Cookie had not returned the books yet because she hadn't read them beyond the first few pages. Every so often, she trundled herself down to the grand library and renewed the books again.

Then one day—after her life changed due to a catastrophic event—she stopped renewing the books. She was a gangster now. She had already accrued fines far greater than the price of the books, but she did not care. She did like the way books looked on her bookshelf. The sight of these books made her feel noble, smart and on the verge of becoming famous.

Her little sister Donny rapped her tiny fist against the outside bedroom door, begging Cookie to come out and play. There was no one else for the little girl to keep company with. Her voice was impassioned and clear. "Please play with me, Cookie!" Cookie imagined Donny slumped outside of her bedroom door and thought of asking her to push a chair against the door so she could reach the latch and unlock it, but it was too much work. And if Johnny was around, the escape attempt would fail. She decided to ignore Donny's pleas. *Please Please*, Donny implored anyone who would listen, until her voice grew distant and faded away.

While the sound of her voice had departed, the little girl's image lingered in Cookie's mind. She loved Donny and at the same time she did not know what to do with her. Donatella "Donny" Colangelo had golden ringlets of hair curling around her head like a halo and blue eyes as translucent as glass. She didn't look Italian or Irish or anything in between. Cookie's parents had abandoned the both of them. The two girls were left on their own to raise themselves.

Cookie felt perpetual guilt over her little sister. She wasn't doing a very good job of raising her because she was doing a pretty piss-poor job of raising herself. Cookie and Donny Colangelo were not ordinary working-class kids growing up in Yonkers. Their mother was crazy, certifiably so, and their father was an Italian guy from the 'hood who had a career in the liquor business with a lifetime option to renew. His hobby playing drums and other percussion instruments for impromptu jam sessions had morphed into a second job that kept him out late most nights.

Cookie didn't know for sure whether she wanted to be a hippie or a gangster and flitted equally between the two personae on whim. She secretly loved one man: *Blind Owl* Alan Wilson. Cookie had not met him. He was so far removed from her world that she might never have the chance to meet him. And yet she was intent on meeting him. If only she met him, her life would be forever changed. The odds are, though, that if she did meet the Blind Owl, he would be frankly uninterested in her.

No breasts, no hips, Concetta Mary Bernadette Colangelo looked every inch of twelve with nothing to spare on top or bottom. Loving only one guy who was totally unavailable to her almost guaranteed she would remain a virgin for life. Unbeknownst to her father, Cookie's virginity was not in danger of being taken away, at least not in the immediate future. She had never even kissed a boy.

Actually, Cookie looked younger than twelve and could be easily mistaken for a young boy. Despite her tomboyishness and androgynous look, she was in no danger of being bothered by most men, not even Roman Catholic clergy, who were the only men daring enough to surreptitiously diddle young boys back in 1969.

Cookie longed to find the right boy to love and felt pressured to acquire a boyfriend, the way one would get hold of a new hit single on a 45 vinyl record. The fate of an Italian girl is not to remain a virgin. Italian girls are driven by a primordial urge to vanquish and immolate anyone who is attracted to them. The objective of all Italian girls is to drive men insane solely because *they* are everywhere and *they* make the rules.

They is a pejorative term and can be applied to any man, regardless of sexual proclivity, age, religion, ethnicity or national origin. *They* were the powers that be and were white. They were the big, old fat dudes sitting in the White House who sent our boys to die in Vietnam. *They* always talked a good game about war except they had not fought a battle or seen combat up close. *They* weren't about sex per se. Sex was window dressing, a fabulous escort who followed them home to get paid. *They*—these white guys—were about power.

Remember, this was 1969 and nobody was looking to come out in public to show-off sexually, except for peeping-toms, old Italian men, and pedophiles, many of whom were Catholic priests. With the exception of *Blind Owl* Alan Wilson, Cookie didn't care for boys, Yonkers boys, especially Yonkers Italian boys, and worried that if she took up with one, not only would she have to eventually relinquish her virginity, but she would be stuck in Yonkers forever.

Speaking of Italian men, Cookie didn't love the fact that her father had locked her in her room during one of the most important events in the twentieth century, Woodstock. Her wings were clipped and she was being denied her rightful place in history. It was August 16, 1969, and everyone knew that history was being made at a rock and roll festival taking place on Max Yasgur's farm in Bethel, New York. One way or another, Cookie Colangelo was determined to get on the road to Woodstock.

Cookie suddenly remembered there was a way to get out. It was risky, but what did she have to lose? She opened her window and stuck her head out where a thick yellow clothesline loomed ahead. Then she looked down to the ground. It was a long way to go, maybe fifteen feet. One wheel of the clothesline was hitched just below her window, and the other wheel was fastened to a big, lonely old Sumac tree across the yard. The tree looked burdened by its fate of having to stand tall on a narrow grassy bank, thick fibrous roots sticking out everywhere, tangling together and forming a bog of peat moss.

Cookie looked down toward the ground and emitted a small, wondrous, girl-like gasp. Bobbing her head like a feral cat, she tried to assess the distance she would jump. The August air was thick and humid, and the sky was belching a clot of grey clouds—all of the conditions perfect for a summer thunderstorm. A mass of small rocks and clusters of brown weeds covered the ground where she might meet an untimely death. She was scared to jump! It was a long way down!

Straddling between her contradictory urges to be a hippie or a gangster, she let the range of tension play out like a new song by Canned Heat. Cookie reckoned the *Blind Owl* faced the same dilemma, fluctuating between being a hippie and a gangster. It was one more reason why he hung around with all of the old black blues musicians. At heart, blues musicians were all gangsters and stuck together *in the life*. Even at twelve, Cookie knew the only way to get a real life was to be a gangster. While she surveyed the ground below the window, she surmised that a mere hippie was scared of heights and would groove on the quiet of her captivity and maybe stoke up a bowl of hash. The gangster, however, was not going to put up with this shit and would make a break for it. *Jump!* she told herself.

Leaning toward the gangster range in her spectrum of earthly role models was not a bad choice for Cookie. Aside from aspiring to be a hippie or a gangster, she was truly a tomboy possessing tremendous athletic ability. Even in the worst-case scenario, dying heroically was better than years of slow death in Yonkers. She was exceptionally well-equipped to jump. She was the best kickball player in the neighborhood and could jump to mighty heights making baskets while playing basketball—although all of these jumps were upward and not to the ground below, where even the best athletes could surely break bones. So she hesitated for a moment, surveying the options. The alternative meant being imprisoned. Taking a risk meant freedom, the road to Woodstock, and a chance to become a bona fide hippie.

She knew the clothesline was strong enough to support her weight. There had been a long winter night two years ago when her parents had a knockdown, drag-out fight. Her mother was running away from her father, who was chasing her. One blow had already lanced the space below her mother's right eye and made a cherry red bruise. Her father was in no better condition with a cut cheek and a bruise visibly swelling where a water glass thrown by her mother had smacked the side of his head. The glass broke from the force of the impact against her father's face and left a pile of shards on the kitchen floor like rubble in the aftermath of war. After Cookie's mother cracked the glass on his face, she ran from him, threw open the window and jumped out. She hung onto the clothesline, which now sagged in the middle with her weight. She clung to the rope with all of her might and shrieked.

It was a frigid night where terror reigned and cold air rushed into Cookie's bedroom. Cookie was sure her mother would die out on the clothesline until her father had the good sense to reel her back inside like a barely dead, flopping fish and drag her in through the window. The whole time, Cookie's mother was screaming, "No Johnny, No Johnny!" Later that night, Cookie's parents made up, and Cookie could hear their amorous activity through a shared bedroom wall where her mother was still crying out, "No Johnny, Nooo Johnny," in a much different tone of voice.

Cookie had no idea why the clothesline had to be hung outside of her bedroom window, but maybe it was fate, where all roads led here so she could go to Woodstock. If her mother could survive the flight on the clothesline on an icy winter night, then Cookie had a chance to make a break for it in the August heat and get to the New York State Thruway.

She closed her eyes and took the plunge. Her weight dragged down the clothesline. She pedaled herself, pumping her arms and legs furiously until she found herself on a soft section of brown thatched lawn and swung in the air, close to the ground. Her brown wavy hair was parted in the middle and sectioned off into two messy braids that were flying around as she bounced on the clothesline. She had always been good at straddling swing-set trapeze rings on the playground, hanging on and swinging hand-to-hand from one ring to the next like a freestyle gymnast. Cookie was as strong in her upper body as she was in her ferocious ability to jump high in the air. Just as she made it to the middle of the clothesline, she felt her arms giving out. The weight of her legs sank heavily, until she was forced to let go, and she fell to the ground in a heap. Then the unexpected happened. Her right knee buckled, as if it had come out of its socket. Cookie howled with pain. It was not the fall that had caused the injury. Her knee had suddenly given out on her just like that, as if it had a will of its own and did not want to go to Woodstock.

She knew she had trick knees. Her knees always went out on her, even if she was just walking. Her knee would have gone out on her if she had just taken baby steps across her bedroom. Her knees let her down, mysteriously and out of the blue, the same way her parents were never there for her when she needed them. Cookie surmised that it had been the same birth defect that she had been born with that gave her trick knees and bad parents. The song *Wipe Out* drifted into her yard and she wished it would go away, but it was always there, background music like a soundtrack for a bad movie.

Growing up in Yonkers was no bed of roses, and most kids dreamed of finding a way out. There were only three ways out of here: education, death or fame. Not everyone was smart enough to stay in school, and dying young and foolishly was an extreme measure. Becoming famous might be a possibility. You could get out of Yonkers by being famous and the only sure road to fame was by becoming a rock star.

Every boy on the block could play *Wipe Out* on the guitar and had thousands of impromptu jam sessions. From garages and basements, yards, parks and parking lots, there was the ubiquitous street sound of drums humping under the twang of three simple chords from an electric guitar. Any boy, talented or not, musically inclined or musically challenged, knew how to play *Wipe Out* and did so with unerring frequency, regardless of the season or the time of day. The rock band The Surfaris might have never known that their song *Wipe Out* was the national anthem for the entire city of Yonkers, circa 1969.

Clutching her wounded trick knee and trying to regain her composure, Cookie stood in her back yard under the lower boughs of the sturdy Sumac tree. One yard over, her neighbor, the bright red-headed hag Fran Ochiogrosso, was craning her neck over a scraggly hedge to see what Cookie was doing. She called out, "Concetta Colangelo, is that you under that tree? Did you fall down and hurt your knee again? Why don't your parents take you to see a doctor about that knee?"

Oh my God, Cookie gasped to herself. She didn't know if Fran had seen her escape from the window, but if she did, she would most certainly tell someone about it, and if she had her druthers she would rat-her-out to her sorry excuse for a father, Johnny Colangelo. Fran Ochiogrosso was more than the neighborhood gossip. She avenged her lot in life by knowing everyone's deep dark secrets and declaring war against the world. Cookie could hear the telephone ringing in her house and she was terrified. That awful Fran Ochiogrosso was probably trying to call her father.

She heard Fran talking loudly, much louder than she would talk on a phone, and Cookie realized that Fran wasn't on the phone at all but yelling across the fence to Louie Santamassino. Soon a shouting match erupted and rose a whole octave higher than the metallic whine of *Wipe Out*. Cookie heard a volley of words that rarely deviated from a successive string of *fucks* that escalated in tone, pitch and frequency. *Fuck you. Fuck you, you mother fucker. Fuck you, you fucking mother fucker, fuck you. Fuck you, just fuck you, you mother fucking, fucking mother fucker, fuck you! You fucking mother, fuck! I said fuck.* The hollering went on this way for a couple of minutes. Then, as quickly as it had erupted, it just stopped.

For as long as anyone remembered, Fran Ochiogrosso and Louie Santamassino had a feud that pre-dated the demise of the Yonkers Trolley. The side yard of Louie Santamassino's house abutted the property lines of Fran Ochiogrosso's back and side yard. Fran's house was much smaller than Louie's mansion style-home, which sat on nearly an acre. No one knew for sure what Louie did for a living. Not that it mattered. He kept to himself and stayed home all day with his German Shepherd, Roscoe. If Louie was still married, no one knew for sure and no one had seen signs of his wife lately. Fran Ochiogrosso made it her mission to know everyone's business and especially Louie Santamassino's. She had a thing for him and kept an eye on him with the intensity of a raptor about to swoop down on its prey.

Cookie hobbled forward, putting more pressure on her buckled knee. It felt like something had torn inside and it hurt, but it had gone back into place on its own. She limped forward through the thatches of high grass and thicket of weeds until she reached the far northern corner of the yard that bordered with a neighboring wall protecting the small Roman Brick home belonging to Bernie and Rose Rosner. Cookie had never formally met the Rosners. The couple kept to themselves and didn't have much to say to anyone. It was rare to see them come out of the house. The last time Cookie had seen the Rosners, they wore straw sun hats while gardening in the late August afternoon. Despite the intense humidity, the Rosners wore long sleeves to conceal the string of numbers tattooed on their forearms. Everyone knew about the numbers and whispered how they had gotten them. *Jewish People, Auschwitz,* they whispered.

Brushing aside bramble, twigs and thin branches, the debris made a snapping noise and hit her in the face. Closing her eyes to avoid getting pierced by a branch, she forged ahead through the whorl of tangled vines where she uncovered a narrow opening that cut through into an adjacent yard and led to the outskirts of the Baptist church. Here was her secret hiding place. A deep stairwell had twenty concrete steps leading down to the basement of the church. She named the secret spot her *Owl Hole*. The *Owl Hole* stairwell was unused, long forgotten and abandoned to thick, gnarly brush, concealing its entrance and its existence from the world. It was down here below, in the bowels of the church's foundation at the bottom of the steps in a basement landing that had grown to become a small natural enclosure flanked by fern and tall grass where anyone or anything could be concealed. Thus its name, the *Owl Hole*.

Cookie had smoked her first joint here. Wrapped in fuchsia-colored, strawberry-flavored rolling paper, the joint had not made her high. When she smoked her second joint, though, wrapped in brown, chocolate-flavored rolling paper, she did enter a new realm of consciousness. It was here in this altered state of mind where Cookie came to the conclusion that getting stoned was not only fun, but straddled gangster hood and hippiedom, the two worlds she explored with equal gusto and reverence.

Her knee hurt while she walked, but not enough to stop her or slow her down. It reminded her that bad things happened to her for no reason and not because she deserved to have something bad happen. She learned this critical lesson in the 6th grade. She never told anyone what happened to her, not even her parents. That catastrophic event forever changed who she was and how she felt about life. It was a secret, so painful it kept hurting her. *Hush,* she told herself. She could tell herself *Stop,* and just like that any thoughts or memories that bothered her would just *Stop.*

She wanted to go down the steps into her secret hiding place and stay there for awhile to think and get her bearings, but there was no time to spare. Woodstock was happening this very minute, and if she didn't get there now, she could miss the whole darn thing. She hobbled out from the church grounds to the sidewalk on the west side of North Broadway, which was dotted with modest wood-frame homes worn by the extreme weather of stiflingly hot summers and cold, harsh winters. All of the homes had fading paint and sported signs of rust in their gutters and looked otherwise unremarkable. The yards were unruly, with overgrown weeds and brown, burned-out patches of grass. Grey metal garbage cans overflowed with litter that had built up over time.

Clutching her hurt knee, Cookie stepped over a pile of rubble—empty bottles of *Royal Crown Cola* and *Yoo-hoo* chocolate drinks, dented *Ballantine Beer* cans, and an empty, crushed, maroon-colored pack of *Pall Mall* cigarettes. There were candy wrappers too, discarded miniature wax-shaped cola bottles, a popular confectionery that used to be full of colored sugar water, empty boxes of candy cigarettes and a mashup of *Blackjack* and *Juicy Fruit* gum wrappers. Clutter and junk littered the front yards as if they were stockpiled in anticipation of an annual visit from the junkman.

Every spring a junkman showed up with a horse drawn cart, although it was hard to believe anyone drove a horse-drawn cart through Yonkers in the late 1960s. No one knew the Junkman's name or where he came from, but every spring he showed up and knocked on doors, asking if he could haul junk from the yards for free. For a small fee, he'd offer to sharpen knives and scissors. Then he'd disappear and be gone, out-of-mind until the next spring, when he'd come back with no notice. Cookie thought next spring he would haul off all that remained here, the old front bumper of a car, a lone head-light, a rusted tricycle missing its handlebars, an old black & white TV, a few wire clothes hangers. The yards on North Broadway were not well tended, but they weren't ghetto ei-ther. Although the ghetto was to the south, ten minutes away, and started on Nepperhan Avenue, the true dividing line be-tween the north and the south, the working class and the ghetto, was Getty Square.

Cookie avoided looking south down Broadway to scope out Christ the King Church and its counterpart—the grade school where she had learned there was no point in being a good girl. The whole concept of being a good girl was something she did not care to discuss with anyone. At first she was in shock over the catastrophic event that had happened to her. Numbness had set in, like spraying *Bactine* on a skinned knee.

Cookie had a habit of wounding her knees when she played sports or when her trick knees went out on her. Scabs formed in the same place on her kneecaps, reopening every time she fell, nicking them and bleeding again like a wound that would never close or completely heal. It always hurt more when a scab scraped off to make an old wound raw. Fortunately, when she jumped out the bedroom window, she had not skinned her knee. Had she done so, the pain in her head and heart would have been too much to bear. Forget about her knee. Her knees were tough. She was going to make them even tougher!

After the big incident at Christ the King School, Cookie felt detached from the whole thing as if it had never happened. Every time it came to mind, she said *stop* to herself and made the recollection, vivid as it was, go away. Cookie was good at putting unpleasant thoughts out of her mind. Then one day in the spring of her seventh grade, a small spark erupted in her heart. This touch of warmth made her feel alive again. As soon as she felt alive, she also felt the pain, which grew acute. More than anything she was embarrassed and sad. She felt grief for her former little girl self, the good girl who had been killed, snuffed out long before her time. The small spark in her heart became a full-fledged fire and engulfed her. She felt like her whole body was on fire and she threw herself on the ground, rocking and rolling across the ground to snuff out the powerful rage that had enveloped her. A flaming hatred burned inside of her, and an enormous power was unleashed on the world. She was an indomitable force to reckon with and would take no prisoners as she cut a mighty swath through the city of Yonkers. In her mounting wrath, she made up her mind. She was going to do exactly what she wanted to do. Anyone or anything that stood in her way would get singed by her fury or altogether destroyed. Imbued with certain strength of conviction, she knew who she was. *I'm a gangster*, Cookie said to herself. *And no one's going to mess with me. Not now. Not ever.*

Two

North Broadway

North Broadway was the northernmost extension of *The Great Broadway*. The *Give my Regards to Broadway* eventually winds up running north from Times Square in Manhattan to Yonkers. Even with its proximity to one of the greatest cities in the world, Yonkers was an ugly stepchild, a fading emblem of prosperity from when the immigrants arrived at the beginning of the twentieth century and was fast becoming a symbol of the racial discord that was sharply dividing America in 1969. Yonkers fell on hard times in the 1960s, when the southern part of the city started deteriorating. The projects and tenements had always been there for as long as anyone could remember, but now the complexion changed from work-ing-class white to the colored people. And everyone, both blacks & whites, started calling Getty Square *Ghetto Square*. Although Yonkers bordered the Bronx and was the fourth largest city in New York state, people stayed in their own neighborhoods. There was a real fear about going outside the *hood*. They might encounter, God forbid, a black person! People with complexions darker-than-olive did not live in this part of town—known as *the North End* and always called *Down the*

End by locals. Everyone knew the darker-than-olive people lived in the projects: Schlobohm, also known as "Slow Bomb," Mulford Gardens, and Cottage Gardens.

Cookie lived only ten minutes away from Schlobohm where her Aunt Mary and Uncle Bill lived—two of the few remaining white folks. She wasn't thinking about her family or the darker-than-olive people; she was only intent on traveling north. She put her thumb out to hitchhike and walked backwards so she could see if anyone coming by would stop and offer her a ride. She was sure the first car that came along would take her straight to Woodstock. But the traffic was non-existent. Her knee had stopped hurting and had settled back into its socket. Until Cookie became a gangster, she had been a wicked tomboy, a natural athlete, and the prospect of falling was not an option. Now she lived with the certainty that at any given moment, her trick knee could just buckle. No one could explain why she had a trick knee. Her parents didn't seem to notice, not even when she had started falling down all the time.

Walking backward on North Broadway did not suit Cookie and made it likely for her to trip on a rut in the broken pavement. She estimated that she was half way to Untermyer Park, where all of the local hippies sat out on the wall. Surely, one of them would know how to get to Woodstock.

Until a year ago she had been a good girl, more than making up for the fact that her mother was sick and her father was never home. She scooped up helicopter seeds that had fallen from Maple trees, and captured lightning bugs, storing them all in Ball glass jars that she collected and added to her science lab in the basement. She used to love lightning bugs and thought the critters were magical and sent to the earth by God. Now she was no longer sure there was a God. And if she never saw another lightning bug, she could care less. *She might even stomp on one if she felt like it*. She crossed her arms defiantly and pulled them close to her body.

On Broadway, she saw a lone wolf of a black boy walking north. His hands were in his pockets, and his head was bowed, so she couldn't see his face. His hair was shorn and shaped close to his scalp in natural tight curls, far too short to be an afro, but slick with pomade that caught a glint of light from the late afternoon August sun. His shirt was bright white, and his shorts were a muted tone of brown almost the same shade as his legs. There was something about the boy that seemed strange, unearthly, an apparition of sorts. Cookie had rarely seen a black boy in the North End. Actually, when she thought about it, she had no memory of anyone black walking on the street alone in this part of town. Not to give the impression that anyone was rich here, but if you were black, you needed to be tethered to someone white, a sponsor, to show it was okay to be black and in the North End. When Cookie spied the black boy, it never occurred to her that one day he might come to be her *owl*, as important a person in her life as the *Blind Owl* Alan Wilson.

She had no experience with black people, except for her kindergarten teacher Mrs. Kerry. *My very first teacher in the whole world.* Next to her parents and God, Mrs. Kerry had been the most important person in her life—for one year.

Cookie lost sight of the young black boy. On North Broadway, a blue Chevy Impala came into view, slowed down and pulled to the side of the road. The driver looked to be older than Cookie's father, but not old enough to be considered an old man. He wore a white sleeveless tank undershirt, splotched with yellow food stains, that barely covered his big belly. Cookie could see that he had a black hairy chest. He leaned his head closer to the passenger window to look at her more closely. He even had hair on his back. And he was sweating profusely. It was August and it was hot. It was so damn hot that a band of sweat had formed in the cleft above his lip. The man looked like he smelled bad.

"Where do you want to go?" he asked, panting for air.

The sight of the creepy old fat guy made Cookie change her mind about thumbing a ride. She crossed her arms over her chest. "None of your business."

"Come on, get in," he growled, nodding at her to get in. "Where'd you say you were going?"

"Woodstock," she squeaked. She had some innate sense to know he would not want to drive her all the way to Woodstock. She looked at him, not moving, hardly breathing. She did not know what to do. But she did have an inkling of what was going to happen next, because it happened all the time.

He placed his right hand on his crotch and rubbed at the bulge in his pants. "How far up the line do you need to go?" he asked.

Cookie made a fussy sound to herself as if it was a firm conviction and folded her arms. "I'm not going nowhere with you!"

The greasy guy was still pumping his primary male appendage in a way that seemed normal—for him. "Is your boyfriend's as long as mine?" he asked.

Without thinking twice, Cookie knew exactly what to say and how to set him straight. "It's longer." She gave him the once-over with a detached sneer. "Much longer."

He seemed taken aback. He wasn't used to being handled that way, and he started the car. Wounded knee and all, Cookie backed away from him and the car, clutched her stomach, groaned, and started running up North Broadway. It was so hot and the air was so thick with humidity, she felt as if she was trying to run underwater or was caught in a huge net. Panting for air, running, and feeling the soreness of her knee, she wanted to run faster but could not, no matter how hard she tried. Cookie didn't know if the hairy guy was following her and she didn't care.

She needed to get to Woodstock, but she also didn't want to be dead, maimed or molested. The harder she tried to run faster, the more she felt like she wasn't going anywhere. One more reason why being a good girl wasn't all it was cracked up to be. From other Italian girls, she heard about the practice of giving guys a hand job as a guaranteed way of protecting one's virginity and keeping them at bay, but she could not bring herself to do such a thing.

Cookie kept walking, keeping her arms pressed to her side. Walking with her head down, she passed modest Roman Brick and old wooden Craftsman-style homes on North Broadway. The front yards were closed off from the street with chain-link fences. Fading flowers and dried-out lawns burnt from the summer sun dotted the patches in between the pavement. She looked up. There was the front of the Rosners' home; the old man Bernie was digging a hole in the side of his yard. He didn't look at Cookie or anyone else on the street. Cookie wondered if he had noticed the hairy guy trying to entice her to get into his car. Probably not, she decided. Besides, it was nobody's B-I-Business but her own.

Next came Louie Santamassino's Tudor fortress perched high on a bank of Greystone overlooking North Broadway. Some rumors claimed Louie Santamassino was involved with gangster-like-stuff: running numbers, rigging bets and loansharking. Louie Santamassino had the only built-in pool in the entire neighborhood. Cookie wanted to swim in the pool but was too scared of him to ask. But things had changed. After the big traumatic incident that had taken place in her life, she wasn't scared of anything or anyone, even Louie Santamassino. Even at twelve, Cookie had developed the uncanny discipline to focus on her mission. If she made it to Untermyer Park, one of the hippies on the wall would know how to get to Woodstock. Then she'd be *On the Road Again*, just like the *Blind Owl*, Alan Wilson.

Another car passed by, and another, but she didn't dare look up. The next car slowed down. For a snap second, she was chilled by the thought that it could be her father, Johnny Colangelo, who had discovered she was gone and had come looking for her. Her heart was racing, but she did not stop walking and did not turn her head. From the corner of her left eye, she saw it was not her father's red Buick Skylark. The car was long and black, a limo. The driver motored down its throttle to a low hum, and pulled over to stop on the side of the road. The limo's motor ebbed to an even lower hum as if it was an expectant, but miraculous, ache waiting for her attention.

Then she saw who was inside the limo. Arky Lovato didn't say a word as he pushed open the passenger door. For an Italian guy, Arky Lovato was a misfit. He didn't belong to either group in the North End, the Freaks or the Greasers. The Freaks were hippies with peace-loving sentiment, but the Greasers were knife-wielding gangsters. It was also a well-known fact that if you scratched any Freak deep enough, you'd find a Greaser. In other words, peace-loving hippie guys could turn on you in an instant. The boys *Down the End*, regardless of their Freak or Greaser affiliation, were mostly Italian or Irish, some Polish, and a few Jews. They all talked tough and wanted to fight big. Arky Lovato was short, on the paunchy side with a cherry-red complexion, marble-shaped brown eyes, and long brown matted hair that looked like it had not been washed in days.

The sight of Arky Lovato made Cookie feel happy. He always had a smile on his face, and he never got flustered. Happy-go-lucky Arky Lovato had always driven an old green Jeep that had a big fake round clock fastened to the front bumper, with its hands set perpetually to six o'clock.

Cookie couldn't believe Arky was driving a limo that appeared to be a funeral hearse. "Where'd you get that limo?" Cookie asked him.

"The Jeep's getting fixed," Arky yelled through the window. "Get in. I'll give you a ride. Where do you want to go?"

"Untermyer Park!" Cookie ran over to the car and got in. Until now she had only been in a limo once to go from the church to St. Joseph's Cemetery for her grandmother's funeral. Inside of Arky's limo, the black leather seat was hot and seared her skin through the open patches over the holes in her blue jeans. She toyed with the round dials on the radio. Instead of dialing in music, there was only the noise of a persistent hiss.

"Leave it alone," Arky, told her. "The radio's not working."

"Neither's the air conditioning," she told him.

"When has anyone's air conditioning worked!" he said, without looking at her. "What were you expecting? A brand new Cadillac!"

"You don't have to yell at me, you know!" Cookie yelled back, sneering to show him just how tough she was.

Cookie looked at Arky while he drove the car and decided that he looked different, like he was putting on weight. He had chubby forearms. His elbows were fleshy and his stomach had thickened and was bulging over the waist of his pants. Cookie saw a thick patch of soft brown fuzz had grown over his reddened cheeks and his lips formed into a red bow-shaped mouth. His Irish pug nose had the most peculiar pointed tip, as if it had been stunted from growing into a full-fledged Italian beak; it was a nose too small for his face. At best, he was a mashup of two distinctly different ethnicities, Irish and Italian, blending into the unformed mass of a typical Yonkers guy.

"Nothing works on this car, except the engine," Arky said. "Even the back window doesn't close all the way."

Cookie turned around in the car and realized that this was not a passenger limo. Her suspicions about the limo were true. It was a hearse that carted around caskets. Dead people.

She shuddered to herself, but she was glad she had run into Arky. His long brown hair bounced on his shoulders while he drove. "I'm going to Woodstock," she told him. "Do you want to take me?"

Arky gave her a slow, sly smile. "What are you going to do at Woodstock?"

Cookie noticed Arky was changing and growing more manly and mature-looking. His thin stubble of a beard looked like it was on the cusp of filling in. He grinned, showing that his front teeth were stained by nicotine and revealing a brown fleck of tobacco. "Woodstock, are you sure? I don't even know where that is. Where is it? Do you know?"

Yonkers was full of Italian guys who acted like they knew everything in the world. They thought they were very smart, but they were dumber than shit. A primary reason why Cookie liked Arky was because he was dumb and he knew it. Consequently, he deferred to Cookie—even though she was so much younger—to make all of the important decisions that were of mutual benefit to the both of them.

"What do you want to do?" Arky asked her. "Where do you want to go? Do you want to stay out all night and hang out at the park?"

"Let's drive as far as we can, then walk the rest of the way," Cookie said.

"To Woodstock?" Arky looked at her as if to assess the situation, which guided him to take a gander at her most active body parts. Aside from wearing jeans covered with seventeen patches, Cookie's white bubble peasant blouse was see-through and showed her bright pink bra. It would be an understatement to say her breasts were buds. Like mad but potent baby bees, two dots poked forth pink points that looked sharp enough to sting.

Arky Lovato had just turned sixteen. The last thing he wanted to do was to be caught with a girl who looked so young that she couldn't even be described as jailbait.

"No, Let's just stay here." He looked at Cookie like he wanted to feel more for her than a desire to protect her—like he was looking out for a kid sister. He looked at her as if he was searching for a way to get worked up enough, albeit horny enough, to want to kiss her... but it was a no-go.

Cookie could have been reading his mind. She shivered, despite the thick humid heat. Cookie had no desire to kiss him. She was not infatuated with Arky. She didn't like him that way. His brown hair was slick and matted and grossed her out. She also noted that his fingernails always seem to have dirt stuck in them. Although she had aspirations to become a hippie, she didn't want a guy to touch her, especially an Italian guy, who couldn't even keep his fingernails clean. She only got into the limo because it was a ticket to get out of Yonkers and on the road to Woodstock. Arky Lovato was a means to an end.

Arky got out of the car, cussing and fuming to himself. He rolled down all of the windows. The back of his shirt was sweaty. "It's too hot to drive all night," he said. "Why don't we take a ride to the reservoir and jump in the water?"

Cookie cursed him with her silence. She crossed her arms and looked out the window. "Let's go, Arky! What have you got to lose? What does anyone got to lose? I'm already in trouble as it is. Let's get in trouble together! As the Blind Owl says, *Lord have mercy on my wicked son*. Think your mother gives a shit if you go to Woodstock? She'd probably be relieved that you are finally getting ready to leave home. It's one less mouth to feed, Arky!"

Everyone knew Arky's mother and grandmother both worked as switchboard operators at St. John's Hospital to support the family. It was shameful for a woman to have to work outside the home in 1969, but Arky's father was dead.

Arky lived with his mother, grandmother, his sister Lizzie, and his grandmother's husband, a fellow called Petey. Arky's grandmother, Anna Carozza, had been married to Petey's brother Bobby Napoli until he died of natural causes. So Petey, the younger brother of Anna's first husband, was really her second husband and uncle to Arky and his little sister Lizzie. Everyone called Petey Napoli *Petey* instead of Mr. Napoli be-cause he behaved like a big, loud kid. Bald and perpetually red-faced, Petey parked cars for a garage close to the Pierre Hotel on the Upper East Side in Manhattan by day, and chased boilermakers, the kind you drink, not oil furnaces, by night. Even though Petey drank too much, everyone loved him because he laughed all the time. And in the summer he took all the neighborhood kids to the Mets games at Shea Stadium on his own *doyme* as he called it, with a Yonkers accent so thick it was almost unintelligible.

Arky's sister, Lizzie Lovato, was so smart she was on the verge of growing up to be a rocket scientist. Lizzie had been Cookie's best friend until the world collapsed—when the good girl had been struck down at the knees, and the gangster was born.

Cookie folded her arms. "I've made up my mind. We're going to Woodstock."

Arky didn't say much. "Yes, ma'am." He could not believe he was taking orders from a twelve-year-old, a girl slightly younger than his kid sister Lizzie.

He got back in the limo. Cookie and Arky rode for awhile, not saying anything. While he drove, he had one hand on the wheel and his other hand on a bota bag full of sangria. He offered some to Cookie. "Want a sip?"

She shook her head no but didn't want to appear to be twelve by telling him she disliked the taste of alcohol.

Cookie didn't want to talk to the jerk. She just wanted a ride, but it looked like Untermyer Park was as far as she was going to get. He turned left to enter a driveway into the far right outskirts of the park that led to an old caretaker's cottage, where he stopped the car but didn't turn off the ignition. The ramshackle cottage was so dilapidated, it was on the verge of collapsing. The cottage was as large as a barn and home to hundreds of feral cats. No one knew how the cats began breeding there but they grew in great numbers. On the driveway lane, two smoky-grey cats with matted fur and yellow eyes were patrolling the front of the cottage, keeping watch, like Vietcong walking point in the jungles of Vietnam.

The grey stone wall in front of Untermyer Park was the hangout for hundreds of kids, hippies, freaks and wannabees, who came from all parts of Yonkers and beyond to engage in no other activity except to get stoned and play guitars or throw

Frisbees. The wall was always populated by a swarm of the long-haired—guys, girls, all reeking of patchouli or jasmine oil under the blue haze of smoke wafting up day or night under the hot Yonkers summer sun. Scoring drugs, getting stoned, and wanting to play in a rock 'n' roll band seemed to meld together in a hum of collaborative activity. The guys wanted to be rock stars and the girls wanted to be groupies. Some of them found their way out of here and left Yonkers forever.

Tonight, though, on August 16, 1969, on the second day of the Woodstock Music Festival, the wall was empty. No one was there. Not a soul.

"Where is everybody?" Arky looked ashen-faced, scared. "I've never seen it this dead before."

In a funny way, Cookie and Arky had no choice but to leave Untermyer Park. Cookie now felt a moral imperative to try to get to Woodstock. No words were spoken, but there was a mutual feeling going on between them. No one wants to suffer the embarrassment of being left behind.

Cookie and Arky were not going to be left behind while everyone else was off being cool! The hearse limo zoomed out of the caretaker's driveway in Untermyer Park, leaving a cloud of dust in its wake. Cookie glanced in the rear view mirror once or twice to see if the limo was being followed. Everyone knew Arky was a pothead and constantly looking to score drugs. She felt very mature sitting in the limo with him while the limo cruised north toward Tarrytown and beyond to the New York State Thruway. She was very much on her own, and doing something special, like going on a bona fide drug run.

Cookie sat back and leaned in for the ride. She rolled down the window and could feel the thick air swelling up her face. Her two braids were coming almost completely undone, unraveling soft tufts of brown hair that were curling up in the humidity. She wasn't being squired around town in a real limo. She reminded herself that it was a funeral hearse. Arky bought the car as a used wreck from Flynn's Funeral

Home. He had taken off the big plastic fake clock from his old jeep and affixed to the front bumper of the limo. The clock's hands were still set perpetually at six o'clock. Everyone on the New York State Thruway would know that Arky's beat-up and dented limo was a druggie-mobile and not a real limo. Everyone in Yonkers knew that aside from high school proms and working class weddings, limos best serve the rich, the famous, and the dead.

Three

On the Road

Once the limo crossed the Tappan Zee Bridge, it veered north on the New York State Thruway. The traffic was heavy, but moving at a steady clip. The license plates on the Thruway came from as far south as Florida and as far west as Colorado and even farther west, California. There were jalopies, Ford Falcons and Ford Mercuries, Plymouth Road Runners, Chevy Camaros, beaters, old vans, pick-up trucks, converted buses, an embarrassment of riches from kids whose parents could afford to give them secondhand cars. Cookie Colangelo and Arky Lovato, however, were the only kids on the road who were cruising on the Thruway in a beat-up funeral hearse.

Arky didn't know the way to Woodstock. He knew the concert was going on somewhere near Bethel and the Catskill Mountains in Sullivan County.

In 1969, there was no Internet, no cell phones or GPS. Arky didn't even have a paper map, and the radio in his hearse wasn't working. Cookie and Arky rode in the protective bubble of other vehicles crammed full of young people who had a wild-eyed look and long, messy hair, some too stoned to know where they were going. When traffic slowed to a crawl, every so often the scent of dope wafted into the hearse from another car. Everyone in the world seemed to be heading to Woodstock.

It was so hot that all of the limo's windows were rolled down. Arky yelled out the window to other cars, asking them where they were heading. "Woodstock," they yelled back.

At Newburgh, Arky got off the Thruway and followed the cavalcade of dented and rusted cars, some painted with rainbows, flowers, and with words like *peace, love,* and *no war,* some looking like they should have been abandoned or splashed with mud and cumulative grime, some hissing steam and smoke from the engine. The traffic was heavy and no one was traveling fast. Together, the metal herd headed west, bumper to bumper, at a moderate speed on Interstate 84.

Cookie was as closed-off from Arky and the world as anyone could be. Her every gesture was as small and as focused as a child who has recently mastered table manners. She was so terrified at what she was doing that her mouth had gone dry and she could not speak—not one word. As much as she had goaded Arky into going on this trip, she realized she was in way over her head. Effectively, she had run away from home, and she did not know what her father would do to her when he found out. Arky wasn't keen on talking, either. He'd mainly mutter curses to himself under his breath. Not much more. His voice was high-pitched, so when he'd say *fuck* or *shit,* he sounded very non-threatening. From that standpoint, Cookie considered him to be a very good traveling companion.

Cookie lit a *Marlboro* and took a long drag, sustaining her indrawn breath the same way she'd smoke a joint. She tossed the match and flicked her ashes out the window carelessly. A few bits flew back in through the passenger window behind her seat. She wanted to be anywhere in the world other than in Yonkers. And she knew in her heart that one day she would leave Yonkers. As soon as she was old enough to run away from home legally, she would be gone.

"I'm outa here," she said.

"What'd you say?" Arky's voice rose a note higher than the crush of road noise.

"Nothing." She busied herself by turning the knobs on the radio all the way up, but nothing happened, and she realized again that the radio did not work. She would have to make her own music in her head. It was hard. Even in her head, she couldn't hold a song, a melody, or a note. Much to her musician father's dismay, Cookie Colangelo had no musical talent whatsoever. She couldn't even dance. And in Yonkers circa 1969, everyone could dance.

Just one more reason why she needed to be at Woodstock. If she could see *Blind Owl* Alan Wilson, just once, talent would flood her mind and fill her heart with a song. Suddenly, her attempt at making music in her head was violently interrupted by the scream of sirens. An emergency vehicle was careening down the road behind them. Arky tried to pull over to the side, but there was no room. Cars were heaped on top of each other. Close to the exit for Monticello, traffic was slowing to a grim crawl. Cookie had not noticed that she and Arky were on a different road until she saw a sign for Route 17. Up ahead, cars had stopped altogether. The emergency vehicle careened into the shoulder and sped ahead, coughing fumes and splashing mud in its wake.

It was raining again; small, misty droplets from a thick bank of humidity had formed a shroud of soft storm. The windshield had fogged up and the wipers squeaked against the glass, sounding like bad brakes trying to stop the car from lurching forward.

Helicopters flew overhead. Cookie leaned out the window and saw that the sky was dotted with small planes, too many to count. The hearse engine hiccupped and vibrated a tinny-sounding bang, but it couldn't be running out of gas. Arky said the tank was full. He reached out the window and patted the car's door, stroking it as if it was a dog he needed to pet to make it behave and perform. "Keep going, old fella. Don't quit on me now when I need you."

Inside the hearse, Cookie felt heat rising from the car's engine. She squirmed in her seat and looked at Arky. "Is it going to be okay?"

Arky didn't answer her. He didn't have to. The car made up its mind for him. It wasn't a matter of running out of gas; the hearse was overheating. Steam rose from the hood, spewing a small gusher of vapor and a trickle of hot water. The engine sputtered one more small cough and died. Arky looked ahead, then on either side of the road. Everyone had stopped. People were getting out of their cars and just abandoning them on the road. A straggly procession of people grew in size and headed up the road like a herd of farm animals. People were asking, *The White Lake. Where is it*?

"Can't we drive on through?" Cookie asked.

In the merging crowd, people were saying, *The New York State Thruway's closed.* One woman carried her young son in her arm and jostled him on the side of her hip. She wore a long, flowing, flowery dress and flat sandals. *Nobody else is going to Woodstock unless we walk the whole way.* Exactly where people were walking to, and how far they had to go, no one seemed to know. No one minded much. *Just leave your car, man, no one's going to take it.* So many people were stoned and walking, meandering forward in tune to the rhythm of music coming from small transistor radios.

Arky looked at Cookie with a touch of desperation. He was feeling sorry he had gone this far. "Got your tickets?"

Cookie stared at him. "Huh?"

"Tickets," Arky said. His voice strained in pitch. "You know, the tickets to get in!"

Cookie looked at Arky as if he was speaking in a language she could not comprehend. "Tickets," she tremored. "There are no tickets."

Arky was red in the face. He was hot and tired and he looked like he was going to cry. "I thought you had tickets! I wouldn't have come all this way unless I thought you had tickets."

"I thought we could buy them here. I brought my allowance," Cookie said.

But Cookie had lied. She didn't get an allowance. She had brought ten bucks stuffed inside her *Marlboro* box. The money came from selling her mother's *ludes* to whomever would buy them.

Arky yelled, "How much did you bring?"

"Be cool," a guy said. The fellow had a long beard and was wearing a straw hat. He came up beside them and smiled, spreading two fingers in the *peace* sign. "Don't worry about tickets, man. Look."

Arky and Cookie were approaching the edge of the concert site, where fences had been pulled down all around. Everyone was getting blow-by-blow reports from voices belting out in the cacophony of the crowd. *All the fences are down, man.* A wall of large planks piled high, some in groups, some lone flanks, looked mowed down by a herd of angry steer. *It's free, man.* The outer edge of the entire field was a mob scene, inhabited by people wading through mud and debris. Everywhere Cookie looked, the ground was covered with empty cans, cartons, and bottles. Her feet swathed in brown leather sandals sank into the earth, and mud oozed in-between her toes. Makeshift tents made from tarps and old blankets dotted the perimeter in front of a meadow where stubbles of fence posts stood like tree stumps hacked down to their roots. There were no ticket booths. Not one. *Look, it's free*, people were saying. *Free.*

Under a weeping willow tree, a medic knelt on the ground beside a young girl sprawled out on a stretcher. Her dress was pulled up and Cookie could see she wasn't wearing any underpants. The emergency road crew vehicle blared red lights. Waterlogged blankets and clothing were crumpled on the ground with litter strewn in a haphazard pattern. Garbage was everywhere. A broken kite made from an American flag lay on the muddy ground, looking like a dead bird that had been shot down in the demilitarized zone in Vietnam.

Portable potty stalls called *Port-o-Sans* were set in rows in the shape of a track field outside of a colossal construction site. Lines had formed in front of the potty cubicles, which stank worse than any heap of garbage or raw sewage that Cookie had ever experienced in her life. She felt faint from the stench and prayed she could just hold it all in and not have to go to the bathroom ever again.

Cookie sloshed through the mud and garbage, trying to restrain herself from crying out aloud how icky her feet felt. She had a thing about her feet, which were so ticklish she could not bear to have them touched. And now here she was sinking her feet into mud and feeling slime oozing in between her toes and in the layer between her soft soles and arches. The balls of her feet felt encased in clay and slapped against the inside of her sandals. A crust of mud had formed above her toes and stuck like glue to her sandal straps. She hated what she was feeling so much that she wanted to go home, but there was no way out of here.

If only she could allow herself to be a free spirit, but she hardly saw a thing around her that delighted her and made her feel more grown-up. She could not shake off the feeling that her feet were saturated with mud. There were so many people, among them girls who, like Cookie, had brown hair parted in the middle and cinched tight in sloppy braids or pigtails. Unlike Cookie, these girl hippies had full breasts and large thatches of hairy bushes. Unbeknownst to anyone, because she was not about to rip off her clothes, Cookie had a small patch of fluff, an intersection of a few soft strands of pubic hair the size of the head of a Q-tip.

"I'm dying of thirst," she told Arky. "See any water fountains?"

Arky handed her his bota bag full of sangria. "Don't drink

the whole thing," he told her. "We're going to need something for the road."

She was so thirsty that she took a sip of the sangria and practically gagged; it was so warm and sour it made her want to throw up. A small gusher of sangria came up from her mouth and fizzed upward into her nose. She started gagging, held her head to the ground and spat. When she looked up, a woman was smiling at her. She had frizzy red hair shaped in the form of a large afro. The word *peace* was written across her left cheek. When she smiled, Cookie could see that she had a gap between her two front teeth and freckles scattered across the bridge of her nose. She handed Cookie an open red and white 12 oz. can of Coke. Cookie took the can and guzzled greedily, feeling a stream of bubbles trickling down the back of her throat.

"I'm Amy," the girl said, holding out a joint and offering Cookie a hit. "Go on. Try it."

"Is it okay, if I give your little sister a toke?" the girl, Amy, asked Arky in a teasing tone.

Arky gave Amy a big, lopsided open mouth. Cookie could tell he liked Amy, but she was totally unprepared for what would happen next. "Fine by me," Arky said. "It's not her first time. And it won't be her last."

Cookie wanted to pass on the joint, but she didn't want to seem uncool. It was hard enough being twelve. She took a hit and began choking up, coughing on the smoke. Her parched throat had been snagged and made raw by the sour sangria. And that really pissed off Cookie because *she knew* how to smoke dope. She spied bands of beaded bangle bracelets going up Amy's arm. Amy looked at Arky and he smiled, showing his uneven and slightly discolored front teeth. *Dang that Arky*, Cookie thought. He smiled back and kept smiling back. He was a regular old smiley face.

There was no doubt about it, Amy and Arky had become instant friends. The next thing Cookie knew, Amy and Arky were sitting down on the ground on a heap of wet blankets, smoking the whole joint. Arky took off his shirt. Amy rolled her pants down to her feet. That's precisely when Cookie knew things were going to get out of control, so she looked around for something to do. Anything other than to sit there and watch the two of them. Everyone was wearing jeans or not wearing clothes at all. There were hairy bushes everywhere. And mostly everyone was white. No black people here. Woodstock was a white man's mecca, a place where a guy could see lots of beautiful, naked hippie girls, all white.

There was a tall, skinny woman blowing bubbles from a small plastic container, the kind often offered as party favors for little kids. Some couples sat on blankets, just staring. In the distance, Cookie thought she could hear music from the festival. She began to hear Canned Heat playing *On the Road Again*, and knew no matter what she did, she would not be able to get close to the *Blind Owl*. There were too many obstacles she had not considered, and too many people in the way to get there. She looked back to find Arky and Amy, who had disappeared under a large floppy blanket. Giving the flying toss of hair, frizzy red and straight brown, merging into one, there was no doubt whatsoever in Cookie's mind that Arky and Amy were balling. Right in front of his kid sister! Just like that.

Even though she wasn't really Arky's sister, she had never felt so alone. Well, not really, because there were far worse things that had already happened. Like the incident in the sixth grade. If she could get through that, then she could get through anything. *Stop*, she commanded herself, to push it out of her mind.

The crowd around Cookie grew thicker until it was elbow-to-elbow. She felt herself almost pressing against the blanket that barely concealed the gyrations of Arky and Amy. The scent of pot was everywhere, and she felt acrid rawness in her lungs because of the irritation left from choking on Amy's joint. She saw a mother sitting on the blanket with a baby's mouth fastened like a clamp on her breast.

Cookie took the opportunity to slide out of her jeans and take off her sandals. She was bound and determined to find a place to wash her feet and get clean. She wandered away from Arky and Amy, but didn't want to stray too far and lose her ride home.

The next camp over was established by a green tarp covering the tops of three wooden stilts, sort of a madcap teepee where everyone was sitting on the muddy ground smoking hash from a brass bowl, sharing stories in slow words and simple sentences. *I don't know where you're coming from, man.* And then whoever was talking stopped and took a space break, forgetting what he was saying. *We are change. It's a planet. Planet earth. We're a planet, not an empire.*

Trying to appear unruffled and cool, Cookie wandered away from the makeshift smoke camp and back where she had left Arky and Amy madly huddling under the blanket. A guy wearing red, white, and blue cotton bell bottoms and no shirt said "Hi," to Cookie. He had a long brown beard and a red bandana tied around his head. "Hi," he said twice.

"Hi," Cookie said. She didn't smile and felt sullen, still parched for thirst. "I'm so thirsty. Do you know where I can get water?"

"I'm Jim." He put his hand out and took her hand in his.

"My name's Cookie."

"Cool." Jim nodded. "Cool name." He sat down beside her on the blanket. "Do you mind my asking...how old you are?"

Cookie had not noticed his girlfriend but now Cookie could not stop staring at her. She wore no top. Her breasts were enormous. "I'm Susie," she smiled sweetly. She wore a long, flowing skirt and a white flower in her hair. Cookie had never seen breasts as large as Susie's. Cookie forced herself to look away, but there were naked breasts everywhere. If Cookie took off her shirt, everyone would know she was twelve.

Jim nodded his head toward Cookie and smiled. "Are you legal?"

"I'm almost sixteen," Cookie lied, and everyone knew it. As put off as she was by Susie's enormous naked breasts, she crossed her arms and asked Jim. "Want to cop some ludes?"

Jim looked at her, squinting like he could not believe someone so young was dealing drugs. "No, man." he said. "Ludes are way too heavy for me. I stick to the natural stuff, pot, hash, mescaline."

"Mushrooms," Susie chimed in, her breasts heaving and shaking so much, Cookie wondered if it was hard for her to breathe. "Just love those shrooms. Magic!"

"Peyote." Jim said *peyote* like *pay-yote* and dropped the *e*. Cookie figured he might be far older than she was, but he was a hick like Country Joe McDonald and the Fish, and not from a city as cool as Yonkers. She popped herself on her own forehead, numbskull that she was, thinking how weird it was to even think for one second it could be cool to be from Yonkers.

Jim volleyed off a round of questions. "Why'd you hit yourself? You didn't take your own ludes, did you? How many did you take? How'd you get here? Who are you meeting up with?"

Cookie shrugged, nodding her head and shoulder in the direction of two sets of muddy feet protruding from the bouncing blankets.

"Oh," Jim said. "I hope it's cool.'

"Cool," Cookie said, but she didn't know if she was being convincing enough to prove she was older than twelve. "He's my bro."

Cool, Jim and Susie both said in a tone that meant boredom with Cookie or maybe boredom with each other. Jim was on the verge of a yawn. Every time his mouth opened, he stifled it by clenching his teeth. Susie stood up and launched in a spontaneous stoned dance, flailing her arms and arching upward to the grey humid sky where the sun did not shine. She danced wildly and picked up speed as if she was a whirling dervish paying tribute to an earth-bound pagan god. Then from nowhere, the wind picked up and it started to rain. And rain. And really rain.

Cookie huddled under a blanket, then squeezed her way into the group with Arky and Amy, who took cover under tarps and three large green trash bags that had been ripped open.

When the rain stopped, she found her way to the lake, where she could wash herself off. She never took off her top or her bra. She wasn't about to show the world that she had not yet grown breasts.

Before she knew it, she and Arky and Amy had formed a happy trio who were walking on the road again. There was no way Cookie was going to make it to the stage, which loomed high and so far in the distance that she would sink into the depth of mud, drown and never be found. She resigned herself to the fact that Woodstock had been totally disappointing and did not give her ample opportunity to meet the *Blind Owl*.

Amy and Arky wore two identical red-matching muscle shirts and baseball hats. They could have been twins, except one was a boy with the first blush of a beard, and the other, a girl with chubby knobs for breasts. Amy was leaning onto Arky and he covered her protectively with a small tarp and a thin mesh blanket. Cookie carried Arky's bota bag and her tie-dyed shoulder sack, both of which were drenched with water and had gone limp in her arms, like two dead animals. Cookie tossed her prized, patched jeans over her shoulder. Sodden with water, the pants dripped down her back. Most alarming, her sandals were nowhere to be found. A normal twelve-year-old girl would have been on the verge of sobbing, but Cookie would never do such a thing. She desperately wanted to go home and complained mightily to Arky, who told her he'd had enough of her complaining. Cookie wanted to click her red shoes together and instantly go home, like Dorothy in *The Wizard of Oz*. Except she wasn't wearing any shoes.

Four

Monday, August 18, 1969

The roads going home to Yonkers were jammed with mud-splashed cars. Throngs of people looked like they needed to take a shower. Looking scruffy was one thing, but smelling bad was quite another. Three days at Woodstock made Cookie feel as though she had overdosed on mud, bushels of human hair on heads and below in the nether regions, and ripped, torn, shredded, and tattered American flags, all of which had been in abundance everywhere. The music was hardly memorable and amounted to a chaotic mish-mash of barely audible rock 'n' roll. Even to Cookie's untrained ear (she could not dance, sing, play an instrument or hold a song in her head), a great deal of the music she heard at Woodstock sounded off-key, intermixed with screeches of feedback, static, and an incoherent mumbling of lyrics that she thought she had heard before but no longer recognized.

She returned to Yonkers, sadly, on Monday, praying her father would not be home, fearing what would happen to her. Conversely, she feared what would not happen to her. The consequences of her flagrant disobedience spanned two extremes, with little possibility of more moderate measures in between.

Either she would be beaten to death or nothing, nothing at all, would happen to her.

All the way home, Arky was tense and in a daze. Cookie didn't talk to him. She was fixated on his dingy teeth and his dopey stare. He had left behind his hat on the ground where the three of them had squatted and camped out. Cookie had lost respect for Arky for picking up Amy and balling her in plain view, in broad daylight. Cookie was also mad at him, but didn't know why. Confused, she recoiled inwardly and shrank from the possibility of his slightest touch. And yet oddly enough, she felt a sense of loss because he had gone off with Amy. She was baffled by her own feelings—and that made her feel cranky and depressed.

Arky dropped Cookie off on the corner of North Broadway and Roberts Lane, so he wouldn't be seen dropping her off in front of her house, which was exactly across the street from his house. Neither of them wanted a chance encounter with either Arky's kid sister, Lizzie Lovato, or Cookie's father, Johnny Colangelo. *See you around*, she told Arky blithely. Arky nodded, with a dull look in his eyes. There was no emotional bloodletting or any indication that their parting was final. Their lives were inextricably linked and tethered together by the many threads of living across the street from each other. Bursting into spontaneous street games of basketball, kick-ball, tag, and hide-and-go-seek, Arky and Cookie were like lawn ornaments, the same as the pelicans, Madonnas, and bird baths lining the front yards of *their hood*. Friends for life and then some, Arky and Cookie had been friends since the early grade school years.

Cookie never knew if Arky ever saw Amy again. Amy wasn't a Yonkers girl, and that mattered to Arky. If she lived somewhere he had to travel to for more than three miles, then Amy was over. He never mentioned what had happened and there was no way of knowing what he felt about her, or Amy, or anything. Cookie could not tell if Arky even had feelings.

He had not yet become one of them, the *they*, the old, paunchy white dudes who ruled the country, but it was painfully apparent he might be well on his way.

She scampered through the overgrown bramble and grass of the grounds of the Baptist Church and quietly tiptoed along the side of the opening to the *Owl Hole* like she was walking point in a war zone trying to avoid a landmine, or worse yet, a sniper in Vietnam. To avoid being seen, Cookie veered sharply into a small woods next to her house. The wooded area was inhabited by thickets of Sumac trees with leaves bloated by the late August humidity. The trees were covered with gnarled hanging vines so thick they looked like they could catch small animals in their web and choke them to death. In the lush undergrowth, a larger thorny bush bloomed with small, sweet-smelling white flowers. She looked at the shape of the leaves and how they paired off with the low-hanging fruit of small white berries. Most people think of the bright red round berries as being poisonous, but that was not the whole truth. Scarlet berries could be the essence of sweet, moist morsels beyond comparison to all other fruits. Consider the color of raspberries, cherries, loganberries, and mulberries. The sight of small white berries, however, was super-scary and as dangerous as a nuclear meltdown—totally radioactive! These non-colored berries belonged to the poison sumac bushes, not to the Sumac, the beautiful trees, and they were lethal.

Radioactive! Cookie had practiced mock fire drills in school, the ones that focused on a nuclear bomb attack and the potential for holocaust instead of a mere fire. Cookie believed what she heard on the news! They were talking about dropping an atomic bomb on Manhattan, which was just twenty miles away! These drills were not meant to be preparation for small fires igniting into full flames from the standard olive green funnel-shaped garbage cans (only one issued to each elementary class room).

A fire from a small classroom garbage can was not really a threat and did not require the kind of drill where you don't evacuate the building in a single file line of scared, rabbity children. Instead, with the nuclear type of drill, you run down the hall, turn toward the wall and put your hands over your head in a locked position. This is so when you disintegrate into vapor, you leave a good trace of shadow image on the wall.

There was a second type of nuclear meltdown drill. Instead of leaving the classroom, going to the hall, turning inward and staring at a chalky-green painted cinderblock wall with your hands over your head in personal surrender, you could crumple to your knees and press into the side of your desk in the yoga position of *child's prayer*, which is not a precursor to the yoga position of *warrior one*. *Child's prayer* is when you tuck yourself into a closed small ball, staying face down, tucking your legs and arms under your torso until you feel you could do a somersault, but would rather not because it's so comforting to curl up into a full-frontal fetal position. Still. Not moving. Calm.

Cookie had learned about the effects of radioactivity, and she knew a radioactive berry when she saw one. Poison sumac bushes bore berries that were white like ghosts, and could not be eaten. She noticed the difference between the evil poison sumac plants that were in the same conspiratorial league with poison ivy and poison oak. Poison sumac plants were so unlike the magnificent Sumac trees that had begun to hatch slightly red-tinged leaves that would soon multiply and intensify in color. She stepped onto a small meadow that was covered by a bumpy carpet of moss, trees, and small stones. She loved this little patch, which was always dark, with sunlight blocked from a shroud of the younger Sumac trees. In June, the flat plane of this wooded area was made fragrant with Lily of the Valley. Cookie liked to pick the delicate white flowers and sought to make a small bouquet but had no one to give them to except herself.

Her mother—*Kitty,* Cookie affectionately called her—didn't like fresh-cut flowers and said the petals brought bugs into the house. The flowers were gone now, and only the remnants of their blade-like leaves had fallen flat to the ground, like slain soldiers in Vietnam.

She traversed the Rosners' grey wall that was made entirely from smooth round rocks and jumped to the lower landing of her front steps, where she crouched low to the ground and shimmied to the outer ledge of jagged rock that dropped down precipitously about twenty feet to the sidewalk, so she could see the street in front of her house. Her father's Buick Skylark was gone. Cookie wasn't surprised to see he wasn't home. He was never home, except on those rare occasions when he dropped in to see if everything was running on its own. She was free to enter by the front door.

Running fast up the front steps, Cookie felt her heart hammering in her chest. In a two-fisted move, she used both of her hands, repeatedly knocking on the front door and simultaneously ringing the doorbell. The front door slowly opened. It was late afternoon, and Donny was still wearing her pink-cotton, puppy-dog speckled pajamas. Her bright blue eyes fringed with impossibly long blonde lashes stared at Cookie's legs and nothing else. Her giggle was exaggerated and she pointed playfully toward Cookie's legs. "Your pants are gone. Liar, liar, your pants must have caught on fire. You don't have any pants on and you were outside. You were outside with no pants on." She jumped up and down. "Liar, liar, your pants burned in a fire."

Cookie was painfully aware that she was only wearing her white, see-through peasant bubble top, a pink bra and pink underpants. Her sandals were lost forever, a casualty of Woodstock. She would never forget her desperate attempt to get the mud off of her feet and pants by jumping into White Lake. When she came out of the lake, her feet were clean but her sandals were gone.

"No pants. No pants. No pants." Donny danced the chaotic bop of a little kid, knocking into the wall and the front door. "You're supposed to be in your room," Donny chortled. "I'm going to tell on you."

"No, you're not." Cookie tugged on Donny's nighty to get her to be quiet. She pushed her way in past Donny and hugged her, pressing her hand over her mouth, trying to get the little girl to hush. Donatella née *Donny* Colangelo was a pest and in need of the mother whose aching presence loomed the minute Cookie had entered the front door, but who was nowhere to be found. Cookie hated the way her little sister followed her everywhere. Her feeling was further complicated by a need to want to protect the little girl and keep her safe.

"Where's Kitty?" Cookie knew better to ask why Donny was still in her pajamas. Their mother was having a spell again. That meant she tended not to do anything other than obey the strange voices she heard in her head.

Donny nodded to the chair in the living room, as if Cookie should have just known where to find her. Even when her mother was sitting in a chair, her body seemed to move gracefully in a lyrical dance as fluid as a waltz.

Kitty Colangelo was one helluva sexy schizophrenic. She wore a sleeveless, low-cut poplin white shirt that showed her ample cleavage to its best advantage. Purple pedal pushers displayed her lovely shapely legs, thighs, calves, and a round bubble bottom that had a dance of its own. Creamy-white skin and dark hair shaped in a bob, the same style worn by Jackie Kennedy in 1964. Dark hair, almost black. Kitty didn't drink, didn't smoke, and ate a healthy diet, favoring vegetables and salad over French fries and potato chips. Kitty Colangelo was perfect in every way, except she was crazy, cuckoo, twisted, bonkers, mad as a shad, and totally insane. Through no fault of her own. It was a chemical thing. Some sort of malfunction of her brain that just did not work like the brains inside of everyone else.

When she wasn't psychotic, Kitty Colangelo had a *Come hither* look in her eyes, and she could be sweet and wise. But today she was *tooting* and her eyes looked black and empty, like she had lost her soul. She had looked this way since Ted Kennedy had driven his car off a bridge at Chappaquiddick Island. She had a thing for the Kennedy family and revered John Kennedy as if he had been the second coming of Christ. As soon as Teddy found himself in trouble and in the news, Kitty had another psychotic break.

Cookie knew history had been made at Woodstock, and that it was a *happening* that belonged to her. In the past thirty days, there had been other historic moments. The Apollo 11 mission had planted astronauts on the moon. The crazy devil worshipper Charles Manson and his family had slaughtered eight people, one of whom was Hollywood actress Sharon Tate. And when Senator Ted Kennedy had driven off a bridge at Chappaquiddick Island, the accident had left a young woman, Mary Jo Kopechne, dead. Of all of the things that had happened, though, the only one that made an impact on Cookie's family life was the incident with Ted Kennedy.

Kitty looked at her daughter, who wasn't wearing any pants and only a shirt and a bra, and emitted a breathy laugh. "What happened to your hair? Is it raining out there? Your hair looks wild and crazy. You should have worn your hair in a pony tail, so it wouldn't fall out so much. Did you drive off the bridge and fall into the water? Like Mary Jo Kopechne?" She kept asking. "You do look deathly pale, like a corpse."

Cookie started to back away from her mother's black-eyed gaze and made a bee-line for the steps leading to her bedroom.

Kitty came after her. She seemed agitated and rubbed her nose like it was itchy. "Did you see anyone?" she asked. "Did you see any of the neighbors on the street? While you were walking home, did you see anyone?"

"No, Kitty," Cookie said, moving quickly up the steps. "I didn't see anyone today. Not a soul."

The pupils of her mother's eyes were enlarged and black, making her look bug-eyed. "Are you sure? Are you sure you didn't see anyone?"

Cookie's voice trailed away. "No," she said as she ran up the steps. "No, Kitty, no one is out there today. It's hot and everyone's gone on vacation."

Kitty came up the steps after Cookie "You have to have your hair all pulled out, ironed straight and put into a pony tail to look like you fit in. If you want to make something of your life, you've got to look like you're a flophouse virgin and not some easy slut of a hot-blooded Italian girl."

Cookie was backing away from her. She was terrified when her mother was tooting, and she didn't mean snorting cocaine. Tooting was another way of saying the woman was having a spell, a full-blown psychotic rant. And unless you've ever been around a true crazy person, you have no idea how scary tooting can be! When she was tooting full-tilt, she called people on the phone, made strange clicking noises with her tongue and talked in a peculiar, gravelly tone—her crazy voice. And while Cookie wasn't scared of anyone or anything, dealing with a psychotic, crazy woman who happened to be her mother was an exception.

Kitty's voice was frantic. "Keep it up and you'll wind up in Poughkeepsie!" She said it like *Po-Kipsee*. In Yonkers, that's the way everyone said *Poughkeepsie* and it meant you were being sent to the nuthouse. The village of Poughkeepsie had a world-class, world-famous mental institution.

Cookie continued to back away from Kitty and pressed herself against her still-locked bedroom door.

"You're going to wind up in Poughkeepsie," Kitty said again.

Cookie slid open the latch on her bedroom door and walked into her room, which looked the same as when she had left it three days ago. She put her head against the door and listened for sounds of her mother, who had gone back downstairs and was now yelling at Donny to put away her crayons, and to quit tearing pages out of her coloring books. The little girl was crying but stopped quickly as if she had been slapped. As agitated as her mother appeared to be, she didn't think she would ever lay a hand on Donny. Something else must have stopped her rant.

Cookie slipped out of her bedroom, closed the door and latched it again. Her mother seemed to be talking to herself, muttering about the Grossos, neighbors who lived a few houses farther down the hill. "*Gootchy, gootchy, I got you, gootchy,*" she was saying. Cookie remembered how her mother had written poems about each of the neighbors and made Cookie go door-to-door delivering her strange, twisted poems. Cookie did as her mother asked, because in some weird way, it made Kitty happy. Cookie knew what she was doing was crazy, but she regarded it as a grave responsibility, the same as if she was serving the neighborhood by delivering a community newspaper.

One poem called *Goosy Lucy* referred to sad, middle-aged dowager Lucy who had never married and sat on her porch all day and rocked in her chair. Another poem was fashioned after the nursery school rhyme *Chicken little, chicken little, the sky is falling*. Cookie could not go home until she delivered the poems. Then, while her mother ironed that night, Cookie was required to go into great detail about what each neighbor said and did upon receiving the poem. Cookie even had to report what they had been wearing at the time. When she could not entertain her mother sufficiently with the truth, she began to embellish the facts. Before long, she was making up stories. Outright lying. Kitty loved her stories. Giggling, getting flushed in the face, she hung on to every word Cookie said.

Cookie told her stories to her mother in the kitchen where Kitty had set up her ironing board. Kitty went about her ironing in the most unusual way. She had a cushy pillowed vanity-style chair where she sat and she ironed. She ironed pants, blouses, sweaters and underpants. And of course she ironed clothes no one had ever thought of ironing, socks, scarves, undies, outies, and everything in-between. She also ironed sheets, pillowcases, and curtains. This woman was an ironing machine! And each night, or those nights when she wasn't totally psychotic, she practiced ironing as if it was high art.

Kitty kept a stash of chocolate and spare change in the family room closet. She'd pull out a random quarter and pay Cookie to tell her more. Cookie didn't think of it at the time, but she detected a pattern. The longer she waited in-between episodes of her storytelling, the more coins Kitty pressed into her hands. Kitty giggled like an excited child, gleefully rubbed her hands together, and waited with bated breath for the next installment of a new story.

Cookie saw that her stories kept her mother entertained and subdued. She didn't need to take medication when she heard Cookie's stories. More importantly, storytelling became a way to grow their bond. Making her mother laugh was as close to her as she could get. And she loved her. How she loved her! Cookie loved when she felt like she connected with her mother. Somehow she had broken through and entered her mother's world. She had also learned to make up stuff and started writing her poems and stories in a black & white composition notebook. She also learned that she could get paid for writing. If her mother tossed her a quarter to get another story, then it was clear proof that her stories were good enough to sell. So this is how Cookie Colangelo began her career as a storyteller.

Tonight, though, after her ordeal of slogging through the muddy grounds of Woodstock, she was in no mood to deal with her mother. She wanted to clean herself off and forget that it had happened at all. Kitty would not be interested in learning about her daughter's experience at Woodstock any more than she was interested in anything about Cookie's life. Cookie certainly had not been able to tell her mother her awful secret. Kitty was only interested in her neighbors—their daily comings and goings, the clothes they wore, the expressions on their faces and the things they said, and especially if they asked Cookie about Kitty. Kitty's grand obsession was with the immediate world around her, the world she wanted to be part of, but could never reach or interact with, in the same way an autistic child is locked in an inner world that cannot be penetrated from the outside.

Cookie tiptoed, one foot in front of the other, toward the bathroom. She was afraid her foot would tweak a floorboard and cause it to squeak. Finally, she made it into the bathroom, locking the door behind her. Tiled in large avocado-colored porcelain squares, the bathroom was unremarkably stark and completely green. Cookie sat on the side of the green bathtub and turned the water on full force. She pulled off her sodden shirt and skinny bra and panties and got into the tub before the water had risen barely an inch. Despite the heat and stifling humidity, she cranked the water as hot as it would go. Her feet were caked with mud, and covered with callouses, cuts, and blisters. The water immediately turned a light shade of grey, the same color as the stone wall in front of Untermyer Park.

Five

Saturday, September 13, 1969

The streets of Yonkers were named after the trees that grew there. Oak, Ash, Elm, Maple, Walnut, Alder, Linden, Mulberry, Birch, Beech, Cypress, Maple, and Willow. There were even street names suggesting the presence of trees: Boxwood, Cherrywood, Greenwood, Arbor, Altonwood, and Grey Oaks. Sumac was an exception. There was no Sumac Street in Yonkers. Sumac was the only type of tree growing in the small patch of woods next to Cookie's house. There in *Cookie's woods*, come autumn, the Sumac trees were regal in their color. In the late summer, however, the grove of Sumacs often appeared to be scruffy, stunted, but bloated with leaves and red berries. Johnny Colangelo considered them to be sorry excuses for trees.

Cookie felt sorry for the Sumacs and thought the trees had gotten a bad rap for no good reason. Every June, a verdant field of Lily of the Valley flared up from the ground in the shade generously provided by the canopy of Sumac trees. Standing no more than six inches tall, and measuring no more than four inches around, the cluster of a hundred or so Lily of the Valley plants dangling their miniature white bell-shaped flowers made the impression of a light-filled meadow. Cookie often described the fragrance of Lily of the Valley as the joy of life—a blend of all things green, sweet and pure. She also recognized that if it had not been for the Sumac trees, Lily of the Valley would not bloom here.

Nestled within the low, tangled gnarl of Sumac Trees, Cookie had another secret hiding place called the *Owl Bowl*. A bunch of branches had become bent and tangled to form layers of a circular thicket that grew in clumps and formed a cave. It was not a true cave, but just the same, Cookie would burrow into the bramble of branches, form a bowl shape, and hide from anyone in Yonkers or even in the world. Cookie didn't know much about real owls and had never seen one, or if she had, the owl had been in captivity in the Bronx Zoo. Her affinity for owls was inspired more by the *Blind Owl* Alan Wilson than for the actual bird.

Growing up in a city like Yonkers didn't lend itself to learning much about animals. There were lots of animals Cookie had never seen close up, including cows, geese, rabbits, sheep, and goats...to name a few. So it wasn't as if she had been owl-deprived. Cookie knew for certain that owls looked intelligent and nested on the ground, or in the old nests abandoned by other birds. Other owls burrowed beneath the ground in tunnels that had been made by gophers, or nested in all kinds of trees; even in Sumac trees, stumps or tall, the living and the dead.

Johnny Colangelo always complained about the rotten Sumac trees and how having so many on his property was a blight, a raging curse that ruined his house. Once again, he had been shortchanged by life. Johnny thought he was short-changed a lot. There was also something to thinking that way that guaranteed he would be shortchanged again in the future. He sat at the dining room table, staring a hole through the empty coffee pot. It was like he wanted to get up and make more coffee, but he was stuck. His focus shifted to the Sumac tree outside the window that was bloated by the cumulative effect of an intensely humid summer that had no end in sight. Even though it was September, the weather was stuck in the thick, dirty air of August, when there was never relief from the sweltering heat.

He tapped his teaspoon in the coffee saucer. "God damn Sumac trees," he said. "They're everywhere. They won't go away and they keep coming back. They're lunatic trees."

Cookie watched him get up from the table, walk through the kitchen, and give Kitty a little pat on the ass. She giggled and said, "No, Johnny." She might have been crazy but she had the most famous heart-shaped ass in the North End. Her natural and easy beauty was part of her overall allure.

No, Johnny, Cookie mimicked to herself, rolling her eyes. In all of the years she had known them, she had never once heard Kitty say *Yes, Johnny*. Nor had she ever seen her father kiss her mother or vice-versa, but they did seem to have a sex life. *Oh, gross*, she said to herself. Who wants to imagine their parents doing it? Even if they had to do it to make sure Cookie was born, it was still pretty disgusting to think about.

"God damn Sumac trees," Johnny said, waking into the living room and out the front door that he left wide open while he stood on the porch, surveying the Sumac trees to the left, or southeast, toward Cookie's beloved small patch of woods, and to the right, due north, where *Goofy Grapefruit* lived. Goofy's house was not ordinary-looking. Large checkerboard squares in red and yellow covered the siding, and makeshift wooden scaffolds were suspended from the upper floors. Neighborhood rumors spread suggesting that Goofy planned to paint pink elephants in the center of each square.

No one knew much about Goofy. Her real name was Helen McDivitt and she lived and worked in Manhattan. She had some sort of clerical job that kept her working overtime in the city. She visited her *house in the country,* as she called it, once or twice a month. She had a green thatched lounge chair, tucked under the awning on the side of the house, where she liked to sunbathe nude. Cookie had never seen her naked. Some of the neighborhood boys ratted her out and tormented her until she put her clothes back on and she never went naked in public again.

Johnny Colangelo stood on the front porch looking down at the houses below. He was smoking an unfiltered *Lucky Strike*, flicking his ashes off the black wrought iron balcony. He liked being high up on the rock that placed him at a slightly higher elevation than everyone else. "Jesus Christ! God damn Sumac trees are everywhere," Johnny said. "Lunatic trees."

To the best of Cookie's recollection, Johnny had topped and thinned the Sumac trees once, the first summer after the family had moved in, when Cookie was eight. He never did it again. Cookie remembered him out there on a 12-foot ladder with a chainsaw, red in the face and sweating profusely, with drops of water rolling off the tip of his big roman nose. The way he was acting, it was like he cut back the branches every day, but he hadn't done anything to the house in five years. Where there used to be green square flats of grass sod had been overtaken by weeds, dandelions, and horsetail clumping together as thick as the indomitable Sumac trees. Johnny was never home, but when he did come back, he acted like he had never been gone in the first place.

"Those god damn trees are growing like a frigging bush in front of that woman's house." He was referring to *Goofy*, but only the kids in the neighborhood called her by that name. "She probably planted them there! The witch! She made them grow crowded like that, for chrissakes! What am I going to do about those trees?!"

Johnny claimed if only the Sumac trees were Maples or Oaks and Elms, his whole life would be different. He'd be a famous jazz musician and get to travel the world instead of having to sell liquor for a living. He called the Sumac trees *lunatic trees* because he was really mad about something else that had nothing to do with the trees.

He also complained about the death in 1954 of the Alexander Smith Carpet Mills (at its peak, the factory had employed over 7,000 people in Yonkers); the Brooklyn Dodgers leaving New York; and the demise of the Yonkers trolley cars. Even though there was every reason to believe that his natural father, Peter Bonanno, died in a trolley car accident, Johnny cited the end of the Yonkers Trolley as one more tragedy in his life. In the middle of the night, about four in the morning, Peter Bonanno's car collided with a trolley that had not been moving at the time. As a matter of fact, the trolley had parked for the night. There was every reason to believe that Peter might have not seen the trolley car until he hit it, and then it was too late. Peter Bonanno was the first cousin of Frank Moretti, who was the second cousin of Johnny Colangelo's adoptive father, but Cookie did not know any of these people and had never verified the facts.

Johnny Colangelo would have you believing the entire city of Yonkers was overrun by trees, because everyone knew the trees sprouted up in between the cracks of great planes of concrete, tenements, walkup flats, and stucco flophouses. He stood on the front porch in front of his house and yelled about Cookie as if someone else from outside the family was listening to him.

"Who knows what this place is," Johnny yelled. "Am I in a city or a suburb or the country? With all of these god damn Sumac trees, I might as well be in the sticks. YONKERS, Yonkers," he bellowed. "I might as well be in the sticks with the hicks and the jigaboos, instead of way up here in my own home that I built with my own two hands!" He held his hands out in front of his face as if he was trying to make himself believe what he was saying. Johnny was always trying to make himself believe his own bullshit, even when his bullshit was true. It's like he could never get enough of a good thing.

Cookie put her hands over her ears. She couldn't believe what an idiot he was and the dumb things he was saying, and what's worse, he wasn't even drunk. If he had been drunk, at least she could say it was the liquor talking and not him.

Out on the street, no one was listening. There were kids out there, but no one looked up. Everyone was used to Johnny Colangelo and his big mouth. Kitty was inside the house, standing at the kitchen sink washing iceberg lettuce, leaf by leaf, and giggling the whole time. Kitty could be like that, swinging from full-blown psychosis to a private moment of humor that she kept all to herself.

Johnny was talking to the whole world about his daughter as if he had an audience, which he did not. "She's a handful," Johnny said. "I don't know what to do with Cookie. I don't know what to do about her mother, either. If you ask me, these women are lunatics just like the trees." His eyes stayed fixated on the vista to the west, where the flat ridge of New Jersey Palisades above the Hudson River looked mostly brown. A few trees though bore the early fall glow of yellow and red leaves.

Cookie looked at her father with a slight touch of venom. She was too annoyed with him to be too filled with rage. She found her father to be sad and stupid, an insipid nuisance, sort of like a pet dog that would not respond to a simple command like *stop barking*.

In Cookie's estimation at that moment, she thought her father was so stupid that no one had ever told him what had happened to her at school. She saw no reason to speak up and tell him what had happened. She knew what his reaction would be. He would blame her! He was an awful father, and a sorry excuse for a man. Forget about the fact that he had fought a war on foreign soil and been deemed a hero, and all of his wop relatives thought he was a big man because he built his own house in the North End of Yonkers. As a father, he was a total washout, dumb, dismal, a big flopping failure.

"What am I going to do with you?" Johnny threw his hands up into the air as if he was seeking an answer from an authority higher than himself—the gods of Yonkers.

Cookie looked at her father, trying to assess whether he had sired the sperm that laid the egg that had become her preliminary genetic prototype—Cookie the zygote, Cookie the embryo, Cookie the fetus, and ultimately, Cookie the baby girl child of Johnny Colangelo, or if, instead, she had been adopted. While she looked at him, she prayed. *Please God, let me be adopted. He is not really my father and she is not really my mother. I don't know who my real parents were, but who-ever they were, they could not be as awful as these people—a goombah and a fairy.*

He was such a complete Neanderthal that he should not be dealing with a female of the species, especially a young girl of indeterminate age. I mean, this guy was Italian, and you know what that means. What kind of success could an Italian guy from Yonkers possibly have understanding any woman, even his own daughter? The situation was hopeless.

"Oh, my God! You're never home anyway! What do you mean: *What am I going to do with you*? You don't have to do anything with me," Cookie said slowly and deliberately, put-ting her hand on her hips in a firm position. "Don't worry. I'll take care of myself. I've already been taking care of myself all of these years. With no thanks to you, I've always taken care of myself." *Harrumph*, she snorted and folded her arms across her chest and locked them together in an embrace. She stood her ground, and held onto her own solidarity with firm con-viction. "I do take care of myself, and with no thanks to you."

Johnny looked like he had been struck in the heart and squinted his eyes as if Cookie was lying, but he seemed un-comfortable. He knew she was telling the truth. He was never home. "Who do you think pays all of the bills around here? I'm never home. I'm never home. Like you don't know how many hours out there I'm working to keep the roof over our heads."

Kitty came to the entrance of the front door and looked at Johnny with mild dismay. Kitty might have been schizo-phrenic, but she had an enormously high level of intelligence,

and when she was lucid she shed insight on the most complicated predicaments. "Don't be like that, Johnny," she said in a
breathy *sotto voce*. "She's just a young girl. And she looks just
like you. Look at her jaw. It's your jawline, Johnny. Can't you
see that? She is your daughter."

Cookie was thoroughly disgusted and swallowed hard to
dispel the knot forming in the back of her throat. Once again
her crazy mother saw an opportunity to prove a sad genetic
reality—Cookie was sired by Johnny Colangelo. Cookie had hit
her limit and had enough of her mother's twisted version of a
paternity game. She gathered up her black & white notebook
and slid a pen into her pocket next to a pack of *Marlboros* and
walked out of the house, slamming the front door behind her.
Slowly she descended the front steps in a perpetual hopping
movement, all thirty-five steps leading down to the street,
where she could hear kids playing in front of her house.

The saddest thing about Johnny was the fact that he was
a victim of life. Everyone in his entire world was either crazy
or had let him down. He never stopped to think that if he just
once stopped blaming other people for his own misfortune, he
might just take control over his own life. He might actually
become a good musician. And it had nothing to do with the
mighty Sumac trees! The trees might have been Cookie's only
friends. Except for maybe the *Blind Owl* Alan Wilson. Cookie
wondered if the *Blind Owl* had parents as warped as her parents. She began to hum a falsetto in her head of the *Blind
Owl's* rendition of *On the Road Again*.

She was on the road again and getting the hell out of
here. The hill in front of Cookie's house was streaked with
oil and grease. The minute she hit the last landing in front
of her house and leapt out to the sidewalks, she was immediately doubled-teamed by her little sister Donny and Arky's
little sister Lizzie Lovato, who were the last two people in the
world she wanted to see. She certainly did not want to hang
out with them. She shrank back and looked for a route out of

there. She pulled a box of *Marlboros* out of her back pocket, took one out and lit it.

"Where've you been?" Donny giggled. Lizzie playfully grabbed a piece of white chalk from the little girl's hand, but she did not seem to care. Lizzie and Donny were drawing a hopscotch board on the ground in the middle of the street. Paying no mind to cars or to the loose dogs forming a stray pack and barking in the middle of the road. The dogs never bit anyone. Except for Louie Santamassino's dog Roscoe, a German Shepherd and a guard dog who protected Louie's yard. Cookie didn't see Roscoe, but she could hear him barking from behind a tall chain link fence at the top of the street. Louie was rich and scary. He might have even been scary-rich—there was no way to know for sure. One thing was certain: all that separated him from the riff-raff was a chain link fence.

Roscoe barked so loudly and violently that for a time it was the only sound from the street. Cookie didn't know if he had ever bitten anyone, but he sure looked like he could. Even though Cookie could not see him and only heard his bark, she did not trust that dog. The rest of the dogs would bark like hell until they became used to the newcomer, but not Roscoe. He bared his fangs and lunged at people and jumped up as if he was scaling the fence. Cookie heard Louie calling him to come home, and his barking immediately stopped.

Fran Ochiogrosso made no secret of the fact that she was snooping. The screen door leading to her porch swung open. Fran was wearing a filmy orange house dress patterned with tropical fruit. Her hair was set in large plastic pink rollers stuck into place with bobby pins. She was holding a dishtowel, and she was scowling.

"That dog's making a racket again," Fran yelled. "I'm trying to work in the kitchen and all I can hear is his barking."

"What's it to you?" Louie yelled at her. "Why don't you turn around and mind your own fucking business! You goddamn busybody!"

Fran turned around and swore. "Goddamn it, Louie, I'm going to report that dog to the pound!" She went back into the house and made a big point of slamming the door shut, but Cookie could still hear her through the open screen. "That dog's vicious, and one day he's going to tear somebody limb from limb!"

"And I hope it's you!" Louie came into view from behind his fence and brushed open a makeshift path among the honeysuckle bushes and conifer hedges. Cookie had never seen him up close. From a distance, he looked meaner than any kid bully she had known. He wasn't tall, by Cookie's reckoning, but he was stocky, with muscular arms and a small hard pot for a belly. His head looked disproportionately large for his body, all jaw with thinning hair, and just one glance from his nasty brown eyes was a threat, not a mark of sincerity. He was wearing a white cotton tank undershirt and dark wool trousers. "Don't you come near my property, you hear me? I don't want no kids around my house. Got that?"

Cookie yelled, "We weren't going anywhere near your property." Then she lowered her voice so he couldn't hear her. "We're just out here minding our own business, and he always has to say something."

"He's not right in the head," Lizzie whispered.

"No one in Yonkers is right in the head," Cookie said. "Haven't you ever noticed that everyone in this whole city is crazy?"

Donny giggled and stuck out her finger in his direction, pointing like she had a lollipop. "He looks funny. Look how big his nose is! He has a schnozzle."

"Better not be doing nothing, or saying things about me behind my back," Louie yelled, "Because if you are, there's no telling what I might do. You trespass on my property and I'll take the law into my own hands. Got that?!"

Cookie sat down on the front steps in front of her house, eyed the two girls and took a long drag on her cigarette. Cookie was feeling left out and at the same time wanted nothing to do with her little sister or Lizzie, who was once her closest friend.

Lizzie stood looking at her and put both of her hands on her hips. "Smoking now?"

"I've been smoking for months. What's it to you?" Cookie blew a smoke ring just to make her point.

Cookie didn't realize that her father was still on the patio outside the front door, camouflaged by the Sumac trees, until he called down to her. "What are you smoking now?" His disembodied voice was an exasperated whine. "You're such a pisser. I can't do nothing with you. Are you really smoking?"

"Since the seventh grade," Donny called up to her father. She gave Cookie a smirk.

"You always were a little snitch," Cookie snapped. She couldn't believe Johnny had been up there the whole time when Louie Santamassino was out there yelling at them for no reason. *Some father*, Cookie thought to herself. How could he save his daughter from harm when he couldn't even save himself? She knew her father was scared of Louie, but didn't know why.

"I ought to come down there and bust your ass," Johnny said. "What are you going to do next? Date colored boys? I ought to knock some sense into you now before it's too late."

Cookie glared upward. "Try it." She couldn't see him through the avalanche of leaves cascading down in front of the house. Then she heard her mother intercede on her behalf. "Oh, come on, Johnny," Kitty said. "Come inside. She's just trying things out. She didn't even know how to inhale. I had to teach her."

"You what?" Johnny said. "You mean to tell me you taught her to smoke! What else are you teaching her to do?"

"Come in here," she said. "Stop making a scene out there, Johnny. The neighbors will hear everything."

The front door slammed shut. "Do we really want to hear the front door slam again? That door is always getting slammed shut. I'm so tired of them. I don't want to be here." Smoke was frothing from Cookie's mouth.

"What's that notebook for?" Lizzie asked.

"None of your business," Cookie snapped. "Not now. Not ever!"

"It's her journal," Donny offered. "She writes all her thoughts in there. I read them too. And she thinks weird things. Weirdo!"

"It's not a journal." Cookie stared at how Donny's nose was too tiny for her face and speculated maybe one day she would grow into it.

"Is too. It's a diary," Donny insisted.

"Not." Cookie stamped her foot on the ground, cradled the notebook to her chest, and closed her eyes. She began counting to herself and imagined how many days it would take for her to leave Yonkers, and where she would go. She was going to run away from home and go to London to attend the Summerhill School, where she could curse, curl up naked around the swimming pool, and go to class only when she felt like it. It was a far cry from Christ the King Elementary School, where the nuns were on a mission to save her soul but to break her spirit. *You're not messing with me ever again*, Cookie said to herself. She wasn't going to think about it—*Stop*. She squeezed her eyes shut tighter still.

She pondered the whole notion of the Summerhill School that existed in a fortress-like structure, a castle in a meadow shrouded by hundreds of trees. She imagined herself living there and going to school, ensconced in something called free thought. Cookie learned about the school in a book called *Summerhill by A.S Neill;* it was a radical approach to education. She stole the book from the Yonkers Carnegie Library in Getty Square. Actually, she had borrowed the book, but it was long overdue, and she had no intention of either returning it or of paying any fines. The book was hers, and she was a thief—a good, noble, and smart thief because she only stole books. And she didn't mean to steal books; it was a matter of long-term borrowing.

She didn't know what free thought was but maybe it meant she could think what she wanted to think. She had a brain. Unlike her mother, who was a mental case, Cookie had a brain to use, to create, and to think. She could think for herself! She had her words. She barely opened one eye and squinted while she took a deep drag of smoke and held it inside like it was pot, until her lungs tickled and she sputtered a small cough.

When she opened her eyes, Lizzie was staring at her. "Look at my mother and grandmother!" Lizzie said. "Smoking turned their teeth yellow and they cough all the time. Smoking is disgusting!"

"Disgusting," Cookie snarled. "You still suck your thumb. Talk about disgusting. Look at you. You have a big buck tooth because you can't stop sucking your thumb."

Cookie saw Lizzie wince and immediately felt bad. She didn't want to hurt Lizzie. She just wanted to let her know that she was *outré* grown-up and had no time for kid stuff.

"You can't get braces for just one tooth." Donny was a pipsqueak, always butting in and interfering. She swung on to the side of a green fire hydrant and ran around it in a circle. "Braces, braces, braces on your face," she squealed.

"My birthday's tomorrow," Lizzie said. "I'll be older than you for a whole month."

"Big deal. And you're still playing hopscotch!" Cookie had gone on to smoke pot and go to Woodstock, and she sold drugs and pined away for boys who were old enough to turn her into jailbait—that is, if boys ever paid any attention to her.

"My birthday's tomorrow. It's Sunday. We don't have to go to school. I'm going to have cake and ice cream. Want to come over?"

Cookie looked up at Lizzie and saw her eyes pleading with her. She had never noticed before, but Lizzie had a round face and wore her brown hair parted on the side. A large chunk of brown hair fell forward onto her face just like the *Blind Owl*.

Cookie knew Lizzie was as smart as the *Blind Owl*. Too bad she was trapped into being a little kid.

"I'm going to your birthday party," Donny said, shaking her head *yes*. She threw a rock onto the hopscotch board, landed on a block for the number six, and started hopping on one leg. The little girl looked open and innocent, and she appeared to be oblivious to everything in the world going on around her. "I'm going to Lizzie's party. I'm going to Lizzie's party," she said in a sing-song.

"Come on," Lizzie said to Cookie. "Petey bought a whole flat of soda in every flavor." She nodded to her house across the street. "There's even fruit punch, blueberry, and root beer."

Lizzie lived directly across from Cookie in a large three-story rambling structure painted a weary shade of olive green and flanked by swatches of burnt umber trim. The house had never been repainted, not in a hundred years, or so Johnny had claimed. The paint was peeling from the siding, showing patches of old yellow wood and signs of decay: the red and brown speckling of dry rot. The front porch seemed to lean heavily toward the right. If you looked at the Lovato house from Cookie's bay window, the entire house was sadly bent on becoming a Leaning Tower of Pisa.

"Please come to my party," Lizzie implored her. "We'll have fun."

"Sure we will," Cookie said sarcastically. She took another deep drag from her *Marlboro*, then stubbed it out on the bottom step and flicked the butt into the street.

"Litterbug, litterbug." Lizzie's mouth was wide open, and Cookie could see her one buck tooth that was growing discolored and almost as green as the tile in her bathroom.

"I can't." Cookie slung her magenta shoulder sack over her shoulder. Cookie lowered her eyes to the ground and examined Lizzie's scuffed-up red Keds, her own tan mouse-colored moccasins, and the small reedy patch of weeds coming up in the middle of the black asphalt street.

Cookie never thought of telling Lizzie what had happened to her. It wasn't like kids talked about those things, fearing if they did, then the same misfortune would befall them. Talking about another kid's bad fortune was sort of like tempting fate. Lizzie didn't go to Christ the King school; she went to St. Mary's Elementary School, close to Getty Square. Still, there was a formidable kid grapevine in the North End. Everyone found out about everything as soon as it happened. Kids played on the street, and one kid found the ear of another, and another, and soon the latest news traveled everywhere in fits, starts, stops, bits, bursts, and pieces, like an old-fashioned telegraph. No one needed a phone. Kids talked to each other.

Cookie didn't think Lizzie would understand. Maybe it was because Cookie was so ashamed of what had happened. *Stop*, she told herself. She had trained herself to put it out of her mind, but every so often, she'd slip up and be right there back reliving the experience that had happened almost two years ago. The memory remained fresh and would not go away until she said *Stop*.

Cookie turned away from Lizzie. "I have other plans," she said, skulking off. "I have places to go and lots of things to do."

Walking down the street, Cookie didn't turn around to see Lizzie's face, but she knew she had probably hurt her feelings. Cookie cared, but at the same time, she didn't care. She didn't have time for feelings, not even her own. As she neared the bottom of the hill, she turned around and saw Lizzie playing hopscotch on the street with her little sister. Lizzie might have been a month older, but she was still acting like a little kid. She was still playing with little kids, for God's sake! How corny was that!

There was a child-like quality about Lizzie that was part of her personality and would never grow up, grow old, or grow cynical. It was as if Lizzie was eternally good and kind. There wasn't a mean bone in her body, and Cookie could never imagine Lizzie telling a lie, to herself or to anyone. She was not of this world, and certainly not of Yonkers. Lizzie was a daft soul soaring in her nerd heart, aspiring to live in a world of science and prehistory, long before humans came to walk the earth. She wanted to study paleontology and travel the world digging up fossils in remote archeological sites.

Her brother Arky, on the other hand, was a total loser, showed no promise and was assured to be a *lifer*—a Yonkers guy forever. It was a lifelong sentence, like being an inmate on Rikers Island or shut away in the nuthouse in Poughkeepsie. Lizzie probably thought Cookie had a crush on Arky. Little did Lizzie know that Cookie just used Arky to get around town in something cooler than a bus. If it hadn't been for Arky, she would never have gotten to Woodstock.

Cookie and Lizzie used to be friends, a little tough, playing street games: kickball, basketball, and football. Cookie spent every afternoon after school at Lizzie's house watching the supernatural soap opera *Dark Shadows* on Channel 7 ABC every day at 4:30. Cookie and Lizzie loved the campy vampire Barnabas Collins, and the beautiful blonde witch Angelique. It was Lizzie who encouraged Cookie to read. The two girls used to swap books. It became a competition to see who could finish a book first. Together, the girls read hundreds of books. Their love of learning manifested itself in very different ways. Lizzie collected rocks, fossils, and bugs. Cookie wrote stories and poetry. Together Cookie and Lizzie put on neighborhood carnivals, posted their flyers everywhere, and then charged other kids admission. Those days were gone.

Lizzie was one of the things Cookie had given up from her old life. Lizzie was a connection to the past—from the way Cookie used to be before the big bad thing that had happened to her. She started to hum *On the Road Again*. When you're forced to straddle the fence between being a gangster or a hippie, there is no room to be a good girl. *Don't cry for me, I'm a good girl gone wrong*, Cookie thought to herself. Then she zipped up the steps through her neighbor's yard that shared her woods full of Sumac trees, trudged through clots of late-summer leaves, twigs, branches, and weeds until in the midst of the thicket, she found the *Owl Bowl* and nestled in to write a word or two about what she was thinking, but not what she was feeling.

Six

Friday, October 17, 1969

Cookie celebrated her thirteenth birthday on a perfect fall day in October. The day had started with the early morning light trickling in through her bedroom window. Facing southwest, the light took on a different color because the window opened up the grove of Sumac trees in the small woods next to her house. Delivering a crushing farewell to summer, the clouds of leaves had turned brilliant hues of scarlet, magenta, red, orange, and the entire palette of a roaring fire in a mighty furnace, moving in the wind and taking on the shape of a storm or smoke, or better yet, the bank of fog suspended above a mountain. She loved October for two reasons: Her birthday came, which meant she was another year closer to leaving Yonkers, and the Sumac trees gave her a gift that no one else could ever hope to compare.

She heard the radio turned down to the lowest volume possible, recapping news about huge crowds of protesters in Washington DC and in Boston. Senator George McGovern gave an anti-war speech to 100,000 people in Boston. The protests were being called National Moratorium Against the War demonstrations.

There wasn't much to eat in the house. Her mother had left a cup of skim milk for her on the dining room table. The cup of milk left there for Donny had been emptied. Cookie didn't know where Kitty was and didn't care. If her mother had remembered it was her birthday, there wasn't much she could have done. Kitty rarely left the house when she wasn't having a spell; it was unthinkable that she would go anywhere when she was *tooting*. Cookie dreaded drinking the milk, but she had to have something in her stomach. More often than not, the milk had spoiled and turned sour. Cookie called it *banana milk*, squeezed her fingers on her nose so she couldn't taste the warm milk, downed the cup in a single gulp, and left for school.

On the pathway into the school yard, Cookie looked for her little sister. The bell rang and the kids formed lines in single file for each grade. She saw Donny in the back of the line, dragging a large blue book bag that dwarfed her size. She was taller than the other second-graders, and her thick blonde hair was turned under in a wild variation of a page boy. She wondered if Kitty had been lucid enough to help Donny get ready for school, or if the little girl had tended to her own needs. It bothered Cookie that she felt so far away from Donny, and even though the girls were sisters living in the same house and had the same parents, she could not get close to her. She could not get close to anyone. She was all alone, remote from the world, cut off from her own feelings and stuck in a silo to keep herself safe inside and to shut out everyone else.

In the privacy of her innermost thoughts, she thought she heard someone say *Happy Birthday*, but she was imagining things. No one cared that it was her birthday. Fifty-one kids crammed together in seven rows of seats made the room stuffy, and reek of the cumulative sweat produced by raging adolescent hormones. The rows were packed so tight that the narrow aisles between them barely had enough room for students to walk to their desks. Cookie walked down the aisle that ran along the far right side of the room, patted her woolen jumper down her bottom to make sure her skirt would not rise up when she sat in her seat, and checked it twice. In a not-too-distant episode, she had failed to pull her dress down, and when she rose to stand, a good sheath of her underpants had been exposed to the boys who sat in the back of the room. They made no secret about what they had seen. That day, Cookie had felt red-hot-flushed shame, from which she had never fully recovered. Only one embarrassing incident among many—and to think it was not even the big traumatic event that had irreversibly changed the course of her life.

Toni Ferlinghetti sat to her immediate left and gave Cookie a nasty smirk. Toni Ferlinghetti was one of the cool girls in the class and clearly, Cookie was not. To make matters worse, Toni Ferlinghetti had grown long, lustrous, jet-black hair and large breasts at the age of ten. Every boy in the class tried to sidle up to Toni for a furtive kiss or to cop a feel, but she would have none of it and delighted in tormenting them. Her method of torment was simple: She would choose a single boy to smile at, giggle with, and chat-it-up for a day, maybe two, but never more than three days in a row. On the third day, a total bitch rose from the ashes of the most beautiful adolescent girl in the world, and she'd drop that boy like a hot potato. Spurning his every move and his every word, she was cold, cunning, and a vicious man-killer. So far, every boy in the class had been given the Toni treatment, and it was only October. She had a chance to perpetuate the cycle multiple times with each of the twenty-seven boys in the class.

Toni deployed the same method to her many girl-pals except the cycle lasted longer than one to three days. She'd choose a best friend for a month and lock into a perpetual love fest. About her chosen girl best friend, she'd croon, "I like her. She's so cute. She's so funny. I love her." Then, as time wore on, Toni made snide side glances, subtle sneers, or worst of all, she rolled her eyes at the same girl who had previously been the apple of her eye and the sole object of her affection. Toni was fickle, though. She didn't choose every girl to be her best friend. Only one out of a gang of four Italian girls had a chance *to be picked.* All other girls were summarily ignored, including Cookie Colangelo, who was not only ignored by Toni Ferlinghetti but out-and-out shunned, picked on, and made fun of in the most teasing and cruel way possible. Toni told Cookie she was a *faggot, a doofus,* and most cruel of all, *too white to be an Italian girl.*

"Got some gum?" Toni whispered to her friend Angela Palumbo, who sat in the seat directly in front of her.

Angela nodded and passed a stick of Wrigley's spearmint gum back to Toni, who quickly removed the black & white wrapper and popped it into her mouth. She leaned forward and whispered in Angela's ear, "Chew it. Pop it into your mouth and chew it."

Cookie couldn't tell if Angela put the gum into her mouth. Angela had a shock of brown frizzy hair that stood on the top of her head like an afro on steroids. She always wore amber-tinted eye glasses that made her look like she should join Sly and the Family Stone or hang out with Janis Joplin and go skiing at Vail.

Afro or not, Angela Palumbo was an Italian girl. In a class of fifty-one students, not one kid was black. Irish, Italian, Polish, Ukrainian, Portuguese, you name it and it was all there, except for Puerto Ricans and Blacks for reasons unknown (no one would talk about why) and Jews, only because they were not Catholic and were destined to go to hell for killing Jesus. *Forget the fact that Jesus was a Jew,* Cookie mused to herself. She hated this place, and she hated Yonkers. She was going to leave this place and never come back. By leaving Yonkers, she thought she would get rid of this place forever. Little did she know that she would never be able to fully excise Yonkers from her mind and exorcise Yonkers from her soul.

Cookie spied Toni Ferlinghetti from the corner of her eye. Toni's mouth was shut but she was chewing the gum, dissolving the sugar at a rapid pace. She stuck her tongue through the gum wad as if she would make a bubble, but she stopped herself from going that far. Toni was a rock star at cracking gum. She had the slam, crack, and pop down to a T and was smart enough never to chew at school, so why she was chewing at school on this day was a mystery waiting to be revealed.

For a moment, Cookie lost track of Toni's movement. Among the girls in the class, Cookie was the *Blind Owl*, the odd-man-out, the girl who knew everything but was never accepted by the cool girls. Cookie made a firm decision, one she would willfully accomplish: as soon as she got to high school, she would wage a successful campaign and immediately become a cool girl.

Cookie watched the back of the evil nun who was writing a math equation on the blackboard. For a crowded room, there was nary a sound, except for the crisp stroke of chalk on the blackboard, an occasional grating squeak, breathing, and if sweat could create sound, it would hum, like a motor about to overheat from exhaustion.

Since the big life-altering event that had forever changed her world, she found math unbearable. Sister Lorraine was her math teacher. *Fangs*, the kids called her. The nun had a face reddened by a skin disorder and short, jagged front teeth, with two extraordinarily long canine teeth that resembled the fangs on a vampire. Everyone was terrified of *Fangs*, to the extent that an entire class remained quiet, hopeful that they would not be found inexplicably guilty and punished. And yet it was impossible for complete quiet to reign.

The collective assembly of fifty-one students crammed into seven rows of desks created a lot of discordant noise. Coughs, sniffles, whispers, snickering, elbow nudges, and shifting legs and arms melded together in a hissing din. It was inevitable that if one sound gained prominence—a cough too loud, a snicker too obvious, or, God forbid, someone should talk out loud or out of turn—Fangs would whirl around to see what the noise was all about. She turned as fast as a cyclone, and her long black veil made a rushing sound like the wind. If you sat in the front of the room, you could feel the air from her veils fan your face. The nun's face was crimson with rage, and her eyes blazed with hatred, roving around the room with lethal precision to find the guilty one who had made too much noise.

It defies reasoning to think anyone in this class would ignore the mandate to be quiet and spark a reign of terror. But kids are kids, and will seek a way to throw off the shackles of tyranny.

So it started. . .*crack, crack, pop*. And again, *crack, crack, crack*. That's all it took. Everything began to happen in unison. Cookie swallowed hard. She looked at Toni, who also swallowed hard. Angela's tiny jaw chomped once and then a half a chew, a clench frozen in place. Fangs swooped all the way around, her head roving like a buoy in water, and zeroed in on Angela Palumbo. With a gust of seismic fury, Fangs whisked down the aisle in-between the two rows where Toni and Cookie sat side by side, stopped in front of Angela, pulled the girl to her feet and held out her hand, stretching her palm open as if it was a receptacle, an ash tray, or a small garbage can. She made Angela lean forward into her hand by pulling her hair and shrieked, "Spit it out!" The girl's gum rolled out of her mouth and into the nun's hand. Fangs yanked Angela's head back and stuck the wad of gum on her nose, then pushed her back down into her desk. "Keep it there for the rest of the day!"

The room stank with the nervous sweat of collective fear. What happened to Angela Palumbo, who sat red-faced and trembling at her desk, a wad of gum stuck on her nose, was not an isolated incident. Any moment, a kid would make the wrong move, or do nothing at all, and get hit, slapped, punched, hair pulled, and a wallop of red-hot-flushed shame.

Cookie turned slowly to eye Toni, who wore a secret smile, like the cat who swallowed the canary. There was no doubt in Cookie's mind that Toni had set up Angela to take a fall. If this is what she did to her friends, imagine what she did to her enemies! Cookie had a strange sense of foreboding that one day she would find out.

When Cookie was on the playground during lunch hour, the sky was blue and full, with golden sun lighting up the tips and edges of scarlet leaves on the hedges and trees. She did not want to be here, not on her birthday, not on any day. Her desk was the old-fashioned kind, where the desktop surface was actually a lid that could be open and shut. Inside the desk, there was storage for books, pencils, and fountain pens. Christ the King Elementary School required the entire student body to use fountain pens with cartridges full of blue ink. On the seat side of the desk, there was another opening to stuff and store books. She put her desk up to get a fresh cartridge for her pen and to make sure her current black & white composition book was there. She had been writing so much that she now had a series of notebooks. When she finished one, she went right on to begin writing in a new one. She was thinking of writing a poem, and referred to it as "blue skies."

She was as bored as bored could be when she heard Fangs order her to put her desk top down. She didn't respond right away. She was lost, but not really lost, dreaming a stanza bellowing the blue skies of her poem. Cookie called her state of mind *drifting* and it was like being stoned, except all her images were clear, and vast numbers of words rolled lyrically from her tongue in a syncopated rhyme, the staccato consonants popping, the same way she wished she could crack her gum. Her mind was creating a world and was set on an exploration far beyond where she was sitting in a crowded, sweat-soaked classroom. She felt sorry for everyone who had to be here at Christ the King Elementary School. Mostly, she felt sorry for herself.

She heard the nun, but only vaguely. This time, Fangs was saying, "Miss Colangelo, if you don't put that desk lid down now, I'll break your arm."

Cookie was closing the desktop lid. Slowly it was coming down and latching into place, but it was too late. Fangs was already there, yanking hard on Cookie's pony tail. The nun was trying to get her up out of her seat. Cookie stood up and with little hesitation, pulled her right arm back into a hook, made a tight fist, and punched the nun on the right side of her face.

Fangs was so stunned, she stood there without moving. Amazed at her own strength and stunned by what she had done, Cookie started to heave into a sob, but no tears came. She felt herself wanting to cry, but could not bring herself to show emotion in such a wretched situation, so she turned on her heels and walked out of the classroom. She soldiered on through the hall, walking down a flight of steps to reach the main floor, navigating a corridor she had walked for many years, headed right into the Principal's Office, and sat down in the waiting area. She was not turning herself in. She sat there and didn't say anything because she was in shock.

Cookie did not remember how long she sat in the anteroom of the Principal's Office. The myriad of emotions that beset her were cruel, came forth in great surging waves and crushed her ability to think clearly. She was horrified by what she had done. She had surprised herself, which one should never do. She was also scared witless to think of the consequences she would be forced to endure, not only from Christ the King School, but from her father, who would not understand why his daughter had hit a nun.

As strange as it might sound, Sister Mary Leticia, the Principal, came into the anteroom and stood still, looking at Cookie. The nun didn't say anything and seemed to be perplexed. Cookie took a minute before standing up, not knowing what to think. The head nun had a clean, round face and wore clear, round glass wire-rimmed spectacles like the Beatle John

Lennon. She didn't reprimand Cookie. She looked alert, like an owl, but not smart like the *Blind Owl*. Her manner was as crisp as a veteran bureaucrat. Somebody or someone had to have given the nun background information about what had happened. For Cookie to get treated nonchalantly after clocking a nun, even if it was Fangs, seemed to be an unlikely outcome. "I looked at your school records and saw today was your birthday. You can leave early," she told Cookie. The nun tried to work the corners of mouth into a sign of encouragement, but a smile would not come. "Happy birthday," she said.

The nun looked neither stern nor kind. She was brisk and businesslike. "Go on," she encouraged Cookie. "Enjoy the beautiful day."

Sister Mary Leticia released Cookie from school an hour and half earlier than the usual dismissal time. Cookie reasoned she was in more trouble than ever. She walked, almost skipped, down Roberts Avenue. It was a beautiful day to have a birthday. Zip humidity, hot in the sun but cool in the shade, the sun was on in full glory, and it was perfect sweater weather. Then she remembered what had happened to her at school the last time it was a beautiful fall day. Her knees felt rubbery and might go out on her, not because of her trick knee syndrome, but because she was still in shock over what she had done to Fangs. The evil nun had it coming. Had Cookie given a birthday gift to herself?

She turned the corner onto Palisade Avenue, stopped at Morsemere Market, and bought a can of Coke and a *Ring Ding* miniature round chocolate cake with icing. She stood on the corner eating her *Ring Ding* while she waited for the Number 2 bus to go to Getty Square. As soon as she finished eating her cake, she thought, *I'm going to have my cake and eat it too*!

Cookie pulled a pack of *Marlboros* from her tie-dyed cloth shoulder sack and lit up a smoke. She waited about five minutes for the bus to show, which arrived in a jettisoned cloud of exhaust with a throaty engine. She stubbed out her cigarette on the ground, careful not to smoosh what remained so she could save the butt for later.

The bus was empty for a Friday, because most kids were still in school and all the adult men were at work. The only people on the bus were old or black. She picked up a copy of the *New York Daily News* that had been left on the seat and scanned the sensational headline *Is Paul Dead?* A rumor was dashing about from coast to coast that Beatle Paul McCartney was dead and had been replaced by a lookalike, a body double named William Campbell. Cookie snickered to herself and wondered if they let William Campbell sing on the *Ed Sullivan Show*. No wonder the Beatles had declined in popularity. Between Yoko Ono, the cuckoo yuck-o, and a rumored dead Paul McCartney, the band was becoming as bubble-gum as the Monkees.

Within minutes, the bus roared up Palisade Avenue, where it soon veered onto Park Avenue and eventually intersected with Ashburton Avenue, which was the gateway to the Schlobohm Housing Project, the ghetto that was growing larger—in everyone's mind—with each passing day. The projects themselves never seemed to change, but everyone acted like they kept growing, a huge, insatiable monster that could not be fed enough. Cookie looked out the window; the Schlobohm Houses were the same unchanging dense pile of dirty brick buildings. The bricks were so filthy, she could not tell for sure whether they were red, yellow or some variable color in-between. The windows on the corner of each building were totally plugged-up with air-conditioning units. No backyards and no front stoops. Cookie saw an amber colored dog tethered to a chain, two medium-sized trees, and a tall wrought iron spiked fence that looked like it was meant to keep some people out and some people in. All the grown-ups in Yonkers worried about the ghetto sprawling far and wide like a fat, canny snake that would eventually come slithering into their own backyards.

Cookie didn't even know anyone black unless she counted one, *one finger on her right hand*, her kindergarten teacher, Mrs. Kerry. In Cookie's four-year-old brain, she did not understand why after Mrs. Kerry left school for the day, she had to always sit in the back of the bus. Cookie thought if she became a teacher, she could sit there too. Then one day, she noticed that all the white people sat up front and only black people sat in the back.

The weirdest thought popped into her mind. The Schlobohm Houses looked like a concentration camp! She imagined that the wrought iron fence had a top border made of twisted barbed wire, so no one could get in and no one could get out. The blacks were allowed to live there, but not allowed to go anywhere else. And that wasn't fair!! She wondered if that's what happened to Mrs. Kerry—that she was behind the wrought-iron fence and not allowed to come out except to teach in a kindergarten class clear across town, close to the Yonkers Raceway at Public School #14.

Before her father built his house in the North End, Cookie used to live in that area. For all that she knew, Mrs. Kerry could be there, rotting away in the projects and not allowed to help little kids anymore. She would be forbidden from walking around the classroom to talk to the little kids, all of whom were white and from working-class families.

In Kindergarten during recess, Mrs. Kerry used to pat Cookie on the forehead head and gently whisper *rest*. Cookie put her little head down on the mat and shut her eyes tight, pretending to be asleep. She was only four years old and wanted to make Mrs. Kerry feel like she was doing a good job. She also didn't want the woman to touch her.

Someone had told Cookie that if she touched Mrs. Kerry, she would turn black. Cookie could not remember who told her that. Her parents? Her parents' friends? The other kids in the class? She thought about it for awhile and it made her scared of Mrs. Kerry. Maybe that's why she closed her eyes tight and pretended to nap on her mat. She knew what they told her wasn't true. As soon as she came home from school, she flew in through the front door and had checked the bathroom mirror to see if she had turned black. It became a game. Every time she came home from school, she headed straight to the bathroom, pretending she had to pee. She peered into the mirror and studied her face from many angles and looked down at her hands. She had not turned black.

Public School #16 was the second time she had gone to a non-Catholic school. When the Colangelos moved to the North End, Cookie could not get into Christ the King and had to be placed on a waiting list. At Public School #16, all her friends were Jewish, and she learned about what had happened during World War II in the Nazi concentration camps. The stepfather of her twin friends, Debbie and Dee Freid, was a Rabbi. Cookie's neighbors, the Rosners, had numbers tattooed on their forearms, and had survived Auschwitz. Cookie had checked out the *Diary of Anne Frank* from the Bookmobile when it made a stop in front of Christ the King. She returned it to the main library in Getty Square. She looked at the pictures in other books of what happened to Jewish people in the concentration camps, and she could not shake the images from her mind. She did not understand why she had learned so much from her Public School #16 teacher Mrs. Chachkes, who was Jewish, when her fifth grade teacher, Sister Joseph Mary, said that Jews were going to hell! *Why?* Cookie wanted to know. *Going to hell for what?* she wanted to scream out. Instead she pulled out her notebook and wrote the title of a poem, *A Thought That Has Crossed My Mind*, and two lines marking the beginning of a poem.

How can there be peace within my mind,
when there is no peace in this world to find?

Seven

Father Dunn

Her arms were bouncing and her body was getting jostled. It was getting hard to write on the bus. She closed the composition book and stuffed it back into her magenta cloth bag. She was taking a bus to her father's office in Getty Square. She fumbled around in the bag for her little robin's egg blue transistor radio. She wanted to turn it on to find out what was going on. She felt around in her bag, rummaging around her *Marlboros*, matches, loose sticks of gum, and a pot of Yardley lip gloss. She turned on the small radio, pressed it to her ear, and tuned in to 77WABC, the bubble gum rock station. *Honky Tonk Women* by the Rolling Stones was playing. The song came out in July, and Cookie loved it so much, she bought the sheet music from Music Man in Getty Square so she could tell what Mick Jagger was singing and sing along with him. She could never understand the words sung by Mick Jagger. He sounded like he had a handful of marbles stuffed in his mouth. She pulled out her ciggy butt, lit it up and blew smoke circles over her head.

Cookie had been riding the bus on her own since she was seven years old—well, almost eight—soon after her family had moved to the North End. In all of her years of riding the bus, she had never ventured to get off at a stop along Nepperhan Avenue. Here, standalone slum dwellings, some with boarded-up windows, lined the streets. These buildings weren't projects; they were old homes that had gone to ruin, been devalued in price, and become the leftovers for the *jungle bunnies* and *coons,* as grown-ups called them, to take new ground.

The bus chugged down the hill, bellowing exhaust fumes strong enough that Cookie felt them trapped in her lungs, along with the smoke from her own cigarette. The bus was throwing off a throaty rumble, like it had a broken muffler, as it veered onto Broadway and finally stopped at Main Street. Her father's office was located in the Yonkers Savings and Loan building in Getty Square. She pulled the cord to let the driver know she wanted the next stop. The bus lurched to a stop. She jumped off the back of the bus and ran though Getty Square. Cookie really didn't want to see her father, but she didn't have a choice. She was in big trouble over Fangs, and thought it best that she should let him know what happened before Sister Mary Letitia called him to the school. In her newfound state of turning thirteen, Cookie thought if she told her side of the story first, then she would have a better chance of minimizing Johnny Colangelo's ire.

Cookie inched open the heavy front door, bypassed the antiquated elevator in the main lobby, and pulled open the door leading to an inner stairwell. The air was cool in the inner sanctum, where grey-veined white marble steps led to the upper floors. People only used the side staircase instead of the elevator when they didn't want to be seen going to the offices upstairs. The only way people knew about those offices on the upper floor was if they had been told by someone. Occupied by a loanshark, a bail bond company, and Johnny Colangelo's liquor sales office, the name of each business was not conspicuously listed in the main lobby directory. Without knocking on the plain, unmarked wooden door, Cookie let herself into the office. The upper half of the door was a grey, fogged pane of glass. No one could look in and no one could see out. The only people who knew about her father's office were those who had a specific reason for being there.

Johnny Colangelo's office was a hotbed of activity, with phones blaring and guys in suits rushing about. Most of Johnny's cronies croaked cigarette smoke and drank cold coffee. They looked desperate, as if they were working their very last job in the world. This was a low-rent office, with a roving receptionist named Millie Mangano, who wore the largest tent dresses in the entire city of Yonkers. Behind her back, Johnny Colangelo told Cookie that Millie's dresses were made by Omar the Tentmaker, but to Millie's face he treated her as if she was the greatest love of his life. And in some ways she was. There was nothing that Johnny Colangelo could ever do to Millie, or to anyone else, that she would not find a way to forgive him.

The instant Millie Mangano saw Cookie at the door, Millie blocked her from coming in until she determined it was okay for her to be there. Millie wore soft, pillowy slippers that squished air when she walked. Cookie often suspected that Millie wore the same outfit to bed at night. She never did know for sure. It's funny how incredibly familiar you can be with someone and yet never have the occasion to see them around bedtime.

Cookie had known Millie Mangano for as many years as she had lived on earth. As of today, that was thirteen years. Cookie kept forgetting that it was her birthday and it should be a special day, a celebration, not a day when she had clocked a nun and had yet to pay the price.

One thing you could say about Millie, though, she had a marvelous sense of propriety. On special occasions and holy days of obligation, she wore a swanky black chiffon shift. Millie was more than the office manager; she was the mother-confessor to Johnny Colangelo. She knew a lot about Johnny, and was entrusted to keep his secrets to herself.

"It's the kid's birthday," she heard Johnny holler. "Let her come in here. Come in. Come in. Come in here," Johnny gesticulated with his arm.

Millie rushed over to Cookie and swatted her heavy arm in the air to usher Cookie into the inner office, where her father sat behind an old wooden desk that looked like it had been badly scarred over time. The surface of the desk was a pastiche of ring stains made by a build-up of tons of coffee cups. A large green glass ashtray sat on the desk and was filled with cigarette buts. Despite the fresh cigarette in Johnny's hand, one butt was still smoldering in the giant ashtray.

Much to Cookie's horror, Johnny wasn't alone. She didn't notice his visitor on first glance because he sat in the farthest corner of the room, tucked so closely against the wall he almost seemed to recede into the dark woodwork. It was the priest from Christ the King. Father Dunn made the impression of being like an imposing bulldog, with a square jaw, broad shoulders and a short neck. He was rumored to have been a boxer before he became a priest, and every young boy at Christ the King School was scared of him. Cookie thought for sure she was in huge trouble. The priest was not disposed to making house calls unless the situation was serious and copious amounts of money were involved. Cookie was sure the priest had come to tell Johnny that she had clocked Fangs, but the priest hardly noticed her.

"Happy birthday, kid," Johnny said. "You Pip. Look everybody, it's the kid. The kid is here!"

When Johnny was in a good mood, he always called Cookie *the kid*. Millie paid Cookie no mind and regarded her as a nuisance. Instead she gushed at Father Dunn, "Can I get anything for you, Father!" She tried to hug the priest. He shrank back from her advances. It was clear that the priest did not appreciate touchy-feely displays of religious devotion.

"Come here, come here, come here, kid." Johnny pulled a wad of bills from his pocket and peeled off a ten-dollar bill.

"It's your birthday. Go and buy yourself an ice cream sundae. What's that ice cream you like? Dolly Madison Ice Cream. How about getting yourself a hot fudge sundae? Why don't you go home? Go back to the North End and go to Urich's and buy yourself an ice cream sundae."

Urich's Stationery and Soda Luncheonette *Down the End* on Palisade Avenue sold newspapers, magazines, and cigarettes, and had an old-fashioned soda fountain where you could buy any type of ice cream sundae, root beer floats, and chocolate egg creams. It used to be Cookie's favorite place to get ice cream. Cookie took the crisp ten-dollar bill from him and stuffed it into her cloth sack without even checking to see if it had made it to the bottom of her bag. She knew she was being dismissed.

Johnny kept the wad of bills out in the open. The bills were in a money clip that was made from a silver dollar, a Ben Franklin dollar. Johnny had that money clip for as far back as Cookie could remember.

She could see the priest eyeing the money on the desk. At that moment, Cookie understood what was going on. Johnny was about to bribe the priest. At that exact moment, the priest inadvertently made eye contact with Johnny, who remained seated at this desk with a King-Kong demeanor, meaning that he was in charge but was about to hit the limits of his patience and blow-up into a huge, chest-thumping rage! From the moment their eyes locked, Cookie knew something was terribly wrong, and it had nothing to do with her.

The priest's eyes stayed fastened on the money. Millie fussed with papers on Johnny's desk, moving her heavy body around the edge of the desk and busying her hands with the quirky movements of a small, nervous dog.

"What's going on?" Cookie asked.

Johnny took a long drag from his cigarette, squinting his eyes to avoid his own smoke. "Nothing," Johnny said. "We're just discussing your Mother. Seems like she's been visiting Father Dunn too much, or something like that."

Cookie rolled her eyes. She felt so embarrassed. The priest was trying to get Johnny to keep Kitty from stalking him at the rectory! The priest rubbed the back of his neck under his stiff white collar. Johnny's ears reddened. He tried to restrain his anger by holding on to the ledge of his desk. Then he stood up and looked at Father Dunn. "I've done everything a man could do. What is it that you want me to do? People come into my office all day long and they want things. They want money. Do you want money? I've already locked Kitty up twice—no, let me see, three, no, four times. I've locked her up four times. What do you want me to do?" he wailed over and over. "My hands are tied," he yelled. "Can't you see that!" He pounded his fists lightly on the desk to make his point.

"Think of how it looks," said the priest.

If Johnny had the power, he would have defrocked him right then and there. "I don't understand what you want, Father. Do you want me to put a fence around you so my wife won't bother you? I don't know where she gets these ideas. She's sick. She's beautiful, but sick. It's a disease. I don't know what causes schizophrenia. No one does. She has a psychiatrist, but he's a whack job too. Do you want money? Is that what you're after? Do you want to build a new church and have me pay for it?"

The priest remained impassive. Johnny must have felt the mounting pressure. He reached for his checkbook on the desk and talked to himself like he was an auctioneer. Calling out dollar amounts that varied and increased, with as much clatter as a seasoned bidder, he was his own auctioneer, but now he became his own number one bidder. Keeping his eye on the priest the whole time, Johnny detected the moment when his bribe proved to be irresistible. The priest forced a smile as contrite as a sick child. Johnny ripped a check from his ledger with a precise crisp tear. The priest took the check and examined it. He shook his head and closed his eyes as if he was praying. He also seemed to be emotionally exhausted.

Finally, he folded the check in half and stuffed it into the folds of his deep, black pocket.

Cookie backed out of the room slowly. No one seemed to notice her advancing retreat. She had to get out of here, and she knew exactly where she would go. *To another secret hiding place.* No one would ever find her there. *Stupid girl*, she kidded herself. It's not like she'd run into somebody's mother, who could claim Cookie was playing hooky from school. Yonkers housewives weren't big on hanging around the library in the afternoons. When Cookie thought about it, she was willing to bet not one mother in her entire neighborhood had been to the library even once! They'd sit around, gossip, drink coffee, and even booze, but not one mother would pack up her hard leather pocketbook and take a trip to the library to get an armful of books.

She ducked out of the office. Not even Millie seemed to pay her much mind. She headed back down the side stairwell and out on to Broadway, where a full autumn sun warmed her cheeks and took the sting out of her grief. She was mad, angry, ashamed, embarrassed, all of these things, but when she looked up and saw the golden sun in a cloudless sky on this crisp October day, which happened to be her birthday, she relished that one small gift.

Eight

The Yonkers Carnegie Library

The Yonkers Carnegie Library sat next to a rather ordinary-looking municipal building, Yonkers City Hall. The library, in contrast to City Hall, was austere and sat high on a bluff that sprawled the expanse of the corner, as if it was a monument to something grand. Its architectural style was *beaux arts*, whatever that would mean to a young girl growing up with a troubled mind, in a troubled home and living in a troubled city. Cookie only knew that the sight of the library gave her the hope that there were wonderful things in the world she had not yet come to know. She might be having an awful time in school, but all of these books housed here spoke to her heart and told her she was learning, she did have a good mind, and just because her mother did not have a brain that worked, it did not mean she herself could not love to learn. Learning would take her out of here, out of Yonkers, away to a new and more promising land, where people took care of one another and made their own stories come alive.

The presence of the library spared her. It was a shield, armor for the battle, a hiding place, a symbol, a torchlight for greatness, a tribute to something she had buried inside of herself that she had yet to uncover and embrace. It made her feel good to be here, like she was doing something brave and noble just by showing up. It was hard to explain, but walking into the library made her feel like she had climbed one rung higher into a realm bathed in golden light that shone on every single thing. This place might as well be called heaven.

She pulled open the heavy wooden door and walked into a small, hushed entry hall. The reception area opened up to a grand main floor desk that was staffed by two women librarians, one with a dark complexion and the other white. She thought for a minute the black librarian could be her kindergarten teacher, Mrs. Kerry, but she didn't want to stare. She had not seen Mrs. Kerry since she was four years old. She did not understand why black people had to live close to Getty Square in the projects, and she lived ten minutes away in a place where blacks could not be seen or heard. Unlike Mrs. Kerry, the librarian wore large, black-framed coke bottle glasses. The other desk clerk greeted Cookie, who tried to force a smile. Given the circumstances of the day, it felt unnatural to be happy, and a smile would not come. So Cookie lowered her eyes as a show of respect.

The room was shaped like an octagon, or so she was told in later years, but on this day in October 1969, she thought of each floor in the library as being round. The first floor was dominated by the circulation desk and reference books. In front of the circulation desk, racks of magazines and an entire row of record albums were up for grabs, first come, first served. Cookie knew not to roam through the records, of old, stuffy classical music. There wasn't a record to be found by *Blind Owl* Alan Wilson, Janis Joplin, Jimi Hendrix, Jim Morrison, or the Rolling Stones. Here she might find waltzes by Chopin or Strauss. No Gershwin, Aaron Copeland, or even Stan Getz. Herb Albert and the Tijuana Brass. Feeling queasy, Cookie peered at the floor and tiptoed across the small white mosaic tiles embedded in the floor in large circles and full triangles.

She stepped within the triangular frame, a decorative border of dark blue mosaic tiles in a classic Greek meander pattern, and walked along until she found the stairwell that led to the second floor.

She climbed the honed, low-luster, grainy white marble steps. Indiscriminate sharp lines bordered the edge of each step. The hall smelled like an old school, the same as Public School #16. The vertical-shaped window had frames forming ten panes of a certain X pattern. Sunlight streamed in through the window and fell on the mosaic floor, where the X shapes now seemed to be transformed by the light into the ethereal images of too many crosses to count. Cookie thought about counting them all, the same way she had compulsively avoided stepping on cracks so she would not break her mother's back. There had been a time when Cookie believed in God and baby Jesus. She had even aspired to be a saint, but all of those notions were before the big mashup that had killed her good girl inclinations forever and changed her life.

When you came right down to it, Cookie learned more about herself during the two years she had spent in public school. Johnny and Kitty sent her to Catholic school as a way to compensate for what they could not do for her. On some level, they both knew they were terrible parents. Johnny and Kitty were not bad people. They were two little kids who embraced their brokenness like a second-hand coat that kept them secure enough to function in the world of grown-ups. Johnny and Kitty thought sending Cookie to Catholic school was giving her a solid-gold background, credentials for the road. *Gumption*, Kitty called it. "You've got to have gumption, backbone to stand up for yourself." *Cajones*, Johnny motioned as if he was yanking his gonads.

Johnny Colangelo did well enough financially to build his own house in the North End. When they first moved into the neighborhood, the nearest Catholic school had a waitlist to get in. Cookie spent her third and fourth grade in Public

School #16, where her teacher, Mrs. Chachkes, came from a Jewish merchant family that sold furniture and lived in south Yonkers. She wore her blonde hair parted on the side in a soft wave that often fell forward and covered her left eye. She told Cookie that she could rhyme well and master long words with complex meanings and was a natural-born writer. That was one reason why Cookie carried a black & white composition book everywhere she went. There were a lot of mean people in Yonkers, but for the most part, Cookie instinctively knew that the young blonde teacher didn't lie to little kids. She believed what Mrs. Chachkes told her about her being a writer.

Cookie slinked into children's room on the second floor of the library, where most of the books were too young for her to read. Intent on being invisible, she avoided the passing glances of a librarian or anyone else she could possibly encounter. At this off-hour of the day, old people and college students roamed the halls, but not in this section, where only young children grappled for the books wrapped in thick plastic see-through covers, and lying open in piles strewn across the tables. She scanned the book covers in bright colors with their big, bold animated images. She kept her head down and put her hands in her pockets. She didn't want to be seen. And even though she was a gangster, now was not the time to announce herself to the world. This was a private place for her to think and quietly wonder why the world was so strange and hostile. Mostly, she just liked being alone.

A young black boy whisked down the aisle across from the children's reading table. He was moving fast, and she did not see his face. He had a book in his hand, which he stuck onto a lower shelf with the precision of a dart, and then scooted into a back room that was only meant for staff. She remembered him from somewhere, but could not pinpoint the place and time. Cookie had no idea what he was doing here, and was annoyed at the sudden intrusion disrupting her private thoughts.

Still intent on remaining undetected, she moved her head slowly and spied the mural, a Lunette painting called *Chivalry* by an artist named David Hutchison. The mural showed knights in armor on horses and in battle. One knight had fallen from his horse and lay sprawled on a heap of battle carnage. Another panel showed a knight kneeling, paying homage to a grand lady. *Milady*, Cookie murmured to herself as if she imagined being the lady, wearing a flowing headpiece and a long, slender gown that glowed like it had been stitched with silken gossamer thread. So much for being a gangster. Milady was a hippie chick. In later years, Cookie would wonder what had become of the murals.

On this day, on Cookie's thirteenth birthday, she found a long, narrow bench in between the rows of bookshelves, low enough so small children could reach all of the books. Nestling in with the books gave her great comfort, like an old security blanket she could wrap around her shoulders. She also thought of Lizzie Lovato for a second and felt bad that she had dumped her friend. She could see the sadness in Lizzie's owlishly round face. Lizzie still stuck her thumb in her mouth, a habit Lizzie had never been able to break. When she was suffering from stress, she retreated into sucking her thumb, a small fact that did not go unnoticed by the neighborhood kids, who ridiculed her when they caught her doing it.

Cookie and Lizzie had spent a lot of time together in the presence of the books. The girls speed-read books and passed them back and forth like chips in a poker game. The girls competed to see who could read faster, and admittedly, Lizzie usually won. Cookie was sorry to lose Lizzie; it was her choice to banish Lizzie from her life. Lizzie Lovato belonged to another realm, a space in time when Cookie thought it was good to play by the rules and be noble and kind. Cookie was changing so fast she did not know who she would become—in the end. She was only certain that one day she would leave Yonkers.

She would make it up to Lizzie Lovato one day, she hoped. She'd take her out for a giant hamburger as big as her face, with everything on it, and an ice cream cone with two scoops dipped in caramel and coated with sprinkles. Right now, Cookie could not share herself with anyone. She didn't want to let anyone inside. She felt like she had a sunburn all over her heart, and if anyone touched her feelings, she would get stung, hurt to the quick, and maybe even die.

Cookie sat down on the bench and opened her black & white composition book. This notebook still had four empty pages left to fill with words. She began to write words, rhyming at first by sound, like thirst, first, hearst, burst, cursed, nursed, and worst; honey, money, runny, funny; and moon, June, loon, ruin, dune, soon, and spoon. She knew the words were spelled differently, and she could distinguish a *t* from a *d* consonant sound, but when she heard them coming together inside of her secret ear, the words rhymed. Her secret ear never failed her; it was the sound and rhythm she heard in her head and the words were directly connected to her magic pen. When she had that magic pen in her hand, it just wrote the most amazing words. She was beginning to feel foolish prattling on about her words, and she stopped rhyming. She had no business being proud about anything, and her ears flushed red with her shame. After all, she had just clocked Fangs. Then she folded her arms and chuckled to herself. The nun had it coming! Cookie wrote in her composition book: *I don't know who else to be except who I am.*

Nine

Monday, December 22, 1969

Cookie decided it was time to get a Christmas tree. It was getting close to Christmas and Johnny Colangelo was gone. It was Johnny's busy time of year. Everyone wanted to order extra liquor for the holidays. Johnny made the rounds—personally going door-to-door—collecting orders from his retail customers. Everything was done face-to-face; a handwritten paper invoice along with a handshake sealed every sale.

Donny followed Cookie around the house, staying close on her heels. "When are we going to get a tree for Christmas?" She clutched a small pink square of cloth in her hands. It was a remnant, the last bit of her favorite blanket, she had dragged everywhere since she was two years old. At one time, the blanket had a thick satin border in a shade of pink brighter than the rest of the blanket. Donny had worn the blanket away. Little pieces had broken off. Now only a square remained, with a fragment of the original border that looked like a shredded pink hair ribbon.

Cookie was annoyed by Donny. She was a pest, a constant nuisance and an insipid little bug who followed Cookie everywhere and treated her as if she was her mother. Cookie did not feel up to the job and at the same time she felt enormous guilt for not being a better sister. *I'm so mixed-up*, she'd write in her black & white notebook. *How can I take care of anyone else when I can't even take care of myself?*

Both girls had gotten used to Johnny Colangelo never being home. Left at the mercy of Kitty Colangelo, who was suffering from a full-blown bout of madness, the girls were wary of Kitty's rants, but loved her in spite of the illness that had beset her. In the midst of her psychosis, Kitty had intermittent moments of sweetness and maternal warmth. She'd swoop Donny up from the ground and into her arms and hug her, kissing her plump red cheeks, telling her she was the most precious child in the world. And she meant it. Kitty had these moments of mental lucidity when all was right with the world and she became a wise and tender mother.

You could tell when Kitty had recovered from a spell. Her transformation from disheveled madwoman to soigné beauty was an overnight miracle. She'd set her hair in rollers to create a shiny waved bob, put on her makeup and dress in clothes stylish enough to invite envy and awe. Johnny Colangelo always said she looked like she had stepped right out of *Vogue*. No one could explain what caused Kitty to cross the line from being a wonderful person to insanity, back and forth and then back again. Like everything else in the world that Cookie loved, and her mother was one, there was a sense of weightlessness and nonchalance she attached to these things that were real, but not so real because she could only embrace them fleetingly like the commas in between words. Cookie viewed her mother's bouts of madness as false stops or breaks so you could catch your breath before taking in the whole concept and image of the next phrase. In her notebook, Cookie wrote that she did not know what caused her mother to swim in and out of an uncertain reality the way an acrobat would do somersaults and suddenly rise to standing after tumbling through the air.

Cookie's earliest notion of beauty was influenced by her mother. Kitty looked like a movie star—Marilyn Monroe with dark hair. She shared Monroe's body type—full breasts and hips, tiny waist, an hour-glass figure. Kitty shared Monroe's special sort of vulnerability too. She suffered from mental maladies, some real, some imagined, but one thing notable about Kitty was she was truly confident in how well she moved. When she went shopping in Yonkers, even in the lazy days of August, she put on a girdle under a light linen summer dress, a spritz *of Chanel No.5* and a dollop of *Elizabeth Arden* lipstick in *Stop Red*. When she climbed onto the bus, she stood in front of the driver long enough for him to give her a slow smile. Then she walked on without paying. The bus driver never stopped her. She was moving forward too beautifully for him to care about collecting twenty-five cents.

It had been a while since Cookie had seen her mother together enough to board the bus and ride for free. The sane moments didn't come frequently enough or last long enough for Kitty to get it together in time to make Christmas happen for her family.

Christmas wasn't going to happen unless Cookie made it happen. Someone had to put up the Christmas lights. When the Colangelos first moved to Arden Place, Johnny was proud of the house he had taken three years to build, and decorated the house with lights and ornaments. Soon he grew restless and found more comfort far away from home. He was supposed to be working, but Cookie never knew for sure what he was really doing.

Looking for Christmas ornaments, Cookie foraged around in the dark corners of the basement. Next to the gas boiler, she found them in a damp concrete nook. Most of the Christmas ornaments were stored in their original box and bore price tags. The boxes smelled of mildew, but all of the ornaments were safely intact.

There was a plastic Santa Claus and reindeer light for the

front steps. There were seventy steps in front of the house; thirty-five steps up to the front door and thirty-five steps going up to the side of the house. She wrapped a string of lights around the wrought iron railing leading up to the front door. She found if she wound the electric cord in and out in a wrap with the same motion, one would serve as the lead patch, and then she was able to get all of the light sockets facing the same way, out to the street. She took a box of cobalt blue bulbs and twisted each one into its own socket. These were the screw-in bulbs and some extinguished their light the moment she twisted them into their sockets. So far she had five bulbs that needed to be replaced. She stood on a chair, unscrewed the over head porch light and plugged in an extension cord, trying to disguise it by running it out along the outside of the railing and plugging it into the string of cobalt blue lights. This was one way Cookie was going to make Christmas. The other way meant she had to get a tree.

The temperature outdoors was in the high thirties, on the verge of freezing, but warmer than it had been the day before. From Thanksgiving until December 8th, Yonkers recently had a cold spell that had lasted fifteen days straight.

It was now or never. Cookie headed down to the North End to Bernie Bento's Hardware Store on Palisade Avenue. Next to the hardware store there was a parking lot that was normally used for cars whose drivers were shopping at Peter Reeves Grocery Store, but now it was almost full of Christmas trees. A stupid Yonkers boy wearing a leather jacket over a dark red flannel shirt with a red handkerchief hanging out of his back pocket didn't so much as give Cookie a glance.

Tommy Parrello was indeed a Yonkers boy, four years older, nearly seventeen. He had a slick mop of black hair, a chiseled nose, large blue eyes, and resembled the pictures of young Greek gods she had seen in history books. The dark shadow around his face suggested he needed to shave. Cookie looked down at the ground, which was damp and covered with pine needles. Tommy Parrello was wearing black *Frye* boots and had a knife stuck in his right boot, presumably to help tie rope around the Christmas trees. Cookie was sure he tucked the knife in his boot all the time. He pretended to be a freak, but deep down inside, he was really a greaser. He was always looking for a fight to show how tough he was, and right now he stood in such a way that indicated he was on alert and seeking the first hint of violence.

Cookie generally did not care much for Yonkers boys, and Tommy Parrello was no different. Except he did have a few things going for him. Aside from his swarthy good looks, he had already broken out of Yonkers. Rumor had it that he had toured Europe hauling music equipment to concert locations for Lou Reed and the Rolling Stones. He was also not a full-blooded Italian, and was half-Irish like Cookie.

Tommy Parrello gave Cookie the once-over as if he was frankly uninterested in her because undoubtedly, despite the fact she had turned thirteen, she still looked every inch of twelve.

Tommy stood in the back corner of the lot, scowling at a young black boy. Tommy wasn't being very helpful. He stood with his arms crossed across his chest, watching him, but making no move to pull out a tree from a large steel pail and hold it upright for him to see. The boy pulled out the tree instead. "How much is this, Sir?" He asked Tommy.

The tree wobbled under the boy's grip. Tommy yanked it away from him, "Can't you see it's two bucks? Look at the tag!"

The black boy turned away from Tommy and spoke softly to Cookie, who was standing within earshot. "I can't wait for it to be Christmas," the boy said aloud. It was clear that he wasn't talking to Tommy.

Tommy snarled to the kid, "Now tell me you don't really believe in Santa Claus!"

The boy didn't say a word. Cookie saw the boy moving lightly on his feet, closer to the counter and farther away from Tommy Parrello.

"Santa, Santa," Tommy mimicked. "Santa is kind of white. What's he going to bring a nappy-haired, ugly fellow like you."

The boy turned around and looked at Cookie. She saw his face was strange and not because of his color. His mouth was open and his upper lip looked like it had been bitten off. His cheeks were chubby, and strangely enough his eyes were a brilliant green. He said *hello* to Cookie because he was being polite, not because he knew her. She gave him a quick little smile that felt like the *Blind Owl* was blinking, another way of saying he was winking at her, like he knew and he was giving her a shot at wisdom or compassion. She couldn't understand what she was feeling; she just knew she was feeling something.

"What's that smile for?" Tommy yelled. "Don't tell me you're a nigger-lover, Cookie Colangelo!"

"Shut up, you slimy greaseball! Leave him alone and shut up! You're mean! Bully! You were always a bully!"

"I'm going to tell your father you're consorting with jungle bunnies! Next thing you know you'll be setting up house with one and having their ugly tar babies all stuck on welfare, ruining Yonkers and turning it into a slum. They're all animals! And you just sucked up to one! You kissed his ass." Then he began to sing, "*I see your hiney, all black and shiny. If you don't eat it, I'm going to beat it.*"

"Come on, break it up!" Bernie Bento, the owner of the hardware store, intervened. Bernie was rumored to be half-Irish, half-Portuguese, and a decent fellow. He gave Tommy Parrello the fisheye, as if he was mightily displeased. He was too much of a good businessman to be standoffish about selling a boy a Christmas tree just because he was black. "Back off, Tommy! I'll take care of this. Why don't you go and sweep the needles into a pile or do something to make yourself useful around here?"

Tommy turned his toe and pointed it into the ground, as if he was staking his turf. By his feet, a pail was full to its brim with fresh-cut tree stumps. "What are they doing in this neighborhood? That's all I want to know. Next thing I know, they'll be turning the North End into another ghetto."

"Do yourself a favor and never mind about this boy. He has just as much a right to be here as the rest of us." Bernie Bento walked away in a huff, leading the boy to another part of the lot where he talked to them politely to see if he wanted to buy the tree the boy had pulled from the stack of trees propped against the brick wall.

Cookie felt sorry for the boy. He wasn't bothering anyone, and he had to take a crapload of shit from a low-life greaser like Tommy Parrello. She was glad to see that Bernie Bento had the decency to lead the boy to the cash register and was giving him first-class service.

"Jesus, I don't want to be nasty or anything, but man, is that kid ugly. God, it hurts to look at him!" Tommy took the opportunity to zero in on Cookie. "Where are your parents, Miss Cookie Colangelo? Where's your father? I need to have a good talk with him to tell him all about your sticking up for the darkies. Still calling yourself Cookie?"

Cookie didn't bother to answer him. She had her heart set on finding a small noble fir, but the lot was running low on good trees. Of the three trees Cookie was interested in, two of them had a core of yellowing needles. The smallest was the best of the three, although it had a larger gap in the middle. Cookie thought she could turn it around and have the gap face the wall. She pulled out the lone tree and prodded it to stand by using her head. Somehow a pine needle got stuck on her lip and she wiped at it. Tommy caught her trying to swat at her face while she was holding onto the tree as if it was her very best friend in the whole world.

"You look so funny," Tommy laughed at her. "You're spitting pine tree needles from your mouth."

"Do something, Tommy!" Bernie Bento yelled. "I'm sick of you standing around all day and doing nothing. Wrap the tree up for her and call it a day."

Cookie handed Tommy five bucks. Expecting change, she held her hand out while he counted three bucks into her hand. He pulled the knife from his boot and cut a long string of brown cord to wrap around the tree to truss it into a cone shape.

Cookie watched the black boy walking out of the lot. For the first time, she noticed that the boy had a *Radio Flyer* wagon to transport the tree. The wagon had rusty parts and squealed in protest under the weight of the tree. No such luck for Cookie; she didn't own a wagon. It bothered her that Tommy had been so mean to the boy just because he was black. She knew it had nothing to do with his deformed mouth. Tommy used the boy's scarred-up mouth as an excuse to pick on him without using the "N" word. Everything Tommy did and did not do with the boy was as if he had called him the "N" word a dozen times. It was unfair, and Cookie knew how it felt to be treated this way.

"How are you going to get this tree home?" Tommy leered at her. His lips were shiny and wet and his breath emitted steam into the cold air.

It wasn't the first time Cookie had dragged a Christmas tree home. She was an old pro. The first time Cookie bought a Christmas tree, she was eight years old and dragged it home, so she could make Christmas for her family when her mother could not. By the time she was ten, she had the sensibility of a twenty-five-year-old woman because if she did not take charge, no one else would.

"Add some extra rope to make a handle sticking out on the bottom of the base," she told Tommy.

"You're going to haul this tree home! That's how the Cookie crumbles," he chided her.

The sun had gone down and a soft haze of fog and drizzle clustered around the floodlight that was temporarily hung on the edge of a metal gutter to illuminate the parking lot. A black, white and red metal sign on the building read *Sherwin-Williams Paints and Varnishes Sold Here*. Cookie liked the sign, which showed a huge glob of red paint covering a rendition of a globe that was as black & white as her composition book. The image was supposed to mean Sherwin-Williams Paints could color the entire earth.

Cookie saw a filmy glow settling in around the streetlamps. While it wasn't that cold, not when compared to the cold snap a few weeks ago, it was the dampness and the thought of the descending darkness that made her shiver. She took the tree by the dangling cord that served as a makeshift handle and dragged it up onto Palisade Avenue, turning left by Morsemere Market, which back in the day had been *Gristedes*, a big grocery store chain in Manhattan. By the time she reached the corner of North Broadway, the rain had started in a steady trickle. It felt cold and icy, like it could turn to snow, but turning to snow would make the whole scene too pretty and too much like the wonderful world some people have when their parents are there to make Christmas for them.

Ten

Saturday, January 24, 1970

Cookie was running away from home but not today. The temperature last night had dipped to a record-breaking -12°F. It was so cold, Cookie had left the water turned on and running at a steady drip in the bathroom and kitchen sinks. She was afraid the pipes would freeze and she'd have to call a plumber to come by with a blow torch to thaw the outside pipes. It had happened once before and given the long cold spell, it could happen again. So far this January had been one of the coldest on record, with an average daily temperature of 12°F. Even with the heat turned up all the way, she could feel the cold air, a stunning chill making her bones ache even though she wore thermal underwear, two pairs of pajama bottoms, a thick robe, two pairs of socks and big fluffy faux fur slippers.

She tried to get into the kitchen to open a can of Campbell's soup and heat it up for herself and Donny. Every time she tried to go into the kitchen, she heard her mother moan and cry out as if she was in pain.

Cookie could not see out of the living room window. The glass was opaque with a thick crust of ice that had bled across the window with no particular pattern except to prevent her from seeing outside. She didn't want to be here. She felt trapped, like a small caged animal. She crept around the shag green carpet of her living room, inching toward the kitchen so she could get something to eat. She suspected that Donny had found a box of stale Oreos and taken them to her room so she wouldn't starve to death. The little girl had been quiet for some time and had not come out of her room. Cookie didn't want to bother her. She didn't know what to tell her, when, or if, things would get better. As soon as the weather warmed up, she was running away from home.

Kitty Colangelo was crazy, but she didn't deserve to be treated this way. And yet no one knew what to do with her or how to help her. Of all the sicknesses in the world, Cookie thought schizophrenia was God's most awful curse. Her mother had stopped her ranting and went into a catatonic state. She laid sprawled out on the sofa in the TV room and stared toward the ceiling as if she was in a trance. Her hair was unkempt, unwashed and knotted into a sloppy bun with a few bobby pins. She wore the same pair of aqua satin pajamas day and night. She didn't eat, drink or move about to do anything. She was beyond reach. And in some ways, at that moment, she was beyond hope.

Johnny Colangelo made a point of staying away from home for longer stretches. He'd come home well after midnight and leave first thing in the morning; that is, if he came home at all. Donny stayed in her room and watched TV. Cookie didn't remember seeing the little girl during the day or after school. In the morning, she vaguely remembered making sure Donny was wearing her uniform and getting out the door to go to school.

The last time Kitty Colangelo had been committed to a mental institution, Cookie learned how to cook. At nights she opened a jar of *Aunt Millie's Spaghetti Sauce* and ladled it over *Ronzoni Spaghetti*. Soon she learned to take ricotta cheese and mozzarella cheese and stir them into the burbling sauce to make a rich concoction and spoon it over short tubular pasta that had been cooked—*al dente* for twelve minutes—in boiling water, to throw it all into a casserole and make baked ziti. She learned how to make a cheese omelet, and oatmeal from scratch, boiling oats from the *Quaker Oats* canister. No one taught her to cook. She just did it as a matter of necessity.

While it was nice to have her mother home from the nut-house, Cookie was frustrated, because she and Donny could not get a proper meal. The girls were not allowed to go into the kitchen. Kitty didn't want anyone in the kitchen; it was her domain. Cookie was terrified if she did go into the kitchen, she'd end up in a knock-down, drag-out fight with her mother. While Cookie was athletic and strong, she was no match for a person who was unequivocally psychotic, and as a result, super human, almost demonic in strength.

Cookie put her head down on the rug. She didn't weep or feel much of anything. No matter what happened, Cookie Colangelo did not cry. Crying was a sure sign of weakness. She was just trying to understand it all, and could not for the life of her figure out why her mother was so sick when she had been so good. She didn't set out in life wanting to be anything other than a good girl.

When Cookie was a child, being good meant climbing steps as quickly as possible without nicking her shins on the way up. For years, Cookie had already been going to the store for her mother, running all of her errands. Kitty Colangelo was afraid of leaving the house. When Cookie was a little kid, she shopped at the grocery store, the hardware store and even did her banking when she was just six years old. Every Friday, she walked on the overpass above the railroad tracks off of Yonkers Avenue to deposit Johnny Colangelo's paycheck. When she entered the Gramatan Bank, the tellers fussed over her, smiling and giggling, because she was so small that she could hardly reach the window to make a deposit. Still, she reached higher, and that meant standing on her tiptoes.

Being good had gotten her nowhere. It did not make her mother well, and only served to get her in trouble every which way she turned.

"Please," Cookie yelled out aloud. She was met with an equally loud moan from her catatonic mother who was flopped on a couch two rooms away.

Cookie's body shuddered with a sudden fresh surge of cold rushing in from the living room bay window. She moved forward, dragging her body along the rug slowly and keeping her breathing low, almost nil. She inched along the rug until she reached three steps leading down into the kitchen. She considered doing a slow slide down the steps and landing softly onto the speckled linoleum kitchen floor. Instead she stayed on the brink of the top step deciding what to do.

On the ground of her freezing-cold living room, she looked eye-level at a long rectangular water radiator that was low to the floor and ran the length of the entire inner wall. Slowly she rose from the ground, pulling her blanket around her, tiptoed toward the cabinets under the oven and opened the door. She reached in to feel around for a can or two or three. Without looking, she could not tell if she was touching a can of green beans or creamed corn, which was maddeningly frustrating when all she wanted was a can of any old kind of soup. She meant to place each one on the floor until she found what she was looking for. The work was slow and tedious. She did not want to make one sound, not even her breath or the movement of her thigh, tucked sideways under her body. She moved each can through the air as softly as a feather-filled pillow and rested each one on the floor. Just when she eyed her prize—a can of *Campbell's Chicken Noodle Soup*—she heard the unmistakable voice of her mother. "What are you doing in my kitchen?" she whispered.

Cookie rose onto her feet, clutching the can between her hands. "We're hungry," she said. "I want to make soup for Donny and me."

"You're not supposed to be in here," Kitty shrieked. Her eyes bulged from their sockets. Kitty had naturally large eyes to begin with, but her madness made them bug-eyed. "Jesus, Mary and Joseph, don't you know you'll get your germs everywhere?" She lunged at Cookie and stuck her nails in her arm. "Give me the can," she screamed.

"I'm not going to let you have it," Cookie pulled it back like a football she was about to pass to a wide receiver.

"Give it to me!" Kitty attacked her, yanking her hair and hitting her in the face. Cookie shoved the kitchen chair in front of her and it became a barrier between them, with Kitty darting from side to side and rushing forward, trying to knock Cookie to the ground. Now the two of them landed at both sides of the table and ran around and around. Kitty heaved herself with all of her might hurdling herself at Cookie, who in turn, shoved the table forward. At the same time, Kitty was trying to push the table forward. The force of both women shoving the table turned it over on its side, dragging the entire wrought iron base, and knocking Kitty down to the floor, where the heavy Formica table top smacked her in the face and she started to cry.

Cookie was horrified, seeing her mother crumpled on the floor under the massive round table. Kitty didn't stir. Cookie thought she had killed her. She knelt down beside her mother. Her mother cried, "You hit me. You hit your own mother." She pulled herself up from the floor. Sobbing uncontrollably, she said, "Wait until your father comes home. And I'll tell him you hit your mother."

Cookie still had the can of soup in her hand. "Get out of here. Go away!" she told her mother. "You go lie down. I'm going to make soup for us."

Donny stood still in the entrance to the kitchen. Cookie did not know how much of the fight she had witnessed, but she had to be scared to death. "This is my kitchen from now on," she told her mother. "We have to eat."

Cookie staked her domain in the kitchen and immediately went to work. She found a can opener in a drawer. Aside from whimpering filling the house, a soft little-girl cry from Donny and the twisted whispering and sobbing of her madwoman mother, the only other sound came from the can being opened and the clang of a small *Revereware* copper bottom pot being placed on top of the gas stove. Cookie turned on the gas, struck a match and ignited a small flame under the small pot.

Soon the kitchen was filled with the scent of hot soup which steamed the inside of the kitchen windows. Cookie made two peanut butter sandwiches to dip in the soup. Donny sat hunched in a small ball in the nook between the counter and the refrigerator, watching Cookie the whole time. There wasn't any reason why the girls couldn't eat. The house was filled with staple kinds of food: cans of vegetables, fruit and soup. A milkman delivered dairy goods every other day. Cookie felt horrified about what had happened to her mother. She replayed the image of her mother crumpled on the floor. The pain cut her to the quick, way down inside where no one should ever have to go. There were no tears, though.

Eleven

Sunday, April 26, 1970

Helicopters rained from the maple trees and settled into sheets on the ground. Cookie picked up a helicopter from the ground, parted its shiny green skin, revealing its inner sheath that was as sticky as scotch tape, and stuck it on the bridge of her nose. She had done this same ritual with helicopters many times before; it was her rite of spring in Yonkers. Even though she was all of thirteen, halfway on the road to turning fourteen, and had smoked pot, sold drugs, hung out with hippies in Untermyer Park, made a trip to Woodstock, was in love with *Blind Owl* Alan Wilson, and openly defied nuns, priests, fat old Italian men, young freak or hippie guys, and crazy women, including the Italian girls and her own mother, she still succumbed to acting like a kid.

When she first spied signs of the thick sheaths of helicopters spinning down from the trees, making the sidewalks slippery with their flattened green wings, she felt compelled to take one apart, cleaving it open in two and wearing it on her nose. For old time's sake, she pretended it was a grasshopper that would suddenly pop off her nose and sprint high into the air. She wasn't completely ready to give up being a kid. It was her childhood, and as much as some had tried to take it away from her, she wasn't going to give it to them, not easily and not without a good fight.

The clocks had been turned ahead by an hour; there would be light in the sky until nearly 8 p.m. Most days this month felt more like March than April; the temperatures hovered in the forties. This year Easter had fallen in March and a surprise snow storm dumped eight inches on Yonkers, and that was after a record-freezing winter. A few nights it had been colder, dropping down into the thirties. It seemed like spring would never come. Then today it was balmy, so spring-like, with clear skies, a full sun, and small baby sprigs of green leaves, blades of grass and tender buds of flowers seemed to be sprouting. Today was the first real day of spring! The earth had come alive and trembled with new growth. Everyone seemed to shuck off their coats like tired old husks so they could feel warmth from the sun touching their skin.

A single sheet of newspaper was rolled up into a wad and thrown into the planting strip in front of her house. The *Yonkers Herald Statesman* was a few days old. Cookie picked it up and read the headline: *The Beatle Thing is over*, Paul McCartney had said. The Beatles had officially broken up. When Paul McCartney stated that he was leaving the band, it was finally over, finished, kaput. Cookie scoffed to herself, every other month, when one of the Beatles said he was leaving the band. Then they'd come out with another new album. She didn't believe them any more than she trusted her parents, her teachers or the Catholic church. She didn't trust anyone. They all lied! Except for the *Blind Owl*. Cookie believed, if she ever met him, he would tell her the truth. Cookie carried a small plastic white cassette player that hummed *Blind Owl*'s falsetto tune *Going Up The Country*. Since late last summer, the song had become the unofficial anthem of Woodstock. She played the song over and over until some parts slowed down because the tape had loosened away from its spool from rewinding it so many times, and she dared not fix it, fearing she would tear the tape in two. It was best to hear it slow in parts and skip a beat than not to hear it at all.

On Arden Place, small wooded areas overgrown with Maple and Sumac trees sat to the side of Cookie's childhood home and in-between other homes. Arden Place itself was a gentle slope, more than a hill, and was located right around the corner from North Broadway and the North End neighborhood. The house that Johnny Colangelo had built was a modest three-bedroom home that had a large open bay window and sat perched on a rocky cliff. With its many steps, several flat planes were landings navigating directional turns, to the left, to the right, then winding around to a final destination, all the way up to the top. Cookie had no problem navigating the steps. She enjoyed seeing how fast she could climb without nicking her shins on concrete.

During the months when the weather was warm, her legs were usually a bloody mess, not so much from falling due to her trick knees but more due to her tomboy nature. Prior to her calling to become a gangster or a hippie, she was one helluva tomboy and scraped her knees on the pavement by sliding to home base in kickball or failing to make a jump while scaling a cliff, a fence or a wall.

The lot where Johnny had built the house was said to be unusable. Johnny never listened to anyone, especially people who said he would never be able to put a house on that lot. Johnny liked proving people wrong. Pure bedrock; there was no way to dig a hole for the foundation. Johnny bought the lot cheap, cheaper than any other lot in Yonkers, he had told Cookie, but she knew what her father said was an exaggeration. Johnny Colangelo made everything seem bigger, richer, rounder, or conversely, uglier, smaller, the worst and more tragic than it really was. He was an Italian guy from Yonkers and he was wired to exaggerate—everything.

Take the actual demolition of the rock. In Johnny's estimation, it was the largest explosion that had ever happened
in Yonkers. More dynamite had been used than in any other
time in history, including the war he had fought in Korea, and
certainly more than was being used in the war in Vietnam.
The force of the explosion was so great that it was heard
all the way up in Poughkeepsie. Although five neighboring
homes had been damaged and suffered cracks in their walls,
no one ever sued Johnny for damages. And this much was
true. Cookie knew no one bothered to sue Johnny because
they thought he was unpredictable. There was no telling what
he might do.

Johnny built the house with his own hands and with the
other boys from the neighborhood, all of whom had a special
skill, bricklaying or masonry, tile work, plumbing, electrical,
carpentry; they knew how to do something well without having
to get paid cash for their work. Johnny repaid them with cases
of liquor—their choice of booze. They wanted *Johnnie Walker
Black* or *J&B Scotch* because they thought it was classy. No
money changed hands.

On any given day, Cookie could walk out her front door
and descend into the street in front of her house and kids all
over the 'hood would just flock together. Soon everyone would
spontaneously erupt into a game. There were no organized
sports in the 'hood. The kids made up games and played out
on the street all day long until the sun went down.

Cookie set her tape cassette player on the lower landing,
the first step leading up to the house, and turned it off. Arky
Lovato came bounding out of the house from across the street.
Fortunately, Lizzie was nowhere to be seen, so Cookie did not
have to deal with her, or so she thought. Within two minutes,
Lizzie was in the street, trailing behind Arky as he stood in
the center of the road on Arden Place. Soon Tommy Parrello
showed up with a ball. Arky's sister Lizzie grabbed the ball
from Tommy and he chased her. Lizzie hit a slick of oil on the

steepest section—the raised bubble section of the road that made it a slope instead of flat ground—and she started skidding. She caught herself before tumbling to the ground. The ball flew out of her hands and Tommy rushed in and caught it. Tommy dribbled the soft ball like it was a basketball, but its skin was thin, and it wasn't stable or weighted like a true basketball, so it wobbled away from him.

Cookie hesitated for a minute. She was done playing on the street. But her reflexes kicked in and she didn't even think about what she was doing. Cookie dove for the ball, grabbed it out from under Tommy and started running with it. Tommy was gaining on her. She dropped the ball and lunged forward, chasing it, ready to kick it, packed all of the force in both her legs until she positioned herself and kicked the ball out of the line of sight, way to the top of the hill.

"I never thought I'd see you playing on the street again!" Lizzie gave her a sullen glance like she was glad, but still feeling the sting from being ignored for so long.

"Wow," Arky Lovato said. He wasn't the only one that felt that way.

Although no one had seen Cookie in action for a long time, at least by kid standards, she had earned a striking reputation. She could outrun any boy and kick a ball to kingdom come. For a minute, Cookie was so charged up, running full speed ahead, she was totally into the blood-pumping pursuit of playing kick ball and forgot that she was a total and abject failure as an authentic Italian girl.

Tommy Parrello called for a time-out. "Let's call for players, pick sides and get a real game going."

The two boys nodded; they wanted to play ball with Cookie. It didn't matter what kind of ball. Kickball, basketball, football, softball. Within minutes, Tommy Parrello could call a game and forty kids would be corralled up to play on the street in loose, ambling teams.

Tommy grabbed the ball and tossed it to Cookie, but she

didn't see it coming. This time it hit her in the chest and bounced. "You're wearing a bra," Tommy shouted. It might have been the first time he noticed that Cookie was growing into a woman. "Cookie Colangelo is wearing a bra! Cookie Colangelo has breasts!"

Cookie was so mad, she was beside herself. His dig cut too deep. It was bad enough that he was making fun of her bra, but she knew she did not have breasts. He had to be able to see that too. It was as plain as day that her bra had the smallest cups in all of Yonkers, and that was no exaggeration. You can't get a smaller cup than a triple A. She took the ball and kicked it so hard, it flew all the way up the hill to the flat street of the back end of Rudolph Terrace, where it bounced against a fence, then shot up in the air over the fence and onto Louie Santamassino's property.

"Fuck, look at what you did, Cookie! How are we going to get the ball?" Tommy glared at her belligerently. "That's my only ball! Anyone have another ball?"

Lizzie crossed her arms and shook her head no.

"Fuck," Arky said. There's no way I'm going onto Louie Santamassino's yard. He'll kill us."

"I'll climb the fence," Cookie said.

Tommy looked at her like she was totally out of her mind. "What, are you crazy?"

Cookie looked at him with a touch of fearlessness, call it *bravata*. "I'm not a sissy like you."

"You're crazy," he said. "You're crazy, a whack job, just like your mother."

"Take it back." Cookie rushed Tommy and pulled back her arm. She was getting ready to punch him in the face. "I said, take it back. If you don't take it back, I'll take a meat cleaver to your face!"

Tommy put his hands up to his face to protect himself, looked at her slyly and gave her a snide smile. "I take it back." He was being a smart-ass and Cookie hated him for it.

Tommy looked at her; this time it was borne of sincerity.

His eyes were a touch liquid and he seemed to take a short sniff as a small sign of gathering courage. "I was really wrong to say that, Cookie. I was just being an asshole. I apologize. I didn't mean it that way. I was just being stupid. I'm a jerk."

Cookie nodded and looked down at the ground. "My mother can't help the way she is. She has an illness. It's not her fault. She was born that way."

"I know," Tommy said. "Mine does too." I can't even live with her. That's why I'm in a foster home."

It was a well known that Tommy Parrello had been taken from his mother because she was too sick to raise her children, and his father was dead. A foster family took him in and gave him a roof over his head—just for the money. Everyone knew they didn't care about Tommy or what happened to him. None of the kids on the block, or their parents, thought much of Tommy's foster parents.

Arky spoke up and saved the day. "All of our parents are whackos, twisted, drunk. They're never home. And when they are home, we don't want to be with them because they're nuts. So we all take care of one each other. Right?"

"Right," Tommy said. "The only time we stay home is when we we're too sick to go outside."

"Or when we get into trouble," Arky said.

"Right." Cookie said. "Now are you done talking yet?! Will you give me a boost over that fence?!"

If she was bold enough to go over the fence to get the ball, who were they to try to stop her? The two boys worked together as a team. Tommy cupped his hands together to create a step to boost Cookie over the fence.

She looked disdainfully at Tommy's hands as if he wasn't giving her enough manpower. "I need the both of you."

Arky stepped forward and cupped his hands too. Cookie nodded to him and placed her right foot into his hands and her left foot into Tommy's hands, while both boys heaved her upward. They pushed her butt up the front facing of the fence to the top. Cookie straddled the fence for an instant before hurdling over to the other side, where she tumbled down and landed in the center of a honeysuckle bush that was a whorl of bramble, tangled twine, green sprigs of thick verdant evergreen and patches of small, creamy white flowers. Her fall into the bush had not been too bad and she was rewarded with the fragrant scent of winter honeysuckle.

A new danger was approaching. She heard the sound of a dog barking ferociously, and it was growing closer. The abundant honeysuckle bush cut off her view from the kids on the other side of the fence. "Are you okay?" Lizzie called out.

"Yeah, fine," Cookie said, but she was wary. A barking dog was coming in her direction. She estimated the bush had lifted her four feet from the ground, but that might not be enough to protect her from the approaching dog. She tried to stand on top of the bush, but her feet were stuck in a quagmire of gnarled vine. Pressing against the fence, she stuck one toe into a chain link pocket and used her hands to pull herself up another six inches. The dog was right there now. His bark violently pounded in her ears. If she fell to the ground, his hot breath was achingly close to her feet; she was sure he would tear her apart. She held on tenaciously, clinging to the chain link to keep herself higher than the dog, who was jumping up in the air. He was so close, she felt his hot panting on the backs of her calves. She did not know how long she would last, clinging on to the fence. Tommy and Arky were calling from the other side of the fence, asking her what was going on and if she had the ball.

If she had been saved from the powerful jaws of the dog, then the worst was yet to come. Louie Santamassino came around the side of the yard, to where she had her face pressed against the chain link fence so tight that the wire mesh had made an imprint in her cheeks.

"What the fuck are you doing on my property?" he yelled. "If I told you once, I told you twice never to fucking come onto my property."

"I'm sorry," Cookie said, without looking at him. "I'm really sorry."

"Sorry," he said. "Sorry? You're sorry! What are you doing on my fucking property?"

She summoned every ounce of strength so she would not cry, but her voice quavered anyway. "I just wanted to get my ball. I kicked it over the fence by mistake. I promise I'll never do it again." She pulled her face away from the fence and tried to look at Louie Santamassino, but she couldn't twist around far enough. "Cross my heart and hope to die," she said.

"Roscoe," Louie called to the dog. "Good boy. Quiet," he commanded him. "Get off my property," Louie said.

"I can't," Cookie said. "I can't climb back over the fence."

"Then come down," Louie said.

"What about the dog?" Cookie cried.

"He'll leave you alone. Get off the fucking fence. You're ruining my honeysuckle vine!"

Cookie slowly slid down the side of the bush and saw for the first time that Roscoe was a large German shepherd, mostly black, with a tan crest running up the center of his chest. His ears were perfect points, and his eyes focused strictly on her while he emitted a low, throaty growl.

Louie had the dog by his chain link collar. "Roscoe, be still," Louie told him.

Louie Santamassino was short, the same size as Cookie. She looked eye-to-eye with him. His mouth was locked in a straight line, like a dash. He was wearing oversized, thick black-framed eye glasses that magnified his brown eyes to the size of two small slippery rocks trying to swim away. Needless to say, he did not look happy. "Get your fucking ball and get out of here."

Cookie searched around the bushes. Every time she made a move, she saw the dog's ears shoot up with greater attention. She did not know who scared her more, the dog or Louie Santamassino. Then she saw him pet the dog and talk to him as if he was a baby. His voice was almost gentle. "Good Roscoe. You're a good dog. Champ. Good dog, Roscoe. Way to go, Roscoe."

"God, I love this dog!" He looked at Cookie. Her ears were on fire. She felt flushed but knew she had not turn red. For some reason, when she was this scared and embarrassed, she became deathly pale, whiter still.

"Where's your father?" Louie asked her.

"I don't know," Cookie said. "I don't know where he is today."

"It's Sunday," Louie said. "Doesn't he take you to church?"

Cookie shook her head. She didn't say anything. She didn't know what to say to Louie. He looked like he was somebody important. She had heard that he was a gangster, but he seemed real nice. She took one small step forward and immediately her knee went out and she was down on the ground. The sudden movement made Roscoe bark. Louie looked confused. "What the hell happened?"

Cookie pretended as though she did not really fall and she was intentionally reaching for something on the ground, or as if she was checking the shoelaces on her *Keds* to see if they were untied. "It's nothing." Cookie sprang up from the ground, clung on to her knee and hobbled forward. "I have a trick knee. It just goes out on me all the time."

"I've never seen anything like that," he said. "Are you sure you're alright?"

Cookie nodded, straightened to stand up and began walking gingerly. She wasn't placing her full weight down on the injured knee. Slowly it melded back into its socket, but not without causing Cookie some pain. Yet she didn't complain or cry out, and did her best to refrain from grimacing.

"I'll walk you to the front yard and you can walk on Broadway to get back home." She was worried about the dog. "Come on," Louie said. "He won't hurt you now. He knows you're not trying to hurt me."

Louie walked with her through a huge expanse of yard, a perfect lawn, with fruit-bearing trees and groves of Sumacs. Poplars were lined against the fence abutting Fran Ochiogrosso's yard. A large built-in swimming pool had not yet been filled with water, and its inner walls had a brilliant blue cast. He led her to the side yard, where there was a grotto full of holy statues and birdbaths.

Cookie was anticipating the sight of Louie Santamassino's Madonna. Few people had seen his Madonna, but everyone knew about it. In this part of town, everyone had lawn ornaments, birds, frogs, squirrels, lambs, bear, and deer, and of course, the occasional owl. The lawn ornaments were larger than life-size, more colorful than they were in nature, replicating the great outdoors in the highest degree of scenic kitsch. The great majority resembled wrought iron pink flamingos and small families of ducks. Louie's yard disparaged generic nature and took on the tone of high holiness, with an eight-foot-tall white marble replica of the Madonna. The Madonna, forbidding, ostentatious, was Kitty's favorite talisman. When she was really tooting, she used to stand on the other side of Louie's fence and engage in casual conversation with the Madonna. Louie didn't seem to mind Kitty hanging around on the other side of his fence and talking to herself. He could be generous that way.

While Cookie's experience with Louie Santamassino wasn't great, it was nowhere nearly as bad as what had happened to her at school, not even close. Louie was crude and threatening, but he seemed reasonable somehow. He didn't want anyone on his property, and that's all there was to it. As she walked down the steps from Louie's house, she realized that she did not have the ball, which made the whole situation that much worse. She made an oath to herself, adding one more to the many oaths she had already made. This was the last time she was going to act like a kid and play on the street. As far as she was concerned, her childhood was done.

Twelve

Sunday, May 10, 1970

At first Cookie did not recognize Fran Ochiogrosso because she was not wearing her school crossing guard uniform. During the school year, from dawn to dusk, she wore her uniform—a square-shaped military cap, a brown uniform of matching shirt and skirt that fell down below her shins almost to her ankles. On this Sunday in May, she was dressed in a filmy aqua shift that was transparent enough to reveal her white girdle and boulder-size white brassiere. Fran had massive breasts, which all three of her daughters had inherited. Fran was coming up the hill, panting a bit, looking faintly out of breath. Her carrot-red hair had been shaped into a stiff bob and was plastered down from hairspray and sweat.

She immediately told Cookie how hot it was, as if she did not know. "We're breaking a record with this heat," she said. "It's 92 degrees! In May! It's only May 10th! What kind of summer are we going to be in for?"

"It's getting dangerous to be a hippie, isn't it?" Fran looked askance at Cookie's bell-bottom jeans with the American flag pasted on her seat.

There was a lot of fear percolating in Yonkers over the

Kent State shootings that had taken place a few days ago. Students at Kent State University, angry about the expansion of the Vietnam war into Cambodia, protested for three nights. On the last night of the protests, the Army Reserve Officers Training Corps building was burned to the ground. The National Guard was called in and martial law was declared. Unarmed college students were shot by the National Guard, killing four and wounding many more.

Cookie thought she was being thickheaded, but she didn't get the direct connection between her American flag on the seat of her pants and the Kent State massacre. She thought Fran would use any excuse at all as a scapegoat so she could complain. Cookie didn't like Fran because she was a snoop and a busybody who wore too much perfume and cackled like a red-headed witch.

"Is it hot or what?" she asked Cookie.

"I hadn't noticed." Cookie pulled her knee up and stood on one leg. Placing her flat foot against a utility pole, she leaned back and leered at Fran.

"I'm going to move to Florida. You mark my words," Fran said. "By the winter of 1971, I'm going to be in Florida and retired."

"Me too," Cookie cried out gleefully.

"You! You think you're going to Florida! You're retiring too? That's enough. Now I've heard it all."

Even at thirteen, Cookie knew the only way to stop an assault from Fran Ochiogrosso was to launch a major offensive strategy. "Where are you coming from? You didn't go to church dressed like that, I hope, and show your undies to Father Dunn!"

Every woman in the neighborhood was in love with Father Dunn, even Cookie's own mother. The priest was well-built, square-jawed and, unlike most of the husbands in the North End, Father Dunn didn't drink, gamble, swear or boast about *nothing*. If he had a sloppy belly, he hid it exceedingly well. You could hide a lot under a long black garment. There was something about the quasi-handsome priest that made some Yonkers mavens want to drop their panties. It might have been because the priest was purportedly unavailable to their advances. It was safe to flirt with Father Dunn. Except for the crazy antics of Kitty Colangelo, no one did anything really untoward with the priest. *Or did they*? Cookie wondered.

"Father Dunn?" Cookie crossed her arms and gave Fran a quick wink.

Fran frowned and acted like she had not heard what Cookie had said. "Debbie's home. She's up there." Fran nodded to her house, an old tract house, with weather-worn white siding and a grey shingled roof. Fran grew wild roses in the front yard, which gave her home a cottage-style charm. The most notable feature of Fran's home was the way the lot sloped down from the front of the house to the back where there was a daylight basement and a sliding door leading to a yard. It was here where Fran had spied Cookie fleeing her bedroom through the window and dangling on the clothesline.

With her keen eyesight, Fran kept a perpetual watch on Louie Santamassino. No one knew much about him. He didn't seem to have a job, which was cause for suspicion. In Yonkers, the only people who didn't have jobs were either rich or on welfare. Rumors circulated about Louie. Aside from gossip claiming he was a gangster, there was talk about his wife. Johnny Colangelo said Louie's wife, Greta, was a 200-pound, broad-shouldered, blonde German woman who came from a family that owned a chain of laundromats in the Bronx, but no one had laid eyes on her in nearly three years.

Cookie chided her. "Any news about Louie Santamassino?"

"Louie Santamassino?!" Fran started laughing until she erupted in a throaty smoker's cough. Louie Santamassino is a menace to society. He has no right to live in such a rich house in the middle of hard-working people like us."

"I know you watch him," Cookie suggested slyly. "That's probably why you're wearing that negligée out in public. You're probably hoping you'll run into him.

Well, he lives that way," Cookie pointed up the hill, a few houses beyond where Fran lived.

Cookie opened her pack of *Marlboros* and offered one to Fran.

"What are you doing with cigarettes?"

"These are Johnny's cigarettes," Cookie lied. She lit the cigarette for Fran, who took a long inhale and then spat out, "These are too strong!"

"What's going on with Louie Santamassino?"

"Got caught killing a praying mantis! He did, honest to God, and I'll swear on a stack of bibles." Fran was nodding head emphatically yes. "I saw him do it."

"No sirree," Cookie was incredulous. "Not a praying mantis."

"It's against the law to kill a bug that big. I saw him in the backyard with that big dog he's got."

"Roscoe?"

"Yeah, the German Shepherd. He was on his patio, then he saw the bug. You know how big these bugs can be. There's no mistaking one. It's the biggest bug I've ever seen, and green too. Well, he took a garden hose nozzle, the top part that sprays the water, and just smacked that poor bug into smithereens. I mean, there was nothing left but a green blot of a stain on his patio." Fran's voice was getting raspy and she coughed a little. "Wish I had something to drink," she said. "It's so damn hot."

"Not to change the subject, but did Debbie have her b-b-baby?" Cookie wasn't stuttering on purpose; it just came out that way.

"That's a fresh thing to say," Fran said. "I should slap your face for talking that way. And I would slap your face, but you're not my daughter. Besides, I want you to do a favor for me."

Cookie started walking away from Fran. She couldn't help asking about Debbie who had her third baby. Every other year, Debbie got pregnant and Fran sent her off to an unwed mothers' home where she could give the baby up for adoption. No one had ever seen Debbie Ochiogrosso big and pregnant, but the news traveled fast. Every time she disappeared for awhile, everyone knew she was knocked up again. Fran had two daughters older than Debbie who had married and moved to Florida. Cookie hadn't seen them in years; they never came back to Yonkers. Someday Cookie was going to do the same thing. She was going to leave and never come back, but she wasn't going anywhere near Florida. Moving to Florida was like packing Yonkers in your suitcase and taking it with you.

Fran called after her, "Yonkers is going to the dogs. I can tell you right now, this city's ruined for good. Between the heat and all the niggers, I'm not staying here no more."

Cookie thought Fran was real *Yonkers*. Here she was as hot as a dog in heat, and somehow it was the fault of the blacks, *the niggers*, as she called them. This was the *Yonkers way*, complaining about something that had no bearing on what was really bothering you. *The Yonkers way was finding a good scapegoat to rant about.* She stuck her hand into her shoulder sack, pulled out a *Marlboro* and lit it, to intentionally provoke Fran. Cookie didn't really feel like smoking. The heat made smoking more unpleasant than usual. She thought for sure by smoking she would just get rid of Fran.

"My God, you're smoking now! Next thing you know, you'll be lying in the gutter and consorting with low-lifes."

"How many babies has your daughter, D-D-D-Debbie, had now?" Cookie grinned, baiting her, and counted on her fingers, "One, two, three. Three!! We're up to three! And she's not even seventeen!"

Fran eyed her with venom. "Your time is coming, Concetta Colangelo. You mark my words. How old are you now?

Thirteen. By this time next year, you'll be knocked up too. You know the saddest thing about it?"

Cookie eyed her coldly. "That's not a very nice thing to say."

"Know the saddest thing about your getting knocked up?" Fran folded her arms and gave her a strange smile. "It will be a Negro baby."

Cookie knew she had been dealt a mighty barb. In Yonkers, there wasn't anything worse than using the race card as the ultimate insult. Cookie didn't understand Fran any more than she understood the evil nuns. She didn't want to be at their mercy. And she didn't want Fran to be watching her every move.

"Does your father know that you're smoking? I could tell him, you know."

"Yes," Cookie said. "He found out the other night."

Fran crossed her arms, "What did he say?"

"Not much," Cookie said, and that much was true. Johnny Colangelo didn't get bent out of shape over smoking cigarettes. "You know Johnny. He didn't say much about it."

"Where's your mother?" she asked Cookie. "I hope she's still not writing poems about me." She gave Cookie an unexpectedly large smile. Fran didn't care much for Cookie and even though she was smiling, Cookie could tell she was a phony. Cookie had good radar. She could just sense things about people and always knew when they were sincere or not. There were many things Cookie could not do. She could not sing, dance or play a musical instrument. Since she had landed Fangs as her math teacher, her grades in math and in every other subject had plummeted. She used to be good at math until she switched schools and ended up at Christ the King. Cookie couldn't do much of anything. She could write poetry and stories, though. She had her words.

"I'm going to write a book about this place," Cookie said. "I have talent."

Fran shook her head as if she felt sorry for Cookie. "Your father's never home and your mother's not right in the head,"

Fran said. "Who's taking care of you?"

"My grandmother," Cookie lied. She had not seen her grandmother in months.

"Who's doing your laundry?" Fran asked.

Cookie folded her arms and gazed at the ground. She wore the same jeans with seventeen patches every day when she wasn't wearing a school uniform. Her jeans were another type of uniform, a symbol of who she was, at the crossroads of being a hippie and a gangster. She wasn't going to let Fran Ochiogrosso make her feel awkward and ashamed. She had felt this way before, and knew it wasn't her fault. Then she looked at Fran with a small measure of sincerity. "We send our clothes to the Chinese Laundry."

"The Chinks! No way!" Fran whispered to her, "Aren't your bills really huge?"

Cookie didn't answer her. She turned her back on Fran and walked away. She looked up at her own house and saw that the curtains in the front window had been parted and were now moving back into place. She knew her mother had been watching her the whole time. She dreaded the interrogation that would follow. Kitty would want to know every little detail about what had been said, and exactly how Fran had looked when she said it. Cookie was her mother's foothold in reality, her liaison to an outside world she was unable to live in.

Let it be, Cookie thought. The Beatles had just released an album, *Let it Be*. Unknown to Cookie at the time, *Let it Be* would be the last album ever released by the Beatles. Cookie didn't know how to explain to her mother that even though she had never known a single black kid in her schools, she knew blacks were no different than everyone else. Her first teacher was Mrs. Kerry, who had touched her in some way she could not explain. She wanted a world were humanity knows not of color, shape or form. She wanted Yonkers to be like life in the *Eastside Comedy* and the *Bowery Boys* films. *Let it be.*

She dreaded going into her home. Kitty would be all over her in an instant, ready to belt her or bribe her or baby-talk her, whatever it took for her to get Cookie to weave a new story about Fran. Cookie took the steps, two at a time, watching for more signs of movement in the front window, but the curtains remained still. When she got to the top landing, the front door was wide open. Not a good sign, Cookie thought to herself. She would not have come home at all and would have traveled straight *Down the End* to hang out, but she needed to cop some of her mother's ludes.

She tiptoed into the small hallway and took off her shoes. Kitty didn't allow shoes in the house. She placed her moccasins on the floor so softly that she made no sound. She knew where all the creaks in the floor boards were and walked sideways in a zig-zag to descend into the kitchen, one soft step at a time, until her bare feet landed on smooth linoleum. Then she screamed. Her scream was borne from horror more than fright.

Wearing only a white bra and white cotton panties, her mother was sitting on the kitchen counter. A large soup pot held water that was boiling violently, sending up a cloud funnel of steam that was becoming dense and mushroom-like. The room reeked of bleach, and Cookie saw the white plastic jug marked *Clorox* on the counter next to the stove. Kitty was holding her foot over the top of the pot and scraping her foot with a pumice stone that looked like a jagged chunk of cement. She didn't see Cookie and cried out to herself the words *sin, clean, filth, prostitute, germs, dirty, scumbag, you scumbag,* in no particular order. Cookie knew the words had no meaning to anyone except Kitty, for whom a whole story was being played out in her mind, and in her mind alone.

"Kitty?"

"Get out of here, you dirty cocksucker, you dirty thing," Kitty spat out.

Cookie clutched her arms to stop herself from shaking. "Where's Donny?"

"Donny, Donny," she cried out in a shriek. "She's doing her homework! No, she's not. No she's not! That dirty cock sucking whoremaster, he's come and taken her away! She's going to be a prostitute, a whore for the church! Father Dunn's taking them all in while the girls are young! Cocksuckers!"

Kitty's normally perfect bob of wave-set hair was a matted frizzy mop falling into her eyes, and her face was dripping with sweat. She had picked a good day to boil and pickle her feet. It was as hot as hell out, and there she was, hatched over the top of a pot of boiling pot of water. Cookie didn't know who to call or who to tell about what was going on. No one could help Kitty. Cookie looked at her mother's eyes, which were black and unreachable, her pupils diminished to pin pricks, as if she could no longer see Cookie or Donny or anything in the world, and could only hear the twisted terror that was going on in her head.

"That cocksucker won't leave me alone," she cried. "No matter how clean I make my feet, he keeps coming here, dirtying my curtains. Filthy curtains! Filthy cocksucker."

In later years, Cookie learned a lot about schizophrenia and felt like a veritable walking encyclopedia. She came to know that a schizo's psychotic ranting took on the parameters of their own unique personality. In Kitty's case, much of her prattle was scatological and related to the Catholic Church. "Filthy cocksucking priest!"

Kitty had been growing increasingly delusional for weeks. And lately, Johnny had not come home, not even to check in.

Kitty rubbed harder on the soles of her feet, as if she was removing thick skin and callouses that had plagued her for days. She cried a little, then spewed a string of epithets renouncing the Catholic church, the twelve apostles, the Virgin Mother and Father Dunn. "Cocksuckers," she intoned. "Dirty maggots getting under my pretty white skin!"

Cookie stood there and watched, mesmerized by her

mother scrubbing her feet, alternating one with the other. She was afraid that she would rub them raw, and her feet would start to bleed. She was afraid of pulling her mother off the counter and away from danger. In her madness, Kitty was strong enough to kill or maim, even her own daughter. Madness knew no limits. Kitty could go on like this for days, getting weirder and more disturbed, until she became lost and totally cut-off from reality. She had an obsession with cleanliness: clean things, clean people and clean thoughts. People were not allowed to wear their shoes in the house. Cookie and Donny were not allowed to have friends come in the house to play. Kitty said the kids had germs. People had germs. Priests had germs. The world was full of germs.

Cookie stumbled out of the kitchen. It was hot for May, and having a boiling cauldron on the stove dished up even more heat and made the house feel like an inferno. She peeped around the corner, searching. "Donny?"

She climbed the steps, thinking she'd find her sister in her room. The bedroom door was ajar, so she pushed it open. Donny's bed was piled with crumpled sheets, some twisted like rope and others pushed into wads. The room was a mess, not a little kid's messy room, but a cave that gave refuge to a small, wild creature. The bedding, two grape juice stained pillows, and two pink threadbare blankets were in a heap at the foot of the bed. Cookie kneeled and looked under the bed, where a wasteland of tired-looking stuffed animals, a lone slipper, three stray socks, pink plastic jewelry, pick-up sticks, a toy stethoscope, a pile of wrinkled underwear, a toy pick-up truck, balled wads of junk food wrappers and dust bunnies stared back at her. She stood up and pulled open the closet door. Immediately a barrage of blankets, clothes and board games came tumbling down and hit her in the head. She was under assault from an avalanche of a plastic crib headboard, an electric keyboard, an old cassette tape player and a fairy princess costume Donny had worn for Halloween several years ago. There were all of these bits and pieces from the cruel narrative of Donny's life, but no sign of her.

Cookie slid down the steps, which were carpeted in a worn weave of olive green, and slipped out the side door. She looked in the yard for Donny, but could not tell how long it had been since she saw her. It might have been two days. She tried to recollect the last place and could not pinpoint the precise day and time. She was immediately filled with self-loathing and disgust. Donny could be hurt or gone or worse, and Cookie had not done much to help her. She was so absorbed in her own thoughts that she had not been looking out for her little sister. She didn't believe in the God of the nuns who had harmed her in large and small ways, and yet she found herself praying anyway, striking a bargain with God that if she found Donny, she would never ignore her again.

Some prayer, she thought; it did little to dispel her despair. She walked into the small woods where the Lily of the Valley would soon begin to bloom. The air was so thick with heat that the tender buds on trees glinted and jutted forth in a salute to the slant of sun streaming in between the trees. It was over ninety degrees on this tenth day of May, and her mother was boiling herself to death while her sister was gone, never to be found again.

"Cookie," someone called. "Cookie, is that you?"

Cookie stood on the edge of the woods, on a bank abutting the red brick landing outside of the door that led to the basement. "Cookie," someone said again. "Concetta Mary Bernadette Colangelo, is that you?" She knew it was not Donny. *Bernadette* was not a given name, but one she used because she felt like it. *Someone had to know her really well to know about Bernadette.*

The voice was as old as her grandmother's and crackled with the hesitation of someone who did not want to be found. "Come here, dearie."

Cookie was not convinced of its sincerity. As a matter of

fact, her hearing grew more acute, and although she stayed calm and still, she was on alert, almost blending in with the trees so she could quickly take cover. From out of nowhere, a small pebble grazed the left side of her head and she ducked. Then another rock whizzed by, and another and another. Someone was flinging rocks at her head and missing by only a hair's breadth. She fell to the ground, took cover and placed her hands over the top of her head, in the same pose she had taken during nuclear attack drills at school. As she squatted in a crouched position, she confirmed the direction and stance she would take to spring forward and get out of the line of fire. She made her move, leaping forward in a great broad jump that was a distance greater than her height. She flew through the air and landed across the meadow of the Lily of the Valley, dismayed to think she could have crushed the new growth of its blade-like leaves. Her one foot padded softly, barely touching ground, while she lifted herself in a whorl of jumps out of the small meadow and into the flat plane of grass that belonged to her neighbor's yard. Then she heard a keening sound, strange and high-pitched; it was laughter, and undoubtedly, more than one person was laughing at her.

Cookie stood up from the ground and saw Lizzie Lovato and her own sister laughing and pointing at her. The two of them were having the time of their lives. Donny's face was red and rippling with excitement like a fire hydrant, diverting attention away from her hands, which held a small slingshot. Cookie was so mad, she felt a greater heat and alarm flooding her body. She was going to kill Lizzie and Donny. She took off as fast as her girl-tomboy's legs would take her. She didn't want to rely on her fast sprinting victories of the past, but her well-practiced days and days of kickball games did still serve her well. She was instantly on top of them both, pinning them down on the ground.

"Ouch," Lizzie protested. "Stop it, you're hurting me."

She let go of Lizzie, slapped her on the thigh and as a

second thought, chafed her arm, giving it a quick rap. She picked up Donny from the ground in a giant bear hug and realized her sister had grown. *When had this happened*? Then she shook Donny until she dropped the slingshot to the ground. Cookie picked it up and promptly crushed it in one stomp on the ground. Donny cried out, "No!"

Cookie looked at her and saw someone other than a little girl who had inhabited the body of her sister. She had a piercing revelation that Donny had changed, and not for the better. Donny's nose was no longer too small, and fit perfectly into the contours of her face. On the verge of turning eight years old, Donny's skin was no longer baby-soft and plump, but looked harsh, as if she had grown up too fast and become thick-skinned. Certainly no one was caring about Donny! No one had paid any attention to her! Donny had been like a theater prop in the drama of Cookie's every day life—the baby sister. Now, Donny possessed a brand of toughness more alarming than a venomous snake that had shed its first skin. Donny's blue eyes looked cold and deliberate, as if she had been born to kill anything—any life form that moved. Cookie had been prepared to strike a deal with God to save Donny. Look at what God allowed to happen to Donny! This was the same God who had forsaken her, again.

Thirteen

As Black as Black Can Be

Yonkers was black & white, and there were no shades in be-tween except one—Puerto Rican. If you were Puerto Rican, you were considered neither white nor black, but something else that wasn't necessarily good or bad, just in between. So if you were not Puerto Rican and colored a shade in between black & white, you said you were Puerto Rican. This way there would be no confusion in how you portrayed your identity to the outside world. The blacks lived in south Yonkers, on Nepperhan Avenue, and all around Getty Square, which was slowly taking hold of its new name, *Ghetto Square*. And the Puerto Ricans lived in Cookie's grandmother's neighborhood, west of Herriot Street.

On Cookie's block, there were no black people, not even one. She did not know what to think about being black. It upset her, because she felt funny when she saw a black person. Her father called them *jungle bunnies, niggers, coons* and *jiga-boos*, but when he got to talking to a black jazz musician, everything changed. Suddenly two people, thick as friends, were bonding as close as two people could be, grooving on the experience of making music together, and all traces of their color were gone.

Her parents, and every adult she knew, called them *colored* or *niggers*. The nicer people called them colored, but everyone else called them bad names. Nigger, jungle bunny and coon were usually the names *du jour* and were said in public without any white folk looking askance.

By the spring of 1970, Cookie was in the eighth grade and only a few weeks away from graduation. She had turned into a complete rebel and played hooky from school on more days than she actually went to school. Her rebellion took no specific form and did not have a label. Cookie still did not know if she was a gangster or a hippie and continued to straddle both worlds. As a white chick, she knew that real gangsters were black. Unless, of course, they were goombahs like her father, and Italian. Italian men were an exception to the black gangster rule. Italian men, like black men, were gangsters.

Cookie was aware of her own shortcomings. She was neither black nor male and wrestled with the gangster issue on a daily basis. She was tough enough to ride the IRT subway from the Bronx and through Harlem alone, where blacks were everywhere. Then, in Yonkers, blacks were hidden away and relegated to the tranches of *Ghetto Square* as if it was a secret hiding place as deep as the *Owl Hole*. There were many places in Yonkers where it was not safe for blacks to walk, at night or during the day.

Cookie felt a different type of discrimination. She was shut out. Every time she began to remember what had happened that day at school, she'd say to herself *Stop*. She started hiding so she could train herself to *stop thinking* in a private place where no one would find her. Cookie had hiding places all over the city where she could go to think her strange thoughts and not be bothered by anyone. The *Owl Hole* at the bottom of the unused stairwell behind the Baptist Church was only one hiding place. Some she was willing to share, but not all of them. That would be like giving away everything she owned and treasured without getting anything back.

Another hiding spot was in the tangled gnarl of dense overgrowth, weeds and bramble in the Eagle's Nest of Untermyer Park. She loved going to the park alone because she never knew who she would meet there. The worst thing was to take another girl with her; then she'd have to spend her time talking to a guinea goon girl, also known as a *Gina* who was burbling out of control and keening on the verge of become hysterical. These Italian girls acted like they were menstruating nearly every day. Either that, or they were in heat and determined to give boys a hard-on that was tantamount to a wet dream. In other words, these girls were big on teasing, but not necessarily willing to put out the fires they had intentionally ignited in the loins of young men.

Cookie was fearless about walking into the woods at Untermyer Park. She was fearless about going anywhere. Mostly. Well, here is the truth: Cookie's main ambition was appearing to be fearless even when she was scared inside. Even if she was scared shitless out of her wits, she would not show it. Not showing fear was a habit Cookie had developed long before the horribly big event that had happened to her in school. Cookie was fearless because she was ambitious enough to stand in for her mother, or anyone else who wasn't strong enough to fend for themselves.

Later in life, ambition would someday take Cookie out of Yonkers and to the most wonderful places on earth. Ambition would also take her to the depths of hell, to places where she should not have gone. By the time Cookie was thirteen, though, she had already experienced both heaven and hell whenever she crossed the threshold and gave free reign to her ambition.

So on this day, June 2nd, 1970, Cookie didn't show up at school and instead gave in to her latest whim. Her notion of ambition meant giving something a try and taking a risk, even if the consequences could turn out *really badly*. She did not know how things would turn out, whether she would travel to a wonderful place or end up in hell. As it turns out, she made an important discovery about what it meant to be young, alone and about to embark on an adventure that would change her life.

In the morning, she went out the front door as usual, but doubled-back and slinked up the other set of steps that went to the basement on the side of the house. She stopped briefly and looked into the woods where the Lily of Valley had started to bloom. There was no time to waste. The night before, she had left her jeans and shirt in the basement so she could change out of her school uniform and not be identified as a truant Catholic school girl. Armed with a pack of *Marlboros*, matches, and a pack of *Juicy Fruit* gum, she made her way *Down the End*.

Her covert preparation was completely unnecessary. Neither of her parents were in possession of minds sound enough to be monitoring her whereabouts. Some small part of her inside wanted to believe her parents might notice she was playing hooky from school, when the reality was the opposite. Johnny was never home, and Kitty was certifiably disturbed enough to be committed, if only someone would take the time to get her hospitalized.

Cookie was a trouper. Despite the realities of her parents' neglect, she took every precaution to not get caught and stole away through the woods and backyards until she passed the Owl Hole, ran across Broadway and finally arrived, a bit out of breath, *Down the End*. Palisade Avenue was inhabited by a string of retail stores, two grocery stores, Palisade Pizzeria, a dry cleaner, a bank, a liquor store and *the Chinks,* which is the name Johnny called the Chinese Laundry. Two luncheonettes both had genuine soda fountains dispensing soft drinks, egg creams, and hot fudge sundaes. The more popular soda fountain, Urich's, carried Dolly Madison ice cream.

At Morsemere Grocery Market, she bought a can of Coke and a *Ring Ding* for breakfast. In the grocery store, the radio blared the number-one hit song of the week *Everything Is Beautiful* by Ray Stevens. No one said anything to her in the store or wanted to know why she was not in school. Through no fault of her own, Cookie had already developed a bad reputation. Everyone knew her mother was crazy, and her father was mostly an absent goombah. Consequently, no one wanted to know what Cookie was doing. Whatever she was doing had to mean she was up to no good. There were a few gossip-mongers who assaulted Cookie from time to time, but mostly everyone stayed clear of her tendency to foment rebellion. No one had the gumption to block Cookie from her mission to become famous. There was no doubt about it. Cookie did not smile a lot. Quite the contrary. She twisted her small mouth into a perpetual sneer. She practiced jutting out her lip in the mirror to see how tough she could look.

Energized by her massive sugar rush, she zoomed on North Broadway toward Untermyer Park. She lit a *Marlboro* and puffed smoke heavily through her mouth and nose. From the south side close to the road, she entered the park and walked by the dilapidated caretaker's cottage that looked on the verge of caving in. Broken rafters and floorboards sat in piles in front of the wooden structure. Both massive doors were flung open and appeared to be falling down and away from the doorframe. Propped up against the outer wall, both doors had become permanently stuck in the ground and could not be further opened or shut.

Cookie walked over to the entrance of the caretaker's cottage, but did not venture in. An enormous orange tabby guarded the door with the fierceness of a livid sentinel and hissed at her. She had not yet summoned the courage to walk through the open doors. Standing in front, she saw the movement of hundreds of feral cats, some among the ugliest cats she had ever seen in her life. Two fat cats, grey and white striped, lunged toward the doors and hissed at her as if she was an outsider, the enemy. Feral they might be, but their bond with each other was stronger than death and an omen, for the day would come when they would all die together.

No one cared about the ugly cats, who could have been pretty and lovable if someone took care of them. Years later, long after Cookie had fled Yonkers, she had heard that all of the cats were destroyed and the caretaker's cottage had been torn down to pave the way for restoring the park. *Philanthropic rejuvenation,* they called it in the news. The bottom portion of the park intersected with the Croton Aqueduct and was close to the trash-filled, rat-infested banks of the Hudson River. There was no doubt that the colony of cats kept the rodent population remarkably under control. There was a time when the caretaker's cottage functioned as if it was a big barn and was home to hundreds of cats who literally bred buckets of kittens totally unfettered and out of control in a big hissing and spitting mass of matted fur, with claws and teeth as sharp as thin knives.

Yonkers had a legacy for killing cats. In a bizarre news story, not far from Cookie's old 'hood, and long after her trium-phant departure from home, a 60-year-old man named Rene Carcamo was arrested for hanging 25 dead cats from a tree. The cats had been bludgeoned to death and placed in plastic trash bags. Some of the dead cats were left on the ground. The story was memorialized forever as the *Yonkers 25*.

Many years later, interest grew in preserving the archi-tectural integrity of Untermyer Park, and there were many funding efforts being made to restore its original glory as a garden to behold. The park's deteriorating grandeur camou-flaged many secrets. Harboring feral cats wildly abandoned and cruelly neglected was only one secret. There were others. The park was a refuge, a wasteland to get wasted for fledgling hippies, wannabees, rebel upstarts who smoked pot, dropped acid, and did drug deals while tossing Frisbees, playing guitars and balling their brains out. Years later, the park could not conceal that in the midst of its sweet verdant lawns and ach-ingly beautiful gazebos and mosaic walls there were pockets of darkness, animal sacrifices, satanic mills, and devil worship.

On this day in June, 1970, Cookie meandered across the great lawn and disappeared into the woods. She did not know that danger was always traveling with her. The stories of dead animals and devil cults was already happening there and very present, burbling beneath the surface and among the people she encountered. Although at the time she did not know just how dark things were. Nor could she have known. Had she known, it is doubtful that she would have ventured into the woods alone.

At age 13, Cookie Colangelo was tough, fearless and street wise. And even though she had already navigated the subways through the Bronx and wallowed in the mud at Woodstock, she wasn't stupid. Cookie could count on being clever, resourceful, and wildly rebellious, but never stupid. Stupid she was not, and would never be. She made that oath to herself with as much conviction as her oath to one day become famous and to get out of Yonkers. *Like I'm outta here*, she said to herself, again in the form of a mantra.

On the trail to the Eagle's Nest, Cookie was confident about where she was going because she had mastered this trek a dozen times. It was a beaten path worn down by marauders more than it was a proper trail. For years it had not been maintained. The path was not yet swollen with weeds and bramble because it was only early June and summer had not yet set in. Later in August, the cluster of weeds would grow so thick that it was hardly possible to walk, and Cookie would have to stomp her way through or wait until the fall when everything died. Cookie looked for wildflowers, cornflower blue and shaped in the form of bells, with shallow roots, growing in this moist place. Her feet padded over moss and her nose tickled from the seeds of the Eastern cottonwood trees that floated in the air like clouds of fluff. The seeds were made up from hair fibers and caught light from the sun filtering in through the trees. Cookie reached out, trying to catch them like fireflies. She had made the mistake once of reaching for a firefly and was stung by a bee. Not that she really wanted to catch a seed puff. She just wanted some companion, a touch-stone along the way and on this journey to the Eagle's Nest.

The original Untermyer Park was once a palatial es-tate owned by the wealthy international lawyer Samuel Untermyer. It was rumored that Samuel Untermyer had been the only go-between the United States and Germany after dip-lomatic relations had broken down before the onset of World War II. Thus the connection to Baden-Baden and Hitler's lair in the Alps. The story of the Eagle's Nest was a Yonkers urban legend. Cookie's father told her that the Eagle's Nest was named after Hitler's secret lair in Baden-Baden. In Cookie's thirteen-year-old mind, she accepted the rumors about Samuel Untermyer to be a likely causal connection.

Sprawling for miles, the original Untermyer Estate and Gardens was a beautiful, unusual and elegant European-style park, with mosaic-lined pools and walkways, classical Greco-Roman sculpture, Doric pillars, and gazebos, all over-looking the Hudson River. Johnny Colangelo told Cookie that Untermyer's children could not afford to pay the property taxes, so they donated the entire estate to the city of Yonkers with the intention of having it turned into a public park. How much of this was true, Cookie did not know. Filled with numerous Roman amphitheaters, intricate Carrara marble archways and latticed tile work, the park symbolized the last vestige of Yonkers as *the city of gracious living*.

Cookie wasn't obsessed with the notion of *gracious living*. She only knew the park harkened to another era, a gilded era, and now the place was falling apart. The columns, walls and pools had faded and were crumbling. The gazebos and *the thousand steps* leading down to the Aqueduct were overrun with weeds and choked with layers of garbage. The only con-cession made by the city to take care of the park was when the main lawn area in the front of the park was mowed. The whole place had fallen into neglect and had become a monument to ruin and decay.

Unlike Hitler's grand alpine homestead tucked into the Bavarian Alps, the Eagle's Nest in Untermyer Park was a large gazebo located in the midst of untamed woods. From the caretaker's cottage, the path to get there was jagged and treacherous. Cookie ambled down a rocky path and kept her eyes fastened to the ground to see where she was going. Rocks of all sizes and weeds clogged the arterial. The ground was littered with beer cans and empty bottles of fortified wine— *Boone's Farm Apple Wine* and *Mad Dog 20-20* were the prominent brands.

Cookie thought her descent into the woods would be worthwhile. Sooner or later, she would make it to her destination and begin her climb to reach the inside of the gazebo. She stubbed her *Marlboro* out on a random rock jutting up from the side of the trail, unwrapped two sticks of *Juicy Fruit* gum and popped them into her mouth. Chewing hard and ferociously, she was eager to dissolve the sugar until the gum lost its flavor because then it was in prime condition to crack. Everyone knows you can't crack your gum until its flavor is gone. Cookie was trying to teach herself to crack her gum. All of the other Italian girls seemed to have taken gum cracking to a higher level—an art form—and could fire off a rapid-fire succession of pops. Cookie was lucky if she could emit just one crack and if she did it was totally random, an accidental pop.

The path was empty and through the slats in between trees, the Eagle's Nest loomed ahead in the distance. On a normal time of day, after school or at night, she'd see people passing by, coming and going on the trail. Some were hippies or neighborhood kids. Occasionally, there were strangers. Should a stranger approach, Cookie's radar went way up and she was on guard to run, kick, scratch, punch, whatever it took to keep herself free from harm. Cookie braced herself to run. She could run fast. This year in a relay race, she had outrun Toni Ferlinghetti, who had always been the fastest girl in the class until she grew breasts. Cookie smirked to herself. Even though Cookie wanted to grow breasts of her own, there was a downside to growing jumbo breasts.

She walked for about ten minutes, but today the journey seemed longer. Not a soul was in sight, and the emptiness of the path made Cookie feel guarded. She always said to herself that if anything bad happened to her, it would occur when no one was looking and no one was around. Today she felt that way, so alone. She was beyond the possibility for anyone to hear her, should she cry or call out for help. Cookie had always felt alone, no matter whether she was in the realm of the familiar or somewhere new, strange, and uncharted terrain previously unexplored. Her thoughts didn't catapult her into full-fledged fear, but she stopped focusing on the ground and hit an uneven patch of tree roots that caused her to twist her ankle; inevitably, her knee gave out. She landed softly on the ground and cursed her trick knee. She could always count on it to let her down. She didn't so much as whimper and pulled herself up quickly, hardly seeing anyone else around her who could have helped her to her feet. She brushed the soil off the back of her pants and moved on.

The gum in her mouth had finally divested itself of sugar and was fairly flavorless. She began practicing her cracking and tucked the gum in small natural crevices in her molars. So far nothing had happened, not even a light puff or pop. God, she felt like such a faggot, a doofus, she couldn't even crack gum like an ordinary Italian girl. And one of her molars had already shed most of its natural crown and was a flat plane of hurt in the back of her mouth. She didn't know, then, that most of her back teeth were falling apart.

Below the gazebo, a base of rocks in many sizes, large boulders, some sharp and jagged and sharp or misshapen; others were smoothly rounded or worn from weather and were piled on top of one another, forming what appeared to be a solid foundation. Stuck together over time and suffering from little erosion, the base of the gazebo was an intricate pile of boulders made to fit together by a master stone mason. Large hunks of grey rock were obelisk-shaped, conical-shaped or laid in thick flat panes and protruding like mushrooms, giant flying saucers, random planetary objects and miniature mountains. This was the Eagle's Nest.

Cookie later learned the Eagle's Nest had been given other names like the *Temple of Love* when it was being restored under the guiding light of tons of money and gentrification. Untermyer Park was changing and going uptown, the same way new neighborhoods were getting a come up in Manhattan and a 'hood like *Hell's Kitchen* could suddenly be renamed *Clinton*.

She headed up the trail that wound around the rock-latched and locked foundation. The trail was craggy and narrow enough for Cookie to tread softly and carefully. Now was not a time to go down with her trick knee. There was no guard rail of any sort and a misstep could mean a plummet off the side of the ledge and, while that did not guarantee or even hint at instant death, Cookie did not want to take the plunge. It would hurt worse than her trick knee. She found herself chewing more furiously and tried to tuck her gum into a pocket in her left molar to form an air pocket that could pop. Much to her dismay, a piece of her tooth broke off and got stuck in the gum, like ground glass. Another tooth was falling apart. Some time ago, it had started to hurt and throb with pain.

As Cookie wended her way around the trail, she remembered playing tag and touch football with the other kids in the 'hood in the woods that led to the site where the big house or the Untermyer mansion once stood and later had been torn down. The demolition had happened long before Cookie's time. She and the kids from the 'hood ran screaming and cutting through the woods, going around in circles and coming in through the back end of the park. The whole gang of kids scampered on the same narrow footpath where Cookie was now climbing. Their game of touch football morphed into plain old tag, where everyone started running and screaming.

The next minute, Cookie grabbled Devin Dooley so hard from behind that he came reeling backward in in an unplanned somersault and landed at the bottom of the cliff. He was sprawled out on his back and trying to cry and could not because he had the wind knocked out of him. Cookie felt ashamed of herself and leaned over him trying to make him okay and before she knew it, Devin was laughing and saying he wanted to marry her. She could swear that had only happened a year ago. And she did not know what had happened since then. She had gone from being a tomboy to a hippie or gangster girl who wanted to grow breasts.

While she ambled up the last leg of her climb up to the inside of the nest, she was humming to herself and feeling grateful about the fact that Devin Dooley had survived his fall; it meant slipping off of the Eagle's Nest did not mean death. It just meant landing the right way. As she jumped off the narrow ledge and into the gazebo, where it surrounded her view to the sky like a great umbrella, she felt grateful that she did not have to wade through a jungle to get here. The weeds were just now coming to life. She spat the lump of gum out of her mouth and watched it fall to the ground, where it disappeared below into the dry-caked soil.

It had not rained in a while, which was unusual for this time of year. Yonkers was beset with sudden squalls of rain and humidity all year long, especially in June, when the humid air was thick enough to curl Cookie's hair. Every day had been muggy, but not too hot, and it did not rain. The rain would be welcome relief to put an end to the cloying humidity. She hated the humidity because her hair was in loose frizzy ringlets, and her skin felt like an oil slick.

Normally, Cookie liked to be alone in her hiding places, but the Eagle's Nest, as remote as it was, hardly qualified as a hiding place. She was out in the middle of the woods in a rundown public park that no one watched over. Untermyer Park didn't have any guards or attendants. At all hours of the day, anyone could come here, and not everyone had good intentions. She found the stillness a bit unsettling. It was nine or ten in the morning. Cookie didn't wear a watch, but guessed it had been more than an hour since she ate her *Ring Ding* and smoked her first cigarette of the day. She felt another presence in the woods. A person or an animal? She wasn't sure.

As much as she hated to admit it, she had put herself at risk. No one knew she had gone here. There were days when she could be gone for hours, and no one noticed. With her mother in and out of mental institutions, she rarely noticed the comings and goings of a fresh thirteen-year-old girl. Cookie's father straddled between his day job in the liquor business and his weekends and nights dedicated to music. Her little sister Donny was sitting in a third grade classroom, oblivious to the absence of her big sister. If she didn't see her in the playground, she would figure that Cookie was late for school again. Everyone knew that Cookie Colangelo was perpetually tardy or absent—playing hooky.

It dawned on Cookie that no one cared what happened to her. Someone could grab her and take her away to be a sex slave in New Jersey, or kill her in the woods and bury her body in the devil's cave down by the Aqueduct. She would never be heard from again. Not that it mattered; she hadn't done much with her life anyway. To calm her nerves, she pulled out her pack of *Marlboros*, lit one, and stubbed the head of the match out in the rock. A twig snapped and she stopped grinding the match, let it fall to the ground, and listened. There was the sound of more snaps.

Looking out over the gazebo to see who or what was out there, she didn't stand up because she wanted to see them before they saw her. She didn't mind the thought of someone else being there, but the woods were creepy. A small shock wave settled in her stomach and moved upwards to her heart. There was a crunch of tin, as if someone had stepped on a beer can. The woods were littered with cans and bottles, especially *Ballantine Beer* and *Coca Cola*. Her mind was skedaddling through jumpy, distorted images while her heart was skipping small flurries to half-beats played by Jethro Tull in *Sweet Dream*. She decided to leave the Eagle's Nest before someone found her and trapped her there. If she made it back down into the woods, she could run fast and get away.

Moving forward on all fours, she felt like a small primate, a monkey or a chimpanzee. She inched forward with seamless athletic grace, careful to keep her movement controlled, stirring up little dust from the cake-dry-ground, where she moved forward onto her knees in a slow crawl. Cookie had not heard another strange sound in a while, but she wasn't taking any chances. Every turn that wound around the base of the Eagle's Nest descended to a lower level and revealed a new vista into the bank of woods. She looked upward toward the sky through the patch of trees; the sun was hidden behind dense grey clouds. Tufted cottonwood seeds floated through the air, transparent and weightless, like cotton puffs catching narrow bands of light and showing off their fragile threads.

Cookie wanted to reach out and grab the seeds by the handful to ward off harm and danger. The path seemed to widen in its circle wending around the massive rock fortress. She thought of stopping to catch her breath and how foolish she was being, when it could just be a small feral cat in the woods, and not a person at all. Aware that her jeans were getting soiled from crawling on the ground, she told herself that new holes would be good and meant she could add two more patches.

A shadow flitted by close to the side of her head. Her heart jumped and began racing. She continued to creep forward, seeing that shadow and feeling the air move. She sprang to her feet and began running on the last round of the path, spiraling downward. Her heart was pounding; her legs were carrying her forward as fast as she could go. She began to scream, shrieking in a strange keening noise. She felt someone behind her, turned and jumped, barreling headfirst into the body of something that appeared to be subhuman. Charging straight ahead like an angry animal in a herd, she plowed right into it and knocked it against the wall into a small nook in the large rocks that formed a hollow indentation of a small cave on the final ledge. The subhuman was sprawled on the ground and crying, "Please don't hit me. Please, leave me alone."

The heap on the ground sat up and trembled. "Please leave me alone!" He was a boy! A black boy! Wearing large, over-sized, black-framed eyeglasses, he was so ugly that Cookie felt sorrier for him than she was stunned at the upset of his surprising appearance and her victory in tackling him. His mouth was deformed; a chunk of his upper lip was missing and there was an open gap up to the bottom of his nose. He was a monster!

She screamed. Then he screamed. She stood still, screaming her head off. He jumped up from the ground and put his hand over her mouth. His hand smelled like cherry pop. "Please don't scream," he said, "you're scaring me." She wriggled away from him. His body was small and wiry. "Get your hand off my mouth!"

He certainly was not a big black dude. He was somewhere in-between black & white, but in Cookie's world, he was as black as black can be. They were the same height, and his eyes were huge and magnified by his glasses—they seemed to be bulging from his head. He stood there shaking, cowering like a small boy. Then it dawned on Cookie that his eyeglasses were exactly the same kind worn by the *Blind Owl*. She had never seen a black boy as funny-looking as he was. No doubt about it, this black boy was scared, and no menace to Cookie or to anyone. He cried, "Promise me you won't scream. I'm in enough trouble already."

Cookie and the boy were two mismatched animals who had clearly startled one another, and yet there was some sort of mutual connection between them as if each had recognized within the other a realm of the familiar. She would have been scared of him just because he was strange and black, but his eyeglasses made him seem harmless, and diffused any chance that he could be a potential threat. In a weird way, she found his glasses to be endearing, and yet she did not think she should be standing in the woods with a black boy. Except for her kindergarten teacher and people riding on the bus, she did not get a chance to see many black people up close and personal. Instead of feeling scared, her curiosity got the best of her. If there were any consequences to be had, she would have to deal with them in her own way on her own time. After her life-altering disastrous episode in the sixth grade, she would never be scared the same way again.

"Who are you?" Cookie asked.

The boy seemed uncomfortable and squirmed, looking down at his shoes like he was feeling real awkward. Cookie noticed his shoes were *Hush Puppies*, a forgotten brand only worn by the most uncool kids. His *Hush Puppies* were tan suede slip-ons. Without a mark or a scuff, his shoes looked brand-spanking new.

"Want one?" She offered him a *Marlboro*.

Much to her surprise, he took it. She struck a match and cupped it, lighting the cigarette for him. He drew in his first puff. Cookie watched the stream of smoke oozing from the indentation above his lip, a sight so ugly she had to look away.

The heightened sense of danger Cookie had been feeling was wearing off. Instead Cookie moved closer to the boy, peering at him as if he was an alien life form. And in some ways, he was. "What's wrong with your mouth? Did someone hit you with a lit bottle rocket?"

The boy shook his head and took another deep drag from the cigarette.

"Sure it's okay if you smoke? With your mouth and all? What happened to your lip? Did you get bitten by a dog or something?" Cookie moved away from him and leaned up against the side of old Sumac tree. "I'm not sure I should be talking to you like this. You're a stranger. And black."

The boy wiped the back of his hand across his eyes to remove any trace of tears." "It's called a harelip," he said. "I was born this way."

Aside from his deformed mouth, he had green eyes and his skin was the color of a smooth chestnut. "Sometimes, I scare people because they've never seen a harelip before."

The distance between them took on an unearthly quiet. Both seemed to be listening to the sound of their own hearts. There was no occasional crack of a branch, the crunch of a can or some other noise like wind in the woods. All alone, just the two of them. Neither one knowing a thing about the other. He had ruined her plans. She had intended to spend most of the day hiding in the park. Now if she left, she would have to find another hiding place. Cookie didn't know what to say to him. She looked at him again and stared so long because she knew he wasn't uncomfortable under her gaze. He was so ugly that he was cute in an endearing way, like a stuffed animal no one else in the world wanted, but she would bring home and take care of it.

Cookie wanted to get away from him as fast as she could. If anyone found her in the woods talking to any boy, no less a black boy, that would be the end of her world as she knew it. People would gossip about her for days. Word would get back to her father, and he would probably have her killed for consorting with a Negro. Although it was okay for Johnny Colangelo to hangout in the jazz clubs on the upper west side of Manhattan and jam with black musicians. There was a double-standard if Cookie ever did see one! Making music together put them all into a different zone, and that annoyed Cookie to no end. More than anything, she hated hypocrisy, and considered the primary offenders to be her father and the Catholic Church. What did the Catholic Church have to do with this? Everything and nothing. Cookie was remembering her dark secret that she was not willing to share with anyone, especially not with this boy who had a deformed mouth and had not yet said his name.

"My name is Herman," the boy said suddenly. "What's yours?"

"Call me Cookie."

"Cookie," the boy smiled, crinkling the uneven gap in his mouth. "Do you have a last name?"

"Do you?" she shot back.

The boy squirmed. He really did not want to say his last name. "I guess," he said.

"What, are you in trouble with the law?" Cookie loved to make wild accusations. "What did you say your name was? She prodded the boy, not understanding a boy who didn't want to say his name. "Come on," she cajoled him. "What's your full name?"

"Lynch," he said. "I'm Herman Lynch."

Cookie looked at him quizzically. "Lynch. What's the big deal?"

Herman looked at her as if she was dense. "L-Lynch. Get it?"

"Lynch?" Cookie said rhetorically. "Like, oh..." Suddenly, the lights went on. "Like hanging from a tree." Then she looked at him more closely. "You are in trouble with the law, aren't you?"

"No," Herman said. "I'm not."

"Well, it's not like Yonkers is the south or something. Like South Yonkers is not Alabama. "Ha ha," she mimicked laughing. "There are lots of blacks here."

"Are not," Herman insisted.

"Are too," Cookie insisted, with the Miss Bossy stance of putting her hands on her hips.

"Not so," Herman said. "Not in North Yonkers."

"Then why are you here? Do you live here?" Cookie zoomed in on him, firing away a round of questions as if she was wielding a machine gun. "Why aren't you in school? Aren't you supposed to be in school? What grade are you in? What school do you go to, and why are you in this park all by yourself anyway?" Cookie put her hands on her hips again. She was expecting answers, and quickly. Feeling herself growing impatient, she fancied herself a small feral cat on the verge of making a pounce.

Cookie jumped off the ledge from the bottom of the Eagle's Nest and landed in a crouched position on the winding path leading down the hill. Using the full strength of her knees and thighs, she shimmied forth in a walking squat. She didn't worry about her trick knees going out. Her knees were as strong and resilient, like rubber bands, in every position except for walking! Because once she stood up and took one or two steps forward, the third step unhinged her trick knee so quickly that the sudden shock and force sent her sprawling onto the ground.

"What happened?" Herman looked at her with disbelief. "You just fell. Just like that. Are you okay?" He reached to help her get up, but Cookie swatted at his arm to push him away.

"Don't you talk to me like that and make fun of me!" Cookie grabbed onto a worn granite pillar and pulled herself up from the ground. She gave Herman a belligerent once over. "Don't make fun of my knees. You do that, and I'll make fun of your mouth!"

Herman grew quiet and tears welled up in his eyes. Cookie stared at him with wonder. "What's wrong?" she said quietly to herself and slapped her hand lightly against her head. "What I said was wrong. There I go again. I'm always saying something wrong. I did it again. I thought you were making fun of me."

Herman closed his eyes and shook his head. "No, I don't make fun of people. I'm not like that. Think with a mouth like mine, I go around making fun of people? I know how it feels. And it doesn't feel good."

Cookie could see a tear squeeze through his shut left eye and sit on the top of his eyelashes, glistening like a diminutive jewel. She quickly tried to backpedal and undo the harm she had caused. "I didn't mean to hurt your feelings. I thought you were making fun of me, and I've had it with my knees."

Cookie didn't know what to do. She had never made a boy cry, especially a black boy. She felt really bad for him.

"My mother just died," Herman said softly. "The day before yesterday, she died. They were going to take me away from her anyway, but then she died." He started to really cry then, a trickle of large drops ran down his face, and it was awful, with his nose running and all.

"Don't you have a father?" Cookie asked him.

Herman shook his head. "I have my grandma, that's all, and some cousins."

Cookie wanted to tell him there were times when she wished her mother was dead, or she wished she had a different mother, but she didn't say anything. It always made her feel funny when she met a kid who had a dead mother or a dead father. It made her feel like she had lost someone too, and she didn't like that feeling. When you come right down to it, the thought of a kid having a dead mother made Cookie feel like she had butterflies in her stomach.

Herman seemed ready to leave and fidgeted while he spoke. "I have to go home. They want to put me in a foster home. But I'm not staying with people who are going to take money for it. I want to stay with my grandmother. Even though she can afford to have me living with her, some people in the county think she's too old and want to put me somewhere else."

Herman picked up a small slender stick from the ground and thrashed it through the weeds to make the path smooth. As the two of them walked through the woods together, the boy did not say much. Cookie and Herman had touched a chord in each other that remained unspoken and sort of mysterious. And as much as there was a need to come to a greater understanding, the odds were that Cookie and the boy would never run into each other again. This was a one-time happenstance that really didn't mean anything in the grander scheme of things. Soon Cookie and Herman reached the clearing that led to the grand lawn of Untermyer Park where there were fountains, the statue of a winged sphinx, with the worn head of a man and the body of a lion, mosaics, and columns with spires to the sky.

Cookie wanted to ask him what had happened to his mother, but never had a chance and she did not really want to know. Thinking about losing a parent was too awful. It was one thing if a parent was never home, but quite another if the parent was dead. "I'm real sorry about your Mother," she said softly.

Herman nodded and looked at her as if to thank her for understanding.

"Gotta go now."

With that, he was quickly on his way, ambling down the same trail both of them had walked from the Eagle's Nest. Cookie saw him racing through the woods, zooming with his stick, and holding it out in front of him like a divining rod, pushing back the weeds. In the distance, she could see his baby afro bobbing down the trail that opened to the magnificent view of the Hudson River against the backdrop of the New Jersey Palisades. The Palisades, a line of steep cliffs bordering the western edge of the Hudson River, were home to the world's first FM *radio* tower. Herman's fuzzy black head sharply descended out of view, and then he was gone. Cookie stood there and watched the woods for a long time. By now, Herman was probably moving toward the Aqueduct, Warburton Avenue, the train tracks and eventually down to the Hudson River and somewhere beyond, to a place he called home.

Fourteen

Saturday, July 18, 1970

Cookie checked herself in the mirror to make sure she had not turned black. Right after she met Herman Lynch, she raced home and stopped in front of the first mirror in the small entry foyer. The mirror was about a foot long, framed in bronze metal, oval in shape and narrow. She turned her face from side to side and tilted up her chin. She was white, sadly white, and so ashamed of herself for believing a dreadful lie that was too awful to be called an *old wives' tale*. The whole notion about being touched by a black person kept popping into her head nearly a month after she had met Herman. He wasn't dirty or bad or wicked, or any of the things grown-ups said about black people. She did not understand them any more than she understood what it meant to be black in Yonkers, on July 18, 1970.

Herman had touched her in some way she could not explain, and it had not made her black. He was so scared and so alone that it made her tremble for him. Still, she checked herself in the mirror, because it would be no fun turning black against her will. If she was going to turn black, it had to be of her own choosing. She felt sorry for Herman Lynch. She also felt sorry for herself. When you came right down to it, Cookie felt sorry for the whole human race. Here we were, all stuck together in this cauldron of confusion and loneliness, and it just wasn't fair.

Once when Cookie was eleven, shortly after she had suffered her earth-shattering event, she put on a pair of prescription eyeglasses that Kitty had stuffed away into a drawer long ago. Almost shaped like cat-eyes, the glasses had black horn-rimmed frames with clear almond-shaped lens. Her mother might be crazy, but she was too vain to wear eyeglasses and preferred walking around, looking at life as if it was an Impressionist painting rather than put on ugly glasses that corrected her nearsightedness. Cookie wore Kitty's glasses to see if she could feel what it was like to be sight-impaired. She popped on transistor radio ear phones as if the plugs were hearing aids, so she could get a sense for being hard-of-hearing or flat-out deaf. She ripped the metal backing from a barrette and stuck it into her mouth across her upper front teeth as a symbol that she had lost her ability to speak. Then she took a cane so she could feel what it was like to be lame.

She hobbled *Down the End*, went into Morsemere Market and bought a can of *Coke*. She wanted to know what it felt like to be handicapped. Instead of learning what it was like to be handicapped, she still felt like Cookie, a good girl who had gone wrong, but who still cared about the things that happened outside of herself, and especially when ridiculously bad things happened to other people.

Cookie didn't know what made her have a brand of compassion and a capacity for suffering that made her different from most people. Her chance meeting with Herman was a month ago, and she had not seen the black boy anywhere since then. It was as if he had vanished or had never been there at all. Maybe she had conjured him up, the same way she made up her rhymes, poems and stories in her notebooks. Any time she picked up her pen, words shot out like magic bullets, nailing fleeting thoughts into perfect sentences.

Two weeks before Cookie graduated from eighth grade, Fangs gave the entire class an unusual assignment. She stood in front of the room and proclaimed the importance of what she wanted the students to do. When Fangs described the assignment, her tone was more than imperious; it was down-right condescending. She mocked her students, "I want you to write a poem without once using the letter e. You do not have to rhyme, but you cannot use the letter e. Then she paused, almost as if she was being thoughtful, and looked at the class with a grim smirk that showed her fangs. "I doubt any of you will be able to do this assignment, but it will prevent you from being idle." Fangs' front teeth were so broken, jagged and irregularly-shaped, it made her appear as though she was smiling even when she was not.

Cookie walked off with her current black & white notebook and thought about the poem, but the words did not imme-diately manifest themselves in her mind, and she could not "hear" a poem. She sat in the *Owl Bowl* all by herself and mostly dreamed about a time when she used to have feelings. She thought about the *Blind Owl* Alan Wilson and how his feelings must be unimaginably powerful. Janis Joplin sang a long cry through everything that broke her raw heart. Jimi Hendrix whined and vibrated at an octave higher than any one she had ever known, Jim Morrison rocked his hips and moved like a snake, exuding an energy Cookie had yet to understand. Mick Jagger had feelings that morphed into a whole lot of pent-up anger; rage was one feeling, maybe the only feeling, she could embrace.

She sat there so long that the twigs forming the basin of the *Owl Bowl* started pinching her bottom and were digging into her flesh, leaving a slight imprint. She propelled herself out of the *Owl Bowl* in a burst, leaving a wake of snapping twigs, pretending she was Mick Jagger singing *Jumpin' Jack*

Flash. She ran flying through the neighboring yards, leaping in the air, shimmying from side-to-side as if she was dancing an amazing rapid-fire turning waltz. Hurling herself over bushes, rocks and small trees, she ran faster than she had ever run before. It did not matter how far she had gone or how far she had to go; the running freed her from something inside and made her true to herself. While she ran, she suddenly knew a poem was forming. It was coming, and there was no holding it back. She ran until she reached the corner of North Broadway and descended down the hidden staircase into the bowels of the *Owl Hole.* During her run to victory, her knee had never given out, not once. She was on a roll, Rock and Roll and moving to the beat of *Jumpin' Jack Flash.*

Cookie did not realize the significance of the song until she stopped moving. Once she hit the square grass and weeded turf covering the bottom landing of the *Owl Hole,* she sat there, crouched low to the ground like a watchful cat, an owl, or the *Blind Owl,* if only he could see. Her heart was racing so fast, it seemed to be skipping beats. The title of one of her favorite songs in the whole world, *Jumpin' Jack Flash* did not have the letter e. This was the same form of the poem she needed to write.

The poem without the letter e came with the words tumbling out on paper and touching upon the outer edge of her feelings that she still had yet to understand. From her journey through the *Owl Bowl* in the woods to the hidden *Owl Hole* at the bottom of the steps at the Baptist Church, the poem revealed itself.

I Ran

I ran from unknown victory.
I ran from immortal infinity.
I ran from tranquil mysticism.
I ran from jubilation in its sorrow.
I ran from truth, fading in shadows of doom.

I ran from a short past so far away.
I ran from a raging storm in its own fury.
I ran from compassion only to find hostility.
I ran only to know I could not run
From limitations surrounding my soul.

When Cookie returned to school, Fangs asked the class to turn in the assignment, but no one could do it. It was one week before graduation, and no one cared. The students of the eighth-grade class of Christ the King School in 1970 were terrified, but knew nothing would stand in the way of graduation. Except Cookie had something yet to prove. She walked up to the nun's desk; it was in the back of the classroom, ensconced next to the window that looked out on the terrible playground, where one day in the sixth grade, she had been forced to stand out there, all alone in humiliation. *Stop.*

Cookie dropped the assignment on Fangs' desk. The poem was written by hand with a fountain pen on a sheet of loose-leaf lined paper. It made a pattering sound when it landed on the desk. Fangs didn't say anything to Cookie and didn't even look up at her. It was as if the nun knew it was Cookie and intuited her presence on some uncanny level, the way we can feel someone looking at us even when don't actually see them looking.

"Anyone else?" Fangs asked the class. The room was silent, with the exception of a low grumble from a few boys who collectively could take no more terror from Fangs, and squirmed in their small wooden seats that were jammed together, one on top of the other.

Fangs scanned the poem. Her eyes hardly traveled left to right, but quickly ran down the middle of the page. She looked up and glanced at Cookie before quickly lowering her eyes. "Did you really write this, or did you copy it from somewhere?"

Cookie picked up the poem from the desk. The nun fanned her hand across the top of the desk and tried to hold the paper down. Cookie slid the sheet out from under the nun's hand. "It's not like I could go to the library and find a book in the poetry section named Poems without Using the Letter e!"

The nun shot up from her desk as if she was going to hit Cookie. Fangs was trembling so hard that Cookie could see that the nun was terrified of her. Cookie prepared to defend herself and positioned herself for attack. If Cookie had time to think about it, the fact that the nun was scared of her would have given her some semblance of pleasure, but she was not thinking on that deep a level. Cookie only knew if the nun laid one hand on her, so much as a finger, she was going to choke her to death and shake her nun head as if it was the top of a rag doll. Fangs was crazy, but not stupid. Instinctively, the nun must have known she was in danger. She clutched her hand to her chest, presumably where her heart was located, as if she was having a medical episode. "Don't you ever, ever talk that way to me again."

Cookie smirked at Fangs, took the poem and tore it into two, dropped the halved paper into the wastepaper can and walked out of the classroom. It was the last time she would walk out of that classroom. She never went back to the school again until she participated in the eighth-grade graduation ceremony. In a class of fifty-one students, six other girls wore the same pastel lace dress as the one Cookie had bought at *Lerner's* in the Cross County Shopping Center. Here they were, girls choosing a party dress for graduation, but they were working-class, not poor, but far from rich, and all shopping at the same low-rent store, buying the same dress as if it was another Catholic school-girl uniform.

The Poem without Using the Letter e incident had taken place three weeks ago, and graduation had taken place two weeks ago, but Cookie had not forgotten the big event that had long ago changed the course of her life. It churned through the dark eddies and swamps of her emotions, from the moment she woke up in the morning to the end of every day, until she fell asleep. Every time Cookie's mind returned to the time of her darkest hour, she had to make her mind *Stop*. There was little consolation in the fact that on her thirteenth birthday, she had clocked Fangs and had never even gotten into trouble for it. No one, not even the school principal, had punished Cookie for clocking Fangs. And later, at Fangs' behest, she had been the only one in the class who had written a Poem without using the letter e.

None of these small victories could undo the damage that had been done. Shortly after eighth-grade graduation, rumors quickly circulated that Fangs had left Christ the King School. Some said she had been sent to another school. Others hinted that she had not been sent to another school at all, but she had gone to *Poughkeepsie*. Everyone knew that going to *Poughkeepsie* meant Fangs had been locked up in the crazy ward.

It was July and hot, but funnily enough, no day so far this summer had been as hot as that day at the beginning of May when her mother was on top of the stove, boiling her feet. Cookie left the entry foyer, where the mirror had reassured her that she had not yet turned black. She heard the sound of running water coming from the kitchen and thought it was best to avoid Kitty. She slinked up the stairs to the bedrooms, pushed open the door to Donny's room and saw her lying prone on the bed. She appeared to be asleep. Cookie tiptoed over to the side of the bed and watched the girl. Her eyes were squeezed shut too tight, as if she was just pretending to be fast asleep. Donny's birthday was fast approaching, so maybe she'd take her out for a hot fudge ice cream sundae at Urich's. Donny's legs stuck out like ice cream popsicle sticks from her cotton baby-blue-colored baby doll pajamas. Even though it was warm, Cookie pulled up a crumpled sheet, straightened it out from its tangled ball and covered Donny's bottom, more as a matter of protection than to keep her warm.

She wanted to reach over and touch her sister on the

cheek, but her hand would not move. "Do you want to go and get some ice cream?"

Donny shot up from her fake slumber and shrieked. "I'm faking you! I was really awake the whole time! I knew it was you, and not Mommy!"

"Isn't today your birthday?"

"I'm eight!" Donny pulled herself out of bed. She was groggy and rubbed her eyes. "I've been sleeping late every day." She tugged on her ear. "My ear hurts. I think I have another earache. What time is it, Cookie?"

"I don't know," Cookie said. "Get dressed and we'll go out. I'll buy you a hot fudge ice cream sundae at Urich's."

Cookie suddenly felt uncomfortable; she could not stand to be around her sister. Why had she suggested taking her out for ice cream? She didn't really want to go to Urich's with her. It was almost too much for her to be close to anyone. She wanted to be a good sister, and at the same time she didn't want to be good, not for herself, not for anyone. *Being good will just get me hurt*, she thought. It was best to be bad, because at least then, if you were punished, you knew the reason why. Telling herself to *Stop* when her thoughts started going down this path, Cookie felt like she was slipping away to a murky, undefined place. She turned around and walked out of the room, as though she was floating, not feeling much of anything, except a sort of numbness.

She went into her own bedroom and stood before a mirror that showed much more than her face. She had not turned black, and loathed herself for thinking that way about Herman Lynch, Mrs. Kerry or any other black person. When she was in kindergarten, she kept her distance from Mrs. Kerry, who must have known something was wrong.

The children sat in a circle on small blue foam mats. Mrs. Kerry sat in a small children's chair and told them stories, with her eyes growing large and animated, and her voice changing in tone and pitch as if she was singing a song to each character; all the while, her arms soared through the air like strong but graceful wings. She gave Cookie the job of putting away picture books. Mrs. Kerry smiled, handing Cookie one book, then another and another. She learned how to put them all back on the shelf. Soon she began bringing books to Mrs. Kerry and asking her to read them to the class. Cookie became the keeper of the books.

She looked at herself in the mirror as if she was a complete stranger, as white as anyone could be. Other than straddling the delicate balance beam between being a gangster and a hippie, Cookie didn't know who she was. She was so far away from kindergarten, and light years away from being the keeper of the books. Too much had happened since then.

She wore a peach paisley halter top that showed her softly rounded and perfectly formed belly. She made a small grimace, meant to be a way to poke fun at herself and the woefully bare buds that masqueraded as her breasts. She stuck out her tongue at her own reflection. She tried turning to the side and twisting her torso to see if her buds were sprouting in repose. No such luck. What's worse, she could not even call herself flat-chested. The buds boasted tips as sharp as the points of darning needles. She wondered if she was doomed to be deformed like this for the rest of her life, and eventually turn black too.

In despair, she tried to squeeze her elbows together in front of her chest, hoping that would create the impression of cleavage. Sadly, even as she pressed her palms together with great force, it did not produce an increased breast size.

Cookie thought she looked young, much younger than someone who would soon turn fourteen. Maybe it was her hair. She always wore her hair in a loose pony tail, bunched in a thick fabric-coated rubber band. Trailing mane-like down to the middle of her back, the pony tail was the last vestige of being a "good girl."

Sure enough, the one day she had loosened her hair, disaster had struck. She had gone to school with her long hair pulled free from the band and cascading down the middle of her back. Her hair was a shiny polished chestnut color and caught highlights from the autumn sun. It felt good to have her hair free and catching warmth from the sun. The morning was cold, and traces of frost dusted the tops of leaves, giving them an amber glow. It was the first genuine cold day of the fall, Monday, November 6, 1967. Cookie was in the sixth grade. *Stop*.

With the exception of the ponytail, she had shucked off her good girl demeanor. Now Cookie wore the ponytail, to keep something awful from happening to her. Her ponytail had become a talisman or a lucky charm, warding off evil that would come flying at her from out of nowhere, like a maelstrom of flying saucers piloted by demons, spirits, and that most dangerous of all life forms, nuns.

The first thing she had done after the big event was to stare at herself in the mirror the way she was staring at herself now. But instead of spying on her own image to see if she had turned black, she was trying to understand what she had done wrong. What had she done to invite the terrible thing that had happened to her? Her ponytail was long and carefully waved, exposing a face that looked pinched, white, and like something that old women—grandmothers in particular—would find pretty. Her Italian grandmother was dead. Her Irish grandmother avoided Cookie and Donny, because she did not know what to do about Kitty. Johnny's sister Ro-Ro had been gone from the scene for some time, ever since the day Kitty ate an apple and placed the apple core inside of Ro-Ro's pocketbook. Lots of family members couldn't put up with Kitty's crazy antics and had fled the scene, leaving Johnny all alone to manage his crazy wife.

It was as if being schizophrenic presented a moral dilemma too complex to fix. And it was sad for Cookie and Kitty, and Donny and Johnny too. No one knew what to do. No matter, though, because Cookie had her words. She leaned in closer to the mirror and smirked at her hair, unraveling from a loose pony tail with frizzy tufts that looked like soft downy feathers on a little brown wren. She concentrated on her face where her green eyes stared back at her with mischief, delight, and an unquantifiable form of cleverness. *Clever girl*, she said to herself, sticking out her tongue. "You've got green eyes like kooky Kitty. Must have inherited her madness too."

She told herself that her green eyes gave her supernatural powers and that she had really been cloned from aliens, extra-terrestrials who had come from another planet. So she wasn't human and did not need to live on earth, especially not in the city of Yonkers, which was mostly inhabited by Italian girls, Irish boys, and some variation of lowly mutt-life that had been created in the heat of passion as a result of mixed marriages. For some funny reason, she remembered Herman Lynch. He, too, had green eyes which looked all the more green against the backdrop of his dark skin.

Cookie heard the sound of someone sniffing and turned around. Donny had already caught her staring at herself in the mirror.

"Why do you keep looking at yourself in the mirror?" Donny wanted to know.

"None of your business," Cookie shot back.

"You're always looking at yourself. I think you're getting crazy just like Mommy. Cuckoo, cuckoo clock." Donny pointed her finger against her temple. "Cuckoo," she kept saying.

Cookie shook her head, scowling at Donny. She was an unbearable nuisance who watched every little thing she did and stalked her around the house. Cookie wished she could talk to her little sister, but she did not know what to say. She wished she could confide in Donny, but she was too young to understand. She looked at Donny as if she was pleading for her to help her choose the right words to say. Donny had changed out of her baby doll pajamas and into a pair of wrinkled red pants and a square-shouldered off-white shirt that showed signs of hard play—mud, grass stains and a dash of blue pastel chalk.

"Those are my shorts," Cookie said.

"You weren't wearing them anymore," Donny said, "so I took them. I didn't think you'd mind."

"I didn't say you could have them. The only reason I wasn't wearing them is because my shorts were probably lost in your huge mess of a room." Cookie held out her hand. "Take them off right now and give them back to me."

Donny jumped backwards and hurled herself down the stairs. Cookie stood still and didn't bother to chase her. She felt stupid for saying the wrong thing, but she also wanted to be rid of Donny. At war with herself, Cookie really did not want to take her to Urich's for ice cream. And that made her feel guilty. After all, it was Donny's birthday!

She heard the front door slam shut and she sprung into an alert stance ready to take off, but before she knew it, she was streaking down the stairs and into the hall where she didn't see anyone, not a soul. She called to Donny but there was no response. She went back upstairs and pushed open the door to Donny's room to see what else was in there. Crammed full of books and shoes and toys, empty cartons, squalid piles of clothes, some soiled, some not, in a tangle of sheets, two pillows tucked into the middle of a large lampshade, the room was a monumental mess in progress.

Cookie leaned against the door frame and tried to sigh, but even that took more feeling than she had in reserve. If she had any feelings buried inside, she could not summon even one. Donny was slipping away from her, going off with her own friends and doing her own thing. She didn't know her little sister anymore. Cookie didn't know how long she had stood there, as still as a statue. She wondered if she had lost her heart, or if a heart could die, even if the person was still breathing.

Later that night, Cookie had a dream. Donny and her friends were trapped under water in a swimming pool. Cookie dove down to bring Donny up for air. Then she saw that Donny's friends had encircled her, locking her in a false embrace so she could not move. Cookie could see that Donny was losing air. Cookie tried to yank her away from them, but their grip was too strong, and Cookie could not get her free. When she woke up, she felt panicked and realized she was covered in sweat, but it was July and it was hot. She tiptoed into Donny's room and saw her sprawled on the bed, still wearing the wrinkled red hot pants. A thin slant of light from the moon illuminated her face, which, under the glow of her tangled blonde curls, made her look angelic. Her mouth bore a faint trace of chocolate ice cream.

Fifteen

Tuesday, July 28, 1970

No one was rushing around on this steamy day in late July. The Number 2 bus ran from Tudor Woods in the North End to 242nd Street in the Bronx. Cookie boarded the bus *Down the End* on Palisade Avenue in front of Morsemere Market. She dropped thirty-five cents into the glass-and-metal cash box and moved toward the back. Her knee had been acting funny all morning and she was sure it was on the verge of going out again. She had intended to go to all the way to the back of the bus, but changed her mind and sat in the first row that faced forward behind the two opposing bench seats.

The bus wasn't even one-quarter full. It was too early for the crush of workers commuting home, and most kids were on summer break, sleeping in every day as late as possible to save up enough energy to go *Down the End* and hang-out to all hours of the night. Most of the windows on the bus were open. The air was inert, foul-smelling and rancid, a distinct mixture of carbon monoxide, sweat, urine and garbage. As the bus moved south on Palisade Avenue, the slight scent from swollen green leaves and freshly mowed grass rose a note higher than the other odors before blending in with the city's stench and finally drifting away.

The bus's last stop *Down the End* was in front of the liquor store. Millie Mangano's thighs rubbed together as she
pulled herself by the safety railings up and onto the bus and
hurriedly waddled to find the nearest seat. Then then she saw
Cookie; her face lit up with recognition and she immediately
moved in her direction. Cookie saw Millie holding onto the
metal frame on top of the back of every seat as she made her
way to Cookie, who audibly groaned. The last person Cookie
wanted to talk to was someone who worked with Johnny.

"Where are you going to?" Millie plopped herself down.
As the woman sank into her seat, she almost sat on top of
Cookie's leg. She sidled up to Cookie in a tight, crushing
squeeze, reeking of the undeniably cloying sent of her *Heaven
Sent* perfume.

"Where are you going to?" Millie asked again. "I don't think
I heard you the first time. Did you tell me anything? Are you
going to the Square?"

She meant Getty Square. Old-time Yonkersites always
called it *The Square*. Cookie looked at her without blinking
her eyes and gave her a small, snide smile. The bus seat was
not large enough for both of them, and Millie did not seem to
notice. Millie, who was large enough to take up two seats, was
almost on top of Cookie. She looked down at the two books
sitting on Cookie's lap. "I didn't know you enjoyed reading.
Your father never told me that you like to read. You must be
smart. Maybe one day you'll be a teacher or a nurse."

Cookie shut her eyes. *Teacher or nurse.* "How about
a lawyer or a doctor?" she snarled. "How about if I become
famous instead!"

"Oh, you've got big ideas," Millie said. "I can see you have
big ideas. You're just like Johnny that way. You're a chip off
the old block." She whispered, "If your father had his way,
between you and me, he'd give up his job and only play his
music with those colored musicians in the city."

Cookie stared at the intensity of Millie's glistening pink

lips, which were covered with a bubble-gum shade of *Yardley* lip gloss. She also had a wad of *Kleenex* stuck in between her bosom. Cookie squirmed in her seat. "I'm getting off soon."

"I thought you were going to the Square."

"What gave you that idea?" Cookie snapped.

"The books you're carrying. The library's in the Square, isn't it? I never go there, but I know where it is."

"I have something to do before I go to the library." Cookie was annoyed that she felt obligated to tell Millie what she was doing. If Millie knew the truth, she would be appalled. Cookie folded her arms and contracted her body into a small, tight ball. She felt thorny, as if she had porcupine quills protruding from her back.

As the bus chugged up the hill, Cookie skulked in her seat. She wasn't big on making small talk, especially with a co-lossal busybody like Millie Mangano. Both heading to the same general vicinity in Getty Square, Cookie and Millie had met purely by coincidence and had only one thing in common—a relationship with Johnny Colangelo. Cookie was his daughter, but Millie Mangano wished she could be Johnny's wife.

Millie was tremendously overweight, struggling with the heat and breathing heavily. A narrow band of sweat had formed above her lip. She wore a sleeveless coral-colored chiffon tent dress that exposed her chubby white arms and her massive cleavage. "When I was young, Yonkers was full of factories that hired many young people. But not so much any-more. What are you going to do for work this summer, hon?"

Cookie chewed her gum with intensity and almost popped a small bubble. Instead she felt a piece of her tooth crack off; it felt like a small rock in her mouth. Her molars were falling apart. She swallowed the small fragment of tooth and tried to put it out of her mind. "Guess, I'll get some babysitting jobs." She didn't tell Millie that she didn't need to work at shitty little jobs. The few ludes she sold on the street kept her in *Marlboros*, new halter tops, short-shorts, and gum.

"How do you get your pin money?" Millie asked.

"Cookie looked at her. "Huh?"

"Your mad money to buy the things you want without asking nobody for things. Doesn't your father give you an allowance?"

"He doesn't need to give me money. I make my own money."

"No money, brother, Jesus. How does he do it? Not giving his kid money! Jesus! With all the money he spends in clubs! How do you do it? I've seen you smoking cigarettes, and not the same kind as your father."

Cookie turned her face away from Millie and looked out the window. *Should I tell her the truth,* she scoffed to herself. *Should I tell her: Allow me to introduce myself. My name is Concetta Mary Bernadette Colangelo, but everyone calls me 'Cookie.' I'm a drug dealer.*

Even with the mandate that she had to be tough, there was something about Cookie that was much tougher than the norm. "Excuse me," she said to Millie. "I've got to get off at the next stop." Instead of standing up, Millie turned to the side in her seat so Cookie could pass by, literally climbing over her.

Cookie hopped out of her seat over Millie's thighs and stood up in the aisle, rocking a bit on the moving bus, then reached for the cord and gave it a quick yank. That buzz let the bus driver know she wanted to get off at the next stop.

Millie leaned forward in her seat and yelled to the bus driver, "Let her off. She needs to get to the library."

"We're not even in Getty Square," Millie said. "Sure you should get off now? It's pretty bad around here." She leaned forward and whispered. "There's blacks everywhere. The projects are over there," she nodded out the window where the cluster of yellow brick eight-story Schlobohm buildings looked hot enough to be baking over barbecue coals during the peak of the summer sun.

Cookie couldn't take much more of Millie's prattling about nothing. "Gotta go."

Cookie heard Millie calling to the bus driver, "That girl's not right in the head. Her name's Cookie Colangelo, and she's not right in the head, just like her mother."

Cookie didn't even turn around to look at Millie. There she was, making a grand scene about Cookie because she hated Kitty. She hated Donny, but most of all, she hated Cookie. She wanted Johnny all to herself. Cookie hated it when someone was making a big scene and drawing the kind of attention that she did not want to be drawn to herself. While she wanted to be famous, she did not welcome unwanted attention, sort of like *Greta Garbo*, who worked hard to become famous, but wanted her privacy. *No photos, please*, Cookie thought to herself. *I vant to be alone.*

Cookie bounded off the front of the bus, mindful that her knee was feeling foolish. *Foppish*, she said to herself for no reason at all. *My knee is foppish, like a dandy old man wearing a top hat.* Cookie needed to write it down and put it into her book, as if it fit somewhere in a new poem she was writing. She didn't know what she was thinking about. She was nervous and knew she should not be here in the projects, but she had made plans to meet Reenie Ruggiero.

On Palisade Avenue, she skipped like a kid one minute, holding onto her two books, both deemed to be rare and treasured tomes, and in the next instant, she thought if anyone messed with her, she could use those same books as bombs, missiles of warfare, hurled at the enemy to knock them out, keeping herself safe. She could outfox nuns, priests, her father, her mother, any Italian girl, all boys, gangsters and Millie Mangano. She was that smart and crazy, like her mother, smart and crazy like a fox.

Cookie thought maybe the *Blind Owl* thought the same way. She felt the sun beating down on her face in a steady sting of hot arrows heating up her cheeks and making her eyesight feel hazy, as if she could not see too far or too well. She walked down the street, passing a whole row of tenement buildings, some brick, some wood, some with bumpy, speckled ugly dirt-brown siding. She knew she was walking east on Ashburton Avenue because the numbers were getting larger. *Growing bigger and bigger, ha-ha*, she said to herself. *YONKERS, Yonkers, the only place where the brick buildings are covered over with coats of paint so badly peeling, they might as well be covered with chalk and soot.*

Cookie was scared and a small lump sat in her throat, but otherwise she felt emotionally flat, like a blank wall. She was moving down the slummiest part of the street, rife with old brick three-story buildings full of small portrait-sized windows, with old wooden frames peeling paint. Chain-link fences drew the boundary between concrete front stoops and the sidewalk, where the same piles of rubbish spilled indiscriminately and formed common pools owned by no one person and at the same time owned by everyone.

She stomped in-between piles of cigarette butts, trash, beer cans, and felt them crunching beneath her feet. Cars cruised the street, going slow and making the exhaustive noise of mufflers in dire need of repair. She felt like she had lost a part of herself that used to be sweet and funny, happy for no reason at all. She had lost her sweetness because she was too afraid to keep it there, even secretly, deep down inside, where nobody knew about it except for her. And now she was here, hardened, not feeling anything except the kind of fear that made her want to survive; and she would survive, no matter what.

She wasn't going to show fear. *You can't own fear if you don't know it.* She was looking for 164 Ashburton Avenue, where Reenie Ruggiero lived with her grandmother, an uncle and an older brother. She looked up at a banner sign for *Yonkers Cash and Gold.* The business had a steel gate garage door that served as its front entrance. The sign said: *Everything we touch turns to cash.* Cookie saw her reflection in the glass of a narrow sliver of an office door. She looked hopeful and studious, with her long ponytail, carrying her

books, her magenta cloth sack slung over her shoulder. The
address was 171 Ashburton Avenue. She had walked too far.
Directly across the street, the Ashburton Pharmacy had a steel
gate garage door. Then it hit her that in another neighborhood in another part of the world, these steel gates would be
made from glass so from the street you could look inside and
see people working. These crime gates stopped thieving and
looting. Cookie was in the midst of jungle bunny town and
starting to feel feverish.

She did not smile at the monstrously large tenement
homes that could put a roof over the heads of twelve children and accommodate many more strays: dogs, cats and kids.
There was always a stray kid or two, orphaned or abandoned,
like Tommy Parrello and Herman Lynch. What happened to
them made her heart ache. Even if Cookie felt sorry for herself
and knew how much she had suffered for not being an Italian
girl, and for having suffered through a traumatic event that
messed up her life, at least she still had two parents. Kitty and
Johnny were damaged and far from perfect, but still Cookie
had two parents.

Cookie found Reenie Ruggiero's address: the brick
building looked old enough to be a three-story tenement. The
sides of the building were white-washed over the obvious fa-
cade of red brick. From outside, Cookie could see that the
frame of one large window was sealed with brick, as if an interior wall had been cemented shut. Cookie stood out in front,
nodding her head to keep watch, seeing who was coming and
who was going. The boys in the 'hood traveled in groups. The
didn't pay her much mind, but when one of them looked in
Cookie's direction, she noticed. The boys eyed her tomboyish
body as if it was a tempting morsel. Toddlers and preschoolers
in bathing suits were tumbling across the concrete stoops
and running under water gushing from an open fire hydrant,
screaming and laughing the way little kids do when having
the most fun ever.

Reenie Ruggiero was nowhere in sight. Out on the street, Cookie looked for a pay phone. She scanned the block, seeing a dry cleaner's and a pizza joint, but there were no signs of a pay phone. Reenie told her once that the phone company, *Ma Bell,* had taken out the pay phones on her block because their pay coin boxes were constantly getting hacked. Cookie walked around the building. In the back a parking lot was full of black kids, mostly guys, some shooting baskets. The rusted guts of a car had been stripped for parts and left abandoned on the side of the yard. Two fire escapes loomed overhead and were suspended in the air, like the giant wrought iron cages that have traps to capture wild animals. Seeing the swarm of black faces eyeing her, *wanting to know who she was and what she was doing,* made Cookie not look at any one person too long. She certainly didn't make eye contact with anyone. She was more than an outsider; she felt like the dumbest honky motherfucker who had ever walked the block. When she saw someone familiar, she was so astonished that she turned around and ran toward the front of the building. She heard the boys laughing at her hasty exit.

It was Herman Lynch! She was sure he had seen her, but she did not have the gumption to talk to him, not when he was with his own kind. *"You have to have gumption,"* Kitty had always told her. *"Gumption is another way of saying you have guts. It's also called backbone, and if you have it, you can stand up to anything."* Kitty might have been crazy, but she could occasionally say something that was piercingly smart, a keeper phrase to take on the road.

But Cookie felt low on gumption today. She wasn't about to go over and start talking to Herman Lynch when he was with his friends. By now, she had no choice but to knock on the front door and go inside the building. The front entrance looked like it had been nice at one time. Vintage wood cornices and decorative crown molding framed the door. There was no doorbell and nowhere to knock. She pushed the door and creaked it open to reveal an interior hall that was dark, with walls of exposed brick. With so little light coming in, the hall was cool in temperature, but smelled like old wood and cooking odors.

She looked for a directory of people who lived there, but no one named Ruggiero was listed. She didn't know if she should start knocking on doors and thought it was a clumsy way to find one family among the nine who lived here, but there was no other way. Unless she stood outside the building and waited for someone to come by. Just when she was about to give up, the front door opened, and in walked someone she had never expected to see here.

Herman Lynch grinned at her. His upturned mouth made his harelip seem less pronounced. "How did you enjoy those books?"

Cookie was all business and without mercy. "I've got sixteen ludes. I'll give them to you for two bucks a-piece. I promised them to somebody else, but first come, first served."

Herman looked at her with his big eyes. Even in the dim hall light, his eyes were about as green as anything she had ever seen.

"I'm not looking for no ludes. Who told you that? After what happened to my mom, I don't touch that kind of stuff. Besides, I know where to get ludes for a buck a piece. That's if I wanted that stuff. And I don't."

"I'll give you all sixteen ludes for thirty bucks." Cookie put one hand on her hip. Her other arm raised and lowered the books as if she was moving a mighty elevator. She was showing him the full brunt of their weight. "You can resell the ludes to stupid white people who come here looking for it!"

"Damn," Herman said. "I don't think you heard me. I don't want the stuff." He moved closer to Cookie and examined the books, she held on her arm. Herman was black and weird-looking, but his proximity to Cookie didn't trouble her. Herman was weird in a good way that she could not explain.

He took a step back away from her as if he was about to deliver bad news. "You're reading Dostoyevsky and selling dope! What do you think I am? Your sorry-assed nigger?!"

"No!" Now Cookie felt embarrassed. "I don't say things like that." She puffed out her chest as if she was offended. "I don't think that way, either. I came here to find Reenie Ruggiero. Do you know her?"

"Yeah, I know Reenie. Everybody knows Reenie. She lives up there," Herman pointed to stairs. "She's on the third floor. You can go on up. Nobody's going to stop you. Just say you live here. Sooner or later, everybody lives here. We're not in the projects, but we're not in a good part of town, either. Know what I mean?"

Cookie cradled the books up to her chest and looked at Herman as if she meant to thank him, but didn't say anything. Then she turned, veering her leg out to the side on a sharp angle to run up the steps. It was inevitable that her knee should protest from going in the direction where she wanted it to go! And sure enough, her knee was coming unhinged, dislocating, and in the force that ensued, she fell in a kneeling position, making a loud thump on the second floor landing.

"Are you okay?" Herman started up the worn wood steps, stopped, then looked at her.

"I've got a trick knee, that's all. It goes out on me all the time."

Herman stood on the first floor landing, looked up at her and put his hands on his hips. "When did that start happening to you?"

Cookie was so annoyed with him. "I used to be the best kick ball player in the whole North End!"

"Used to be?" Herman asked. "Why'd you stop playing kickball?"

"I don't want to talk about it!" She wasn't about to tell Herman that she stopped playing kickball long ago. Kickball was for little kids, not gangsters or hippies.

"You move like a natural-born athlete, but if you don't take care of yourself, your knees are going to let you down. Real nasty too."

Cookie picked herself up and stood like a flamingo, tucking her injured knee up in a bent position. "Thanks," she grumbled, then turned and continued to hobble in small, but increasingly stronger, hops and jumps up the steps. Once her knee popped back into place it was as good as new.

"You should learn to dance," Herman said. "If you learned to dance, your knees would get strong and stop doing that."

"Yeah, right," Cookie said sarcastically. "Dance."

"Seriously," Herman said. "You need to build strong muscles around your knees. When your knees go out like that, it means you are just hyper-flexible, kind of like being double-jointed. If you're not going to play kickball, do something else besides walking for a change!"

As Cookie climbed the steps to the third floor, the wood treads on the steps grew increasingly worn where big strips of paint had peeled off. With no fans or air conditioning, the hallway seemed to be getting hotter and felt confined. The hall was dimly lit; a threadbare light bulb dangled from the ceiling by a loose cord that had unraveled from its socket. The wooden bannister was shaky and the spindles holding it together were streaked with old splinters of paint. She held onto the banister lightly, so that it would not come apart altogether. Under the touch of her sweaty hand, the wood felt dry, like it was disintegrating and turning to sawdust. The newel post on the top of the third floor landing was covered with graffiti, engraved with crudely carved initials, hearts, swastikas and a closed fist, and it shook, threatening to collapse.

On the third floor, there were two apartments marked 3A and 3B, sculpted in crude wrought iron, and neither door showed the name of the family that lived there. "Which one?" Cookie yelled down to Herman, but he must have left because he did not answer her.

The doors did not have bells or knockers. Cookie knocked on the nearest door, 3A, and bit her lower lip, tasting the faint trace of *Yardley Pot o' Gloss*. She knocked again, then heard the sound of chains and latches opening, as a grim older Italian woman answered the door. She couldn't have been more than four feet tall. Her hair was salt and pepper in a mass of tight springy coils that resembled a small afro. Cookie figured she was Reenie's grandmother. "I'm Cookie," she said, "Reenie's friend. Is Reenie home? I was supposed to meet her here."

The old woman, who still hadn't opened the door wider than a crack, looked at Cookie suspiciously and spoke with a thick Italian accent. "Reenie's not up yet. She's still in bed."

Cookie spoke through the slight crack between the door and the peeling molding that framed it. "She told me to come over today. Can I come in and see her?"

The old woman sighed, made the sign of the cross and closed the door. For a second, Cookie thought she was trying to get rid of her. Now Cookie could see why she had not opened the door more than a crack. Cookie heard the old woman unlatching an extra chain lock. Then she opened the door all the way.

At first Cookie thought she had never been inside of a tenement apartment but then she realized it had only been a long time. She didn't connect Reenie's apartment to the tenement where her grandmother lived on Herriot Street. Maybe it was because her grandmother's shabby tenement had always been in the family and no one paid rent. Reenie's apartment was different; it was low-income housing and a lot of the people who lived here were on welfare.

Cookie stepped right into the living room, which had a large overstuffed sofa with a trundle bed sticking out below, and a matching armchair. A small black & white TV was on, with the sound turned low. Cookie recognized the soap opera *As the World Turns* flickering on the screen and the static of a commercial interruption from *Tasty Cake*. The apartment was tiny and cramped and made her feel as if her small house in the North End was manse-like, larger than life and real rich, richer than anything else she had ever known. The old woman motioned to a closed bedroom door lacquered with shiny olive green oil paint. A large letter-size school calendar was crookedly tacked to the door as if it had been a careless afterthought. Cookie didn't bother to knock, pushed open the door and walked in.

Three beds were crammed into the room. Even though the shades were pulled down and there was little light, the walls looked in need of new paint. Reenie was wearing bikini underpants with tiny flowers and a peach-colored bra. She had a crumpled sheet in between her legs. "Reenie," Cookie called to her. "Get up."

The old woman stood in the open doorway. "She's been like this all summer. She doesn't do nothing. She's good for nothing."

"Oh, shut up," Reenie pulled her pillow over her head to muffle her voice. "There's nowhere to go and nothing to do."

"It's your own fault," the old woman said. "You do nothing but bring trouble on yourself. Maybe you can talk some sense into her," the old woman said to Cookie. "Look, she's got books and she's reading them even though there's no school and it's the summer." She left and closed the door behind her.

Cookie watched the door to make sure the old woman was gone. Reenie sat up on the side of the bed. Her long brown frizzy hair fell forward and covered her eyes. She was one of the few Italian girls who let her hair get frizzy. Reenie liked the nappy-haired look and did little to try to control it. Most Italian girls, the ones who did not have straight hair, wrapped their hair in sheaths around their head, or used giant rollers, to smooth their long tresses into hippie hairdos. Kinky hair or not, Reenie possessed the chief attribute of all young Italian girls; she had enormous breasts. Although Cookie was the same age as Reenie, the girl could easily pass for eighteen.

"I'm getting my period," Reenie complained. "I'm swelling up, getting fat and my boobs hurt."

Cookie still had not had her first period, and she didn't want to talk about it. "I have something for you," she said, pulling a small plastic baggie from her cloth shoulder sack and holding the ludes up for Reenie to see. "Sixteen," she said. "Two bucks a piece."

Reenie tossed back her hair to stop it from falling into her eyes. "That's too much. I know where to get them for a buck."

"But these are real. My ludes are from Nepperhan Avenue Pharmacy. These weren't cooked up by some freak in his home laboratory and cut with rat poison. These are as one hundred percent pure and unadulterated as a bar of *Ivory* soap. You see, my ludes float," Cookie shook the bag, rattling the peach pills. "You'll float, too."

Cookie held out her hand. "Come on, give me my money, honey. You asked me for them. Here are your ludes."

"I don't have that much money," Reenie said. "Let me think about it."

"Thirty bucks," Cookie said. "That's my final offer."

"Okay," Reenie said. She hung her head to the side and looked up at Cookie, almost as suspiciously as the way her grandmother had looked at her when she first arrived at the front door. "Give me a day and I'll get the money from Billy Dee."

Although Cookie knew Billy Dee was Reenie's older brother and a good bet, there was no way she was handing over a bag of genuine ludes without cold cash in her hand. "I'll wait," Cookie said. "I'm going to go to the library to take back my books and stop back here on the way home. You've got yourself an hour to come up with the dough."

Cookie stood up and let herself out of Reenie's room and into the living room, where the old woman sat dozing on the couch in front of the tiny TV. "It was so nice to see you," she said, walking away, hardly looking at Reenie's grandmother. "Have a nice day."

Cookie might have been a gangster and a hippie, but she still had good manners, especially with old people. And with that, Cookie walked out of the apartment and headed to Getty Square and the library.

Ludes were normally prescribed to crazy housewives who couldn't sleep. Most of the drugs Kitty used were over-the-counter prescription anti-psychotic medications. Johnny had struck a deal with Nicky Santoro, the pharmacist at the Nepperhan Avenue Pharmacy. Nicky gave Johnny drugs— whatever he wanted, and Johnny was always trying something new—to quell Kitty's schizophrenia. In turn, Johnny gave Nicky a case of liquor: *Seagram's 7,* extra special delivery once a month.

Johnny slipped the ludes to Kitty because none of the pills the shrinks had prescribed for her had worked. Cookie had tried a lude once. She didn't like the feeling, and it only made her remember the horrible thing that had happened to her and changed her life. The effects of the lude made her feel like what had happened did not matter, that it did not hurt so bad. But actually, it did matter. A lot. And that's all the time she had to give to the whole thing today.

Sixteen

Star-crossed Lovers

Everywhere Cookie went, she kept bumping into him. *Down the End*, on the wall at Untermyer Park, in Getty Square and oddly enough, at the Yonkers Carnegie Library, Herman Lynch turned up everywhere. En route to the library, Cookie decided to make one extra stop. She hurried to get to her father's office and didn't remember walking or running; most likely, she moved in a combination alternating between the two. She was in an altered state of mind and intent on getting to where she needed, as fast as her two legs would carry her.

Forgetting about provoking her trick knee, she inadvertently took Herman's advice to work her muscles and picked up her legs, bending and stretching her knees in a magnificent sequence of goose steps. She ran through Getty Square and vaguely saw a curtain moving in the second-floor apartment of a turn-of-the-century tenement building that probably had eight layers of chipped linoleum on every floor in every room.

On Main Street, she stopped in front of Knepfer's Toyland and decided to have a smoke. She pulled out a *Marlboro* from her cloth shoulder sack, lit it and took a long drag. In the storefront window sixteen Madame Alexander dolls with painted faces, red lips and pink cheeks, stared back at her with large unblinking eyes. She knew there were sixteen dolls, because on a different day, a lazy day when she had time to kill, she had counted the antique dolls and noted the different colors of petit point and lace the same way she looked at the different colors of people. The store had a sign for a Doll Hospital: *Get your favorite doll restored and repaired.* Cookie thought if she had been a doll, she could just check in and have her heart reattached in a place where it used to be. She tried to recall the lyrics to the nursery school rhyme Humpty Dumpty. *Humpty Dumpty sat on a wall, Humpty Dumpty had a great fall. All the king's horses and all the king's men Couldn't put Humpty together again.*

Cookie didn't know where she was going, or who she was becoming. She only knew: I have no choice but to be who I am.

In the distance, she heard someone crying out, "Paulie!" A boy, about three, was running up ahead on the sidewalk. His mother savagely scooped him up from the ground and spanked him hard on the bottom. She heard the child cry, "stop," and her admonishment, "I told you, you shoulda been good." The mother screamed in between whacks. Cookie had a sudden urge to vomit, but she held back and told herself *Stop.* She had seen hundreds of kids spanked by their parents, but never before had she reacted so violently, wrestling with the intrusion of bile rising in her throat. She stared at the painted faces of the Madame Alexander dolls and spotted a lone Gina doll sitting off to the side. Even the dolls showed her no mercy.

She rushed into the Savings and Loan Building and panted while she raced up the marble steps. In the office reception area, she was surprised to see Millie Mangano. Millie didn't even feign kindness. She looked at Cookie with accusatory eyes and adjusted her eyeglasses to tilt on the tip of her nose. "Still got those books, I see. I'm starting to think you're pretending to be somebody you're not. You carry those books around trying to make it look like you're smart, but there you are, going down into the colored neighborhood."

She cast her eyes downward, and kept them focused in a way that made them appear to be closed. "What were you doing all this time? You mean it took you this long to walk to the Square? I saw you on the bus two hours ago."

Cookie realized that her relationship with Millie had taken a turn for the worse. "It's none of your business where I've been, especially when I never know where my father is. Think about it."

If Millie was shocked, she didn't let on. "Your father's not here," she said without looking up. "And I don't know when I'm expecting him back."

"I'll wait," Cookie gasped. "I need to see him."

Cookie was trying to come up with an excuse for being there in the middle of the day, but Millie said nothing and walked away. Cookie sat down at Johnny's big oak desk in the far corner of the office. The drawers were open and looked like they had been ransacked, but being messy was Johnny's operating style. Mounds of paper were piled high in chaotic heaps of stacks, threatening eruption. Cookie skimmed through the papers on her father's desk even though she wasn't supposed to be snooping. There were lots of bills, of which Cookie could not discern one from another. She was mainly struck by the photographs of her and Donny. Smiling, innocent girls dressed and veiled in bride-like white from their first holy communion, and later from Cookie's Confirmation. There were no pictures of Cookie after she had reached adolescence. It was nothing personal. That's when trouble had set in. Johnny was gone most of the time and Kitty—well, Kitty had her troubles. *Some mother*, Cookie thought to herself. She loved her so much that she wanted to save her from the disease that ravaged her mind, body and soul.

On Johnny's desk, there were many photographs of Kitty Colangelo, mostly headshots in the muted shades of early photo color. Kitty, formal—wearing a lace schoolgirl collar poking out from a navy blue argyle sweater. Kitty, sociable— sitting in front of the soda fountain at Woolworth's. Kitty, working—framed by the teller's cage at the Gramatan Bank in Bronxville. Kitty, bride—wearing a wedding veil, crowned with thousands of tiny seed pearls. Kitty, knockout—in her entirety filling out a foamy-pink swimsuit in a cheesecake pose.

In 1952, Kitty had gone to Atlantic City and paraded in the boardwalk revue. In those days, Atlantic City was the working-class Riviera for New York, New Jersey and Philadelphia. Kitty could have been a star. She could have been Miss America. She was that good-looking and that photogenic. That was Kitty Colangelo, a regular oiled goddess, sunning herself on the yellow sand, looking as delicate and as creamy as the inside of a young conch shell. She had the celluloid dimension of another Norma Jean Baker prior to her platinum blonde transformation into Marilyn Monroe. There was no outward sign of cancer, gangrene or illness, exposing the classic lines of a woman nicknamed *Black Irish Beauty*. No one knew there were voices in her head because she smiled with beautiful white teeth. There were no pictures of Kitty looking crazy.

Sometimes Cookie worried about becoming crazy. Fran Ochiogrosso called her crazy once. She said Cookie was weird and crazy, like her mother. Then she took it back, because she knew the accusation had cut Cookie to the quick.

Cookie had enough thoughts to fill up a new notebook, but she still needed to find the words, and in a strange way, she had the confidence that the words would come. She picked up her two library books and walked out of the office, hoping Millie would not notice her leaving. She made it all the way to the outer office thinking, she had dodged a bullet, when she heard Millie calling after her. "Your father's at the studio," she said. "He's in the city playing with those colored musicians. Just thought you'd want to know."

Millie walked into the outer office and placed her hands

on her hips as if she had squared off and reconciled with some sort of conflict within herself. "More than any other thing in this world, Johnny loves his music. It's the only thing that keeps his own demons at bay. Just thought you ought to know. It doesn't mean he doesn't love you. He's had a hard life. He does love you, and tries to do the best he can."

Cookie wasn't moved by Millie's confession. She felt strangely empty. She knew there was something wrong with Johnny, as much as there was hard evidence about what was wrong with Kitty. At least Kitty had been committed to the crazy ward umpteen times and everyone knew she was schizophrenic. Not so with Johnny; he wasn't diagnosed with anything. He was just normal-crazy like everyone else in Yonkers.

"It's because of Korea," Millie said. "And other stuff too."

Cookie walked out of the office and quietly closed the door. She knew part of her father's story. At 20, this Italian working-class boy from Yonkers found himself in the Marine Corps, on the front lines in Korea, in the 1st Battalion of the 1st Marine Division. Marching north to the Yalu River during the Chosin Reservoir Campaign in 1950, he was one among the 12,000 marines who were surrounded by 60,000 Chinese soldiers. When she asked him how he survived, Johnny said, "I kept charging forward, but I kept my head down." Cookie knew the war had done something bad to him, but she wasn't quite sure what it was. She only knew he went ballistic every time he saw the Vietnam war protesters and called them names. The war in Vietnam brought up something terrible for him, and he hated the patch of the American flag that Cookie had sewn onto the seat of her pants.

Cookie walked along Broadway, allowing the rumble of the traffic to drown out her thoughts so she could stop thinking for awhile. She needed to have a break from herself, and that notion made her laugh. Imagine taking a break from my own mind! When she reached the foot of the library stairs, she felt the weight from the humidity and heat come crashing down around her. She was thirsty and sweating from every pore of her body. It had been hours since she had anything to drink. She climbed the steps, feeling weary and looking forward to entering the cool lobby of the library. She heaved open the heavy oak door and stepped into the cool anteroom and found the water fountain on the left side of the front entrance. Before she approached the main reception desk in the great room, she stopped and took a long drink from the water fountain.

When she looked up, she wiped excess water from her face. She had been so thirsty that she had guzzled the water and splashed some clear up into her nose. There he was again! Make no mistake, Herman Lynch was carrying a stack of books up to the main reception desk. He didn't see Cookie but she sure saw him. Then she realized the connection. He worked here! How on earth did Herman Lynch get a job at the library! It was astonishing the way he kept showing up in all of her favorite places: The Eagle's Nest at Untermyer Park and now the library. She'd seen him in the ghetto, but that felt normal. Before she knew it, he'd be showing up in her *Owl Hole*, and that would not be okay!

Cookie quickly rushed to place her overdue books in a bin next to the front reception desk. By this time, Herman saw her and quickly darted up to her side and offered to take them from her. Cookie let him have the books. Then she turned around and headed up to the second floor, to the children's reading room. She knew she was too old to be here, but it gave her comfort to look at the murals and to sit on the small chairs. She felt like if she sat here long enough she would heal some part of her younger self that had been stolen from her. She looked at the picture books, flipping open the pages of *The Velveteen Rabbit*.

Herman came into the room and sat down beside her. "Your reading is way beyond that, Cookie."

"What do you know about my reading level?"

"Seriously, what are you doing with little kids' books?" Herman looked at her incredulously. His harelip had grown on her. She hardly noticed it any more. It was simply part of him. "Dostoyevsky is a far cry from *The Velveteen Rabbit.*" Then he leaned forward and whispered. "You shouldn't be dealing drugs. Ludes are real bad for you."

"I'm not using drugs," Cookie said. "I just sell them. I'm an entrepreneur."

Herman started laughing, "Entrepreneur! Now I've heard everything. You're a funny-ass honky motherfucker."

"Honky," Herman slapped his leg. "And I mean honky." He looked up at the mural on the wall showing knights on horses fighting in battle. He pointed repeatedly to one panel showing a fair noble woman laying her hands on the top of a knight's head who knelt before her. "*Guinevere* had *green eyes* like yours, milady, like yours."

Cookie shook her head and smiled at him. "Don't you ever get tired of being a cut-up? Besides, I think your eyes are greener than mine."

"No, I don't," Herman said, squirming in the small chair. "Mine just look greener because I'm a nigger."

"You're not supposed to say that word!"

"Can too," Herman said, jumping up out of his seat. "Because I'm a nigger and if I like you enough, maybe one day I'll let you call me a nigger too." He gesticulated with his hands in a language of his own. "That's just the way it is."

Cookie didn't know what to say. He had skirted right over the race issue and made it okay to say the most derogatory word of all. She didn't understand him. She thought it was best left for her to find new words to describe the whole thing in her black & white notebook.

"How'd you get this job?"

"My grandmother works here at the circulation desk," he said, pacing in front of the low table. "She pays me a few dollars for doing chores. She says it keeps me off the streets."

"Does it? Do you stay out of trouble?" Cookie gave him a stern look, as if he could not possibly be telling the truth.

Herman's smile was accentuated and emboldened by his harelip. "I'm going to be a dancer. And man can I dance."

Herman rocked forward, bending and straightening his knees. "You should be doing this too," he said, motioning for Cookie to bend her knees. At first, Cookie was reluctant, but Herman kept prodding her. "Move those knees," he told her. You're too young to be falling down stairs all the time. Get moving, Cookie girl."

Herman launched into a soft-shoe shuffle. His footwork was fancy and fast, so fast, she could feel air moving like a fan around his feet. He seemed to be tap dancing, but he was wearing *Hush Puppies* with soft soles. His feet moved so rapidly and with such precision, that he barely left the floor before he was already on to the next ten steps. He put his hand out to Cookie and made her follow his moves.

"Bend your knees, now straighten and contract them. Feel that muscle around your knee-caps, "he said, grinning and spinning. "Use it. Use those muscles. Work it. Go on, work it. Use it good!"

"I can't sing, can't play music, "Cookie protested. "And I can't dance."

"That's not true! Anyone can dance!" Herman picked up his tempo and waved his arms in the air. "Look at you go there! All you have to do is move. Keep moving!"

Cookie was struggling to keep up with him, and grateful that the moccasins on her feet were as soft-soled as Herman's *Hush Puppies*; otherwise, the clatter would have invited a librarian to come see what all the commotion was about. She struggled to keep up with him. "My knee's going to go out on me."

"No, it won't," Herman said, leading her with two hands, and before long they were dancing so fast it had turned into a jitterbug. Both of them were moving to a tempo set by Herman and the music he heard in his head. Cookie could not hear what he was hearing and tried as hard as she could to keep up with him.

"Bend those knees," Herman said. Then he held his leg straight out in front of him to show her what it meant to contract the muscle. "See how tight this muscle gets! All you've got to do is straighten your leg, then bend it." His dancing picked up even faster. "And you've got to do it again and again and again. Flex your foot, straighten that leg, point your toe, bend that knee as far as you can. More. More. Tighter. There you go! Did you feel that?"

Cookie nodded to him, and did what he told her to do. She could barely feel her knees, what he meant, and what he was telling her to do, but so far, with all of the movement, her trick knee had not buckled, not once. All told, Cookie and Herman must have danced for only three minutes, but for Cookie, it felt like an eternity. She liked it and yet she hated it. Mostly she hated it, because she was afraid a librarian would come in and yell at them.

In all the time Cookie and Herman were dancing, no one else had come into the children's reading room. During the summer months, the children's reading room was frequently empty. Cookie and Herman had the place to themselves. The city had a bookmobile that scheduled stops all over the city, even in the ghetto areas on the west side of Yonkers.

In the next few weeks, Herman and Cookie ran into each other often, most of the time at the library. Herman talked about a lot of different things. Cookie talked about how great books move people. She tried to call Herman *nigger,* but couldn't bring herself to do it, and he affectionately called her *honky*. Herman offered to get any books that Cookie wanted from the library. "I'll check them out on my own card, and bring them to you," he told her. And most of all, he pushed her to keep practicing her deep knee bends.

Cookie confided in Herman that all of her suffering was for a reason, and meant if she could connect with another person, that would help her find meaning in life. She also told Herman she intended, one day, to leave Yonkers and to become famous. Herman said he had already left Yonkers in his own mind long ago. In this thing called art, suffering, and finding meaning, one ultimately finds true love. Cookie didn't know what true love was; Herman said he didn't know what true love was, either. Cookie told Herman the closest thing to true love she had known was with *Blind Owl* Alan Wilson. Herman told her he would love to play the harmonica like the *Blind Owl*, but having a hare lip made it impossible. Cookie showed him a poem she had written and explained how her suffering helped her to find her own words. Cookie and Herman began sharing important secrets that they had never told to anyone else. Unthinkable as it might seem, the black boy with a harelip from Ashburton Avenue and the working-class Italian girl from the North End became friends.

Seventeen

You

Johnny Colangelo had come home again. Not that he had been gone and completely out of the picture. Instead of rising before dawn and returning long after midnight, he sat at the dining room table as if all along he had been there as a permanent fixture, as vigilant as an overhead lamp. Johnny's brown hair curled around his head in a tight wild bush. He was a dead ringer for the Welsh pop singer Tom Jones. Looking at Johnny oozing heat and masculine power, Cookie expected him to stand up, unbutton his front shirt down to his navel and belt out a refrain from the passionate hit song *Delilah*.

"You look like Tom Jones," Cookie chided him. She giggled and laughed.

"You really do look like him."

Johnny looked pissed and squinted his eyes as if he was shielding them from direct sunlight, but he was only pretending to be annoyed. He was more than pleased; he was flattered, and enjoyed bearing a resemblance to a celebrity, especially a popular musician.

"Everyone says you look like Tom Jones," Donny giggled. "Tom Jones. My father looks like Tom Jones." She sidled up to Johnny so close that Cookie expected her to jump up on his lap, but Johnny wasn't that kind of father. He had a hard time showing any affection, even a small hug or some small term of endearment. For him to say *I love you* was the most remote of all possibilities.

"Tom Jones! Don't give me that shit," Johnny said. He grunted and cleared his throat. "Do you know where your mother is?"

Donny shook her head no, closed her eyes, and then stuck her fingers in her ears. "What's that all about?" She kept shaking her head. "Mommy's gone crazy."

"Don't you have something better to do? Like play outside? You're always in the house. Why don't you go out and play some games? Do something!"

Donny knew she had been banished, and scampered off.

Johnny looked at Cookie and winked. "She's a pest," he said. "She needs to stay outside and play. It will do her good."

Johnny's voice was rich and baritone, blending the musicality of a man who loved to sing. Cookie didn't know for sure if her father could sing. If he could, she hadn't heard him. Her Daddy was a percussionist—a thumper, in the heavy back end of rhythm, jazz and the blues. Cookie knew for sure when Johnny was gone, which was most of the time, he was hanging out with the boys in the band at Lynn Oliver's studio on the upper west side of Manhattan.

Despite the reference to Tom Jones, the final piano crescendo of Gershwin's *American in Paris* blared from the stereo tucked away in the living room, trailing away until it was gone. As long as Cookie could remember, music was perpetually on, and was another way of saying Kitty was home. The Hi-Fi stereo console was ensconced in a massive wooden cabinet and set to WPAT-FM, broadcast from Paterson, New Jersey. Johnny loved hearing music and it seemed to soothe Kitty's psychotic spells.

Cookie and Johnny were in the back of the house in a combination dining room and TV room. In one half of the room, there was a TV, couch and a chair. A dining room table with chairs took up the other half. Her father sat at the other end of the dining room table, which was covered with a yellow plastic table cloth. The music from the stereo now blared a honey-soothing melody by Stan Getz. Johnny was drinking coffee, one cup after the other, from a squat round see-through glass coffee pot that showed its inner metal works. He loved Martinson's coffee – extra fine grains in the blue can. He'd make a whole pot of eight cups and drink the whole thing by himself.

Kitty Colangelo didn't drink coffee, claiming it stained her teeth. Even though she was crazy, she had a keen under-standing of her stunning beauty and the impact it made on every man who crossed her path, including Father Dunn, the parish priest who was said to be smitten with Mrs. Myrtle Shep, the church organist.

"There was a lot of organ playing going on there." And Johnny did not mean the musical instrument. Johnny did not like the idea that his wife seemed to be obsessed with a priest. "I don't get the priest stuff at all. He's not even a good priest."

Kitty was in the kitchen talking to herself. She couldn't be seen, but she could be heard from everywhere in the house. She was babbling about priests, sinners and the church bells ringing too long, chiming on until her ear-drums threatened to blow up. Kitty was having a spell, which was not uncommon and could go on for days. Her voice ranged from sinister whispers and hellion cries to whoops and chirps, and then she'd begin weeping.

Cookie was fixated on the sight of her black & white composition book. Somehow her notebook—the one that contained her innermost private thoughts, her poems and the beginnings of her book—had landed on the dining room table. Every so often, Johnny's formidably muscular forearm grazed across the cover of the notebook. He had confiscated the notebook, not knowing it was only one in a series of many. He kept picking it up, then putting it down. Fanning the pages, he behaved with far greater suspicion than his obviously paranoid wife.

Johnny whispered to Cookie, "What's going on there between your mother and this priest?"

Cookie closed her eyes and looked away. She felt sorry for her father. Saying Johnny Colangelo had a hard life was a mild understatement.

From the other room, Kitty Colangelo was mumbling and wailing. Most of what she said was incoherent and loony. Then she'd belt out a whole sentence. "There's not much to our marriage; we cohabitate!"

"Oh *Madone.* I don't know why she says these things and thinks these things." Johnny whispered again. "A priest! Where does she come up with these things?"

"Because she's crazy," Cookie said. "She can't help it. She was born this way."

Not only did she have to endure growing up under the whacked-out tutelage of a crazy mother, but her father was no help whatsoever. Why did she have to console him? It should have been the other way around. At thirteen, Cookie understood that her father did not know what to do about his wife, and she felt sorry for him. Everyone else did too.

"Know what I think?" Johnny Colangelo was always tapping his finger on his temple, as if he was smart or something. That annoyed Cookie to no end. She did not think he was smart, not even a whit. "No, sure you don't," he answered himself. "You always think you're so goddamn smart. But I didn't live this long for nothing. I've seen it all. If that priest is doing something with my wife, I have no problem knocking the crap out of him, and her, the both of them."

"Please leave me alone," Kitty cried out. "Please, please, please," she shrieked. I don't want to hear no more bells. Please," she started crying in a high pitch and her voice kept rising. "Please go away."

"Keep your voice down," Cookie whispered to her father.

"She can hear you from there. She may be crazy, but her hearing is excellent."

"What am I supposed to do? I don't know what I'm going to do. Those pills I got from Nicky aren't working."

Johnny Colangelo was referring to the deal he had with Nicky Santoro at the Nepperhan Avenue Pharmacy.

"Maybe those pills from the shrink are no good," Cookie suggested. She hoped and prayed to herself that he'd get more ludes. She could make even more money. Ludes were so in! Everyone would buy them, and her mother would finally shut up! The solution would be good for her, good for her mother, good for her father, good for everyone. It was a win-win. "Why don't you get her more ludes? She's much happier on ludes," Cookie insisted.

"You think you know everything," he said. "And you know nothing. Nothing. What do you think you know about prescription drugs? I take your mother to that whacked-out shrink in Harlem and all he does is charge me a hundred bucks an hour to put her on more pills."

Cookie hated it when her father was sanctimonious, holier-than-thou. No wonder her mother was chasing after a priest. Johnny Colangelo was usually gone for days or weeks. Cookie heard his car pulling up late at night and by the time she woke up in the morning, he was gone. On the weekends, after playing with the boys in the band, he came home late. He wasn't a bum or a totally absentee father. He just had a life outside of the home that did not include Cookie, Donny or his crazy but beautiful wife, Kitty. When he occasionally returned, he'd suddenly decide he needed to focus exclusively on his daughter. He'd beam the spotlight on her with a high dose of toxic light. She was forced to submit to examination under his *Italian father-style* interrogation.

Johnny thought he was being the most observant, caring, interested concerned-about-his-daughter father who had ever walked the main streets of Yonkers. From Cookie's perspective, she saw him as a grand inquisitor who was intent on tormenting her. She could not wait for him to leave and go back to *his life*. As soon as he chastised Cookie sufficiently by punishing for deeds both real and imagined, the spotlight was turned off and he resumed his party boy life outside of the home. Playing music, chasing women, drinking and gambling, Johnny was one of the boys from the old Italian neighborhood, which was more a state of mind than it was a mindset derived from living in any actual 'hood in Yonkers.

Johnny grazed his hand across the top of Cookie's black & white notebook that looked grossly out of place on the dining room table. He had tied a towel around his head to mop the sweat away from his forehead and to prevent it from dripping into his eyes. "Jesus, it's hot," he said. "At least it's not too humid today. It's cooled down. The high's 84, but the humidity's not that bad. I can take the heat, but I can't take the goddamn humidity."

He leaned forward and grinned, whispering to Cookie. "Think she's gone to bed and she'll shut up for awhile?"

"Can I go out now?" As if Cookie needed permission. She was just being polite. She was going to do whatever the hell she wanted to do. She moved to get up from the table.

"Sit down," Johnny commanded. "I want to talk to you." He banged on the table as if he was playing the piano keys. He wasn't threatening; it was just his way. He wanted to make a point that would be heard by his daughter. "I've seen the good, and the not-so-good. And all I want is what's good for you."

Playing his fingers like the drums, he strummed and tapped on the table in rhythm with the song. Johnny never stopped moving. He was constantly tapping, rapping, knuckling and waving his arms. Every pore of his body poured out a rhythm and a song.

Cookie squirmed in her chair. She was wearing red short-shorts—called hot pants—and chewing gum while the man went on a wild rant. She knew she had it coming. She hated it when he was about to give her a lecture. It was as if he felt that was the main priority—aside from keeping a roof over their heads—in his part-time career as a father.

"At least I showed up tonight. You could be grateful for that. You should be lucky that I'm your father, and not one of the wacky guys your mother used to date before she met me. Yo, me, Johnny Colangelo. Not that she really knew a guy before she met me."

He leaned back in satisfaction, as if he was proud of what he had said and more importantly, he was proud of the man he was trying to become. He looked at Cookie with a strange sense of wonderment. He was deeply perplexed at having to raise a daughter. He didn't understand different life forms, women, girls, any more than he understood another species like a dog or a cat, a fish and a snake. He didn't understand what made them different.

"I think you need to mind who your friends are," Johnny said, pointing his finger at Cookie. "I know the darkies are taking over the neighborhood, but that doesn't mean you need to be around them or any of those other boys that I've seen you hanging out with."

He picked up Cookie's black & white composition book and waved it in the air. "Shit poems," he said. "These are shit poems. He laid the book on the table and looked at her. "I don't understand why you write about these silly things!"

Cookie felt hurt but she didn't let him know. She wasn't big on sharing her feelings with her father. She shrugged and looked at him sadly. "Why do you hate them?"

"I hate all of them, because these poems are weak. You're complaining all the time. Don't you see how beautiful the world is! Why don't you write about happy things like birds, and the flowers and trees?"

"Which poem do you like the most?"

"Are you kidding me? I don't like none of them. These

poems are bad. Why don't you see the glass half-full instead
of completely empty?" He flipped through the pages and said,
"Who is this *You*? This poem is called *You*! Like it's about a
boy. *You*. Who is this guy named *You*?"

Johnny read Cookie's poem out loud. "*You*," it's called.
"Here, I'm going to read from it, so it will help me understand
you better. *You*." Then he began reading.

> *When I see you my heart bursts into a tremendous fire*
> *You are the fulfilling dream of my every desire*
> *You don't even know my name just my unhappy face*

"Good," Johnny commented on the line. "He doesn't know your
name. GOOD, like let's keep it that way. He doesn't know your
name and you stay UNHAPPY. Got that kiddo? Eh? Am I
right? You can stay unhappy. No wonder why he doesn't want
to know you! You've got an unhappy face. What guy wants to
know a broad with an unhappy face? But then if you get rid
of the unhappy face and he wants to know then we've got a
whole different problem!" He read on.

> *But we both have something that we both love that strange*
> *familiar place.*
> *You have something that every person could wish for*
> *But just seeing you I could not ask for more*
> *I have a strange feeling that I have loved you and you have*
> *loved me in another time*
> *But I rejected you because people said our love was a sinful*
> *crime*
> *Now you have rejected me,*
> *So you could be as happy as a bird flying free.*

When Johnny read the whole poem, he looked up at Cookie
and said, "This is disturbing. Very disturbing. You think you
had another life. What are you, a heathen or something? Don't

you realize it's a mortal sin to think this way, that you had another life other than the one you have right now!"

Johnny leaned forward and danced his fingers across the table like he was intent on being as sincere as a snake. "I really have to ask you something, Cookie, who's this boy YOU? Who is he? Is he a boy in this neighborhood? Come on, tell me. Who is this YOU?"

"Alan Wilson," Cookie said "*Blind Owl* Alan Wilson. His birthday was on Saturday, July 4th. I wrote the poem for him."

"So he's one of these rock 'n' roll guys? Help me to understand this, Cookie. Are you hanging out with these rock band guys? These musician guys are the worst. Musicians are very bad boys. I know," he leaned into the table like he was trying to make the biggest point of his life. "I know these musician types are all very bad. Musicians only think of themselves and their music. All these guys think about is their music."

Then he looked right at her, squinting his eyes as if he had pincers that could stab. "Is he black?"

Cookie shook her head.

"Then who is this Blonde Owl Wilson?" Johnny's eyes squinted to a narrow slant. "Does this owl guy hang out with black musicians? Is it a nigger band?"

"Blind Owl Wilson. I've never met him, and he's white."

"Good, let's keep it like that."

She couldn't believe he was talking to her this way. Her poetry was none of his business. And for him to talk about musicians that way. "You're a musician."

"I know." With his finger, Johnny tapped his temple. "That's why I know these things."

"You're a hypocrite of the first degree!" Cookie snatched her notebook out from under his scrutiny and clutched it to her chest.

"Why don't you do something practical, like learn how to play tennis? You'll meet nice boys if you play tennis."

"You mean like the Amakassin Club?"

"There you go again, busting my balls, Cookie. You're just like your mother that way!"

The Amakassin Club was a private club in North Yonkers that had a swimming pool and tennis courts. Shortly after Johnny had built his house, he applied to be a member, but was turned down. There was no reason given. Johnny took it to heart. After all his hard work, he was ostracized as low-life, the son of an Italian immigrant. His rejected application to the Amakassin Club only bolstered his feelings of shame; he was guilty of being born on the wrong side of the tracks, an unpardonable and grievous error, from which he had no chance to recover. It goes without saying, everyone in Yonkers had been born on the wrong side of the tracks. Johnny Colangelo was no exception.

"Did you have to be that way? Did you have to bring up the Amakassin Club?" Johnny looked sincerely pained. He pointed at Cookie's notebook. "Also, you shouldn't be saying bad things about our president."

"You don't even like him. Tricky Dicky," Cookie said in a snotty voice.

"Yeah, you're right. But he's still the President, kiddo, and don't forget it. And this other stuff about the war in Vietnam and the hippies. I don't get it. It's not how I raised you to be, Cookie. You dishonor me when you say what you do and think the way you think."

Kitty walked into the dining room. Her eyes were bugged out of her head. "We called you Cookie because when you were a little girl, you loved cookies. Zwieback was your first cookie. And that's the way the cookie crumbles." She rubbed her fingers maniacally along the sides of her nose as if she was trying to stop from sneezing and giggled.

"Jesus, would you stop talking like that, Kitty?"

Kitty took his coffee pot from the table and smashed it on the floor, "Look what you made me do," she cried out. "The pope's done leaning on me. I'm not going to take it no more.

"You see what she does? I don't know what to do with her!"
Then he looked at Cookie with tears in his eyes. "I have to take
her into the hospital. Your mother. She's sick. She's not getting
better. I don't know what to do." He looked at Cookie, im-
ploring her. His blue eyes were rimmed red, and tears started
to form in the corners, glistening in the creases, growing into
drops. "What do you think I should do with her? What's a man
supposed to do?" He threw his hands up in the air as if he was
beseeching God or some higher power to intercede. "What's a
man supposed to do? I've done everything a man could do."

He looked at Cookie as if maybe she had the answer. It was
a remote possibility, but Johnny was willing to try anything.
Cookie didn't think at that moment. She didn't try to help him.
She had enough trouble being herself, not to mention trying to
understand a crazy person, even if that crazy person happened
to be her mother, someone she loved, someone she loved so
much that it hurt inside out and outside in. She loved Kitty
more than she had ever loved a pet, her sister or her father,
but there wasn't anything she could do for her.

Eighteen

Tuesday, August 4, 1970

Cookie didn't have a way to communicate with Herman Lynch. She didn't know his phone number. She didn't even know if he had a phone. Nor did she intend to phone him. She didn't know exactly where he lived. Not that she had reason to contact him. From time to time, out of the blue, she thought about him, but did not know why. One thing Cookie had realized about herself from an early age was her propensity to passionately embroil herself in mini-obsessions. Her obsessions were thoroughly consuming, far-ranging, always eclectic and a bit strange. In the seventh grade, she was obsessed with Einstein's theory of relativity. She went to the Carnegie Library in Getty Square and asked the woman working at the circulation desk where she might find the book. When Cookie checked out *Einstein's Theory of Relativity*, the librarian did not bat an eye. For the seventh-grade school science fair, Cookie's project focused on the concept of *time.*

Her science teacher Peter Battaglia smirked to himself when he reviewed her posters about space, time, and her poor artistic rendition of lopsided planets revolving around a childishly scrawled yellow sun, replete with spokes of fiery orange and red rays. Her inability to draw anything beyond a basic stick figure, and at that, not very well, was on par with her inability to sing, dance or play a musical instrument, but all of her negative attributes did not preclude her ability to think well. And of course she had her words. When her mother was lucid, she told Cookie she had inherited the talent to be musical from her father. At school, every instrument she tried, and she tried to play many, left her wanting something else to do. The funny thing was, she wondered, if she saw Herman Lynch again, he might actually teach her to dance. She did like moving and continued to practice deep knee bends just to see what could happen and if it would fix her trick knees.

As for her seventh-grade science experiment, Cookie had been prepared to offer her presentation—an explanation of how we could travel in outer space and not age—when Mr. Battaglia rudely interrupted her. He stopped her cold from talking about Einstein or his theory of relativity. His tone was caustic and he called her by her last name *Colangelo*. He asked her how long a day was in the Book of Genesis when God created the earth. Cookie was literally stumped. She had not thought about a biblical day as the 24-hour period of time that it takes for the earth to rotate on its axis around the sun, and told him so. "The biblical day is an artful interpretation of time," she told him. Although she had labored for many months learning about time, Mr. Battaglia gave her a B. Cookie was not completely dismayed or surprised by a mere B for so much work! Mr. Battaglia had never liked her ever since the big event happened to her in the 6th grade. Talk about the convergence of the past and present being one and the same! Like a grand example of Einstein's theory of relativity! Mr. Battaglia had seen what had happened to her on that infamous day, November 6, 1967. After the incident, she had to report to him and he told her to write an essay about why she should never talk during a fire drill. He also could not look her in the eye. When she thought about it, Mr. Battaglia never looked her in the eye again.

Even as she walked north on Broadway under the glare of the harsh afternoon sun, what had happened to her in the sixth grade would never go away! That event from her past would live with her all of the days of her life. She could not shake it or wish it away. It is what it is, and that's all there is to say about it. *Stop*!

Another obsession of Cookie's focused on her exploration of the entire landscape of Untermyer Park. She couldn't go to the moon, but she could explore every craggy nook and cave. She knew she should not go there, but the park invited her like seductive bait and bade her to visit as a resolute temptation; it was a place of taboo that could never be avoided because this was where ultimately, she would find and know herself.

The sign read: **Untermyer Park, Parks Department, the City of Yonkers** in small, neat, white letters against a mud brown muted background. She spied a smaller sign that stated, *Yonkers, The City of Gracious Living,* and chuckled to herself. She did not know how the catch-phrase implying gracious living measured against her reality of everyday or ordinary life in Yonkers. The image of Johnny sitting at the dining room table, slurping down *spaghetti aglio e oli,* wearing only his boxer trunks and an olive oil-splattered undershirt, did not conjure the picture of a charmed existence. In fact, she could not think of one person in the entire city of Yonkers who could be considered the epitome of gracious living—any way you looked at it—east or west of the Hudson River. *Sorry,* she snickered to herself. *Yonkers is not an elegant place.*

Yonkers is not an elegant place—even if you were the children of Samuel Untermyer, who were rumored to have frittered away his fortune and left the property to the city because the family could not afford to pay the hefty taxes on this prime parcel of land overlooking the Hudson River and the ninth wonder of the world—the New Jersey Palisades. Cookie knew this rumor had to be well-founded. Rich people don't give away something for nothing. Only five acres of the park remained from the original estate. The rest of the land had been parceled off and subdivided into the lots that marked the middle-class homes dotting the outlying neighborhood and the large complex for St. John's Riverside Hospital. The main house had been demolished years before Cookie's birth. The only original structure that remained was the caretaker's cottage currently inhabited by hundreds of wild cats—scrawny and ragged, feral creatures—who propagated madly and thrived on vermin and garbage. The vile, hissing creatures were known to have attacked people without warning and without provocation.

Cookie shuddered as she walked up the gravel driveway that ran alongside the caretaker's cottage and into the great lawn. What would she do if a pack of starving stray cats suddenly charged at her? She'd take her cloth shoulder sack and use it as a weapon to thwack them hard on the head. If wild cats dared to mess with Cookie Colangelo, she'd make them pay. She'd crack open their feral skulls the same way she cracked eggs on the edge of a frying pan to make a cheese omelet.

This confidence in her ability to fend off wild cats gave her strength to sort through one of the biggest dilemmas of her life. How could she go home tonight? How could she go home and face her father after he made fun of her poems and accused her of inviting the advances of boys, sight unseen? She would be lucky if a boy had asked her out. It was as if her father did not see her in the light of reality: she looked twelve, and not a single boy in the entire North End was interested in her. She had not done anything wrong to invite Johnny's suspicions. She had never even kissed a boy. Not really. Not properly. When she was younger, and when the boys were younger, there had been little kisses, pecks and pats, glances and hugs, but no ardent making out. Cookie Colangelo was a complete and total virgin.

Cookie had her ideas about loving a boy but these thoughts were all directed toward the *Blind Owl*. Aside from him, she had other interests too: Einstein's theory of relativity, the

Summerhill School in England, Sumac trees and Herman Lynch. For reasons she did not understand, she had added Herman Lynch to her short list of obsessions. Regarding the whole notion of obsessions, the apple did not fall far from the tree. Johnny Colangelo had a flaming obsession with his daughter's honor and even though he was never home, he had an unnatural fear that she would get knocked up before she had finished high school. Johnny forbade Cookie from riding in cars with boys of any age or variety. To an Italian father who had caroused his way through the fifties, cars were really just beds on wheels. Johnny was preoccupied with the concept of good girls and bad girls, whores and Madonnas, and yet his wife Kitty belonged in a category of her own. He was insanely jealous of his wife and nothing irked him more than her obsession with the priest Father Dunn.

Cookie was almost all the way into the park. She stubbed her toe into the gravel path and kicked up dust and empty junk food bags of *Wise Potato Chips* and *Frito-Lays*. She could hear music squealing in the distance; guitars, banjos and a flute, clashing sounds, all shrill discordant notes; no one was playing the same song. Cookie was thinking about the time Kitty was crying because Johnny had accused her of bedding the Puerto Rican plumber who had taken four hours to mend and weld leaky pipes. Johnny said, "It should have only taken two hours and he charges me two extra hours for nailing my wife. I've gotta pay extra for his work on my wife's pipes! How does that make me look? Think I'm going to put up with this! Do I look stupid or something?"

From then on, Kitty made Cookie stay home from school to serve as a witness whenever she called in any service repairman, even the Sears washing machine man who looked like his face had been punched-in by a bag of bolts. Cookie doubted Kitty had an interlude with the plumber or any other man, even the priest. Johnny always suggested that Kitty might be fooling around and it became a running gag between them.

"No, Johnny. No, Johnny," Kitty always wailed. "You're the only man I've ever had. You're the only man I've ever wanted!"

Cookie tried to tell herself that Kitty had lost her mind over Johnny's wild suspicions, but she knew better. Kitty was sick, and it was no one's fault, no one except God.

What about me? Cookie thought to herself. Every night as she lay in bed during those delicious sleepy, still moments just before she drifted into sleep, she hugged her body and caressed herself as if she was her own boyfriend, pretending her own arms belonged to the *Blind Owl. What was going to happen when it happened for real?* It wasn't fair that she had to live in terror at the prospect of being kissed and stroked until she tingled all over. She wanted to know what it was like to be loved. *How could her father stand in the way of these feelings that felt so good and natural?*

Cookie glanced quickly at people, the hippies all over the place. Some sleeping naturally or passed-out from some un-bidden stage of a drug-induced high, some staring and sitting in yoga positions intent on welcoming an unwanted mantra; hippies were everywhere. The great lawn of the park was teeming with hippies sitting on park benches, under the groves of trees that bordered the crumbling palatial fortress type wall, on the gentle slope that people called *the hillside*, and strewn around, sprawling on their backs or lying prone, flat on their torsos, heads up like cobras or sideways, all over the meadow that led to the woods and wound down to the Eagle's Nest—the place where she had first met Herman Lynch.

A woman in a fuchsia, tie-dyed sari danced to the strange lilting tune emitted from a silver flute while she swirled yards of cotton broadcloth, leaving a wake of patchouli that got stuck in the humid air like a polluted cloud. Cookie could only see the backs of people and could not see their identities to figure out if she knew them. The great lawn was covered with groups of people clustered together like musical grapes, jamming music with many more instruments than banjos, guitars and flutes. Mandolins, bongo drums and rare lutes enhanced the wailing fracas, where everyone seemed to be playing something, but not everyone had talent, making for a graceless cacophony of noise.

Cookie skimmed through the entire perimeter of the great lawn, never stopping for too long. Everyone was older than she was, and she felt as awkward as if she was in the fifth grade and entering their turf for the first time. She remembered that day in school when she had first entered Christ the King. The students had just finished a math exam, and the papers had been graded. Sister Joseph Mary held Cookie's test paper high in the air to show the class that Cookie had the highest score.

The nun said to the class, "How could you let this girl who just came here from a public school get a higher grade than you?!"

Some compliment, Cookie thought. She did not know then that many years from now when she looked back at her life, she would regard the two years she had spent at School #16 as the golden years of her childhood. Everything went downhill when she returned to Catholic school and entered Christ the King in the fifth grade. All of the cool Italian girls had already formed a clique that did not let in an outsider like Cookie Colangelo. It was one lesson in humiliation after another. By the time she ended up with Fangs as her math teacher in the sixth grade, she stopped doing well in math. I'm not really good at anything, she thought. She sat down on the ground, the same way she slinked down into her seat at school.

Cookie felt uncomfortable in the park. She knew she was not cool at all. She didn't know how to make new friends, any more than she knew how to relate to her older friends like Lizzie Lovato. She liked to think she had outgrown Lizzie but her alienation was more than that. Cookie knew that she herself had changed. She was different somehow, and there was no going back to the girl she used to be. With her ragged,

patched blue jeans and taupe macramé head band, her clothes
fit in, but she did not. She didn't fit in anywhere. She wanted
to run from the park, but there was nowhere to go. She was
sitting under a large tree that had lost all of its leaves. It was
too hot for a tree to be in the midst of a cold-weather blight.
She noticed the color and shape of the leaves that had fallen
to the ground like a knotty blanket of gold wool. It was most
certainly an elm tree and with all of the dead elms that had
perished through disease, it might have been one of the last
elms left standing.

Some of the older guys played Frisbee on the great lawn.
The plastic blue disk seemed to be whirring closer and closer
in the air above the ground and close to Cookie's elm tree. The
guys didn't seem to mind Cookie, and hardly ever caught the
Frisbee that was flying so close to her head. She thought she
ought to leave, but that would have meant defeat, and she
was determined to stay. The sweet, acrid scent of pot wafted
by in the air and occasionally intermingled with strong incense. The pack of hippies sitting on the park benches that
dotted the gravel path to the inner courtyard were obviously
smoking. Cookie wanted to join them, but she felt too shy
to wander over and stand on the outskirts until one of them
noticed her and offered her a toke. She thought, *I'm not really
good at anything, but I have my words*. She pulled her black
& white notebook out of her shoulder sack and began writing
a new poem:

Gone for Awhile
How many joints did I have today?
Enough to send me far away.
I am in the land of deep *contentfulness*, not even a bird
can fly as high.
I even said excuse me when I bumped into the cop that
just walked by.
So here I am way up in space.
In the mirror, I can't even see my face.

Now I'm beginning to feel sad.
Even my friend is feeling bad.
I'm coming down, down, down.
My head feels heavy like the weight of a crown
Or like a boat beginning to sink.
Weird thoughts are running through my mind, I can't
even think!
Even though my head feels like lead.
Next time I smoke I won't remember what I've just said.

While Cookie pondered her poem, two things immediately happened. The blue Frisbee grazed the top of her head, smacked against the lower boughs of the elm tree and landed close to her knees. She also heard the unmistakable sound of Marvin Gaye's song *I Heard It Through The Grapevine;* its low rumble of base notes blared higher than all the other music being played in the park. It was as if someone had brought a portable stereo, which was impossible because there was nothing with a volume louder than a tape cassette player or a transistor radio. One of the hippie guys was running toward her, laughing, motioning for her to toss the Frisbee in his direction. Cookie was too stunned to move, not because the Frisbee had scuffed her head; she didn't know the first thing about tossing the Frisbee and didn't want to blow it on the first try. The hippie guy walked toward her with an unlit cigarette dangling from his lower lip. He looked at her appraisingly—why didn't she pick up on his cue? Didn't she want to have fun? Her looked her over as if he was noting her jeans and her pink paisley halter top that barely concealed her two tiny darts. He smiled and patted Cookie on the top of her head as if she was a cute puppy.

He plucked the Frisbee from the ground in front of her feet and tossed it into the air in a single seamless movement. Suddenly, Cookie noticed how beautiful he was; he looked exactly like the *Blind Owl*. Long enough to cover his ears and bowl-shaped around his round face, his hair was a very dark shade of brown that accentuated his smooth blue eyes. Cookie was mesmerized by his eyes for a moment and thought he had gotten a lot of mileage out of those eyes. She estimated he was in his early 20s. A slim track of adorable freckles neatly arranged across the bridge of his nose seemed to move in suspended animation as he chewed on the filter of his unlit Marlboro. "Got a light?" He talked like Vic Morrow in the popular TV show "Combat."

Cookie smiled and shook her head. She felt embarrassed, and moved to pull her matches out of her cloth shoulder sack, but she wasn't quick enough for him. As a parting shot, he crinkled his perfect *Blind Owl* features into a grin, then strolled off. Cookie didn't even know his name. He walked over to the pot smokers on the bench and grubbed a light without saying a word. He simply stuck his cigarette out and a bubble-eyed hippie chick struck a match and cupped her hands around his cigarette with intensity and flush-faced devotion, while he puffed to light up and exhaled a heap of smoke into her face, which she did not seem to mind; she giggled, hiccupping stoned excitement as if she felt honored to be in his presence.

Marvin Gaye's *I Heard It Through The Grapevine* grew louder. Cookie turned her head slightly to see where the music was coming from. She stood up from under the elm tree that protected her from the hot August sun, only because its trunk cast a long, thin shadow that made up for its loss of leaves. She wandered aimlessly, trying to find the source of the music as if it was a magnet leading her to a new place in time. She felt like she had been here a million times before and was only going around in the same circle. The path grew narrow and had no gravel. Rugged and overgrown with weeds and bramble, two muddy tracts hardly defined a safe or functional trail into the woods. She heard the sound of a diminutive mew and leaned down. Underneath the brush, a frantic kitten was trying to claw its way out of an empty coffee can. Cookie stopped to look at the skinny, limp creature that bore more resemblance to a rodent than a cat. She kicked the coffee can over on its side to aid its efforts. Instead of being grateful, the little cat retracted its matted head, spat a terrible hiss and shot off in the direction of the caretaker's cottage, which was at the opposite end of the park.

Still in pursuit of the music, she walked by the decomposing walled garden that led down *The Thousand Steps* and toward an area lower into the woods where there was another Amphitheater. Although the staircase bore a bombastic name, the fragments of fifty or so broken steps were all that remained. The thousand steps were hardly steps, but long landings stretching many yards, dropping down and descending like one lengthy plateau after another, all choked with litter, the detritus of long nights of wild partying, empty bottles of hard liquor, grain alcohol and fortified wine, all designed to get you drunk fast and cheap. The northern part of the walled garden had fallen into ruins. Large chunks of the wall had broken off and left rough, gaping holes that could have been punched in by angry fists. The large marble columns had turned yellow and sighed of neglect. The mosaic tiles where she was treading were fading and coming up from the ground like misshapen old stones that no longer had a reason to be there.

This area was off the beaten track, shrouded by dense, tall trees and the wild undergrowth of stinging nettles, dandelions, ferns and horsetail. Cookie didn't venture this far out of the main area of the park and away from the great lawn. It was a scary part of the park, and while Cookie did not show fear, she reasoned that she didn't venture this deeply into the bowels of the park unless she had a good reason, and that reason stood before her, as clear an expectation as anything else she had ever known.

Herman Lynch grinned at her. On the ground by his side, he had a giant radio, larger than any radio Cookie had ever seen. It was booming with Marvin Gaye and Tammi Terrell singing *Ain't No Mountain High Enough*.

Herman turned down the volume on his radio. "What are you doing down here? No one comes down here this far during the day, and at night the peeps who come down here are drinking and doing other stuff too. All up to no good, as far as I can tell."

Herman and Cookie stood across from one another in the decaying Amphitheatre that was no tribute to the ancient civilization of Rome, but clear evidence of the city of Yonkers' sad and willful neglect of Untermyer Park. Herman and Cookie circled the circumference of the Amphitheatre, stopping every so often to look at one another as if it was new and fresh, a look for the first time.

"Where'd you get that radio?" Cookie asked him, folding her arms and looking at him from the side of her eye. "I've never seen a radio that big. Did you steal it?"

Her question hung in the air and provoked a silence between them that grew and made them both uncomfortable.

Herman stopped walking and looked at her. The hurt was evident in his eyes. "What are you getting at?"

"I thought you were on welfare. You live in the projects." Cookie was embarrassed and tried not show it. "My mistake. I'm sorry. I didn't mean it that way."

"You think I can't afford cool things because I'm a poor nigger, right?"

Cookie looked at the ground and saw Herman's feet. He was wearing a brand-new pair of golden fawn-colored *Hush Puppies*. "I would never use a word like that."

"Nigger?" Herman smiled. "My friends…we call ourselves *niggers*." Herman pointed to himself. "And we're proud of it."

"It's wrong, Cookie said. "I cringe when I hear grown-ups saying it."

"Grown-ups saying stuff like that, they don't know what they're talking about. Especially white grown-ups." Then

Herman smiled at her. "Unless I want you to call me a nigger. Then it's okay."

Cookie felt ashamed of herself. "I was wrong. I shouldn't have brought it up. I'm known for always saying the wrong thing." She stood still and tried to say something but she couldn't. She felt so awkward for saying the wrong thing. Once again she had put her foot in her mouth. She thought at times like this it was best to be planning on writing a new poem, something that made sense of this whole thing.

"You can call me a nigger," Herman smiled. "And I'll call you a bad-ass honky, because that's what you are!"

Cookie started to laugh. "I can't."

"Yes, you can. Seriously," Herman said. "When I ask you to call me a nigger, I mean it. It's because we own it. We call ourselves niggers. We own it. And no honky is going to shame us into thinking bad things about ourselves. We are our own niggers, and proud of it. Got that?"

Herman walked up along side Cookie and held out his arm next to her arm. "Man, are you white. I think you are the whitest person I've ever seen."

"The Italian girls at school tell me I'm too white to be Italian."

Herman flashed her a smile that made the upper portion of his harelip look like the inside of a tender paw. "The guys in my hood say I'm not black enough." He was growing soft stubble, the first vestige of a moustache. She didn't mind him being so close to her. With other boys, she felt like they were too close for comfort and about to pounce on her. With Herman, she felt different, like he was good and kind, and he had her back.

"When I tell you to call me a nigger, you do it. Got that?" Herman jutted his forehead forward and nodded, bobbing his head and looking around then back at Cookie to make sure she understood him. "Got it, honky?"

Cookie smiled at him. "Okay, where'd you get the giant radio?"

"From Amsterdam. My grandmother knows this man who comes into the library and he always goes on trips to the Netherlands. He brought this back for me. It's a Radiorecorder."

Cookie had never heard of a Radiorecorder. She had never seen a radio like the one owned by Herman Lynch. It was a long, rectangular box about a foot and a half long. With one large box-shaped speaker and three tuning knobs on the right; one knob controlled the volume. A tape cassette player took up most of the left side of the box, and the top horizontal bar had buttons and a dial for tuning AM and FM radio stations. Later in her life, Cookie would see them everywhere. And although later they became more technologically sophisticated, light-weight and were called *boom boxes* or *ghetto blasters*, Cookie always remembered Herman as the first to have one.

"Radiorecorder!" Cookie didn't know why, but she felt like jumping in the air. "I heard it all over the park. It's louder than all those guitars and flutes put together!"

"Have you been doing your knee bends, Miss Cookie?" Herman started rocking and bending his knees forward and back like mini-lunges, or plié squats in parallel position, with his knees directly over his feet, which were pointing straight ahead. Then he shifted into second position, his legs forming the shape of a triangle, with each foot pointing in opposite directions. Bending and straightening, going low and rising up.

"While you go low," Herman said, "your whole body is rising higher. See what I mean by that, Cookie girl?" He kept demonstrating, prodding Cookie to keep her back straight and bend her knees until he stopped counting. "Want to hear some real music?"

"I'm getting tired," Cookie said. "It's so hot."

"We haven't even started to dance!" Herman cranked up the volume on his radio. Marvin Gaye's *I Heard It Through The Grapevine* blared so loud, there seemed to be an echo reverberating in the wooded area surrounding the Amphitheatre.

"I come down here and practice my dancing all by myself. Let me show you some of my moves."

Herman was moving in a rapid rhythm that syncopated the wildest beat of swing. Flailing his arms in a full extension sideways and forward and backward then around the clock in a full circle, he was moving beyond the speed of a windmill and shimmying up and down, low to the ground, when his footwork kicked high in the air. And while he was still shimmying, he jumped full-throttle into the air, and twirling around in a single turn, then into two double axis turns, pulling a reverse turn that kept him pivoting in the air until he leapt forward and did a full somersault in the air, then reversed his curled leap, flipping backward. He landed in a semi-squat that sent his knees plunging down, barely touching ground before he sprang back into the air, where his feet crisscrossed, one extending over the other in a random grapevine that slid sideways, on both sides, going back and forth, with two more kicks fully extending in the air. He touched down on the ground in a side move that kept traveling sideways, with force so great that it would have taken any baseball player in the world into a fierce slide toward home base. Only this wasn't baseball. This was pure dance!

Cookie was moving now too. Dancing side by side, she mirrored his every move, at least the ones she could keep up with. Because she was mirroring him, she was about two seconds off with every next step. Cookie's dance moves were jerky, out of step and out of rhythm, the delayed reaction all beginners have when learning a new dance routine for the first time. She kept up with him, though, until she began to synchronize with him at the same pace, hitting the same moves at the same time. Cookie was almost completely out of breath, not because she lacked the endurance; she was feeling so exuberant, the same way she used to feel when she was being a tomboy, playing kickball out on the street and kicking a ball clear beyond the outfield and up into the trees, over the fence and into

Louie Santamassino's backyard. She felt that good and that alive again, and it was as if that big bad November event that made her say *Stop* all the time had never happened at all.

She wasn't going to tell herself to *Stop* now. Their moves grew repetitive and predictable, shimmying from side to side in long grapevines traversing the entire expanse of the Amphitheatre, tumbling into rapid-fire waltz turns and springing into leaps traveling forward, then backward. Their final touch was lifting off in a jump straight into the air like arrows repeatedly shooting upward, while clasping their hands under their bent knees that were still airborne, then coming down and beating the ground before leaping straight up into the air again, clapping their hands high over their heads in a holy charge and a celebration of pure joy.

The dance mirrored everything Cookie knew to be deep in her soul. Herman and Cookie danced in tandem and side to side creating the most intense form of groove that had ever been practiced deep in the woods of Untermyer Park. And until this day, no one has danced there quite like the way Herman and Cookie danced on the afternoon of that hot August day.

Herman turned his radio off and smiled at Cookie. It was time for him to go home. "Honky, you did real good." He waited for her response, prodding her with his hands, motioning for her to *come on and give it to him*. "Come on, Cookie say it. Just get it out there in the open."

Cookie shook her head and closed her eyes. Sweat rippled along the crest of her forehead and drizzled down to the bridge of her nose. She didn't realize how hot she was until she had stopped moving. She was so sweaty that her skimpy halter and blue jeans clung to her body. No matter how much Herman prodded her, she couldn't bring herself to say a word she found to be offensive, and even though it was said aloud by every white person she had ever known, including her own parents, that didn't make it right, and didn't mean it was going to come from her own mouth.

"Say it." Herman tilted his head down, dropped his jaw and looked at her as if he was intent on being real serious. "If you say it, it will never come between us." His eyes implored her as if he was making a genuine promise.

Tears came to Cookie's eyes and she could feel them stinging the bottom of her lids. She nodded to him. "You're not going to get me to say that word to you, no matter what you do."

Herman smiled and started heading further down, much deeper down into the woods. He put one hand out in front to push away the branches and bramble. Then he turned around briefly and waved goodbye to Cookie.

"Where are you going?" Cooked asked him.

"I like walking home on Warburton," Herman said. "No one looks at me the way they do when I walk alone on North Broadway. Up here, they look at me like I don't belong here. You know, it's the North End, and niggers aren't supposed to be here. If I'm alone, I'm a target to get beat-up, and if I'm with my friends, they think we're going to steal something or mug somebody."

Cookie saw the back of his head bobbing down into the woods. She noticed how the sunlight lit up the tendrils of his hair in a paler shade of red and almost made it seem like he had a halo glowing around his head. She didn't bother to ask him when he would be back. She knew she would see him again, as surely as she knew she was a cross between a gangster and a hippie, and then some. Herman turned around and called up to her. "Don't ever come down here all by yourself," he yelled. "The Devil's Cave's down here, and I think lots of bad things are going on, like drugs and weirdos. Some of the weirdest dudes I've ever seen have been down here."

Cookie nodded to him. "See you." She had heard bad things about what went on deep in the woods. People were shooting up and mainlining smack. The crumbling walls leading to the aqueduct were covered with graffiti, and dirty needles had been found everywhere. Even the feral cats didn't venture down to this edge of the woods, where only lost souls seemed to walk. In later years, the Devil's Cave became the site of animal sacrifices, satanic cults and the stomping ground of David Berkowitz, also known as the *Son of Sam*, but by the time all of these revelations emerged, Cookie had long grown up and gone away.

Cookie turned and walked up the landing leading to the north edge of the park. Her knees felt strong and certain. Since she started doing the deep knee bends, her knees had not gone out on her. Not once. When she arrived at the walled garden, she skipped across the mosaic tiles, feeling a small pocket of joy in her heart and in her troubled soul, and ran back toward the great lawn, passing the long, narrow pool that had been drained of water; its basin was stained, full of rusted metal pockmarks. It was sad that the city didn't maintain the park when it had been left as a gift for people to enjoy. If the fountains and pools were working, Cookie would jump into the water and cool down from her fantastic dance.

In the great lawn by the park benches, The *Blind Owl lookalike* was nodding to a wild-eyed skinny man who looked like Charles Manson, except when he smiled, Cookie could see he had no teeth. A third guy who looked like David Crosby of *Crosby, Stills and Nash* joined them. She heard the Charles Manson-looking guy yell, "Crazy Davie, how are you doing, man!" Cookie figured his name was *Crazy Dave*, and as it turned out that was his name.

A small crowd started to form around the three guys. Cookie did not know what was going on, but all of sudden, the hippie guys turned around and all eyes were on her. The energy of their gaze pierced through her body like an automatic assault weapon; it was that sudden, intense and dangerous. She walked by the outer fringes of the crowd and tried to be invisible, but she heard snatches of their conversation. *It's better than what I got in New Paltz. It's the real thing. Ludes. She's got ludes. Real ludes, Man.*

The *Blind Owl lookalike* smiled at Cookie. His pert nose turned upward and showed his fine aquiline image in repose. "What have you been up to?"

Cookie was taken aback. In her heart, she knew he wasn't interested in her. She also knew she had at least ten ludes in her cloth shoulder sack. The fake *Blind Owl* came up to her, put his arm around her waist and smiled as if he had been waiting for her all of his life. "Isn't your name Cookie?"

She nodded and swallowed hard. She was so embarrassed she could die and at the same time this was an unimaginable victory. She could not believe this older, hunk hippie guy was befriending her; not in her wildest dreams would this happen. Well, maybe, yeah, in her dreams. This guy was beyond beautiful and his arm was wrapped around her waist that had been made damp from her dance.

The fake *Blind Owl* leaned down and whispered in her ear. "The word is you have some good ludes. Am I hearing the right thing?" His eyes were blue, intense and sincere. He was gorgeous.

His question both thrilled and repulsed her. All these older cool people, hippies proclaiming peace and love, were taking an interest in her. It was happening before her very eyes. Then she heard the word *Nark* and it was an ominous warning of what could possibly happen to her. "She's probably a Nark," someone said.

And that's all it took. The small crowd shifted focus. An assortment of stoned eyes drifted toward Cookie Colangelo. She stared at them as if she felt guilt for being underage and an outsider, but no one was going to mess with her. These guys might be hippies, but she could be a gangster. She forced a smile and said, "Hello."

They looked at her as if she had indeed confirmed their worst suspicions. The bell bottoms and thin halter top hardly disguised the fact that she looked twelve. Cookie knew she was in a tight position, and needed to do everything in her power to make a good impression.

Her voice was so calm it bordered on monotone. "My name is Concetta Mary Bernadette Colangelo, but everyone calls me 'Cookie.' If you want ludes, I'll give you ten for twenty-five bucks." She took a deep breath and looked at all three of them, one by one, in the eye. "That's the best price I've got."

The toothless Charles Manson dude pointed his finger in the air like the Charles Dickens demonic ghost of Christmas Future and asked, "Are you a Nark?"

Cookie knew her smile was quivering, but she forced herself to get tougher. "Nark, Nark! How could you think I'm a nark! I'm not even fourteen years old!"

The guys stared at her points, both of them, as if this feature was too dire to be the main attraction and looked away in embarrassment. Then they looked back at her face and as hot as she was, unbeknownst to Cookie, she was very beautiful in a child-like sort of way. Her brown hair had thickened in the humidity and came undone from her pony tail, settling like a mantilla framing her soft white face and rolling away from her shoulders.

Crazy Dave started laughing and so did the *Blind Owl* lookalike, who stepped forward and patted Cookie on her arm. She looked at his feet. He was wearing white tennis shoes. Then she slowly looked upward. His jeans were faded to just the right shade of blue, and he wore a pale yellow work shirt under a worn army jacket. "She's just some Catholic school-girl chick," he said to the group. Then he looked at her. "Cookie, right? Cute name," he smiled showing her his white, even *Chiclet* teeth.

He seemed satisfied with her innocence and looked at her with a touch of boyish compassion. It's not that he loved her, but he came to her side, for reasons that were not clear to Cookie. Maybe she reminded him of his youngest sister. With two words, he soothed the paranoia of the moment. "She's cool."

There was a slight delayed reaction between the time she pulled the ludes from her shoulder sack and sold them to the *Blind Owl* dude. She let him have them for twenty bucks, which was her standard rate and not discounted. She took them out of her vial and counted them into the palm of his hand, then handed the vial back to him so he could use it for his own stash. Gradually, everyone seemed happy, content and grooved their way into giving Cookie a pleasant smirk of acceptance.

Crazy Dave lunged forward and nudged the fake *Blind Owl* on his arm. "Can I have one of those ludes, man? Just one. If it's a good lude, it will take me out.

Fake Blind Owl popped a tab into Crazy Dave's hand; he boasted, purely for show. "Just watch this," he said. He popped the tab into his mouth and swallowed with great exaggeration. His mouth opened as wide as the entrance to the Lincoln Tunnel and he stuck out his tongue like a drawbridge to show that the lude was gone. "Look, it's gone, man."

"I can see that." Cookie felt foolish and inched her way forward, then to the side, then back to the *Blind Owlish*-looking guy. He didn't seem to mind that she was leaving. She would go home for now. Being hassled in a public park by guys much older than she was made the prospect of going home seem attractive.

As she chugged down the gravel walkway and away from the great lawn, she flitted past the caretaker's cottage, not wanting to see the hissing herd of wild cats, and ran toward the front of the park and to Broadway. From the corner of her eye, she detected new movement and felt someone's eyes fastened on her. On the long granite boulder wall, known as *The Wall,* that bordered the front of the park, Toni Ferlinghetti had staked her position. With only two Italian girl soldiers at her side, the reigning Queen Bee of Italian girls did not seem nearly so powerful. The wall where they sat was three feet high and fashioned like those still standing in many parts of

New York from Revolutionary times. The long wall of speckled granite stretched for a quarter of a mile and marked the outer perimeter of the park; it was one reason why this area of Yonkers had at one time been known as *Greystone*.

The whole notion of Einstein's theory of relativity popped into her head, and it was as if the past, the present and the future were converging at this very instant. Cookie immediately understood why the trio of Italian girls was sitting on the wall. They didn't have the gumption to venture inside the park. Their self-imposed exile on the wall made it clear that they weren't making the hippie scene any better than Cookie Colangelo had been trying to make the scene. Toni pondered Cookie for a second, as though she might actually say hello, but she was too cool to make an overture this early in the game. She smiled in a quirky sort of way, then nudged her soldiers off the wall and down to the sidewalk on North Broadway.

Cookie snickered to herself. After a really bad day, she had found some success. She had danced mightily without her knees going out on her, made twenty bucks from the sale of Kitty's ludes, found a friend in Herman Lynch, and gave the impression to Toni Ferlinghetti that she had an "in" with the hippies at Untermyer Park. Cookie knew Italian girls had to stay on top of the coolest things that were happening. It was part of their DNA. No doubt about it. Untermyer Park was the coolest thing happening in the North End of Yonkers, and Cookie Colangelo had been seen walking out of the park alone, like she was a lot cooler than Toni Ferlinghetti. For the first time in her life, Cookie felt as if she was in charge of her own destiny. It was always a question of timing, force of will, gravity and a smidgen of luck that wasn't luck at all, because everything she had done in life so far prepared her to be here at this time and in this place.

Nineteen

Thursday, September 3, 1970

Yonkers always looked worst in September. The dog days of August were over and the blight of September had set in. The streets and sidewalks were crumbling from the aftermath of the long, punishing wave of heat and humidity. Thick with carbon monoxide and soot from cars and city grime, the humid air enveloped Cookie's body like a dirty sheet. Cookie was walking on Palisade Avenue, cruising the strip *Down the End*, looking for something to do, which meant she was up to no good. She still didn't know the name of the fake Blind Owl guy she had met at the Park, but it didn't matter. He wasn't the genuine article, the real deal, *Blind Owl* Alan Wilson.

Today she wanted to be tall and sultry in the heat. In another week, she would be entering the ninth grade at Sacred Heart High School or *the Heart*, as it was called by every one. The four-inch kelly green platform shoes she had borrowed from her mother were a whole size too small and pinched her feet. She had gotten her peach-colored hot pants on sale in Getty Square at the five-and-dime store *H. L. Green*. Her shoulder sack had grown too worn to be reliable and threatened to unravel at the seams. From Mimi's in Getty Square, she bought a brown hand-tooled leather Hippie shoulder bag that was etched with delicate flowers and had a brass buckle. Buying her own clothes with her own money was a luxury afforded by her entrepreneurial pursuit with ludes. Her white bubble blouse was the same she had worn a year ago at Woodstock, only underneath she wore a tiny floral bra with size triple A cups.

It had been a whole year since she had gone to Woodstock, and much to her dismay, she still wore the same size bra. Her breasts had not grown a bit.

Cookie had kept going to *W.T. Grant's,* another five-and-dime store in Getty Square to try on new bras, or *brassieres* as Kitty Colangelo called them. So far Cookie had amassed three bras, one in hot-pink or fuchsia, a floral pattern with flowers in many colors and as small and as delicate as lobelia, and one in pure white to wear under her Catholic school girl uniform blouses. Much to Cookie's humiliation, Kitty Colangelo referred to her daughter's bras as *training bras.* Kitty sported breasts the size of a comely 32 C cup and had a 22-inch waist, one that, Kitty had claimed, had been ruined by childbearing. Kitty claimed that before she had children, her waist measured 18 inches round, the same as Scarlett O'Hara's in the fictitious classic *Gone with the Wind.*

Cookie could hardly walk in the heels, squeezing her feet like hot Italian sausage stuffed into casings. She was careful to look at the ground so she wouldn't trip on the jagged sidewalk that was uneven in patches and full of broken concrete, gaping holes and ruts. She wanted to be anywhere other than here, and tried to dream of a day when she'd be long gone and Yonkers would be a forgotten memory. She didn't feel right dreaming about things, not even when it came time to write down her poems—and other secret writings—in her black & white notebooks. She couldn't dream like other people. The notion of dreaming made her feel like she was thinking crazy, like her mother Kathleen *"Kitty"* née Murphy Colangelo.

By the time Cookie turned thirteen, her mother had been committed to a mental institution four times. The pattern was always the same. First, her psychosis grew so acute that she embarked on a campaign of harassing friends, family, neighbors, churchgoers and the public at large. Johnny put up with her antics that only impacted friends and family, but once her tirade crossed into the public domain, he'd bundle her into his car and haul her up to Grasslands in Valhalla, New York. Johnny didn't like Grasslands and soon had her moved into a private Catholic hospital, St. Vincent's in Harrison, New York. Kitty Colangelo spent three weeks in the hospital. Never more than three weeks, not less than three weeks. It was always exactly three weeks.

Kitty's three-week stints in the mental hospital were a source of pride for her. She'd always say, "I always come home after three weeks. Some people are there forever and then some, but I'm not that crazy. I always come home in three weeks." She'd tell everyone, "I always come home in three weeks." There was some aspect—that can't be defined—about the schizophrenic brain that made her repeat herself. Kitty Colangelo said the same things a lot. She was stuck on the same track—a broken record that skipped and was trapped mid-song or a refrain repeating too often in a poorly constructed poem.

Cookie swore she'd never be like her mother. Not even for a minute. Not ever. Cookie would rather be dead than beautiful, but crazy, like Kitty.

The loud call of *Cookie* came from nowhere and was so startling that she almost wet her pants. Cookie knew who it was without looking. She stared at herself in the reflection of the glass outside of Hedy's Luncheonette. She hated the way she looked and surmised that at thirteen, she was probably the only Italian girl in the world who had developed into little more than a square chunk of maidenhood. She had no breasts, a thick solid waist, and a fat block for a face. She looked very much like a female version of the *Blind Owl* Alan Wilson, one more reason why she was besotted with him. Cookie and The Owl were both simultaneously cool but very uncool—*doofs*. Cookie prided herself on being a person of high intelligence and talent, just like the *Blind Owl*, who was amazingly accomplished as a high-pitched, falsetto blues singer and a blues-rock musician. So, despite her absence of Italian girl goddess attributes, Cookie still had high self-esteem and considered herself to be a pretty darn good drug dealer. Her steady supply of ludes had given her a minor reputation and made her famous for something other than possession of adolescent beauty.

People were going in and out of the luncheonette. Most of the guys were Con-Ed workers grabbing their coffee regular. Known for its fried egg sandwiches and chocolate egg creams, Hedy's Luncheonette had a grill and a real soda fountain. The owner, Henry, was a big burly Polish guy and his wife Hedy wore black coke bottle-framed eyeglasses and kept the place spotless. Oonah, a small, nervous woman with a white-blonde pixie cut, scurried around the counter, looking to please the owners, who found disapproval with everything she did. At the end of her day shift, Oonah took off her apron and sat at the counter on the very last stool in the luncheonette. Even when she wasn't working there, she was a regular.

More than any other newspaper, the *New York Daily News* was the top seller on the news stand at *Hedy's Luncheonette*. Most of the regulars flipped open the pages and headed straight to the sports section. Even the *New York Post* was too sophisticated for the regulars. At the end of the day, heaps of *The New York Times* were the only newspapers left in the news stand.

Cookie heard that god-awful voice—it was the red-headed hag Fran Ochiogrosso and she was coming toward her. Cookie started walking away from her. From the corner of her right eye, she spied the candy section inside of Hedy's Luncheonette dominated by 10-cent Hershey Bars and, much to her horror,

Fran Ochiogrosso storming out of the luncheonette, hot on Cookie's trail. Cookie began walking faster. She heard Fran call out, "Cookie Colangelo, I need to talk to you."

Cookie began running and not looking at the ground. Never mind that she was wearing four-inch kelly green platform shoes that grazed a wobbly line through an oil-slicked pavement. Cookie felt herself slipping and on the verge of falling. In slow motion, she started a long slide on the sidewalk. Her arms swam frantically through the air, trying to reach the sky for balance. She reached for utility poles and garbage cans with equal effort and finally stopped the slide. She landed squarely upright, her feet encased in the green platform shoes, stuck together in a perfect 90-degree position, with her knees turned out and slightly bent. Cookie was rendered speechless and assessed the situation. She had been inches from getting splayed and sprawling out on the sidewalk in a heap, like a crumpled linebacker. But this time, her trick knees did not betray her and let her down. Somehow her knees had become stronger. The brief encounter with the utility pole had not left her totally unscathed. Her peach hot pants sported a long messy mark of black grease that ran down to her calves. So much for being sultry.

At the sight of the grease on her leg, Cookie hollered at Fran Ochiogrosso, "Shit! Look what happened to my pants!" She beat her fists on the pole with the type of rage that belied her image as a nice young Catholic schoolgirl.

"I'm sorry," Fran said. "It's just that..." she stopped mid sentence as if she had forgotten what she meant to say, but she hadn't really forgotten. Fran looked at her with pity. "I was just trying to find out what's going on with your mother."

Cookie trembled and bit her lower lip, trying to suppress the truth until she could stand it no more. "It's none of your business."

The pupils of Fran's eyes grew large and looked more black than brown, one-part venom and the other part showing she really believed what she said no matter how small-minded it made her seem. "The way your mother carries on, bothering everyone, she's made it everyone's business."

Even though Cookie felt hurt, she did not cry. There was no way in hell she'd cry. Kitty wasn't home. She was gone. Johnny had packed her off to the hospital. The night before, he bundled her in a blanket and called the ambulance to take her to Grasslands. Last night it was hotter than hell, but Kitty was in a blanket because she had torn off her clothes and run outdoors. Being naked wasn't a quest for freedom or a desire to experience the more sensual side of her nature. Kitty thought her clothes had caught fire and were singeing her skin, turning her organs to charred remains.

"Everyone knows Kitty's crazy," Fran said. "Your mother's a real sick girl."

A small crowd of onlookers had formed on the outskirts of where Cookie and Fran stood next to the utility pole, but didn't linger long enough for Cookie to recognize who they were. From their perspective, there wasn't much to see. There was no blood; no injuries had been sustained, except for Cookie's pride. Even though Fran and Cookie had postured themselves as intent on killing one another, a real fight had not taken place. "I don't have anything to tell you, Fran. My mother's in the hospital, and that's all I know."

She held up her knees, bending one and then the other, then standing on one leg in a slightly locked knee position like the pink plastic flamingos that graced some of the front lawns in the neighborhood. Fran groaned; not hearing the details of what had happened to Kitty was too painful. "That's all you've got for me? Don't you know anything else? She is your mother!"

Cookie was moving and Fran was right alongside her. Walking south on Palisade Avenue, Cookie pulled up her knees to exercise them in a full range of motion which made her look like she was doing a goosestep in platform shoes. Fran mimicked her movement. She was teasing Cookie. Every time Cookie pulled up her bent knees high into the air, Fran tried to do the same thing but could not raise her knees very high. Cookie peered off to the side, behind a thinning hedge and looked eye-to-eye with the chiseled serenity of a statue of the Madonna. Cookie was standing in the front of the Christ the King convent, where Fangs lived. There was no point in discussing Fangs, at least not now. Cookie still had not been able to tell anyone what had happened to her when she was a little kid in the sixth grade. Now she was on the verge of being a high school girl, and what happened to her back then no longer seemed to matter, or so she told herself.

The street was teeming with cars and kids on bikes. A small crowd of guys had formed in the front of Donaghey's Pub and spilled out on the sidewalk in front of Palisade Pizzeria, where one of the owners, Tony, stood out front. Tony was a new arrival to America, fresh off the boat from Sicily. He had a thick accent and always wore *Chef Whites* and an apron stained red with splotches of tomato sauce. Still standing in front of the convent, Cookie half-expected Fangs to swoosh out the front door. Feeling lower than low, Cookie's frame of mind suddenly plummeted and her anger surfaced and soared. She remembered the humiliation she had suffered at the hands of Fangs. "I don't want to be here," Cookie told Fran. "Get me out of here before I go off and kill someone in a fit of murderous rage."

"How could you say such a thing, Cookie Colangelo? You're standing right in front of the Madonna. The fucking Virgin Mary, for crissakes."

Cookie wanted to know, "What's the Madonna got to do with it?

Somehow standing eye-to-eye with all that holiness provided Fran with the overwhelming urge to be even meaner. "You shouldn't wear shoes like that. You don't know how to walk in them. You're a tomboy and girls like you should never try to stand up in a pair of platform shoes, no less walk in them!"

Fran blessed herself, "There, I said it," she said to herself. "I've never been smart enough to keep my mouth shut."

"Ochiogrosso! Big Eyes! That's what your name means in Italian! Gross Big Fat Eyes! Isn't that so! You're always nosing into everyone else's business!"

Fran looked at her disdainfully, as if she was ruefully studying the aftermath of the wreck of a car she had once loved. In a weird way, she loved Cookie like a daughter, and in an even weirder way, Fran was the mother Cookie should have had.

"It's those shoes," Fran said. "I think those shoes have gone to your head. You shouldn't wear such high heels to walk *Down the End*. Those shoes are what you call *knock me down and fuck me shoes*. Do you know what that means?"

Cookie tried to hide her embarrassment, and looked at Fran with great hatred. "Quit picking on my shoes, you faggot!" She would never admit it: not only was she a virgin, but she hadn't even had her first period! "Faggot," Cookie yelled again.

Faggot in 1970 didn't mean you were gay. It could mean you were queer, which could be gay, but it might also mean you were strange, introverted, very uncool—a mere doof, and frequently had nothing to do with sexuality.

"Fag-got! You really shouldn't dye your hair so red. The poison has gone to your brain and made you insane."

Cookie was desperately trying to be a regular girl, soft, silly and underripe to perfection, like a hard peach covered with too much fuzz. The kelly green platform shoes were only part of the ensemble. Heavy black eyeliner and caked-on black mascara and *Yardley Pot o' Gloss* in a shimmering shade of *red shriek* completed her sultry look. And she reeked of *Ambush* Spray Cologne. To top it off, Cookie had dyed two single strands of her soft brown hair; stripped to bleach blonde and woven like the inverse of raccoon stripes, framing both sides of her face like a picture postcard that said, *ruin me, ruin me now, ruin me for life*—the mantra of every bad Catholic school-girl who had gotten knocked up before her time.

Fran cocked her fist like a warning and shook it at Cookie, "You're really something. You're going to end up crazy like your mother."

As far as Cookie was concerned, that was the last straw. She could put up with Fran's abuse, so long as it was hurled at random and nothing personal, but the mention of her mother made her angry and she stomped off in her platform shoes like a sulking bull. She hated Fran with all of her might, and most of all, she wished her mother was dead. Cookie wouldn't have minded becoming famous for being a princess or for being the girlfriend of the *Blind Owl*, but she didn't want to be known for being the daughter of a bona fide lunatic. She thought she should say a brief prayer for uttering the word death in the same breath as her mother. Instead, she fastened her eyes to the sidewalk and avoided walking on the sharp cracks so she wouldn't break her mother's back. She didn't want to wish her mother dead. She loved Kitty more than any other person in the world. It was sad and confusing; Cookie was all mixed up.

Despite her almost trick knee mishap, she was back to her antics and showing off her athleticism. She jumped over the cracks on the concrete sidewalk, from slab to slab, always landing dead center. Drawn by her energy like an electrical charge, dried leaves and blades of grass stuck to the sides of her platform soles and heels.

"Aren't you going to tell me about your mother?" Fran asked in a whining, nasal tone of voice. She was seeking a confession of some sort. Cookie had almost forgotten that the woman was still there.

Cookie felt very sorry that she had come this far with Fran Ochiogrosso. She did not want to talk about her mother to anyone. Her mother had been acting especially peculiar lately, and Cookie did not know who to turn to. She did know that baring her innermost thoughts to Fran was not an option.

Cookie stopped walking but she didn't turn around to face Fran. "I was adopted."

"I think I see where this is going," Fran said.

"No, you don't." Cookie turned around and faced her. She put her nose up in the air. "My parents are actually the King and Queen of a small principality. I was kidnapped by the Weathermen and the Black Panthers, and held for ransom. I was mixed up with the baby of some hippie girl. Princess Caroline of Monaco is really a hippie chick, and I am really royal."

Fran was taken aback. "Really?"

"Really." Cookie was droll like a fortuneteller on the boardwalk in Atlantic City who is so used to lying, the creases in her forehead permanently furrowed. She looked at Fran with contempt, as though all her money and worldly possessions were held securely in the palm of her hand. "One day, I will be famous. You mark my words, the name Cookie Colangelo will be uttered by people everywhere from Nashville, Tennessee, to Bangor, Maine. Take that! Stick it in your pipe and smoke it!"

Speaking of pipes and smoking, Cookie saw Reenie Ruggerio snaking down the soft underbelly of Palisade Avenue and heading in Cookie's direction *Down the End*. Reenie had sold Cookie her first nickel bag of pot, and many more since then, to smoke in Cookie's secret *Owl Hole* behind the Calvary Baptist Church on North Broadway. Everyone knew Reenie Ruggerio had an older brother, Billy Dee, who dealt drugs between the North End and Getty Square. Cookie hadn't see Reenie since she had gone to her apartment and sold her a pile of ludes.

Cookie let go a wild whoop, screaming at the pitch that girls only use when spending themselves emotionally. More devastating than a secret handshake, it is an utterance so offensive that it would blow out the eardrums of most ordinary people. Fortunately, girls only keen at close range. This particular keen had a dual purpose. It was meant to get Reenie Ruggerio's attention and, at the same time, drive away Fran Ochiogrosso.

Fran shook her head and looked at Cookie with great sadness. Cookie looked pleased with the results of her keening.

"No shit, Fran Ochiogrosso, I'm not going to talk about my mother to you or to anyone."

Fran and Cookie looked at each other and smiled a long time, offering each other the sentiment of purple hearts for the wounds suffered in the line of ordinary fracas. Cookie was the first to break visceral eye contact. She looked down at her kelly green platform shoes with contempt. "These shoes are too small for me, but guess what, my trick knee didn't go out on me."

Fran nodded. "Your mother should take you to the doctor and get it looked at."

"I don't want to be told that I have palsy," Cookie said. She screwed up her face in the most god-awful facial contortion, stuck out her tongue, stooped like a hunchback and limped, off leaving Fran looking bewildered and not knowing what to do, standing in front of *The Chinks*. The Chinks was really named *Young's Chinese Laundry*, but no one called it by its rightful name or even knew that it had one. It didn't dawn on Cookie that it might not be the name of the place until she noticed the name *Young's Chinese Laundry* on the receipts when she picked up her father's shirts.

"I'm here if you ever want to talk," Fran called after her. Her hands were on her hips and she looked stern. "I'm here, just so you know. We're neighbors. Don't be a stranger. You can knock on my door anytime, Cookie Colangelo."

What if I don't want to, and have no intention of, ever knocking on your door, Cookie thought to herself. She felt humiliated, but she would never show it, not in a million years. What happened to her mother was none of Fran's business.

What happened to Kitty Colangelo turned out to be everyone's business. Kitty had a penchant for creating drama that rose to the level of high spectacle. Cookie didn't want to waste any more time talking about her mother. Fortunately, Reenie Ruggerio was a welcome diversion that swept upon her in a sudden storm of angry black curls, long, naked tanned legs protruding from under the shortest orange hot pants in the world, in a humid cloud reeking of jasmine oil. Reenie intentionally tried to make her hair nappy by waving it and plastering a long bang down the side of her face. Everyone knew Reenie Ruggiero loved everything black and was intent on sun-tanning herself until she, herself, turned black. Even Fran knew Reenie had an obsession going on with all things black, and especially loved black boys.

"Now I can see trouble brewing with those two," Fran yelled at no one in particular, but she was out of Cookie's sight and had gone into *The Chinks* on the corner of Palisade and Chase, muttering something about having to pick up her husband's shirts for work, which was not possible because she did not have a husband.

Cookie could not for the life of her figure out why Fran put so much energy into obsessing about Kitty when her own daughters, all three of them, had created scandals of their own making.

"How is screaming Meemee?" Reenie crooned in her ear in a confidential tone. "I heard she got the whole neighborhood up last night. There were sirens, police cars, and an ambulance. Did they use a strait-jacket, or what?"

"Forget it, Reenie!" Cookie glared at her. "I don't want to talk about it."

Reenie never knew when to stop. She went for the jugular. "Did they use one of those giant hypodermic needles that they use on elephants and wild boar in the African jungle? I saw one on 'Wild Kingdom' and it was scary."

"I said shut up."

Reenie gesticulated with her hands and pointed her fingers in the shape of arrows. "Those needles are so long and pointy. I wish they'd use one on me. Think of how high I'd get, and for free!"

"Shut up!"

"You wouldn't even have to get close to her to stick her with it."

Cookie leaned in, nudging her. "Come on, stop it."

Reenie was not really her friend. She was one of her primary consumers of ludes. And occasionally, Reenie supplied Cookie with pot; it was a mutually beneficial relationship, cemented by the two things they had in common: drug use and Sacred Heart High School. Reenie was making fun of Cookie. She jabbed the air wildly with an enormous imaginary needle. "As long as you stuck her hard, you'd knock her out." Her voice bordered on the sinister as she whispered into Cookie's ear, "You could wear her *Chanel No. 5* any time you want."

Cookie kicked up her shoe from the pavement. "I've got her shoes and that's all I've ever really wanted. Her shoes. Except her feet are too small for me."

"I hope you don't end up crazy like her," Reenie giggled until she could see Cookie had grown quiet and that she might be causing her pain to say mean and hopeless things about her mother. Reenie propped up her hip next to a mailbox, as if she needed support to strike a pose, and lit a cigarette. Cookie opened her shoulder bag and pulled out her own *Marlboro*, lit it and took a long drag. The smoke clung in the humid air over their heads like a noxious cloud.

"Nice bag," Reenie said. "How'd you afford it? Let me guess," she said snidely. Everyone knew Cookie had a small business that was part-time but lucrative.

Fran Ochiogrosso walked out of *The Chinks* carrying two perfectly rectangular-shaped bundles wrapped with brown paper and tied in the center with white string. Even though Johnny sent all his shirts to be cleaned at *The Chinks,* he especially didn't like the Chinese, and said when he was on the front lines in Korea, they kept coming and coming and just when he thought they had stopped, they kept coming and coming. The more Cookie thought about it, the more she realized Johnny didn't like any race or ethnic group, including his own. His favorite pejorative was *greasy guinea pig*, which had an almost lyrical quality. He also liked *grease ball, grape-stomper, meatball, Mingia,* which meant dick in Italian and, *Spaghetto,* which was an Italian who acted black, and defined Miss Reenie Ruggiero to a T.

"Who's going to cook your dinner?" Fran yelled. "With your mother gone and all, don't tell me your father's going to do right by you and Donny. Is your grandma going to be looking in on you girls?"

"Why is she always bugging into everyone's business?" Reenie mumbled under her breath. "She's so weird and nosy. She's scary."

Cookie hadn't thought far enough along to think about where her next meal was going to come from. Cookie had been helping herself to her own meals for some time. She and Donny were not starving, and it was unfair that Fran would make them seem like orphans.

Cookie fought back tears like a champ. She'd never cry. She was too proud to cry. If she was the crybaby type, Reenie would not want to hang out with her. Reenie didn't cry, either. It was another thing they had in common along with their mutual interest in drugs and their newly minted status as Sacred Heart freshman girls. Reenie kept bumping into Cookie, not so much because she was clumsy, but, more likely, she was off-balance from her habitual use of ludes. The girls cut through the asphalt playground in the back of Christ the King Elementary School, walked together in silence and eventually reached North Broadway.

Without discussion, Cookie thought the two of them were heading to the secret stairwell leading to the *Owl Hole* behind the Baptist Church. Cookie tried to remember how her mother ended up in the nuthouse. As the summer wore on, Kitty developed a passion for reading, rereading and obsessing over the Christ the King Church Sunday bulletins. She committed entire passages of church buzz to memory and recited them with the oratory flair of a twisted Method actor.

On command, she'd answer her own voices and launch into frenetic renditions of religious devotion while she was doing the simple tasks of vacuuming or washing dishes. "Fatha, Fatha, Fatha," she'd say, "I got you by the balls, your prick and your cock bull. You play pussy foot with me. You play with yourself and make the sign of the cross, nine genuflections before the stations of the cross, curtsying without your panties. Jesus, Mary and Joseph. Your long red cassock has sperm on the back. Fatha, Fatha, Fatha. Don't you know why there's a big monkey on your back."

The woman was clearly losing her mind, but the most obvious symptom was outer-directed. Kitty Colangelo had fallen in love with Father Dunn, the rector of Christ the King Church.

Cookie silently followed Reenie to the curbside in front of the Baptist Church, where she scuffed the tip of her platform shoe out to the road and into the soft underbelly of a tar baby. It was so damn hot that the road had formed lumps from the city's unsuccessful bid to patch up potholes. The potholes had been filled with black tar, darker than the regular shade of asphalt, and in the heat, the tar lumps had softened to the texture of taffy. Cookie called them *tar* babies and was sure she had written a poem about them in one of her notebooks. Shifting her giant platform heel into the soft tar, it started to sink in and get stuck, like in quicksand. Both girls stared at her sinking heel as if it was a drowning victim neither girl cared to save.

A beat-up Chevy convertible whisked down Broadway, blaring a loud horn. The girls looked up and at each other, blushing, until a similar thought seemed to have occurred to both of them at the same time. The girls realized that their blushing was for no good reason. Cookie knew she wasn't skilled enough to flirt with a car moving that fast down Broadway. She loosened her heel from the grip of the tar baby.

"My mother had these shoes in a box in her closet for ten years, and look what I did to them in two hours." Cookie lifted her foot into the air to assess the damage. The green shoe was peppered with pebbles and feathered with leaves and grass stuck to small clots of angry black tar. Reenie wasn't looking at Cookie's shoes; she was watching the street. Her voice was snotty: "Don't worry; it's only Tommy Parrello."

"Tommy Parrello," Cookie said, rolling her eyes. "Mr. beat it, meat it. I told you he went to Europe with the Rolling Stones and worked backstage. I told you that a long time ago." Cookie acted nonchalant about the prospect of running into Tommy Parrello, but in reality he exuded a maleness, a guy-sort of energy, that she was simultaneously attracted to and repulsed by. She hadn't seen Tommy Parrello since the spring, when she had burst into a spontaneous game of kickball and had kicked the ball into Louie Santamassino's yard. Cookie didn't like Tommy Parrello, but he made her feel funny, as if he could charm her into doing something she did not want to do, like pull down her pants and say it was her idea.

Reenie shook her head. "To me, he's just a regular guy and that means white."

It was 1970, and pure scandal to think of an Italian girl balling a black boy. No one had ever seen Reenie with a black boy, but she made her preference known by the way she talked.

The Chevy braked and parked on the side of the road up ahead, where the girls would soon have to pass. Cookie plucked her fingers through her thick curly hair as if she was adjusting the shiny quills on a porcupine. "How do I look?"

Reenie jabbed her elbow into Cookie's side. "You look real stupid in those shoes."

Cookie latched onto Reenie 's arm and dragged the whole half of her body close to the ground with the force of a nose tackle. "Thanks a lot, faggot."

"Stop it, you're hurting me," Reenie protested. Cookie pinned Reenie's arms behind her back. The blue veins under her tanned skin started to puff up and a rosy color burst into her cheeks. "Tell me that Tommy Parrello is cute, and you want him more than you want to meet Jimi Hendrix."

Reenie nodded. "Yeah, right. Think I'm going to go for that!"

"If I tell you he's cute, you will believe it too." Cookie tightened her hold around Reenie's arms. "How cute is he?"

"Very." Reenie nodded twice, and it must have been a satisfactory answer, because Cookie released her from her powerful clutch. Reenie looked stunned at the brute force of this Cookie monster in peach hot pants and kelly green platform shoes.

Cookie convinced herself that when she was mad, there was no force on earth more powerful.

Allow me to introduce myself. My name is Concetta Mary Bernadette Colangelo, but everyone calls me "Cookie." I'm scrappy enough to remove your left eyeball, your right lung, your trail of entrails (your guts) and your whole heart, as if only a small part of this organ could ever satisfy me? Aside from being a gangster, I am a hippie too. But don't buy into any of this hippie, peace and love shit. I am the toughest chick in the entire North End, maybe even the world. Don't mess with me. Got that?

The girls walked with their noses up in the air and their feet almost on tiptoe, exuding a budding form of feminine grace that was young and inexperienced but potent in a girly sort of way. Their hips gyrated ever so slightly as if this sway and bop had taken on a life of its own. It was truly amazing: anticipating and knowing that in a matter of a few seconds the girls would come face-to-face with a real cute boy. The closer the girls got to the Chevy, the slower and more careful their steps became, unlike their small hearts that quickened with the tempo of a newborn baby. Cookie's trick knees seemed to have healed under Herman's guidance, and had regained their natural ease of gliding in and out of their sockets with curious comfort.

Cookie was certain that Tommy Parrello was the unseen driver of the Chevy and told Reenie, "No one ever drives the

Chevy, except for Tommy Parrello. He paid for the car himself after working two consecutive summers at the A&P as a clerk in the meat department. Every time I went shopping, he was in the meat section wearing the same coverall bib saturated with more blood than you'd see in the average *Chiller Theater* flick on Channel Nine. Under the eerie glow of the A&P Supermarket fluorescent lighting, his fingers looked like wax, and permanently yellowed to the same shade of a fat chicken."

"I'm not having those greasy yellow fingers touch me," Reenie said. "Hope you know that!"

"He's very much an older guy," Cookie shot back. "Almost seventeen."

"He's too old for you and too white for me," Reenie said.

Cookie was obviously taken aback and clasped the crest of her white bubble blouse. *He must like me! Otherwise he would not have stopped the car,* she thought. She peeked out to the side and nodded up ahead, to note that the Chevy was real close, and getting closer. Until today, Tommy Parrello never seemed to notice Cookie. She had seen him last week, sitting in Palisade Pizzeria, eating a slice smothered with olives, sausage and extra cheese. She had heard him put in his order at the counter. He never bothered to look up to notice Cookie. Then he got up and went over to the jukebox and played "Lonely Days, Lonely Nights" by the Bee Gees. Cookie especially liked the line: *Where would I be without my woman?* Cookie was hooked. If things didn't work out with the *Blind Owl* Alan Wilson, Tommy Parrello could be a backup, and she could be his woman.

As the girls moved in on the Chevy, Cookie convinced herself that Tommy could see that she was growing up and becoming a beautiful Italian girl. Cookie shook her head. Even as much as she wanted to convince herself to be as delusional as her mother, she could not. Most of Tommy's girlfriends were beautiful, dark-haired and dark-skinned, like Toni

Ferlinghetti, the leader of the Italian girls. Other than the *Blind Owl*, Tommy was her first inkling of a romantic interest. Cookie began to convince herself that by some odd twists and turns in life, call it a quirk of fate, Tommy had fallen in love with her and was right there now, waiting for her to walk by so he could take her on a spontaneous date. She considered the possibility that he had been in love with her for years, and was just waiting for her to come of age, old enough to go on dates to *the city,* which is what all Yonkers working-class girls called Manhattan. And almost all Yonkers girls were too scared to venture into *the city* by themselves.

Going out on a date to *the city* with Tommy was about to happen! Cookie convinced herself. She was old enough to hang out. Old enough to kiss French style a la *French kiss.* Old enough to give and get hickies. Old enough to wear turtleneck shirts to cover up hickies. Old enough to allow an occasional feel. Old enough to allow an occasional feel outside of her bra. Old enough to allow an occasional feel inside of her bra. Old enough to grind. Cookie wanted to stop! She wanted to stop now, before things got too out of hand. And she hadn't even gone to the city yet. All of these suppositions, raw imaginings, were brewing in the tender bud of her thirteen-year-old mind.

It was a good thing she had dispelled these thoughts because every single notion had percolated in vain. Tommy Parrello was nowhere in sight.

"He's not black," Reenie said.

"Duh," Cookie said. "He's not Tommy Parrello either."

He's white," Reenie said. "Real white."

Arky Lovato reappeared in their lives with a cowlick popping up on the back of his head, like an adolescent boy who had woken up after his last wet dream. He had a big grin on his face as he leaned over to the passenger side of the car and peered at the two girls.

"Arky Lovato," she nodded to Reenie and folded her arms across her chest.

"Where's Tommy?" Cookie asked him. "What are you doing with his car?"

Arky was hanging out of the Chevy window, waving and flailing his arms. Cookie thought he looked real stupid, and yet the attention made her feel wanted and almost pretty. But having Arky Lovato make you feel pretty cancelled the pride in the situation and made her feel mostly awkward. Even though Arky was almost seventeen, he acted like a little boy. Besides, Cookie had never forgiven him for picking up the strange hippie chick Amy at Woodstock. Cookie shuddered because of the gross memory of Arky and Amy balling right in front of her, with about as much finesse as it takes to take a dump in a public place.

"What are you doing with Tommy's car?"

Arky looked immensely pleased with himself. He had a knack for scoring cars, for a day or a week, or maybe a month. It wasn't until after the trip to Woodstock that he confessed to Cookie that the funeral hearse had actually been a loaner owned by an old Italian man who lived in Nepera Park.

"I've got the Chevy for the afternoon," Arky said. "Where do you want to go?"

Cookie's feet were squeezed from the too-tight platform shoes. She closed her eyes and grimaced from the pain. "How about a ride all over, you know, like, *Down the End*?"

Reenie started to net nervous about the prospect of getting into the car with this gimp and tried to be diplomatic. "Do you have a license? Can I see it?"

Arky rolled his eyes, started the car's powerful eight-cylinder engine and revved the engine for maximum effect. "Come on, no one will care. What are you afraid of, anyway?"

The girls looked at one another without talking, but their eyes conveyed little. Taking a ride with Arky Lovato wasn't a bad way to spend the next fifteen minutes, especially when Cookie had already gone the distance with him. Riding around the North End in a Chevy was a far cry from going all the way to Woodstock in a funeral hearse. Arky was pounding the steering wheel to the beat of the tail end of Iron Butterfly's *Ina Gadda da Vida* blaring from the car radio. It was going to be a long ride. Bumpy too.

Cookie wedged into the front seat close to Arky so Reenie could sit next to the window. The scent of their sweat comingled with a blend of stale cigarettes, carbon monoxide and the waning strength of Cookie's *Ambush* perfume. Cookie pulled her *Yardley Pot o' Gloss* from her leather bag and dipped her finger in to make her lips shine. She rubbed the residue of the lip gloss on the waist of her pants in the rim behind a belt loop, so the sticky goo could not be detected. The radio in the Chevy was dialed in and loud. The music stopped and the news broke into the instant static of white noise as if the needle on the dial was stuck between two stations. A commercial jingle played *Goobers are delicious peanuts covered with chocolate. Raisinettes are raisins covered with chocolate too.*

Reenie sang along with the jingle and laughed, "I'm just a white raisinette," she said, "white on the outside and dark inside."

Cookie and Reenie climbed out of the front seat and into the back of the Chevy and sat high above the seat on a ledge cushioned by the collapsed convertible roof. Despite the dangers of being in a car driven by a stoner, Cookie and Reenie had arrived. Riding *Down the End* in a car driven by an older boy meant instant recognition by the coolest kids on the block. It didn't matter that Arky Lovato didn't strike fire in the heart of girls or boys. With the exception of the girl, Amy, he had picked up at Woodstock, Cookie had never seen him getting it on with another girl. Woodstock did that to people. The Woodstock experience was so surreal that it gave him an altered perspective of reality.

While Arky was lucky enough to get laid at Woodstock, he was done in Yonkers, especially *Down the End*. Cookie thought of Arky as a prop in a spectacle. He was a warm male body propped up behind the steering wheel, *chauffeuring* them around town. Cookie and Reenie wanted to be seen, and look grown up. And both girls were using Arky Lovato to arrive at that perception. Ha! This was what was in their minds on this muggy, crappy day in September.

Arky Lovato was driving the car so slowly that it might as well have been driving itself. Every retail front had its own crowd in silos that to this day still exist in Yonkers and in working class neighborhoods everywhere. Back then, there were three silos: the Freaks, the Greasers and the Hippies. The Greaser boys loved to fight. The Hippie boys loved to love. And the Freaks loved to fight and love, whatever came first. The neighborhood bar, Donaghey's Pub, had an abundance of freaks hanging around. These guys had regular blue-collar jobs, punching time clocks. Most of the guys spilling outside stood in front of the pub on the sidewalk, looking for a fight. Some kind of confrontation. It wasn't about winning, but whining, complaining up a storm and bullshitting. Whining after a long day of working a shitty job and a longer night of drinking in desperation made them feel comfortable. Drunk, stoned, or some combination too lethal to mention—none of that mattered. These guys lived to hang-out in the 'hood and watch the world go by.

Next door, the Palisade Pizzeria had the lousiest pizza in Yonkers, maybe in the world. The crust was tough, the sauce was watery and bitter and the cheese was stringy. The neighborhood kids were mean to Tony. Right to his face, the North End Italian boys called him *wop, guido* and *greenhorn.* Anyway, Tony didn't seem to mind kids hanging out and not eating his pizza. The pizzeria was always jam-packed with the bad kids. Tony probably figured that looking busy was good for business or else he didn't know any better. He didn't know how to tell the squatters to leave; he didn't speak much English. The kids who hung out at the pizza place were rebels, did drugs, got into fights and aspired to do bad things. Some kids sat there all day and all night hanging out, which is a working-class way of saying the kids looking to talk to anyone who would listen.

Although Cookie frequently thought about bad things like embarking on a career as a gangster, she knew deep down inside that she wasn't really bad, she was just misunderstood. The pizza place was full. Cookie didn't wave to the kids sitting inside. In the winter months, the storefront window was fogged-up. Heat from the big brick oven and the lack of ventilation streaked the window with steam. Tonight, though, you could see in and the place was full. The Palisade Pizzeria might have had the lousiest pizza in Yonkers, but it did have one redeeming quality: a jukebox. And what a jukebox it was. The music vibrated all day long. Every guy who came into the pizza place played a personally preferred popular prize song, or just a tune that the guy liked a lot. Cookie wished she had met *Blind Owl* in front of a jukebox, and she imagined which letter and number he'd push on the console to play his own song, *On the Road Again.*

The next landmark hangout on the strip was the Palisade Avenue parking lot. Cookie's stomach churned for an instant. Behind two parked cars, in the farthermost corner of the lot, a guy was wrapped around a girl. His body blocked her face, concealing her identity. His body pressed against hers, which was pushed against the metal ridge of the parking lot bumper. He was kissing her with big, slobbering gulps, the way teenage guys kiss girls for the first time. Cookie could see his large tongue sliding in and out of the girl's mouth and muttered to herself, *He's a wet kisser, for sure.* Cookie didn't know how to French kiss and was afraid to think what would happen the first time she tried. What if the guy dribbled spittle onto her chin, and left red welts around her mouth and hickies all over her neck? Kissing a bad kisser was not the solution to not knowing how to kiss.

If you don't count any of the local grocery markets, the delis or beauty parlors, the last great spot on the strip was

Urich's, where there was an old-fashioned soda fountain with bright green stools that swiveled. The good kids hung out at Urich's. There wasn't much in the way of trouble to get into while sipping a vanilla egg cream and talking to the two guys who owned the place about who was winning in the World Series. Cookie thought about stopping in for a hot fudge sundae. Cookie's favorite confection was mint chocolate chip ice cream covered with hot fudge sauce, for sixty-five cents. As the Chevy cruised south and chugged toward the hill on Palisade Avenue, no one on the street seemed too impressed by the Chevy or the two giggling girls, trying to make the scene with the practiced smiles of beauty queens gliding by on a parade float. The news was background noise, and Cookie was intent on changing the channel. She dove forward into the front seat and said to Arky, "Mind if I change the station?"

Arky didn't even seem to hear Cookie. His attention was completely captured by Toni Ferlinghetti standing on the street corner in front of *The Chinks Laundry*. It was no co-incidence that Toni Ferlinghetti kept showing up *Down the End*. She seemed to be intent on stealing Arky away from Cookie, and everyone else, so she could have her own private chauffeur. Toni was wearing a midriff blouse that made her breasts look like two swollen Pomelos. She flashed a smile at Arky that was only meant to torment him. And torment him it did. He stopped the car without looking down at the ignition, but kept the motor running. It's not like he had a chance with Toni Ferlinghetti. No one had a chance with her.

Cookie heard vague words on the radio that were alarming. At first she thought she had not heard them at all and that it was a mistake. Then she heard his name again. *Alan Wilson. Canned Heat.* She thought she heard that Alan Wilson had died. He had been found dead in Topanga Canyon, California. She could not be sure of what she had heard. It could not have been true. The newscast was interrupted by a catchy jingle for *Diet Rite Cola. Everybody likes it. Diet Rite Cola Good for you and children too. Because it hasn't got any sugar at all … new Diet Rite Cola!* Cookie tried turning the dial to find another news report. She lurched forward in her seat and bolted her fists to the dashboard. "I have to get out," she suddenly yelled. Arky and Reenie tried to find out what was wrong, but Cookie paid them no mind. *I have to go*, she kept saying. Her voice remained calm, but inside she felt a lump rise in the back of her throat and stay there stuck, like she was in a dream, wanting to scream, but she was paralyzed with fear and no sound would come out of her mouth.

Arky had already pulled to the side of the road on Palisade Avenue in the Number 2 Bus Stop so he could further check out Toni Ferlinghetti. Reenie tried to get out of the car with Cookie, but Cookie had already climbed over her and pushed the door open. She didn't say anything to anyone about what was happening and where she was going, because she did not know. She left Reenie standing there all by herself while Arky revved the car's motor. A thin stream of blue-grey smoke from the muffler curled into the air like an angry snake and coiled close to Toni Ferlinghetti, who had a smile that did not quit. Cookie was on the sidewalk, walking. She did not know where to get the news. She pulled her tiny robin's egg blue transistor radio out of her brown leather shoulder bag and tried to tune into some news. The radio was AM; she turned the dial, flitting through eight stations. Her miniature battery-powered transistor radio picked up the news, but finding the news station she had heard blaring from the car was impossible, and the news brief she had heard was over. She did not know what had happened, or if anything had happened at all. She did not know where to go to tune in to the news. And most of all, she did not know how the *Blind Owl* Alan Wilson had died. It was all a horrible mistake.

Twenty

Blind Owl Flies the Coop

Blind Owl Alan Wilson had been found dead. His body was discovered in the back yard behind fellow musician Bob Hite's house in Topanga Canyon, California. For five days and over the Labor Day weekend, Cookie tried to find out what had happened to him and why he had died. Getting good information was impossible. She stayed glued to the TV, trying to get news, but news about the *Blind Owl* wasn't forthcoming. Walter Cronkite gave an eloquent summary on TV of the one-year anniversary of the My Lai Massacre in Vietnam. It had been one year since Lt. William Calley had been charged with premeditated murder in the death of 109 Vietnamese civilians, including unarmed men, women and children. Other news reported the United States 101st Airborne Division and the South Vietnamese 1st Infantry Division launched Operation Jefferson Glenn in the Thừa Thiên-Huế Province in Vietnam. Black & white clips showed flag-draped boxes arriving at the Oakland Army Base Airport in California. Anti-war protesters led small pockets of riots in cities and on college campuses, although larger campus protests were subdued and small-scale in the wake of the Kent State shootings that killed four college students.

Johnny Colangelo was on the verge of tears, and not because of the dead *Blind Owl*. He walked around the house moaning, "What's going to happen to Green Bay?" Aside from the Pittsburgh Steelers, the Green Bay Packers were Johnny's favorite pro-football team. "He's the greatest ever," Johnny cried out. "He was only fifty-seven years old. How could this have happened? Fifty-seven!"

The Blind Owl's death was eclipsed by the sudden death of Vince Lombardi. Both men had died on the same day. Vince Lombardi was often said to be the greatest football coach who had ever lived. Lombardi had been head coach of the Green Bay Packers during their peak championship years in the 1960s. The death of Vince Lombardi made Johnny take note of the expansion of the Sumac trees on the south side of the house. The trees' green leaves were beginning to turn color and bore a faint tinge of red.

Johnny saw a long leafy bough impinging against the downspout and on the verge of touching the window. "Goddamn Sumacs," he cried. "Those trees are trying to take over the house!" He left the house and slammed the door behind him.

There was hardly any mention of the *Blind Owl* in the *New York Daily News*, *The New York Post* or *the Yonkers Herald Statesman*. The longest write-up was in *The New York Times*. A few paragraphs mentioned where he was born, his immediate survivors and his most famous songs, *Going Up the Country* and *On the Road Again*. The preliminary autopsy reports were inconclusive. It could not be determined whether the *Blind Owl* had killed himself on purpose, or if he had suffered from an accidental overdose of barbiturates. Foul play had been ruled out.

It would be another month before *Rolling Stone* magazine covered the story of his death, and the cheap teeny-bopper magazines like *Tiger Beat* and *Sixteen* covered bubble-gum music like the Monkees and the Cowsills, and weren't interested in someone as odd and offbeat as the intelligent and hyper-talented *Blind Owl* Alan Wilson.

The day after Labor Day, Cookie started high school. She walked in the front door of Sacred Heart in her stiff cranberry plaid wool skirt and short-sleeved cotton blouse, feeling like she bore a vague resemblance to a Haitian shrunken head that had devoured her entire body. Her loafers squeaked on the drab olive-colored, highly polished linoleum floors of the A-building. The floors were gleaming, and she could clearly see the reflection of her face because she kept her head down. She did not want to look up and see anyone. Old or new? Old classmates had come in from Christ the King, but Cookie had not paid attention to the adolescent litany of who was who. Other kids had come from schools all over the city, but most had come from Sacred Heart's elementary school. Her homeroom class had thirty-four girls, all of whom Cookie regarded as mean girls. Even if they weren't innately mean, everyone was forced to be, on some level, extremely cruel. It was a matter of survival.

The Blind Owl had flown the coop. Every time Cookie thought about him, she felt like she had been punched in the stomach. The pain rose and fell like a wave pounding the surf repeatedly in a storm, or in the aftermath of an earthquake. Even though she was a master of experiencing pain, and creating meaning over pain, and wanting to work to transform it into another small poem, she fell short in her ability to describe the pain of losing her owl. Sure, she had been punched and had the wind knocked out of her stomach, but before this had happened at school, at home, or playing with the other kids on the block. All those other times had been mostly physical. This time it was different. *Blind Owl* had died, and she wished she was dead too.

She tried to convince herself that the *Blind Owl* might only have been playing a joke. She thought of owls as being intelligent, highly evolved and predatory, but she also thought owls were capricious; jokesters, not as tricky as ravens and crows, but owls could play a joke just the same. She thought the *Blind Owl* might have engineered another *Paul is dead* movement, the same way the rumor circled the earth last fall, claiming that Beatle Paul McCartney had died and had been replaced by a lookalike. The *Blind Owl* could have the same thing and one day, hopefully soon, he could come back from the dead and say the whole thing was a joke, a publicity stunt intended to sell more albums. Cookie could not be certain of anything, and there was no way to tell for sure.

By the second week of school, Cookie started cutting classes, and worked on earning herself a bad reputation. Kitty was still in the nuthouse and Johnny never came home except to change his clothes. Cookie knew he had been around, because he left the brown paper wrapper from the *Chinks Laundry* in plain sight on the kitchen counter, where he wrote a note to Cookie in broad, black strokes that said she could charge whatever groceries she needed at Peter Reeves on Palisade Avenue and run a tab. Cookie also remembered that Lizzie Lovato's fourteenth birthday had come and gone without Cookie saying anything about it, not even a simple *Happy Birthday* wish. She couldn't bring herself to talk to Lizzie. She was too close to something that was raw inside of Cookie and she did not know what to do about it, except to stay away from her. And she was thankful that Lizzie had chosen to go to a different high school, Blessed Sacrament Academy, which was an all-girl school where the nuns were cloistered and not allowed to leave the convent without getting a special dispensation from the Pope.

Some mornings, after Cookie checked to make sure that Donny had made it to her fourth grade class at Christ the King, Cookie wandered through the back woods of Untermyer Park, which was mostly empty now that school was back in session. She was looking for something, but did not know what it was or how to find a way to move on. The *Blind Owl* had flown the coop and he wasn't coming back. She stayed mostly to herself, close to home, occasionally slipping down into the *Owl Hole* to think. In this safe, secret, almost sacred place, she brought her black & white notebook in case new words would come, but the pages remained empty. She was too sad to write. One day late in the afternoon after school, Reenie Ruggerio showed up with a nickel bag of pot. Reenie was the only other person in Yonkers who knew about the *Owl Hole* only because this was where, in the past, the two of them had always smoked pot together.

Reenie started rolling a joint in bright pink, strawberry-flavored rolling paper, but Cookie wasn't interested. Of every shape, size, variety, type and name imaginable, she had altogether lost interest in drugs. Drugs hardly kept her mother sane and had killed the *Blind Owl*. She didn't even want to sell drugs any more. She was feeling that bad. Reenie lit the joint, which began burning fast, took a short toke and handed it to Cookie.

Cookie shook her head no.

Reenie was still holding in smoke, "Go on," she rasped. "Take a hit."

Cookie thought about it. She wasn't in the mood to get high, but Reenie was being real kind by making the trek down the steepest steps in Yonkers and into the *Owl Hole*.

"I think I feel real bad," Cookie said.

"Uh-duh," Reenie said. "I know how bad you feel. I'd feel the same way if something happened to Jimi Hendrix."

Cookie nodded to be polite, respectful of how Reenie felt about Jimi Hendrix. Cookie wasn't a fan of Jimi Hendrix. His electric guitar emitted a rhythm that she could not internalize and make her own. Jimi Hendrix's grating squeal left her ears sore and she was unable to ratchet up the sound to a tune that could make her body move in an attempt to dance. She knew Reenie loved Hendrix, and could see why. The boys in the North End held him to be the greatest instrumental guitarist who had ever lived, and if you liked that kind of music, then Jimi Hendrix was almost as legendary as BB King.

Cookie grabbed the joint from Reenie and took a toke. The moment she held in her breath she felt the effects of the pot, and her thoughts lifted to a place where she thought she might be eventually be okay, but there was no way of telling for sure. "I'm getting stoned. So quickly," she said. She forgot about her idea to completely turn her back on all drugs. She could do that anytime, but for now she just had to get through this time by putting one foot in front of another. Almost hypnotically, she stood up and started doing slow knee bends and weaving her hands over her head.

Reenie started to laugh and smoke came out of her nose. "Why are you doing that?"

"Herman Lynch taught me," Cookie said. "And ever since I started doing them every day, my knees don't go out on me anymore. He knew how to fix my trick knees."

"Cool," Reenie said. "Too bad he's so ugly or I'd like him." She passed the joint back to Cookie. "He lives with his grandmother." She eyed Cookie dead-on through a wisp of smoke. "He's got a harelip."

"I don't even see it no more," Cookie said. "He looks fine to me."

"You don't like him, do you? Ewww...," Reenie emitted disgust. "I couldn't imagine kissing a boy with a harelip. He looks like a wild animal bit him on the mouth."

"I don't like him that way." Cookie squirmed uncomfortably. Here she was grieving over the loss of the Owl, the love of her life, and Reenie was talking about her kissing another boy. It made her feel sick inside. "I like him because he's different."

"He's different, alright," Reenie agreed. "He's a Goober, kind of light inside like a peanut covered in chocolate."

"You mean an Oreo," Cookie put her hand over her mouth and laughed.

"Goober," Reenie insisted. She sang the jingle. "*Goobers are delicious peanuts covered with chocolate. Raisinettes are raisins covered with chocolate too.* He's always by himself, and his grandmother is real strict. She works at the library." Reenie belched a small puff of smoke and handed Cookie the joint.

Cookie took another hit. In almost no time at all, the joint was burning down and becoming a fat little roach. "Ouch," she said. "Got a roach clip, Reenie?"

"Go on, pinch me with a clip," Reenie laughed. "Never did have a roach clip. Never did want one. Roach clip, is that what you call it? What is it?"

"Loosely translated, a roach clip is a serrated tooth metal clip for holding the butt of a joint."

"Loosely translated from what? You've read too many books, white girl. Cookie Colangelo, you act like all your books and your learning's going to save your life or something. The stuff you say is like the slogans on the sides of the bookmobiles."

Reenie tossed her head back, pushed her long black fringe of hair away from her face and laughed. "I'd rather smoke hash. Don't have to worry about your fingers getting burned or making them smell ridiculously like pot."

Cookie took one last drag that singed her fingers, stung her eyes and made her cough. She dropped all that was left of the butt to the ground and stamped on it as if indeed it was a genuine cockroach that she felt compelled to kill. "Enough of that."

She sat down on the floor of the *Owl Hole,* which was pebble-rock textured bare concrete covered with patches of grass and weeds coming up in between cracks in the pavement. "Oh man, Reenie, I don't know what was in that joint, but it gave me one hell of a whitey."

"No shit," Reenie said. "It's just regular pot. I think it's your frame of mind. You're feeling bad about the Owl."

"I'm so dizzy and I feel sick," Cookie said.

A *whitey* is a bad reaction to smoking pot that is more common to first-time smokers, but it can also happen at random, and it made Cookie dizzy, nauseous and feel like she was on the verge of vomiting. The name whitey comes from how pale the skin gets due to a rapid plummet in blood pressure. All of the blood had drained from Cookie's face.

"You do look white," Reenie said. "But you always look white. Too white."

Cookie sat there for a long time. She was conscious of Reenie talking to her and wanting her to come up the steps so the two of them could take a walk *Down the End* and hang out together, but mostly Cookie didn't move and she didn't say anything. She didn't feel like she needed to move at all. She sat there for a long time and stared. She was blanking in and out of consciousness. She was aware of Reenie being there beside her, but she could not move. Reenie prodded her arm once, then harder, more than a nudge and almost a push. Still, Cookie did not move or talk or cry or think. She could not move at all. She stayed that way so long, she did not realize Reenie had given up on her and left her there sitting *all by myself*, she said to herself until she passed out. *I'm all by myself.*

It started to grow dark, and she didn't know how long she had been there. The light was dim. The sun must have gone down. She could see the faint trace of the grass and the black wrought iron hand rail that ran along the edge of the steps. Soon it grew cooler, and she curled up on her side in a ball so she wouldn't have to get up and go anywhere. She was coming down from her high and craving something sugary to eat. She remembered Reenie singing the jingle for *Goobers and Raisinettes,* and wished she had a box. She heard voices coming from above at the top of the camouflaged stairwell that led down to the *Owl Hole,* but could not make out a shape or form, or recognize the voices. She felt a tinge of alarm to think her hideaway had been discovered, or worse; someone could trap her down here and not have the best of intentions. There was only one way in and one way out, up and down the crumbling concrete steps.

She sat up on alert for whoever was there. Her hair fell out of her pony tail and into her eyes. She brushed away her hair from her face so she could see. She made out two people bounding fast down the steps. One body leaped high in the air and jumped off the steps, right down into the center of the landing, and stood above Cookie. The boy put out his hand to offer Cookie help up from the ground. Even in the dark, she could see that it was Herman Lynch, and Reenie Ruggiero stood by his side.

Cookie stood up and looked at Herman. "How'd you know I was here? This is my place and nobody else's." She turned to Reenie. "Where did you find him? You're too afraid to go to the projects."

No matter how much Reenie had professed to love everything black, she was still afraid to hang out in the projects: Schlobohm, Mulford Gardens and Cottage Gardens. Everyone was afraid of the projects. Even the people who lived there were afraid. Somehow Reenie found Herman and told him that Cookie was in a bad way.

Reenie nodded to Herman and shook her head. "He doesn't live in the projects. He lives in my building."

Herman nodded to Reenie. "She told me where you were."

"I told him," Reenie said. "It's not good for you to be alone." Reenie tapped Herman on the shoulder. "I'm going to go and leave you two alone to talk," she said. "Cookie, don't worry, things will be okay. You've gotta be tough. Like me," Reenie smiled.

"Give me a break," Cookie said.

"Tell her what you told me," Reenie said to Herman.

Herman looked at Cookie. He didn't have to say what she thought he was thinking, *I know the Blind Owl was important to you, and I'm sorry*. He didn't say anything. The look in his eyes spoke and it was true, truer than anything she had known. He understood what she was going through.

Cookie lowered her eyes and nodded. She wanted to cry, but there were no tears to be found, not one. She nodded her head a few more times before looking up at Herman. "Thanks."

"I know how you feel," Herman said.

"Do you!" Cookie said belligerently. She felt like popping him in the nose, and made a small fist. "I'd give you a big fat lip too, except you don't have one. What do you know!"

"You shouldn't have brought him here," Cookie yelled at Reenie. "Now he'll know my secret hiding place and use it all the time too."

"Think I'm going," Reenie said. She headed toward the steps and didn't look back, not even when Cookie, yelled at her, "Thanks. Thanks a lot, Reenie. You've gone and made things a whole lot worse."

Herman looked at Cookie. She noticed he was not wearing his glasses. The street light from North Broadway flashed on and illuminated his light-colored eyes. "Cookie, there's something I need to tell you." He took a deep breath before saying anything else. He grew real quiet and looked out toward the fluorescent strobe of light from Broadway, then back at Cookie. "I don't think the Owl meant to die."

Cookie was feeling angry, more than she had ever known, except the last vestige of being high quelled her thoughts of turning violent. "How do you know?"

"I think he was feeling bad. I think he was feeling too much pain. I think he was just trying to stop the pain and took too much. He didn't mean to OD. He just took too much to try and stop the pain."

Cookie looked up at him. "I read every news bulletin I could get my hands on." She sniffed as if she had an automatic reflex making her toughen up, and repressing any release that could allow her to cry. "No one knows for sure why he died."

Herman sighed and looked around, then put his hands in his pockets. With the aid of low-wattage fluorescent light, Cookie could see that his pants were tan army khakis and his shirt was black and had a football player wearing a golden yellow helmet with deep green stripes. The name of the team on his t-shirt was the Green Bay Packers.

"The same thing happened to my mother," Herman said softly. "She couldn't handle being a young mother with no job and no man, so she started shooting up. All the dealers came to the projects. They'd drive by in their big fancy cars, selling smack. They preyed on us, man. She didn't mean to die. She didn't want to die. She was feeling bad. She got her hands on some bad stuff. She OD'd. She didn't want to die. She loved my grandmother. She loved me."

Cookie stood motionless. She was hardly breathing. She heard Herman tell her again. "It was an accident," he said. "Sometimes you can take downers and you get stoned, but it's not enough, the pain doesn't stop, so you take more, but you're stoned and you don't remember how many you've taken and how many more you could take without it killing you, so you end up taking too much. And then you're dead."

Cookie thought about it, the pain of it all, and it was no fun. Life was no fun. Herman nudged her toward the steps to go home. "You need to sleep. Go home and get some rest, Cookie."

Cookie looked at him the way she had never looked at anyone else before. She loved Herman Lynch. He could talk to her like no one else could. "I think I want to stay here for a while and think."

"Okay," Herman said. "I understand. Just don't stay too long. It's getting late." When he smiled, she only saw the gleam of his teeth; his harelip was invisible in the dark, accented by a slight sprig of fluorescent light. His harelip had become a hidden wound that you would only know about if you knew him. He smiled that cute way, turning up the corners of his mouth. Then he turned to leave and she saw him climbing up out of the *Owl Hole*, taking two steps at a time, sometimes three.

"Thanks," she called after him.

Tonight, the first nip of autumn chill was in the air. She sat on the very last step, pulled her notebook out of her shoulder bag and opened to a blank page. She wanted to write about the Blind Owl and what he meant to her. He was shy and lonely, smart and wise. Even though she had never met him, he was more real to her than any other person she had ever known. She thought he would understand her feelings in a way that no one else ever could. *Go off and live in a cave. There is nobody there to tell you how to behave. Life is hard, everybody knows. So find your peace where only nature grows. I am here in this Owl Hole with a pen as my only friend. Tonight, I write this poem for you my Owl to say goodbye and to help my heart mend.*

Twenty-one

Trees Like Sun

A sudden awareness struck Cookie in the form of a double feature playing at Loew's Movie Theater in Getty Square. Only this double feature was going on inside her head. She saw two important events happening at the same time and if she didn't take action soon, then something bad could happen. Herman was off his beaten path and she did not know if he knew how to get down to Warburton Avenue from the Owl Hole. Cookie remembered he had not been wearing his glasses. Normally, he descended deep into the woods by the Devil's Cave at the bottom of Untermyer Park. The site of a lone black boy cutting through the North End and heading west to the Hudson River was as rare a sighting as a real owl building a nest above Urich's on Palisade Avenue. It just wasn't going to happen and there was no telling how those tough Yonkers guys hanging out in front of Donaghey's Pub would treat a black boy with a harelip.

The second movie playing in Cookie's head was about Donny and how she was going home to an empty house where there was little or nothing to eat. Kitty was still in the hospital, and there was no telling when Johnny would come back home. While Cookie knew Donny could fend for herself, she did not need to commit another mandatory act of bravery to end her first week of school in the fourth grade.

Cookie sprang up from the ground of the Owl Hole so fast that she became dizzy. She quickly ran up the steps, taking them two at a time the same way Herman had done. The effects of the joint had completely worn off. She was grazing through the woods and bramble, plowing over small blighted shrubs when she had a funny feeling about the direction Herman could have gone, and if she was right, he would run headlong into Louie Santamassino and his German Shepherd guard dog Roscoe, baring teeth and all.

Cookie tore through the backyard belonging to Fran Ochiogrosso and to the chain link fence that marked the boundaries of Louie's property with as much certainty as his dog who peed the perimeter on a daily basis. Cookie called Herman's name, repeatedly, not in a frantic way but just to see if she had been right about the direction he could have gone, and if so, she didn't want to alarm him too soon. If she was right about his being there, he would call back hello.

Going around the far right corner of Fran's house, Cookie saw her flaming red-haired head pop into the kitchen window. The light was on in the kitchen, and Fran seemed to be standing behind the sink doing dishes. She was wearing tight pink foam rollers, and a cigarette dangled from her ultra-red lips. Even when she was wearing a house dress, Fran never went without wearing her cherry-red matte lipstick. Cookie tiptoed along a small alley around the back of the house and crept close to the exterior wall so Fran could not see her. She stopped calling for Herman until she made it to the other side. The top of the block was covered with honeysuckle bushes that had long faded in the heat and had gone dormant in anticipation of the fall. She pressed herself against the fence and softly called Herman's name several times. She was about to give up when she heard a lyrical rustling as gentle as a whisper. She called his name again and this time, there was no mistake, she heard him call her name in response.

"Cookie," he whispered. "Cookie, is that you?"

"Yes, over here," Cookie whispered back. "Where are you?" She clung to the fence and stuck her foot into a metal slat to pull herself up higher so she could try to peer over to the other side.

"Here. By the tree."

Cookie could not see him, nor could she tell for sure the direction from which his voice was coming. "Herman?" She pulled herself higher into another slat on the fence. "I hope you're not in Louie Santamassino's yard. He'll kill you!"

"Oh, man, you don't want to see this." Herman came into view on the other side of the honeysuckle vine that grew in tangled knots, embedding itself in a wide bank of evergreen hedges. Herman's head popped up and he whispered, "That man's dog is dead and he's crying. It's a pitiful sight if I've ever seen one."

"Come over here," Cookie whispered. "Can you jump the fence?"

"Sure, no problem." Herman jumped up into two middle slats on the fence and propelled himself over, as if he was making a pole vault jump without having to use a pole. He came down onto the ground and made a squashed indentation in the honeysuckle quagmire, stood upright and faced Cookie. "That man there," he said, pointing, "lost his dog. He's sitting there in the back yard crying because the dog is lying on his side and he's dead. I've never seen a grown man cry like that before. You'd think that dog was his only friend. Man, it's a really bad thing to see. Man, is it *uggh-lee*. You don't want to see it."

"Let me see."

Herman cupped his hands together so he could hoist her up over the fence. Cookie stood on one leg and hurled her other leg up over the top of the fence. She came crashing down into the bushes that bounced her body around as if she was on a trampoline. Far more elegant in his approach, Herman catapulted over the fence in a single clean leap.

Cookie and Herman leaned into the hedge, partially concealing themselves behind a magnificent, ancient Maple tree. The tree was a whole world unto itself and had two trunks that either had divided into two separate root systems over time, or there had always been two trees from the beginning, growing strong and close together, each bearing its own weight and finding a way to reach the sun. Many broad limbs shot out from the base of the two trunks, bending outward to form a canopy of branches that were covered with infinite varieties of moss, fern and new saplings.

Louie Santamassino sat on the ground in front of the dog's body. It was not apparent what had killed Roscoe; the dog appeared to be sleeping. Louie Santamassino wept with the raw emotion of a small boy who could not be consoled. He called the dog's name, Roscoe, while tears streamed down his cheeks. Racked with sobs, he cradled his arms across his chest, rocking forward as if it was the only way he could comfort himself. Cookie had never seen a grown man cry. Well, that wasn't true. Come to think of it, she had seen Johnny cry once, but only once, and it was so scary that she never wanted to see it happen again.

Louie knelt forward on his hands and knees as if he was about to pray. Instead he took a large plastic tarp and slowly wrapped it around the body of his dead dog. He took an ordinary round garden shovel and when he began to dig, the blade of the shovel did not penetrate the earth and hit the ground, making a thudding metallic sound. Louie left for a minute and came back with a large, angry pick, with which he hacked at the ground, sending dirt, clumps of soil and rocks exploding into the air. Then he began to dig again and soon formed a large hole in the ground where he could bury his dead dog. Cookie nudged Herman as if to say, *Let's get out of here.* Even without his glasses on, Herman's eyes were huge, and she wondered how he was able to see well enough to have stumbled on poor Louie Santamassino preparing to bury his dead dog.

When Herman and Cookie climbed back over the fence and were safely away from Louie's yard, Cookie spotted Fran Ochiogrosso standing on the street corner, looking as if she had just seen a ghost. She did not even bother to say hello. Cookie realized Fran must have also seen Louie burying his dog. She stalked Louie in a most unnatural way, for some reason Cookie did not understand. Fran was always into everyone's business, and it made no sense.

Cookie nodded to Herman to follow her and to walk together down the gentle slope of Arden Place, "If you want to get down to Warburton Avenue, you can walk all the way down Rudolph until you hit the Circle, then you just keep going down, down until you hit the Aqueduct." Cookie pointed in the direction of the Hudson River.

Herman laughed, "Cookie, you are too funny. I think by now I can find my way to the river. It's kind of a big river and I can see it from here."

"With the trees being so full of leaves right now, I didn't think you'd find your way. You can hardly see the river," she smiled. "You don't even have your glasses on."

"I'm not needing them as much," Herman said. "Whatever's wrong with my eyes is starting to get better."

"Sounds like a sorry-assed excuse to me if I ever heard one!"

Herman grinned and started walking backward and away from her. "You see, you're starting to seem like your old self again." He pointed at her with both hands, "And keep doing those knee bends to keep your legs strong and not popping out all the time."

Cookie turned around to walk home on her own, but staring her right in the face, Fran Ochiogrosso met her with a wagging pointer finger. "Who's that colored boy you're with,

Cookie? Isn't it enough that your mother's in the hospital that you're spending your time sneaking around with a Negro boy?"

Cookie wanted to kill her then and there, but she didn't. "He's my friend," Cookie said, defiantly sticking out her tongue. "You probably don't even know what a friend is! And never even had one!"

Fran's pink curlers bounced while she yelled at her, "You have no business being around the colored! Wait until your father finds out about this!"

Cookie turned her back on Fran and kept walking until she made it home. She wondered what had happened to Louie's dog, and it occurred to her that maybe Fran had poisoned Roscoe. Fran hated Louie and especially hated his dog. She saw Johnny's Buick Skylark in front of the house and knew that if he was home this early, there had to be trouble brewing. The front door was unlocked.

Pushing open the door and tiptoeing into the house, she tried to be as unobtrusive as possible, and as much as she wanted to disappear into her bedroom, she was starving and needed to eat. She could fix everyone supper—that was a bright idea! She headed to the kitchen through the living room. From the kitchen, she saw Johnny sitting at the dining room table.

Johnny looked up at her as if he was ashamed. He was red in the face, not from the sun, but from what Cookie recognized to be the flush of deep embarrassment. Immediately, Cookie felt as though she had been caught doing something wrong. He probably caught wind that she had been seen hanging out with Herman Lynch. Her own feelings of shame flooded her being, not because she was wrong, but because she was being made to feel wrong. Her shoulders slumped, and her shoulder bag slipped onto the floor. She felt guilty without having had a chance to tell her side of the story. She should not have to feel guilty. She had not done anything wrong. She was so consumed with shame and guilt that she did not see what was really troubling Johnny.

"Will you look at her?" Johnny said. "Look at what's happened to your sister."

Donny was wearing her baby doll pajamas, which had been made to look more blue than usual because everything else about her was pink and red. Her face, neck, arms and hands were covered from head to toe in pink calamine lotion. Her eyes were almost swollen shut, and her lips were three times larger than their usual size. Her ears were scarlet-tinged and thickened from inflammation. Angry-looking scabs oozed a thin watery fluid from underneath some of the open patches of calamine lotion. She was sipping from a sealed-off, self-contained plastic baby *Sippy cup* that had a built-in straw. She looked at Cookie and stopped sipping for a minute, then with the straw she began blowing bubbles into her cup. "I'm allergic," she said. "And it hurts to go to the bathroom."

"Poison Sumac," Johnny said. "Those goddamn Sumac trees. I should have taken them down a long time ago. Look what those trees have done to Donny! She's broken-out everywhere, for crissakes!"

Cookie was too exhausted to explain to Johnny the difference between poison sumac vines and the majestic red leaf-tinged Sumac trees that circled their home. She knew how stubborn Johnny could be, and how much work it would take for him to understand a simple, but different way of thinking. She might be able to convince a normal person of the basics of Sumac botany in five minutes, but with Johnny, there was no telling how long it would take, or if he would ever come around at all. She slipped out of the room and went to bed, where she immediately fell asleep.

By morning, Cookie woke from a deep, exhausted sleep. Her dreams had been troubling, the sort that are close enough to reality to be more real than a dream and hinted at the turmoil that chased her everywhere. In her dream, a red-and-white *Coca Cola* can was perched precariously on the cornice of Fran Ochiogrosso's fence that abutted Louie Santamassino's yard. The can grew to resemble Fran's head, and was pulled back by some unknown force, until she bared her teeth and growled at Roscoe, who was barking up a storm. Fran's head expanded into the giant head of a black & white high-hat-hooded Dominican nun, who laughed at her with the throaty engine of a chainsaw. The disembodied chainsaw sliced through the air and cut Roscoe into two.

It was the sound of a real chainsaw that had woke Cookie from her sleep. Outside her window, she could see smoke rising in the air. A low-humming rumble, some intermittent fits and stops of mechanical coughing, then the full throttle gunning of a motor screeched, mitting out all other sounds of that morning.

Cookie jumped out of bed and ran outside to see what was happening. Johnny was brandishing a chainsaw in the air; its whirring blade was cutting down the smallest branches and leaving only bare boughs on the trees in her beloved woods. The air was filled with Rorschach-patterned clots of smoke, and the raw stench of gasoline.

"Stop! What are you doing?" Cookie screamed. "You can't cut down these trees."

Johnny snorted so hard that his blue eyes flashed fire. "Look what these trees did to your sister."

"You're wrong!" Cookie was frantic. "It's not the trees that are poisonous! The trees didn't cause her rash! It's not the same thing! You're wrong!" She yelled.

Johnny whacked the chainsaw and took down a large bough. Landing in a loud crash, the bough was laden with sheaths of scarlet etched leaves that had been on the verge of turning into the glow of red fire.

"Will you please stop!" she cried. "Poison sumac is a vine. It's not a tree! Please stop! You don't know what you're doing!"

"Get out of here," Johnny yelled. He climbed up on to a twelve-foot aluminum ladder. "You're going to get hurt!" He looked down at her. "You always think you know everything! Get out of here and go watch your sister!"

Cookie cradled the bottom of the ladder. "Please!" she yelled, looking up at him. "Poison sumac grows low to the ground. It's a vine! It's got white berries! It's low. It's low! It's a weed, not a tree! It's not a tree!"

"Get out of here!" Johnny waved the chainsaw in the air, threatening her. "Don't make me come down from this ladder!"

Cookie backed away moving toward the house, watching her father with horror. "It's not the Sumac trees!" she cried. "Sumac trees! The trees are not poisonous. Sumac means red! Because the trees have red leaves. The trees have red leaves in the fall!" She wanted to cry and shed real tears, but could not; the tears were not there. It was as if her tears had gone away forever. "The trees are not poisonous! The Sumac trees are not poisonous. Beautiful trees. The trees look like the sun!"

Cookie could not stop him. She did not know what to do. In all of the years she had been with her father, she had never seen him so full of rage. It was as if the Sumac trees had borne the cumulative pain of every single thing that had gone wrong in his life. She repeated over and over, *the trees are not poison sumac*. She repeated *beautiful trees* until she felt as though she had turned on the verge of code blue to counter his red-hot emotion. But he had not heard anything she had said, even if it was the truth. He was fixated on something. And even if Cookie could show him he was being stupid, he could not let go of his belief that the Sumac trees were the root cause of all of the problems he had encountered from the beginning of time.

Johnny had turned into a madman. Sweat poured from his face, droplets fanning out from his nose, dripping down his neck and falling to the ground. Johnny was powerfully built, with a broad back and thick arms that rippled with dense muscle. Sweat and soot covered his back and neck, and small flecks of wood were stuck in his hair. The scream of the chainsaw gyrated, belting out a long, thin tail of smoke that ballooned into the shape of a mighty comet. Johnny's face was red with rage and screwed up into uncontrollable hatred. His body shook and his sweat flew into the air with the force of a rogue rain shower.

He wielded the chainsaw as if he was in Korea again, shooting a powerful M-1 automatic machine gun. He was under enemy fire, and in his path, he would leave no one standing. He wanted to live and they were trying to rob him of his life. They were not going to kill him! He'd kill them first. He was out of his mind with rage, and enjoyed the feeling. In blind, blood-simple fury, he sacked limbs, boughs, branches that once bore the sheaths of crimson and scarlet glory, butchering them, hacking them to pieces and leaving them lying slaughtered on the ground where Lily of the Valley once grew. Twigs, leaves, bramble fell from the sky in an avalanche of disemboweled trees, and soon debris covered the earth. He murdered the Sumac trees, every last one.

By the end of the day, all that remained of the Sumac trees were stumps, hardly standing and cut down to the ground. Having surrendered to their decapitation without a struggle and without a fight, only the last remnants of a massacre were left behind. Gone now were the boughs dipping in the wind under the weight of intensely brilliant red leaves and the blazing scarlet promise of another fall. Gone was a touchstone for Cookie to find one more reason to be alive and look forward to her next birthday. She had failed in her mission to tell Johnny that the Sumac trees were noble, full of soul and the wisdom of the ages, and were in no way responsible for what had happened to Donny. Poison sumac was a nasty plant, and not at all related to the proud trees that had once talked to her and stunned the North End neighborhood with their beauty. And as much as Johnny had slayed the trees as innocent victims, he had not gotten rid of the real enemy, the poison sumac vines that still lived low to the ground and the poison that still lived inside of him.

Twenty-two

Friday, September 18, 1970

There was a slight chill in the air. Cookie sniffed and detected the distinct mixture of car exhaust, cigarette smoke and the sweet smell of decay from the brittle leaves that had fallen to the ground. She kicked at the leaves and felt them crunch under feet. She was last in the long loose processional line of ninth-grade students who were walking from church to the school. Cookie clutched her black & white composition book and stomped in-between piles of soot blackened leaves. While she was in church, she had scribbled down her thoughts on paper.

Welcome to the hood! I'm glad you decided to visit here. I've been wanting you to come by to say hello and to pay your respect to me. Allow me to introduce myself. My name is Concetta Mary Bernadette Colangelo, but everyone calls me Cookie. I'm scrappy enough to remove your left eyeball, your right lung, your trail of entrails (your guts) and your whole heart, as if only a small part of this organ could ever satisfy me? Don't ever piss me off! No one's going to mess with me. I'm from Yonkers and I'm not scared of anything.

Since the *Blind Owl* had died, she had begun work on her first novel, in his honor. So far her book had too few pages and no title. Post-dead *Blind Owl,* along with the demise of the Sumac trees, she hadn't felt like writing anything. She still practiced her knee bends and ran into Herman Lynch in the most unusual places, including the *Owl Hole.* The *Owl Bowl* that had been in her woods had gone the way of the dead Sumac trees. It too had been destroyed during Johnny's rampage.

Cookie felt claustrophobic in the crowd of bodies swarming around her. The sight of fat jack o'lanterns and other proud gourds lined up in rows on front porches did not make her happy. Fall meant nothing more than dirty mounds of leaves heaped high on both sides of the street for three months. September, October, November. Today, it was September 18, 1970. In two more months, the leaves would disintegrate into mulch under a fine layer of dirty frost. Then the snow would come.

On the other side of the street from Shonnard Place, the sight of little kids tumbling across the lawn like baby basketballs did not make her smile. She was reminded of Donny, who would get home before she did and no one would be there to greet her. Left home alone, Donny would often sit outside on the front steps and wait for Cookie to get there. Today, Donny would have to wait even longer. It was only the second week of school, and Cookie was already in enough trouble to warrant having to serve a period of mandatory detention, the dreaded jail sentence foisted upon bad Catholic schoolgirls.

Her attention drifted to the street, where all of the houses looked identical. Small ranch-style, Roman brick homes flanking both sides of the street made it look like Queens or Staten Island. Newer than the tenement-infested homes of the Bronx and South Yonkers, the homes in North Yonkers had less character than homes in Manhattan or Brooklyn, and every square inch of brick and wood was of average quality, decidedly modest and working-class.

The students' uniforms were color-coded by grade in narrow plaid patterns of green, navy, maroon and grey. Cookie was a freshman, so her uniform was maroon plaid and her wool skirt felt itchy against her white skin. Cookie had an uncanny fascination with scent. Her ability to distinguish the complex range of scent was an acute distraction. The cumulative crush of sweaty wool emanating from the cluster of skirts smelled like the inside of *LuDell's Uniform Store* in the heart of the ghetto, down on South Broadway. Cookie had a notion that it would be fun to set fire to LuDell's. Come next fall, thousands of Catholic girls would be roaming the city wearing the disguise of ordinary street clothes. Unfortunately, LuDell's did not burn to the ground, and while she walked, the coarse wool prickled the back of Cookie's knees and her outer thighs.

She had been late for school this morning, and last week she had played hooky twice. Today she had to go to two hours of detention before she could go home. It was only the second week of school, and already she had been cast in the role as a troublemaker. She could tell that by the way the nuns' beady eyes zeroed in on her the moment she walked into the class-room, and roved constantly in her direction throughout the class period, fastening on her as if she had some sort of magnetic bad-girl attraction.

Gloom, doom and depression. She wanted to stop, take a break and write in her black & white notebook, but if she stopped in the line even for an instant, the nuns would nab her. She was in enough trouble already. To pass the time and to avoid talking to anyone, she counted the jagged potholes on the street. Some of them were patched up by city road crews last summer in a half-hearted attempt at urban renewal. The filled-in holes looked dark and lumpy, like deformed hard clots of coal. Next summer, the road crews would be back to repair their own shoddy workmanship. They'd make bigger, better, all new and improved variations of black tar babies. Only the next time around, they'd dig up entire sections of the road and get paid time and a half for not doing the job right the first time. Cookie thought of how the name tar baby had come about, and if it was something she should mention to Herman to ask him if the name was one more nasty way to describe black people.

Everyone in this city had a scam going on, just to survive and *make ends meet*—that's what all of the grownups said, and they should know, because they were stuck here. Cookie still could not believe they used to call Yonkers *the city of gracious living*. In Cookie's mind, Yonkers was *the city of dangerous living*, a ghetto. She tried to imagine a different world, the one she wrote about in her black & white composition book. In this world, the starched smiles of old nuns were preserved in jars of formaldehyde, and potholes never formed. In this world, there would be lots of clean gold leaves fluttering in the wind, and horse drawn buggies that moved on wooden wheels. The buggies would transport kids to the kinds of schools that never heard of cliques and race riots. Everyone would wear crisp white man-tailored shirts under crew neck woolen sweaters over new blue jeans; and penny loafers, stuffed with real pennies.

On the way home from school, the girls would share apples and their skin would glow from the buggy ride in the open autumn air. Cookie could hear the wooden wheels clacking original, but traditional-sounding, names like a picture postcard from colonial New England. Everyone would have pretty teeth that looked white and shiny without the backdrop of olive-toned skin. These girls had one-syllable last names: King, Lamb, Cole, Prince, Pence, Burns, Smith, Jones and Knight. Of course, those were the last names of many of the black people living in south Yonkers. Truth be told, there was another story explaining why blacks ended up poor and living in the ghettos of south Yonkers and the Bronx, bearing one-syllable Anglo names, and it had more to do with slavery than the Emancipation Proclamation.

In Cookie's black & white composition book, her friends did not have last names like Columbo, DiOreo, DiLorenzo, De Luca, Gallo, Mancini, Palumbo, Bruno, Scarpino, Lombardo, Lombardi and Boscone, all of whom were herding around her, intentionally obnoxious or not, bumping into her and laughing. There was no mistaking it. They were messing with her on purpose! They were laughing right at her!

Cookie was paralyzed, trying to catch her breath and figure out what to do. None of these girls seemed to like her and she couldn't stand the thought of another calculated snub, or worse yet, if they said something nasty to her. Cookie was tough, but she was outnumbered. A heathen pack reeking of sweaty wool skirts, cotton blouses, pots of *Yardley* lip gloss and chewing gum, pushed into her. At least three girls were cracking their gum in short staccato pops that sounded like a chorus of dim-witted firecrackers.

"What's with the ponytail," Cookie Colangelo? Your hair looks too flat for your fat face."

"Her face is round, not fat," one of the girls squealed. "She has a face as round as a pumpkin. Pumpkin face! How do you like Halloween, pumpkin face?"

"She's so white. Look at how white she is!"

Cookie's eyes met the eyes of her accuser. The girls were led by Toni Ferlinghetti who was the most beautiful adolescent Italian girl in Yonkers. At fourteen, Toni Ferlinghetti was so developed and so well-endowed that she looked like a cross between Sophia Loren and Virna Lisa, a sight so overwhelming it was enough to make grown men weep. Toni Ferlinghetti looked at Cookie Colangelo, but not through the corner of her eyes. Instead, her eyes narrowed to the slits of a measured wise-guy side glance, probing to find Cookie's weakness.

Toni was pleased to find freshman Cookie Colangelo with her long brown ponytail and pale white skin standing completely still, in awe of her magnificent presence. The other Italian girls avoided making eye contact with Cookie and waited until they had direct approval from their leader. They waited patiently for Toni's response, observing every telltale sign that would signal her acceptance or rejection of Cookie Colangelo.

Toni's amber doe eyes widened into a blank trajectory, and

her upper lip curled into a detached sneer; the fate of Cookie Colangelo was sealed. They looked at each other in a mass toss of espresso colored hair. They smirked. They giggled. A sea of maroon plaid wool fanned open and parted around Cookie as if she was a dead Sumac tree stump marked by hollow roots. The girls laughed at Cookie Colangelo as if she was too white, half-Irish, and did not deserve to have an Italian last name.

"How'd you get an Italian name, Cookie Colangelo?" Toni Ferlinghetti asked. "Someone must have switched her at birth at the hospital," she said to the other girls. And they laughed.

Cookie wanted to yell "Enough" at the top of her lungs, but she didn't want to draw attention to one of the loneliest moments of her life. They had turned onto Convent Place, where the monstrously large buildings of Sacred Heart High School had windows mimicking watchful eyes that were staring at her frail and girlish body as if it was a birdlike morsel. Soon this place would devour her. She hated this school.

From the corner of her eye, Mike Trapani was looking at her, grinning. Since school had started, he was always showing up unexpectedly in the playground where everyone went outside for lunch-hour smokes, and in Lennon Park, where everyone smoked dope after school. Mike Trapani was a freshman boy, with robust red cheeks covered with warm brown fuzz. Built enormously to be chubby for life, he had a thick pom of brown hair and a tiny beak of a nose.

Of all the life forms in this world, she especially loathed sloppy Italian boys. Mike came up to her side as if he was trying to detect if she wore perfume. Cookie instantly realized he was her height, but easily three times her weight. He quickly reached up underneath her jacket, probed her back to find a bra strap and snapped it. "Gotcha," he said. "Just checking to see if you're wearing a bra yet."

"Get out of here," Cookie yelled at him. He bore no signs of adolescence except for a small band of dark fuzz above his big mouth. "Catch you after school, Cookie?"

Cookie hurried ahead to get away from him and joined the outer flanks of the Italian girls, who did not so much as nary a nod to show that Cookie was alive and in their midst.

She tried to think of happy things, such as her notebook where she wrote the thoughts that would save her life. She felt fortunate that the character in her book had a beautiful name—Andrea Verrone. Her last name had only two syllables: Verrone. Ver-Own, sort of like *Her Own,* in Cookie's limited understanding of French. The last e was silent. She had a thing for the letter e. She could use the letter e in the most artful and interesting ways or not use it at all.

In the world of horse drawn carriages and apple-cheeked happiness, she passed for a WASP girl. A WASP girl did not have to seek the approval of a greaseball wop like Toni Ferlinghetti. In the world of WASPdom, Cookie's white skin would be revered. She'd prosper. She'd be one of them. She'd be famous. And when she died, she might have to go to hell with the Jews, and everyone else who was not Catholic, but that's the price you pay for being free from the bondage of the Italian girls.

Cookie clutched her notebook as if she was afraid someone would take it away from her. She didn't feel right, dreaming about freedom. She couldn't dream like other people. It made her think she was thinking like her mother. Kitty was still in the hospital, and not coming home any time soon. She'd never be like her mother. Not even for a minute. Not ever. Cookie would rather be dead than to be beautiful with large breasts, and crazy. Come to think of it, the Queen Bee Italian girl Toni Ferlinghetti had the same hour-glass-shaped body as Kitty Colangelo. In fact, the more Cookie thought about it, Toni Ferlinghetti could pass herself off as Kitty's daughter.

The shrill scream, *No, oh my God, no* came from nowhere and was so startling that Cookie dropped her notebook to the ground, where it landed close to the edge of a puddle of stagnant water. She dove to retrieve it while the line of kids *plowed ahead* of her. She heard the murmur of voices running through the crowd. *Jimi Hendrix. Jimi Hendrix.* Then *Jimi Hendrix is dead.* The words started coming together faster and faster, the way words do when a rumor travels through a crowd. *Jimi. Jimi. Drugs. Paris. OD'd* and *Overdose.* The rumor was traveling fast, and it began to sound an awful lot like it was the truth. The famous black guitarist Jimi Hendrix was dead.

Cookie immediately thought of Reenie and scrambled ahead, plunging into the midst of the other Italian girls to find her. If she felt awkward about being aggressive, she didn't let on, and would not admit it to herself. She had this uncanny ability to turn off her emotions and barrel ahead. She wanted to know what had happened, and she was intent on finding out. *What's going on*, she kept asking anyone would listen. *Where's Reenie? Have you seen Reenie Ruggiero?* Girls were crying, and some boys were using their hands to mimic playing a guitar.

"Who's Reenie Ruggiero?" Toni drew her hands up to cover her mouth. "You mean you don't know what happened," she mumbled. Her eyes grew larger while she looked at Cookie with a mixture of incredulity and haughtiness. Toni prided herself at always being *in the know*, and the girls she surrounded herself with had no other purpose than to act as minions to her greatness. She gesticulated her arms as if she was a priest delivering a sermon. "Jimi Hendrix is dead. His body was found in a hotel in Paris."

Toni folded her arms and continued her sermon in an imperious tone. "I don't like his music, but half the boys I know want to be just like him."

Cookie frantically scanned the faces in the crowd, searching for Reenie. "Has anyone seen Reenie?"

Cookie knew since grade school Reenie had proclaimed herself to be a lover of all things black: soul food, black music, the Black Panthers, Bobby Seale, the *Black is Beautiful* movement, the first black Congresswoman, Shirley Chisholm, and especially Jimi Hendrix.

Anna Maria Scarpino stepped forward like an acolyte serving Toni Ferlinghetti by providing her with inside information. "Raoul Montego hung out with Jimi Hendrix when he came to visit here last summer. That's why there was a photo of him in Jimi Hendrix's *Band of Gypsies* album."

The son of a preacher, Raoul Montego was a something of a Yonkers legend in the 1970s and on the road to making it out of Yonkers. The photo showed Raoul Montego under a lone spotlight in the audience of the Fillmore East in New York City, where the *Band of Gypsies* album was recorded. Only someone who was in the good graces of Jimi Hendrix could get to be featured in his *Band of Gypsies* album. There was no doubt about it, Raoul Montego had become a legend in his own time.

"So what's the big deal!" Toni stomped her foot on the ground. "I didn't like his music." Cookie knew the truth about Toni Ferlinghetti. What she really didn't like about Jimi Hendrix was the fact that he was black. Sacred Heart School had a few black kids. Out of 1,200 students, a handful, maybe a dozen, were black and they were not acknowledged by Toni Ferlinghetti, any more than she acknowledged the woeful existence of the too-white Italian girl Cookie Colangelo.

"Jimi Hendrix is black. Raoul Montego's black." Toni said, as if no one had noticed that one small detail. "They're both coons! What am I supposed to care about niggers or something?" She hissed under her breath. "I just don't like his music. I don't have to like it. I like the Allman Brothers and Led Zeppelin. They are my main bands."

"The Allman Brothers," the Italian girls crooned, nodding, still carrying on like a glee club of sob sisters.

"My main guys," Toni herself seemed to be on the verge of swooning.

Cookie knew that these girls didn't care so much about anything, not even the passing of Jimi Hendrix. They were

Italian girls, and they were passionately in love with only two things: themselves and drama. They would cry about anything.

Trying to find Reenie, Cookie pushed her way through throngs of crying girls. She moved through the crowd, shoving people to the side, motioning them to get out of her way.

It was easy to spot Reenie. All the other Italian girls straightened their hair. It takes a certain toughness to sleep with empty beer cans on top of your head just to get *Big Sexy Hair*. Some Italian girls ironed their hair the way their mothers ironed cotton bed sheets. Reenie's hair was parted on the side in a thick wavy weave verging on frizzy in a mock attempt to create an afro. Cookie found her leaning against the trunk of an ancient Maple tree.

While all the other Italian girls were bawling their eyes out, Reenie wasn't crying. She stood there, her eyes un-blinking, not seeing anything. Her too-tan face was pinched in pain. She was in shock. *Sly and the Family Stone* stickers were stuck all over her red leatherette-and-plaid book bag. Her small red lunchbox was lying on the ground, as if she had dropped it by mistake.

Cookie picked up her lunchbox and handed it to her. "Are you okay, Reenie?"

The girl's eyes looked vacant, like the lights had turned off, and she seemed to be holding her breath. She didn't take the lunchbox from Cookie's hands, so Cookie set it down on the ground by her feet.

"Oh shit, look who's coming," Toni shrieked. "Let's get out of here; he's going to say, we're loitering and up to no good."

The Italian girls scattered apart like racing storm clouds, moving as fast as they could so they could not be identified by the Vice Principal, Frank Della Croce, also known as *Mr. DC*.

Cookie failed to heed the early warning system, and was stuck with the fallout. Mr. DC swooped in-between Cookie and Reenie Ruggerio. He looked at Reenie and nodded, then turned his attention exclusively on Cookie. "Getting into trouble again,

Colangelo! Aren't you supposed to be in the building by now? What's the matter with you? You're supposed to be in detention, and instead, you're out here trying to get another girl in trouble!"

"I'm just trying to talk to her!" Cookie protested. She didn't know how to explain to him that her friend was devastated over the death of Jimi Hendrix and she wanted to be there for her. "Please, let me talk to her!"

"Just ignore her," he yelled at Reenie, who stood still and was in shock like the tender rendering of a young tree who had shed its leaves for the first time. "Got that! Colangelo is a bad influence."

"You're coming with me, Colangelo." Mr. DC grabbed Cookie by the collar of her uniform jacket and prodded her toward the front door of the school. "Get moving, Colangelo. Get inside now, before you have another two hours of detention."

She didn't like the rough way Mr. DC handled her. She shrugged her shoulder, trying to remove the imprint of his touch. She turned back to see what had happened to Reenie, but she was gone. Cookie trudged into the entrance of the building. Instead of heading to her lockers in the A-building, she skipped backwards, retreated to the older B-building and searched for a seat in the detention room. It was the second week of school and she had already served two hours. Detention meant sitting still at a desk. No writing. No reading. No homework. She was stuck doing nothing.

She opened the door leading into a small classroom that was crammed full of desks. There were rows of desks six lines across, ten desks to a line. Each desk had a flat top for writing and a side compartment to stuff in one's books and meager possessions. Girls were not allowed to keep makeup or cigarettes at their desk. Cookie craved a *Marlboro*. She had a pack in her locker. Most of the Italian girls met together first thing in the morning in front of school or in the school parking lot to have a smoke. Cookie kept her black & white notebook on top of the desk. If she had a chance, she would sneak in a sentence or two about Andrea Verrone, the main character in her new book.

Mr. DC sat on a raised chair in front of the class. He had slicked back his dark brown hair with Brylcreem in a greasy pompadour that looked wet and shiny, with a few strands falling forward onto his forehead. Sharp nose, small brown eyes and 1950s greaser-style hair, he looked to be Italian, the older generation before the rise of hippies, bell bottoms and the war in Vietnam. He was so uncool. All of the boys Cookie liked wore extra long bell bottoms that dragged along the ground. Mr. DC wore pants so short that they exposed his doofus athletic socks. He was a dork, a throw-back to another era before the summer of love in Haight Ashbury and the Woodstock Music Festival changed the world. He looked around the room while he read the names of the students who were in the detention room. He seemed to be searching for something and found Cookie Colangelo before he even said her name. He stared at her like he had a grand plan. Then he called her last name. "Colangelo, big clown," he said. "Big clown. You're a big clown, Colangelo."

Cookie sat in her seat and looked neither right nor left. She especially avoided the gaze of Mr. DC who seemed to be trying to make eye contact.

Mr. DC scanned his list for who was next and called out, "Mary Mancuso."

Mary suddenly sat upright with rapt attention. She wore the green plaid of a sophomore, and had dark brown hair that was parted in the middle, with two streaks of bleached blonde hair falling forward on both sides of her face. She rose from her desk and let her arms hang on either side of her torso like she was ashamed of herself. She was looking down at the floor as if she was waiting for Mr. DC to give her permission to leave.

"Go on, Mancuso," he said. "Just because your brother died, doesn't mean you get time off for good behavior. Sit down."

"For those of you who don't know, Mary Mancuso's brother...," his voice trailed off. "What was his name?"

"Frank," the girl said softly.

"Nice name, I like it. Where did I hear that name before?" Mr. DC scoffed. He was kidding her because his name was Frank too. "What you should know is that Frank Mancuso was killed in action in Vietnam. He was serving our great country to protect our freedom. When you get a chance, please offer your prayers for everyone in Mary's family."

Mary Mancuso bowed her head and closed her eyes. The room was so quiet, Cookie thought everyone could hear the sound of her own heart. It wasn't enough for Jimi Hendrix to have died today, and the *Blind Owl* to have died two weeks ago. Death was everywhere, and striking close to home. And while Mary Mancuso's brother had died in place thousands of miles away, Cookie couldn't ignore the fact that the Vietnam War was a symbol of everything she thought was wrong with Yonkers and the injustice in the entire world, including the racial tension, the slums, the nuns, her 'hood, her home and the Italian girls. She did not want to be here, and hoped someday the memory of this day, and every day she spent in Yonkers would be forever erased.

Cookie reached for her notebook and flipped through the pages to find one of her poems. She had written the poem with a *Bic* blue ink ball point pen that skipped across the page. Some of the words in the poem were crossed-out and replaced with new words.

Soldier Boy

You're a soldier boy now, you've learned to kill.
They have made you a murderer with their advanced technique and skill.
You'll fly away in an airplane from your home.
Then you'll be let loose in a jungle free to roam.
A shot from nowhere has hit you in the dark.
In your weary body it has made a fatal mark.

She felt a sudden jerk; a hand had grabbed her by the collar of

her jacket and yanked her out of her seat. Mr. DC had the finesse
of an ill-bred Italian boy from the 'hood, which is a nice way to
suggest that he was a Neanderthal and a complete jerk. With
one hand, he held her by the collar, while his other hand tried to
snatch her black & white composition book, but Cookie wouldn't
let go. She held the book away from him and pressed it against
her chest barely covering the two little knobs she had developed
for breasts. Mr. DC moved slightly to the side and backed off.
He looked around, as if he did not want to get caught grabbing
the notebook that she clutched to her breasts. He nudged her to
the door. "Colangelo, you're coming with me." He turned to the
class. "If I hear one sound, just one sound from this room, then
everyone is staying for an extra hour of detention."

Mr. DC led Cookie through the hall. He had let go of her
collar, but he had not lost sight of the notebook. He walked
ahead, expecting her to follow his lead. Into the orbit of the
circular A-building, he led her into a stairwell and quickly
moved up the steps. Rising higher and higher, Cookie was
going to floors where she had never been. Until now, she had
never known this part of the building even existed. He walked
ahead of her. "Where are we going," she called out, but he did
not answer her. She continued to clutch the black & white
notebook to her chest.

His oversized suit jacket was open and flapped, cape-like,
behind him. Mr. DC led her to a portion of the hall where
the lights had dimmed or were turned off. He stopped for a
moment, turned around and prodded her to stand against a
door. He placed his hand above her head and rested it against
the wall. This was the closest she had ever been to Mr. DC, or
to any man who was not her father. She had been this close
to Herman Lynch, but that didn't count because he was her
dear friend. She felt trapped, and a small lump formed in
her throat. She could smell his scent. He was wearing some
cologne or aftershave. From her forays into the department
stores in Getty Square, she recognized the scent as *Brut,* the

same fragrance that was worn by sports stars like Joe Namath. Wilt Chamberlain and Muhammad Ali. One of Muhammad Ali's lines popped into her head, like a meditation meant to keep her safe. *Float like a butterfly, sting like a bee.*

Mr. DC looked down at her, giving her the once over. "Colangelo, why are you always in detention? School's just started, and you're here all the time. What's the big problem?"

He leaned down, closer still. He was almost eye-level with her now. He lowered his voice and asked, "Are you in love with me? Is that what it is? You figure, by getting into detention, you get to see me? You love me, don't you?" He tried to pull the notebook out of her hands.

But Cookie would not let go. "I'm not giving it to you. You're not getting my notebook. I'll scream at the top of my lungs!" She felt herself on the verge of exploding. She'd kill him before she'd let him get her notebook.

Mr. DC backed up. Whatever she did worked, and he dropped his hand from the wall. She thought that any minute now, he would hit her. It wouldn't be the first time she had been assaulted by a teacher.

He wanted something from her, and if she did not want it, well that was too bad. "You love me," he insisted. He was toying with her. He touched the bottom of her chin and tilted her head up to be closer to his face.

"You were late again." His smile was a tad nasty, a smirk. He was making fun of her. "You like me. Isn't that what's going on with you?"

Cookie turned her head away from him and toward the wall. She closed her eyes and tightened her grip around her notebook.

"Why are you late for school so much? And you're getting in trouble with the sisters all the time."

Cookie didn't want to tell him she was late because she had to get Donny off to school in the morning. She didn't want to talk about her family. "Did you know that Jimi Hendrix is dead?" she asked him.

"Think I care about somebody like that? This country is getting ruined on account of people like that. Know what I mean?"

Cookie opened her eyes and looked at him. For the first time, she noticed his eyes drilling a hole through her, like he was going to harm her. He had a watery gleam in his eyes—two fishy pods of deep pools where there was no soul at the bottom. He was going to hurt her. And there was no way she could get away from him.

Mr. DC looked like he was pretending to care about what happened to her. "Don't you have parents?"

My parents are dead, Cookie wanted to say, but she didn't. Nor did she tell him that her mother was in the hospital, and that she had to take care of Donny because her father worked all the time.

Cookie gave him a hardened look. She felt embarrassed, but she knew what he was asking wasn't right, and it wasn't any of his business. She didn't know why he had taken her into some hidden part of the building where no one else was around. She scoffed, shook her head and tried to chuckle, but it backfired and she ended up making a strained sound like a small snort. She was feeling so awkward that she accidentally began to laugh in his face. She wasn't laughing at him. It was nervous laughter. She was dying inside, but no tears would come, and in this instance, that was a good thing.

He leaned in and pulled her closer to him. She clenched her teeth, narrowed her eyes to a squint and shuddered. She could detect his warm breath that bore the strange scent of an empty stomach belonging to someone who had not eaten all day. The sensation was mildly unpleasant and warm, tickling her nose with an itch she wanted to get rid of, but his face was leaning in toward her, his lips smacking forward. She jerked her face away from him and turned her head sharply to the side. She felt his tongue smash against the side of her cheek. She closed her eyes as if she had indeed been stung by a bee. "Gross," was all she said. She turned ever so slightly to look at him. He was red in the face. *That was so disgusting*, she thought to herself. Then she completely turned her face away from him.

He shoved her forward, a small push that centered on the heart of her black & white composition book. It wasn't enough to hurt her, but it bruised her heart in ways she could not yet explain. Then he stomped off, flapping his jacket and trailing a subtle mixture of *Brut* and *Brylcreem*. Her ears burned with humiliation. She trailed behind Mr. DC, six arm-lengths away, wanting to cry out, call out for something, but she didn't know what she needed. His pace picked up as if he wanted to get away from her. She found herself scrambling to keep up so she wouldn't get into more trouble than she was already in.

Later, she would realize that instead of running to save her life, she had given others the impression that she was chasing after him. This small fact, mounted along with other small incidents, led to her downward spiral and eventual expulsion from school. No one could rescue her from the situation, and she did not know whether she wanted to be rescued. She didn't know what had happened. She didn't know why he had taken her to a remote corner of the building and had tried to kiss her. She didn't know what to say to him now, or ever again. *The fucking greaseball,* she thought to herself. *The audacity to think that she would love him was too much to bear.* It was Friday, September 18, 1970, the day that Jimi Hendrix died, and close to Cookie's fourteenth birthday.

Twenty-three

Schizophrenia Ebbs and Flows

Kitty returned home from the nuthouse with little fanfare, bearing small gifts, a small wooden box edged with hammered bronze metal, lacquered with bright blue buttons, and a pale blue statue of an angel made from plaster of paris. She handed the box to Cookie. "For your *Marlboros* and your hash pipe."

Donny took the angel from Kitty, gave it a kiss and put it in her pocket. Both gifts were art projects Kitty had made while she was in the nuthouse. She had been gone for three weeks and had put on weight. Cookie estimated her mother had gained about twenty pounds, which meant she looked like her normal sexy self. Prior to her hospitalization she had stopped eating, dropped below ninety pounds, and grew skeletal and sunken-eyed. A wild-eyed apparition had cautioned her that all of the food in the house was poisoned, and that if she ate, she would die a slow and agonizing death.

The stereo in the living room played *Autumn Leaves* with one of Johnny's favorite jazz musicians, the saxophonist Cannonball Adderley, who had once played music with Ray Charles. Johnny knew these guys and played music with them on the upper west side of Manhattan.

"I was only gone for three weeks," Kitty said. "They just kept me for three weeks. They keep some people for years. I'm not that bad. A lot of people are worse off than I am. Three weeks is not a long time to be in the hospital."

Kitty moved around the house in sync with the sexy rhythm of *Autumn Leaves*. Music soothed her, and she responded to the tune as if she would begin floating around the house from room to room in a syncopated waltz turn. She was fluid and funny and gracious while she looked at her daughters, as if the girls were the most prized possessions of her life. She said little, but smiled with such kindness and beauty, it transcended the human realm and seemed to have a healing effect on her daughters. Or maybe Cookie and Donny were waiting with bated breath to make sure that Kitty was genuinely in remission, and not faking sanity just to get out of the nuthouse. She had done this before. She didn't like being in the nuthouse, and knew if she just turned in her art projects on time, she'd be released in a jiffy.

Cookie did not know if her mother had emotions like other people. Nothing seemed to bother her and, at the same time, everything bothered her. It was a paradox, difficult to explain, and we could not know it, nor could we entirely understand it, unless we had experienced it first-hand, happening to someone whom we deeply loved. When Cookie told her mother that the *Blind Owl* had died, Kitty's response was sort of a non-response. The expression on her face was flat, or uninterested, or both, and she asked why he was called the *Blind Owl*. "Didn't he have a real name? Who would do something like that to their child?" Then she dismissed all mention of the *Blind Owl* and went on to ask if any of the neighbors had known she had gone to the hospital.

Fran Ochiogrosso was the only one who had asked about Kitty, but Cookie wasn't about to get into a conversation about it, not even when Kitty bribed her, offering her five bucks for any news from the street. As if five bucks even mattered to

Cookie, when she made so much more money dealing Kitty's seemingly inexhaustible supply of ludes.

Kitty dangled a wrinkled five-dollar bill in front of Cookie and smiled at her daughter. "Look at my little Cookie, she's getting all grown up. That ponytail looks nice on you. It shows the shape of your face. I missed you, honey." She came over to Cookie and gave her a small, childish pat on her back.

Cookie stood up and came to her mother's side. She kissed her twice on her warm cheek that bore the sweetish-trace of *Revlon's Love Pat* face powder in a shade of creamy ivory that raised her Mother's remarkably good skin to a sheen of polished perfection. Her lips were coated with *Elizabeth Arden's* matte lipstick in *Stop Red*. Cookie knew the entire contents of Kitty's cosmetics basket: name, color, brand and quantity; little parts of the sum total that made Kitty, her mother, beautiful. Kitty wore the same brands of cosmetics with the same frequency as she repeated the same bizarre disjointed thoughts when she having a spell and on a rant. Kitty's basket contained at least a hundred gold tubes of *Elizabeth Arden* lipstick in the shade of *Stop Red* that had been worn and used down to the nub.

Kitty was turned out today like the great beauty that turned heads, stopped cars in the middle of Getty Square, and got her to ride on the bus for free. She was wearing a rust-color suede jacket that accentuated the red highlights in her dark auburn hair. She rubbed her nose and smiled at Cookie as if she was going to giggle. Then a funny look came over her face. Looking out the window opening up to the south, the light was strong, much brighter than usual, and she squinted her eyes. That is when she noticed. "The trees," she said. "What happened to the trees?"

"Daddy cut them down," Donny said. Her flare-up from the poison sumac was gone, and her pink skin tone had returned to normal. Her blonde hair had grown long into a wild mass of intricately connected corkscrew curls.

"The Sumac trees are not poisonous," Kitty said. "The trees never have been poisonous." She looked at Cookie and shook her head with confusion. "Why didn't you tell him that, Cookie?"

"She tried to tell him," Donny said. "But he wouldn't listen." Donny giggled.

Kitty threw open the side door and went outside, where at first there was only silence, so preternaturally quiet that it could only be a lethal prediction of what was yet to come. Cookie watched the clock on the top of the Magnavox console TV. A few minutes passed. Cookie and Donny looked at each other. It had been quiet for what seemed to be a long time. And yet both girls knew it not would stay quiet forever. Finally, a single bloodcurdling scream pierced though the clearing that opened to the sky. Formerly the home of Sumac trees, the woods were now a morass of misshapen stumps. Kitty cried out, "The trees are all gone! How could he do such a thing! How could he do such a thing! I can't believe there will be no trees this fall! No leaves will turn color!"

Whatever progress Kitty had made at the hospital seemed to go into instant remission. "All of the trees in Yonkers are gone!"

Kitty's deepest passion wasn't for a man, woman, child, beast or material thing; it was for color: living color, full-throttled and miraculous color, unapologetic, raging riots of color, magnificent color, wheel of light, wheel of life. The happiest day of her life was when Johnny brought home a color TV. She liked hippies because of their tendency to wear colorful clothes. She collected jugs and jars in jewel-tone colors. She was in love with color, in all of its variations, in all seasons, giving definition and meaning to all things, living or dead, yawning open to a new season or closing forever in a tight balled fist of darkness. Her entire life was built on the prospect of seeing the first sign of yellow leaves in an explosion of the sunset or the blue cast of morning, showing a world without shadow until the sun rose in a blossoming sky. She called her front bay window a picture window and filled it with orbs of glass in every color, some rich, bold and solidly-pure, others light, pastel and translucent. By the end of the night, she lost energy in her rant, and her final lament was she had never seen a rainbow, not one.

The day before, when Cookie's mother came home, there was one other event that had happened. In addition to her mother coming home from the hospital, Janis Joplin died from a heroin overdose. So much for *Freedom is just another word for nothing left to lose*, Cookie thought. What good is freedom when you're dead?

Things weren't going well for Cookie at *the Heart*. None of the girls, especially the Italian girls, seemed to like her, except for, maybe, Reenie Ruggiero. The boys spoke in a range of squeaks in falsetto to low-sounding bass notes, depending on where they were in the transition from boy to man. She carried her black & white notebook and kept it close to her chest, as if it was both her breastplate and her shield as she rode into battle each day.

In Cookie's homeroom, the loud speaker crackled a small electric hiss just prior to a voice floating overhead, making an announcement. Even though Cookie had only been in the school for a month, she recognized the voice of the principal, Sister Hilda Marie. "Concetta Mary Colangelo, please come to the office," she said. The intercom popped off, making a metallic grating sound as if the microphone on the other end had been accidentally bumped.

Cookie's ears felt hot, as if she had done something wrong. Even if she had not done anything wrong, feeling like she was wrong about everything had become the real story of her life. What she wrote about in her notebook was a subdued reflection of the pain, angst and unfairness of it all that she suffered every day. Forces out of her control made her responsible for everything that went wrong. *I'm not that bad*, she told herself, *and I'm so sick of things that are unfair!* She shook her fist slightly in the air, then lowered her arm and kept her knotty hand from forming a real fist. She pressed her flat palm close to her leg. Cookie was especially angry that the nun had dropped "*Bernadette*" from the litany of her names. It was as if the nun had arbitrarily offed another saint from the *Canon of Saints*.

Concetta was Cookie's given name, and she hated it! *Concetta is the Italian cognate of Concepción, like I'm the fucking Virgin Mary,* Cookie thought to herself. *I hate my parents for giving me this name.* Everyone called her "Cookie," and she hated that name too. Cookie made her sound like she was the extraneous sweet snack that people eat. People might like cookies, but do not need them to live. Go on a diet and the first thing they'll tell you is, no cookies, not one. *God, I hate my name.* Johnny's sister Ro-Ro started calling her *Cookie* because she wanted to get back at Johnny for giving her a nickname. Ro-Ro had also observed that Cookie loved cookies in all shapes and sizes, from basic white bread chocolate chip cookies to *Stella d'oro* Italian biscuits made in the Bronx, and her own homemade pizzelles.

That was Cookie, *Concetta Mary Bernadette Colangelo*. Truth be told, Bernadette was not her given name. It was her Roman Catholic name chosen for her Confirmation. Cookie liked it enough to make it part of her whole name. When she was six, she wanted to be Saint Bernadette of Lourdes. Note that she didn't indicate that she wanted to be like Saint Bernadette. She wanted to actually be Saint Bernadette. Cookie liked the clothes she wore, especially when Jennifer Jones played the role of Saint Bernadette. She wore a woolen head wrap in baby blue, to match the color of her eyes.

Saint Bernadette was so pure, wise, noble, good and true that after she was laid to rest, her body was placed under glass and her flesh turned to wax. The body of St. Bernadette Soubirous is in a glass coffin and on display for all the world to see at the Sanctuary of Our Lady of Lourdes, in Lourdes, France.

Back in her pious Catholic good-girl phase, Cookie used to pray to Saint Bernadette. *Bernadette, you who are a saint, so pure, wise, noble, good and true, help me be good today. Help Mommy get better. Help Daddy come home. Help keep my Donny girl safe.*

Saint Bernadette was dead now. In Cookie's mind, she wasn't preserved in wax and under glass. Bernadette had died the same day Cookie had experienced the earth shattering event that had irreversibly changed her life. Bernadette had died on November 6, 1967, when being a good girl made no difference at all.

Cookie's rubber-soled *Bass Weejuns* squeaked in small skips along the linoleum floor. She took her notebook and brushed it against the flat, pale-green painted cinderblock walls. She took the notebook with her everywhere, just in case she wanted to write something that popped into her head. By the time she arrived at the principal's office, she decided permanently and irrevocably to remove *Bernadette* from her litany of names.

Cookie used to pray to Saint Bernadette, but she wasn't praying now as she approached Sister Hilda Marie's big, fat oval office. She walked into the back room behind the admissions desk, where the nun was seated next to a large stack of paperwork. An open file on her desk had **Colangelo** written in capital letters by a black magic marker. A large black wood crucifix was nailed to the wall behind her chair. The nun said, *"Concetta Mary Bernadette Colangelo."*

Cookie closed her eyes with mock disbelief. "You can drop the *Bernadette*. People just call me Cookie."

Sister Hilda Marie was taken aback. Her face locked into an expression harsher than stern. "Please sit down. I have something important to say to you."

Cookie did as she was told, and hardly swallowed. She realized her palms felt damp for no good reason. Even her feet in her loose-fitting *Bass Weejuns* felt clammy. She wasn't going to allow herself to be scared.

"Let's start with a silent prayer," the nun said. "Silent," she emphasized. The nun bowed her head and closed her eyes. When she looked up, Cookie was looking at her with a mixture of baleful anticipation and confusion, wondering what would come next.

"I'm sorry to tell you this," the nun said slowly, haltingly, "but we've received some bad news." The nun looked away and closed her eyes as if she was uncomfortable. "We've received a report that your brother has been killed in action."

Cookie closed her eyes. She was truly pained, and did not know what to say. "Uh. I don't know." Cookie raised her eyebrows, cleared her throat and tried to say something, but the words would not come.

"He died in Vietnam," the nun continued, "in a place called the Shau Valley, close to the border of Laos."

"I don't have a brother," Cookie haltingly told the nun. "No brother. I don't have a brother."

The nun read from a file on her desk. "His body is being returned to the United States." The nun looked up at Cookie. "Your family will be able to have a Catholic burial."

Cookie shook her head. "I'm sorry, Sister, but I don't have a brother. I've never had a brother."

The nun didn't say anything. She looked down at her file and seemed to be reading, then glanced up at Cookie. She adjusted her clear wire-framed glasses that were balanced on the tip of her nose and scrutinized Cookie. "What about your father?" The nun suggested. "You do have a father, don't you?"

"I do have a father," Cookie said and by saying that, she felt like she had made an ugly admission of guilt.

"Well, of course, you must have a father." The nun shifted in her seat and looked at the large console phone on her desk that had many buttons for extensions to other administrative offices and classrooms. Two orange and yellow lights were blinking as if those lines were in use.

"What's this got to do with my father?"

The nun dropped her head and jutted her jaw forward to make sure Cookie understood the gravity of the situation. "Your father was killed in action in Vietnam."

"Okay," Cookie looked around the room, trying to think of the right thing to say. She felt bad, even though she knew it could not be true…, or was it true? The news stunned her. She had to verify in her own mind, if only for a few seconds, thinking Johnny might have run off on a half-cocked mission to Vietnam. No, it could not be true. It could not be real. There were no jazz studios in the jungles and rice paddies of Vietnam.

"I know my father hasn't been home in a while," she told the nun. "But the last time I saw him he wasn't wearing a uniform or carrying an M-16."

The nun looked at her as if she thought Cookie was lying. "I'm very sorry," the nun insisted. "I will alert Father Dunn. He is your parish priest, isn't he?"

"Sister, you're not listening to me. My father's not dead! You've made a mistake!"

"I think you need to be in a quiet place. The chapel is being used by a large group, so you can't go in there."

"My father's not even in Vietnam!"

The nun shook her head as if she was both sorry and frustrated that Cookie had lost her mind. She did the only thing she could do. She sent Cookie to detention with Mr. DC. "It's room 101," she told Cookie. "You need a place to be quiet so you can gain control over yourself."

The nun picked up the microphone on her desk for the intercom system and called Mr. DC. "Miss Colangelo will be joining your detention for the next hour." Then she turned to Cookie. "Now go. Mr. DC will look after you until your mother arrives."

"I'm not going to detention. My father's not dead and my mother's crazy. You've made a mistake," was all Cookie could say, but the nun would not hear of it.

"You won't be returning to your homeroom today," Sister Hilda Marie said. "Your family will come by to pick you up. Then she spoke into the intercom, presumably to Mr. DC. "Please let me know when she arrives, and if she isn't there in five minutes, I will go looking for her." With a hiss and a click, the intercom went silent.

Cookie wasn't the only Colangelo who went to Sacred Heart High School. When the other *Colangelos* arrived and Sister Hilda Marie learned she had delivered shocking news to the wrong next of kin, she came into the detention room and had Cookie released, without providing any sort of explanation to Mr. DC. So even though Cookie had not done anything wrong, in Mr. DC's eyes she had further established her increasingly stellar track record as a bad girl. No one apologized to Cookie for the case of mistaken identity. It was pushed aside as if it had not happened. In some ways it had not happened, because Cookie responded with her usual methodology of pushing it out of her mind. *Stop*, she told herself and that always worked.

She did resolve to write more anti-war poetry to memorialize her *dead brother* and her *dead father*.

Cookie was more concerned about losing another famous rock star. In one month, the *Blind Owl* was joined in death by Jimi Hendrix and Janis Joplin. Years later, the trio, along with Rolling Stone Brian Jones, would form the foundation of the infamously tragic "27 Club," commemorating the unusually high number of famous musicians who tragically died at age 27.

After school, outside on the wall in front of *the Heart*, everyone was smoking *Marlboros* and talking up the latest news in a sorry string of rock star deaths. Janis Joplin was close to coming out with a new album and had just released a new song on the radio, *Mercedes Benz*.

"I didn't know how she could have had a new song come out on the radio the day before she died," Cookie told Reenie Ruggiero. "*Mercedes Benz.*"

Reenie had no regrets. "She was a black woman trapped in a white body. That's why she killed herself. It hurts too bad when you don't look like what you don't feel inside."

"Tell me about it," Cookie said. "I'm really a gangster and a hippie trapped in this," she said pulling on the lapels of her maroon wool uniform jacket. Cookie began rolling the waistband of her skirt to shorten its length and show some leg. "I've never seen a Mercedes Benz I didn't like. At least I don't think so. I don't even know what one would look like. Where do I find a picture of one, so I know what I'm going to ride in someday when I'm famous?"

"Yes you do," Reenie laughed. "You know what Mercedes look like. Those cars are everywhere in Yonkers!" The two girls laughed at the impossible image of rich cars cruising *Down the End* or through *Ghetto Square*. Both girls jumped around and made clicking noises, pretending to drive, pushing down the buttons to lock their car doors and thwart muggers and murderers. Pretending to *Zoom* and *Vroom*, their hands locked around a steering wheel while their heads were turning, looking into the rear view mirror.

"My uncle Bill used to carry a baseball bat in the back of his car when he made deliveries in south Yonkers," Reenie said. "And he just drove a Nash Rambler." Imagine if he drove a Mercedes Benz. He'd be stripped, his hood, his tires and his radio."

"He'd get rocked around on his wheels and be eaten alive for breakfast," Cookie laughed.

Both girls launched into whining chorus of *Oh Lord, won't you buy me a Mercedes Benz?*

Cookie pondered the reality that Janis Joplin was dead and lying stone-cold in a morgue in Hollywood, California. So much for being famous and a rock star. Another dead rock star made Cookie feel claustrophobic. And yet, if becoming famous was the only way out of Yonkers, she decided then and there she would rather be dead and famous than alive and stuck in Yonkers.

"I'm going to be famous," Cookie blurted out.

"Me too," Reenie agreed.

"Famous you are, Cookie Colangelo. You're famous to me." Mike Trapani sat down on the wall next to Reenie, with his white man-tailored Catholic schoolboy shirt half hanging out from his pants, like it was a sail billowing from a dark pirate ship. "Famous," he said. "Why does everyone want to be a rock star? What's wrong with being a plumber, like my Dad? He went to Saunders. Next year, I'm going to Saunders too."

Saunders High School was a school for boys to learn trades like plumbing or carpentry. At Commerce High School, girls learned how to be office workers and beauticians. By the time Yonkers kids turned fourteen, the kids had to decide whether they were going to learn a trade or go to college, or they could slog through school for two more years and drop out. Most kids in Yonkers were destined to ride in limos only for high school proms, working-class weddings, and funerals. That's the only chance they got to sit in a limousine, looking like they were somebody. The die was cast for the working-class young, regardless whether they became famous and ended up dead.

Mike Trapani did his best to engage Cookie. "Don't you care about the World Series? Who are you going to root for?"

"You first," Reenie said, like she was trying to be polite.

"I asked Cookie," Mike said. "Not you."

Cookie thought he was being nasty to Reenie on purpose. "We asked you first."

"I'm going for the Orioles," Mike said.

"The Reds!" The girls looked at each other and smirked, nudging each other, giving the high-five.

The 1970 World Series pitted the American League champion Baltimore Orioles against the National League champion Cincinnati Reds, but Cookie knew both she and Reenie didn't care about who won, and picked the team Mike Trapani didn't want to win on purpose. Cookie watched Mike Trapani while he lit a *Marlboro* and blew a cotton candy puff of smoke, betraying that he had not been smoking for very long and was trying to be cool.

Cookie was an experienced smoker. When she was 11 years old, she bought her first pack of cigarettes for forty cents at Morsemere Market *Down the End*. She looked at Mike Trapani with disdain and scrutinized every inch of him from his beefy forearms to his thick neck and his thunder thighs, and decided, without asking him to bend over that he had already formed a youthful and premature version of plumber's crack. Cookie thought of telling him to bend over to see his crack rise from the seat of his pants. She could be mean when she wanted to be.

"Saw you chasing after Mr. DC," Mike Trapani chided her. "Why do all the girls have the *hots* for him? I think I'm missing the point or something. Or I'm missing out on something. I just don't get it."

Cookie was beside herself. "You've got it all wrong, Mike Trapani. I think he's a creep." How could she explain the long walk out on the gangplank in the off-limits floor of the A-building when he tried to kiss her and accused her of being in love with him? She gritted her teeth and retched at the memory of his *Brut, Brylcreem* and bad breath. No one would believe her. She was only a freshman in high school. Who was going to take her word over his?

Every day since school had started, Mike Trapani was waiting for her after school and she was sick of it. She didn't know how to get rid of him. Cookie pulled out her red crush proof pack of *Marlboros,* where she also packed her matches. Students could smoke cigarettes anywhere they wanted around the school, even on the playground. Only drinking and drugs were banned, but Lennon Park was a stone's throw away. Every morning, gangs of kids would throng together in the park and smoke pot before school started.

Just before Cookie struck her own match, Mike Trapani beat her to it. He quickly struck a match, cupped his hands, leaned forward and lit her cigarette. He sat down next to her. His big thigh moved close enough to touch her skirt.

"Mr. DC seems like an okay enough guy," Mike said. "He's got it out for you. What is it between you guys?"

Cookie took a long breath and looked away. She couldn't share what happened to her. *Stop*, she told herself and it worked.

"Why are you always carrying that notebook?" He looked over her shoulder as if he was going to reach for it. "What's in it?"

Cookie pulled away from him and moved her notebook to rest on her arm and away from him.

"She's writing a book," Reenie said.

"A book," Mike shot a stream of smoke in her direction. "No kidding. What's it about?"

Cookie shook her head to change the subject. "None of your business."

"No one knows the title," Reenie said. "It's probably about being young and understood."

"Misunderstood," Cookie corrected her.

Ignoring Reenie, Mike looked at Cookie and gave her a big grin that made him look like a wet-kisser. "What do you say? We stay here for a while? Maybe you'll show me your book?"

Cookie's hair felt electrified, unraveling from her pony tail. She reached around the back of her head to see if her rubber band was still intact. Her brown hair was separating into wide sheaths and drifting down to the middle of her back.

Mike lunged forward and put his arm around Cookie's waist. She moved away from him but he moved along her side and she felt this awful realization, true embarrassment; she did not know what to do. He couldn't be for real. Why do boys do this? Why can't they only go after girls who want them? Then Cookie realized no one wanted Mike Trapani. Ramming himself against an unwilling girl was as good as it was going to get.

Reenie did not appreciate being ignored. "I'm outa here." She was so mad, she snorted, stuffed her schoolbooks under her arm and stomped off.

"Please don't leave me, Reenie!"

Reenie turned her head to acknowledge that she had heard her, then gave her a quick fisheye that meant there was no turning back. She didn't bother to turn her head all the way around to look at her and kept moving forward.

"Some friend," Cookie yelled.

Mike snuck his barrel-shaped head onto Cookie's shoulder and crooned into her ear. "Come on and hang out with me for a while."

Cooke felt like she was cornered by a huge, wild animal. She moved ever so slowly, one leg at a time, smoothing down every pleat on her plaid uniform skirt, which felt as open and as wide as a fan. She would pursue a quiet escape from the wall before Mike Trapani made the big push and pawed his way to a wet dream. Her legs were about to jump off the wall, but Mike's squirrely hand toyed with the tassels on her loafers and she almost tripped over his arm. Then he grabbed her ankles and locked them in a firm grip. She thought of the possibility of rescue and looked for her friend, but Reenie Ruggiero was long gone.

It was in the heat of this awkward moment that Mike kissed her neck and tried to cop a feel. He squirmed as though his entire destiny would be measured by his involuntary pelvic spasms rocking forward. He clobbered his head into hers and found himself stopped by her heap of unraveling hair. She knew there was no way she was going to extricate herself from the situation without a physical fight. He put his arm around her waist. She pushed him off. He took her hand. She shook it free. He kissed her cheek and left moist residue. She brushed her cheek with the raw wool sleeve of her uniform jacket. He grinned with a wide-open mouth, showing his teeth yellow with plague. His big, round face moved in so fast, she could feel his hot breath on her chin. His lips puckered-up for final impact and he promptly planted a kiss on the entire area circumventing her mouth and nose.

It was as if someone had thrown battery acid in her face. She wiped her face with both hands, stood up and yelled, "Oh gross!"

The only attention to her yell was from a passing yellow Mustang, now slowing down long enough for Cookie to see the driver. Mr. DC looked at her, shaking his head with revolt, disapproval, and the certain affirmation of what measures he would soon take. Cookie could have died right then and there. Mr. DC narrowed his uncommonly small brown eyes; he had it in for her, and there was no telling what he would do. She was so distracted that she did not see what Mike Trapani was doing. By the time she glanced back to the wall, Mike Trapani held his two hands up in the air and smiled. He was holding onto her notebook and had no intention of letting it go.

Twenty-four

In the Owl Hole

Cookie had come to grips with what Herman Lynch meant to her. He looked funny, but the way he moved physically spoke to the feelings she wrote about in her poems. He was always in motion, stretching out his arms, making them seem yards long and fanning all five of his fingers, opening like flowers and reaching for a generous sun. He walked softly, but at the same time he was impossibly strong and could jump straight up into the air or leap forwards, sometimes backwards, or to the side, with great force, sheer abandon, and totally out of the blue. Every move he made was full of the grace inherent in the way he spoke and looked at life, at all things, and especially the way he looked at Cookie. There was something about him so honest and so vulnerable that he touched her in a place where no one else could.

And yet Herman and Cookie never touched one another in a way that pushed them to become more than friends. As much as Herman showed lyrical beauty in the way he moved, he was as closed with his body as she was closed with her own physicality that had made her a talented physical specimen, a tomboy. Herman and Cookie passed a *Marlboro* back and forth between them as if it was the same as sharing a joint.

Herman and Cookie were hanging out in the *Owl Hole*. Hanging out was more fun than going to a high school dance or a party. When you hung out, you never knew who would turn up or what would happen. There were no rules. Hanging out was more than a way to keep watch and to see who was making the scene; it was a way to keep score of who did what to whom, and a way to talk from your heart and not worry about having the wrong person doing all of the listening, or for that matter, doing all of the talking. Hanging out was more than the best way to be seen; it was the best time to share the stories that needed to be told.

The Owl Hole was a different sort of hangout, though. It was not a public place—to be seen, or where anyone could easily find you. Here you hid. You came here on purpose to hide, to think and to decide when and what you should do to put up with this world. At first, Cookie resented one more person knowing about the existence of the *Owl Hole*. She had been reluctant to share her lair with Reenie Ruggiero, but it was the best place to smoke pot in secrecy. Introducing Herman Lynch to the *Owl Hole* seemed the best way to keep him safely hidden in the white North End neighborhood.

Cookie had told Herman what had happened with Mr. DC at school, and he didn't know what to make of it. "Nothing like that's ever happened to me. What's going on with that dude? I don't understand why he keeps picking on you like that."

"I don't want to go to *the Heart* no more," Cookie said. "Mr. DC has it out for me. The girls hate me, and Mike Trapani took my notebook. I'll never be able to write those poems the same way again. My poems are gone and I don't know how to get my book back."

"You've got to get it back from him," Herman said. "That's not right. Go tell the principal. He can't just take something from you!"

Cookie dropped the butt, stamped it out with her foot and nudged it toward the small graveyard of cigarette butts that had formed on the dirt floor.

Herman nodded and smiled, curling up his entire mouth into the shape of a question mark. "Yo, Cookie? Those guys are all after you, that's all. Forget about it. Take a stand. You can handle it. I'm rooting for you. You're tough. Those dudes have no business messing with you."

"What do they want with me?" Cookie shrugged her shoulders. "I mean I look like I'm twelve."

"No, you don't. Not any more. Look at yourself, girl. You're growing up. Don't you have a mirror where you can see yourself? You're so pretty." Herman stood up and looked at her. "Have you taken a good look at yourself lately?"

"It's not true! I'll hit you for saying that, Herman. I don't appreciate bullshit. Never have and never will."

"Take a good look at yourself, girl, and you'll see what I'm talking about. Those guys are after you. That Mr. DC dude and the mama's boy who took your book."

"How do you know he's a mama's boy?"

"Because no boy can get that fat unless he's got a big mama who wants to make him big too." Herman laughed, then he looked at her and grinned. "You're pretty. Must have gotten it from your Mama."

Cookie slugged him on the shoulder, not enough to hurt him, but it startled him. "How could you say such a thing to me! I thought you were my friend!"

"I am your friend." Herman paced around the length of the *Owl Hole* then jumped up on the ledge of the landing and walked the edge, using his arms to balance himself as if he was walking a tightrope. "Just because you're my friend. I can tell you things. I can tell you things that I think are true. Like I see you and think you're real pretty. Your eyes are green and you've got nice hair. And you're built incredibly well. Mighty fine. You're a good looking girl, Cookie Colangelo."

Herman jumped from the ledge and landed squarely on the ground, kicking up a few clumps of dirt and twigs. He sat across from Cookie and crossed his arms. Even though he was sitting, he seemed to be positioning himself to move again. He was always in motion. He waved his arms overhead and then used his hands to trace his feelings in the air. "When I see a beautiful woman, I say to myself, now will you look at her. My, she's beautiful. That's a mighty-fine looking, beautiful woman."

Herman leapt to standing, then turned all the way around in a full circle before sitting back down. "But I feel the same way when I see a man who's handsome. I say to myself that's a mighty fine-looking guy. And I think he's beautiful too. And," he hesitated. "And," he said again. "I like him." He looked at Cookie as if he was saying: *Do you know what I'm trying to say to you?*

Cookie nodded like she understood, but she really didn't understand what he was saying. She didn't know what he was getting at, but she knew whatever it was, it was okay with her.

He looked at Cookie. "I'm not so much attracted to any one person, or guy. I don't know what that means. I don't know what that makes me."

Cookie looked at him and bit her lip. She shook her head. She did not know what he was trying to say, and yet on another level, she did know what he was trying to say. She knew he was saying something really important, but she didn't know how to define what it was.

Herman clasped his hands by his sides and started moving again, swinging his arms like levers. "I don't know what I'm trying to say either. I'm confused about what I feel. I just know that I don't feel that I'm like other guys."

"You're not like other guys," Cookie said. "You're better than that."

"Look, Cookie, I don't believe anyone feels about you the way I do." He looked at her. "You're my friend."

Cookie understood Herman and she nodded to him. "You're my friend too.

"You're not just my friend. You're my only friend." He was walking around, picking up speed into a subtle skip, moving his feet more than any other part of his body. "There are things I want to say to you now, you know. But I don't know how to say them. Maybe you're the one who's going to save me. Maybe you're the one who's going to show me it's okay for me to be who I am." He stopped and looked at her. "I trust you, Cookie. I think of you like I think of my grandmother. I know you're looking out for me."

"No one else is there for us," Cookie laughed. "Maybe we're going to save one another."

No one said anything about leaving, and Herman and Cookie both walked up the steps as if one knew what the other was thinking. As she surfaced from the *Owl Hole*, Cookie sniffed like she thought her nose was running. If what she was feeling was a crying kind of tear or two coming on, she told herself *Stop* and it worked, but it was a little harder to make it stop this time. Herman must have known she was feeling something because he hugged her and gave her a small kiss on the side of her head. His kiss made a funny smacking sound because of his malformed lip. "You're strong, honky. Those guys, don't let them make you crazy or bring you down. You're too good for that."

Herman walked toward North Broadway. He was slightly ahead of her and turned around and looked at her. "What are you going to say? Come on, Cookie!" He stood up and held his arms open, outstretched and reaching to the sky. "What am I? Name it? Come on."

Cookie shook her head, flashing her ponytail across the middle of her back. "I can't."

Herman looked at her for a piercing instant and made contact. "Cookie?"

She got the message and shook her head. "No."

"We all need someone to help us get though tough times. Don't ever forget that. We might be people, but we're really owls. We sit, we watch and we listen. We're always watching. We wait, we wait patiently, then we fly though the air and get what we want." With his arms, he made swooping motions. "Always remember that. When we watch, we figure it all out and know exactly what to do."

Cookie and Herman left the *Owl Hole* together and soared up the secret steps with as much prowess as eastern screech owls fleeing a nest. The North End was only ten minutes from the ghetto, but it might as well have been in another part of the world. Cookie's working-class neighborhood was full of modest homes where not one adult was educated or a professional. No one was a *white-collar worker*, as Kitty had called them. The only *rich* home in the neighborhood belonged to Louie Santamassino. No one was sure how Louie got so rich, and there didn't seem any point in asking too many questions about it. Some women worked outside the home, but their jobs were menial, and these women were shamefully branded as *having to work to make ends meet*. Fran Ochiogrosso was one. She worked as a school crossing guard because her husband was dead.

"I don't feel like I fit in around here." Herman was gesturing in a way that meant he couldn't limit himself to walking. He was always on the verge of twisting or turning, in long-limbed fluidity, stretching the arc of his back like a cat who could dance. And from what Cookie could see, man, could he dance.

Later that day, the two of them left the North End and walked on Walsh Road around the Schlobohm Housing Project *Slow Bomb*. Cookie and Herman were in the heart of the Yonkers Ghetto. Yonkers is different from other cities, and especially New York City, where the rich and poor sit shoulder-to-shoulder in subways and share the same streets. Yonkers is deeply stratified by neighborhood tranches that coexist, but do not meld together. Getty Square or *Ghetto Square* is only a few minutes from the wealthy Park Hill section, but the inhabitants of both areas rarely cross the line. Boundaries marked by skin color and money put an emotional fence around who gets in and who can't get out.

Herman didn't live in the projects, but the only thing he could see from his apartment, which was in the same building as where Reenie Ruggiero lived, were the projects. Cookie had not talked to Reenie since Mike Trapani butted in between them. Girls hate it when a boy shows up and favors one girl more than the other. Even if the girl doesn't like the boy, it still makes her feel bad about herself, as if she has been rejected. Being the one who's been picked like a prom queen is no fun, either. Even though Reenie had to know how much Cookie hated what Mike Trapani had been doing, she still acted like she was feeling rejected. No girl likes being the odd one out, the outcast.

"Why do boys do this?" Cookie wondered aloud to Herman. She had told him what had gone down with Reenie.

"And that's ug-leee, Herman said. "You've got to get your notebook back from that dude."

Herman told Cookie that large groups of kids usually hung-out in the large lot in front of his apartment building, but today mostly everyone was gone. A couple of guys standing close to the sidewalk nodded to Herman and he waved back. He led Cookie to the side entrance of the brick building, across from a narrow alley and next to a side street, Ritters Lane. It's not as if Cookie and Herman were avoiding being seen together. The side entrance was a more direct path to where Herman lived on the first floor. He told Cookie that he expected his grandmother to be around, and although the TV was on, no one was home. Cookie looked around the living room that was dominated by a large overstuffed sofa and book cases. She had never seen so many books in one room. The only other furniture was an armchair with a matching cassock stool and a standing lamp to read by the light. She heard the ticking of a large clock and saw where it was neatly placed on a shelf in the middle of a row of hardbound books.

"My grandmother has so many books that we always have to live on a lower floor." Herman smiled. "It takes too many trips to carry all these boxes up the steps." Herman didn't say anything when he left and disappeared into a kitchen located off of the small living room, or he might have gone to the bathroom.

The sound on the TV was turned down low, but Cookie could see President Nixon giving a televised speech. She strained to hear what he was saying. He seemed to be proposing a cease-fire in Vietnam. Then she heard another sound, whimpering, the crying of a dog. Then she heard a yippy bark. Herman surprised her, walking into the room, carrying a puppy in his arms. "Check it out," he said. The dog had supple floppy ears but the brown and black markings and pointed nose of a German Shepherd.

Cookie took the dog from his arms and hugged him. She put him on the rug, where he ran around in a circle, barking, wagging his tail. He tried to nip at her heels, but they were safely ensconced in her thick-soled *Keds*.

"I think he's starting to teethe," Herman picked him up and held him up to see the inside of his mouth. He cradled him with one arm and playfully placed his fingers in the puppy's mouth so he could chew on them. Then he set him down on the floor where he ran, bounding, on his paws.

"Look how big his paws are," Cookie said. "He's going to be big."

"Do you want him?" Herman asked.

Cookie noticed Herman had put his black-framed glasses on. As much as Cookie would have loved to take the puppy home, she couldn't. A dog would send Kitty over the edge. She couldn't handle pets of any kind, especially dogs. In the past, Cookie had tried. Herman made it clear that he couldn't have a dog in the apartment. Having a large dog would get them kicked out. Cookie didn't understand what he was doing with a dog in the first place. As cute as the puppy was, he started to piddle on the floor right in front of the TV, where on the screen images flickered a wave of anti-war protesters marching on Washington, D.C.

Herman used a paper towel and was cleaning up a small wet circle left on the rug. "I found him in the alley off Summit Street. Somebody dumped him there. Probably left him in a dumpster for dead. Poor puppy. People are always dumping off animals here because we're close to the projects. Cats. Dogs. You name it. When people don't want their animals, they're too lazy to take them to the shelter. Anything that's still alive, but unwanted, ends up here."

Herman and Cookie wondered who might want the puppy and give him a good home. Cookie suggested Reenie, but Herman reminded her that she lived in the same building. They considered other possibilities, but it was a short list. Cookie and Herman didn't know that many people well enough to gift them with a puppy; neither of them had many friends. Amazingly, the name of a potential new owner for the puppy occurred to them both at the same time.

The front entrance of Louie Santamassino's mammoth home faced North Broadway and was located half way between Christ the King School and Untermyer Park. From the street level, the house sat relatively high up from the street on a small cliff, and was constructed entirely of greystone, the chief architectural hallmark of North Yonkers that had once connoted the grandeur of *the city of gracious living*. Although the house looked imposing from the street below, the truly spectacular feature of the home was the sheer size of the property it sat on. Nearly an acre, the backyard of the home was a park-like setting full of Maple, Oak, Sumac and Cedar trees. All year round, varieties of lilies and roses bloomed in the yard, and a professional gardener attended the grounds to keep the lawn green and trim.

The puppy was not doing well on a short leash, so Herman picked him up and rang the doorbell, which resounded like the alto chime sound of a grandfather clock. "Never heard nothing like that before. That's fancy." His eyes were magnified by his coke bottle black-framed glasses as he looked in through the narrow glass window next to the front entry door.

The glass in the front door was etched with the shape of art deco blocks and the branches of trees. No one came to the door, not immediately, and Cookie and Herman waited, not saying anything. It occurred to them that the puppy could be left there by tying his leash to the front doorknob. Both of them seemed to know what the other was thinking, but neither of them posed the question about whether they should just leave the dog there.

Cookie thought it just wasn't right to abandon the dog. As far as anyone knew, the puppy had already been left behind once or twice, and Cookie knew how that felt—to be abandoned. So did Herman. After all, his mother was dead and her mother might as well be dead. And it made Cookie feel guilty for even thinking that way.

When Louie Santamassino came to the door, he didn't immediately open it and invite them in. Cookie could see the shadow of his image close to the narrow glass window. There had to be a peephole that Cookie and Herman could not see. Herman figured Louie had to be seeing them from some other view finder. A mirror? A camera? Cookie looked above the door frame; it was made from a type of wood she had never seen before, and did know its name. One day, Cookie would learn that the door was not made from wood at all, but was a variation of a *Browning Vault Door* and the glass Cookie was seeing was not regular glass at all, but bulletproof.

Louie Santamassino took so long opening the door that Cookie and Herman looked at each other, concerned, debating the wisdom of what they were doing. Then Louie was at the door, standing there, not smiling, but not angry. If Louie

Santamassino was showing any emotion, it could only be defined as confusion. He seemed more confused with himself than he was confused by finding two kids on his front steps. Cookie had rehearsed what she was going to say to him, but now she felt herself oddly at a loss for words. The puppy squirmed in Herman's arms, whimpering and wagging his tail at Louie. He didn't smile, but somehow the flat expression on his face, and his short stitch of a mouth made him seem almost friendly and approachable, as if, ultimately, he would have the last laugh over everyone else, and the final word. Herman handed him the dog and Louie took him in his arms. He nodded at the two of them, took the dog inside, cradled the puppy close to his chest, then looked at them one more time, nodded like he understood something on a deeper, human level, and slowly closed the door. Herman and Cookie stood still, looking at the closed door, for what seemed to be a few minutes, but it probably wasn't that long. Time always feels like it lasts longer when a situation is particularly frightening, even if it's scary in a good way.

Twenty-five

Into the Heart

There was nothing great about being a good girl. As far as Cookie was concerned, giving up a bunch of fun stuff, bad stuff, the stuff that you really wanted to do, didn't reap a reward. Being good didn't stop you from living in hell on earth. Being good did not mean you got to be a saint. Even if you were saintly good, *they* didn't let you be a saint for as long as you wanted. There seemed to be a fairly complex system making up *they*, those who decided the fates of saints, sinners and young Catholic girls. The row of nuns sitting in the front pew of Sacred Heart Church were not *they*. The nuns were the guards in the prison and prisoners themselves, the same as everyone else, including Cookie Colangelo and all of the other Italian girls in Yonkers.

The incense in the church was overwhelming. The priests were decked-out in formal vestments. The mass was treated as if it was a holy day of obligation, but it was only Friday and the saint being honored was one she had never heard of before—*Saint Theophane Venard*. Cookie was crammed into the pew between Toni Ferlinghetti and Angela Palumbo who kept whispering and giggling, leaning over behind her back.

Cookie had not gone anywhere near Toni Ferlinghetti since August when she had climbed into a car with her and Arky Lovato and went to the Sprain Brook Reservoir. It was a hot summer night, and Toni surprised everyone by peeling off her shorts and tank top to reveal she was wearing the tiniest fuchsia bikini. Cookie, who didn't own a bikini, stripped down to her underwear, cotton panties and her raspberry training bra. For the sake of comparison, without a doubt, Toni had the better body and at thirteen she looked like a bathing suit model for Cosmopolitan magazine. For reasons unknown, Toni Ferlinghetti pushed Cookie into the water.

Cookie didn't see it coming and hit her head on the concrete slab bordering the edge of the reservoir. Next thing Cookie knew, she was tumbling downward under the water. She felt a rough hand, and Arky Lovato was dragging her out of the water by her shirt, which was wet and glued to her small frame. As she came up for air, the first face she saw was no angel. It was Toni Ferlinghetti, snarling at her as if she had jumped into the reservoir of her own volition and hit her head because she was clumsy. Forget the fact that Toni had pushed Cookie into the water and Cookie would have been sucked down the watery black hole to her death. Cookie figured Toni probably did not even remember that she did such a thing. Sociopaths have no memory of their foul deeds.

Cookie did not know how she had managed to get wedged in between Toni Ferlinghetti and Angela Palumbo. She wasn't being careful. She wasn't paying attention to where she was when the long processional line filed into the church. Whenever she was in the midst of the Italian girls, she had to mind her placement and her position, as if it was a military maneuver; it was a matter of survival. Now she was stuck. She looked across the way into the rows of pews where the boys had been segregated from the girls. Mike Trapani caught her gaze and gave her a big smile while taking his hand and lifting it as though he was going to wave. Instead, she saw he had raised his hand high enough for her to see her notebook. She wasn't going to play that game with him. He could keep the damn notebook. She crossed her arms and glared at him. She had so many more words left inside of her that she did not need the ones he had stolen from her.

Behind Cookie's back, Toni Ferlinghetti prodded Angela Palumbo with her hand and giggled. Toni snapped her head forward with the jerking motion of a jack-in-the-box, suppressed a chortle and emitted a small snort. They kept whispering and giggling, leaning over and leaning forward. Cookie didn't know what the Italian girls thought was so funny. Then her eyes followed the devious jet trails left behind by Toni and Angela, which brought her to gaze upon Colleen Colacurcio, who had been born deformed. Colleen had short brown hair, pale olive skin, and little wings for arms. Knobby elbows protruded from her shoulders and made her look like she was a bird, perpetually in flight. She was a *thalidomide baby*, one of the babies, among many, who were born deformed because their mother had taken a drug—thalidomide—not knowing it would cause birth defects. There had been a lot of those babies born around the same year Cookie had been born. Colleen Colacurcio was in good shape, considering. She could have been born without arms and legs or fingers sticking up from the back of her head instead of from her shoulders.

Toni was waving and flapping her arms subtly, and putting only minimal effort into her attempts to fly by using her elbows. Angela was more than amused and showed her appreciation by flapping her wings in return. This went on for a few minutes; back and forth they flapped and giggled. Cookie was stuck in the middle between them and considered what she should do. That morning she had been late for school again, which meant she had two more hours of detention. What difference would it make if did one more bad thing? Cookie was so disgusted by the way Toni was making fun of Colleen Colacurcio that she did not think and agonize about what she was about to do. It was purely instinctual. She took her elbow and landed one swift jab in Toni's stomach. Toni emitted a shocked gasp. Cookie did not look left or right, and certainly did not look at Toni. She did not move at all, and scarcely breathed. There was no way she was going to put up with someone making fun of a girl who had simply been born that way.

Toni didn't retaliate, and Cookie wasn't about to see what she would do. She was also willing to bet Angela had not seen what she had done. Even though she knew sooner or later Toni would take revenge on her, it did not lessen the satisfaction she felt, knowing that she had stuck up for someone who did not deserve to be mistreated.

For most of the afternoon, the ninth grade girls of *the Heart*, had been shoved against an altar rail. The priest in the pulpit droned on forever about saints who had lost their sainthood. *They* were kicking saints off of the saint list. Their names were being removed from the *Canon of Saints* without a trace. Cookie felt a sense of loss. She had especially liked the sound of their names, Saint Lucy and Saint Christopher. Every car visor in Yonkers had a clip-on medal of Saint Christopher, the patron saint of travelers. There was a whole ton of metal clips that weren't going to work magic any more, no matter how hard anybody prayed. Saint Ursula, who led holy virgins on a pilgrimage, was slaughtered by the Huns. Saint Nicholas, aka Saint Nick—gone. *They* even dumped Santa Claus!

The priest didn't mention what the saints had done to achieve sainthood. Forget about having to give up the basic necessities in life, like necking with boys, wearing short skirts and blue eye shadow. Most likely these saints had endured more than one lion attack, a few prime torture sessions, the rack and the screw. All of that suffering, and for what? You get a little recognition for a couple hundred years, then they tell you to pack your halo and go home, like the whole thing never happened.

Now if you could be a bona fide saint and get delisted, what did this mean for ordinary women? Half of the grown-up women in Yonkers could be called martyrs. Cookie was reminded of her father's sisters, Cookie's old Italian aunts, Ro-Ro, Sally and Spanky. Chubby, barely over four feet in height, the aunts had moles embedded in the fleshiest part of their cheeks. At weddings, funerals and family gatherings, they'd cluster together like a string of spicy hot sausage. They loved to weep and moan with the passion of real martyrs. And they were happiest when the pain was self-inflicted by the habitual beating on their breasts. They wheezed and sputtered a lot while they said a staccato stream of Sicilian curse words, at the same time they wrapped rosary beads around their knuckles, the way boxers wrap their knuckles before a fight. They'd gnarl their knobby little hands into clenched fists and beat...beat...beat... their breasts with the soulful precision of the sign of the cross. All of that suffering for what?

The aunts also insisted on calling Cookie by her formal name, "Concetta." They'd say, "When are you going to do better in school and hang around with the right friends? Look at yourself. Soon you'll be hanging around Nepperhan Avenue with the jungle bunnies." The aunts never came around and visited any more because they didn't know what to do with Kitty. Ordinary Yonkers martyrdom was *de rigeur,* but not exceptional enough to qualify for sainthood.

Playing by the rules was for other people, but not for Cookie Colangelo. By the time she made her way home from school, she realized that Kitty might be crazy, but she didn't play by the rules. And for that one reason alone, Cookie admired her mother. Kitty Colangelo had gumption. Cookie did not know what was more traumatic, having a really awful thing happen once or having a succession of small bad things happen over a long and drawn-out period of time. So far, in her fourteenth year of life, she had experienced all forms of trauma, but maybe there was nothing exceptional about it.

Maybe everyone experienced a steady stream of rotten stuff in their lives. Maybe everyone should be recognized as a saint and not let *they* delist them.

Twenty-six

Friday, November 6, 1970

Today marked the three-year anniversary of Cookie's big November event. The details of what had happened that day were so repetitive in her mind that it sounded like an advertising campaign for a store-wide clearance sale. She wasn't recounting the memory of what had happened, because if she had, she would have told herself to *Stop*. Instead, she reflected on what had happened to her since then. She had changed. Even her appearance had begun to change. She turned sideways to her bedroom mirror and examined her body in repose, then swiveled back, returning to a full frontal view. There was no denying it. Herman had insinuated as much, but he was too much of a gentleman to say it outright. Her two sharp points had become bumps and promised to be fledgling breasts like the ones owned by all the other Italian girls in Yonkers. She no longer looked twelve.

She didn't rejoice at her changing body. Guys like Mike Trapani and Mr. DC were hitting on her, and it was happening more often. It felt so weird to have guys pursue her when she wanted nothing to do with them. In her mind, sometimes she'd give them a chance. She tried to imagine that she liked them, but then she was repulsed by her own willingness to try to like them. She wanted to like someone, but since the *Blind Owl* died, no one had replaced him. Herman was her new owl, but it was a different kind of love than she had experienced for the *Blind Owl* Alan Wilson.

In the mirror, she saw the same green eyes staring back at her. She had a knowing look. She was street wise. No one could pull a fast one on her. She was nobody's fool and nobody's patsy. For the rest of her life, she would be a fighter, and wise; she'd always have gumption, and if you have gumption, you have guts.

Being fourteen brought a whole new set of problems and it seemed to be turning out that's just the way life is—no matter what she did or where she went in Yonkers, she would encounter problems. *Yonkers is such bullshit,* she said to herself.

She walked out of her bedroom and was met by Donny at the top of the steps. She pointed to the side of her head, giving Cookie *the cuckoo, she's crazy* hand signal.

"Now Mommy's depressed," Donny said. "She's always sitting at her ironing board, but she's not ironing anything. She's not doing anything."

"Well, at least she's not screaming," Cookie said.

Cookie took great care to approach her mother. This wasn't an exercise of walking on eggshells. Cookie likened her journey with her mother's madness to walking softly, but carrying a big enough stick so she could defend her own life. Kitty had two faces to her madness. It was like flipping a coin to see which one would manifest itself. Flip a coin and *Heads* was full-blown raging psychosis, scatological rants about body fluids, sexual functioning, and fixations originating in Catholic dogma with mad delusions about priests, nuns, bishops, cardinals, the Pope and the saints. *Heads* could be a violent place for Kitty. Even if she didn't physically hurt herself or someone else, she made liberal use of her violent mouth. The other side of the coin, *Tails,* transported Kitty to a catatonic state, where she was emotionally non-responsive, listless, sat still, stared out the window, and joined the tribe of the walking dead.

On this day, Cookie found Kitty hovering somewhere between heads and tails, the living and the dead. Kitty sat on an armchair in the living room, looking out the window to the woods where the fiery Sumac trees once stood. The stereo was on, and tuned to WPAT-FM 93.1 Paterson, NJ, playing easy listening, popular jazz as background music. The station played romantic string orchestrations. No vocals. It was as if Kitty enjoyed listening to music without vocals so other people's words did not compete with the voices she heard in her head.

"It's November," Kitty said. "The leaves would have fallen to the ground by now anyway. So it doesn't matter that the trees are gone."

Kitty had just enough energy to do something about her despair. She seemed agitated, sitting there on the chair, crossing and uncrossing her legs. She stretched them out to rest on a stool. "They only kept me at the hospital for three weeks. I've never been there longer than three weeks. Not like some of those hard-core cases. They're really whacked out." She fidgeted with her feet as if she had uncomfortable electric impulses in her legs and kept moving them, back and forth, like scissors. Cookie knew it was her medication that made Kitty get restless legs. She smiled weakly at Cookie, "How are you, honey? You don't look well. What's gotten into you? You're not letting people get to you, are you?"

Cookie sat by Kitty's feet on the floor. "Kitty, I've come to see how you are." Cookie looked up at her mother and spoke softly. "Are you still my Kitty?"

Kitty's eyes were reddened, filled slightly with tears, yet at the same time, she smiled. "Yes, I'm still your Kitty. I'll always be your Kitty."

"Then you're still my Kitty," Cookie said in a firm voice, as if she was again making a commitment to her mother.

The *Kitty* exchange had been a ritual between them that went back longer than Cookie could remember. From the beginning, she had set herself forth as her mother's protector, the one who would take care of Kitty into old age.

Cookie looked up at her mother and patted her leg. "How are you feeling?"

Kitty didn't respond. She placed her hands in her lap and looked down at them, as if she was trying to determine whether these hands were attached to the rest of her body. She was deep in thought, or not thinking at all, but lost in some faraway place. Her crying had petered out. Her small display of sadness had never been too obvious in the first place. You'd have to know Kitty really well to know she had been crying. Cookie knew; she knew her mother, her moods, her changeable nature, what was real, what was not, what was important to her and what never bothered her at all.

Some mothers would care that their daughter smoked cigarettes, or pot; sold ludes and hung out with a black boy and an Italian girl who wanted to be black, but Kitty didn't mind those things so much. Kitty cared about the destruction of the colorful Sumac more than she cared about going to Cookie's school to meet with teachers and to pick up her progress report. Kitty always assumed Cookie was doing well in school. In all the years Cookie had been in school, Kitty had never met any of her daughter's teachers, not one.

Even though it had been three years since Cookie's awful episode at school, she had never told Kitty what had happened. She would never tell her. Cookie could take care of herself. Kitty thought Cookie had gumption, backbone, she called it. Kitty was proud of her daughter and Cookie knew that.

Her mother's words came out slowly, as though she had thought carefully about what she wanted to say. "I'm doing the best that I can, but I know it's not enough."

Kitty might be sick, but that didn't stop her from having courage. She looked at Cookie with eyes that were kind and flickered with a trace of wisdom, the recognition that she was neither afraid nor ashamed to tell the truth. "I know I'm not what I should be," she said and took a long pause, breathing, then talking as if she meant to be emphatic in a slow, sonorous sort of way. "That's why you have to stick up for yourself. You have to have gumption. Always stick up for yourself, no matter what."

Cookie rose slowly from the floor and came to her mother's side. She leaned down and kissed her on the cheek, then she hugged her. She hugged her mother so long that she didn't want to be the one to break away. To Cookie, Kitty had a sweet, clean scent like *Ivory Soap* mixed with the soft petals of a non-fragrant flower, a mum, a daisy, or a dahlia. While Cookie was hugging her, Kitty patted her daughter's cheek. Kitty was unable to initiate affection with kisses or hugs, but could respond with a gentle patting motion like she was a shy child, or autistic. Cookie knew her mother believed that her daughter would do the things in life she was incapable of doing.

On a conventional scale, the Yonkers barometer of good women and good mothers, Kitty had been stunted in growth in the same way as if she had been savagely cut down like a Sumac tree. Long ago, she dropped out of high school, and later quit working at a bank, gave up acting like a mother or a wife, and now couldn't leave the house to run a simple errand. She couldn't do things that most people took for granted. She was overrun by the voices in her head that tormented her, night and day, day and night, body, mind and soul, assuming schizophrenics have a soul, and most do. In another place and time, away from Yonkers, her mother might be the village shaman, a holy woman, and eventually a saint. She'd be *Saint Kitty Colangelo of Yonkers*. Kitty Colangelo was crazy, but she didn't deserve to be this way. Schizophrenia was nobody's fault.

Neither was being born white or black. You were just born that way. You didn't get a menu and place an order with some higher being, asking to be born. And sometimes you were born at the wrong time in the wrong place and all the lemons lined up and you ended up like the Rosners, shielding the concentration camp numbers on their arms from prying eyes, or your mother takes the wrong drug while she's pregnant and you end up being born with wings for arms, like Colleen Colacurcio. Long ago, someone told Cookie that if she touched her kindergarten teacher she would turn black too. She didn't know who she was more scared of, Mrs. Kerry or the person who told her that.

YONKERS, Yonkers! Johnny always said, making fun of the place where he lived. If Johnny had his way, he'd live in Harlem with his crony musician friends. He felt as out of place in Yonkers as much as Cookie felt that she did not want to live in the North End. Johnny was trying to play by the rules, doing all the right middle class things he thought he was supposed to do. He built himself a big house high on a rock, where his family could live. He sent his daughters to the neighborhood Catholic school. He worked hard every day of his life trying to get ahead. Okay, Kitty Colangelo was not *June Cleaver*, but he couldn't help that. No matter what Johnny did or how hard he tried, he didn't fit in. *They* wouldn't let him belong to the Amakassin Club, even though he had the money to join. Who was *they*? *Shit if I know*, Cookie thought to herself. *They* didn't like any body who looked *different, or thought different or stood out. They* were just mean, spiteful and looking for somebody to blame. *They* wanted to pin their whole load of shit on somebody, so *They* did not have to take a good look inside of themselves. *Fuck them,* Cookie said to herself.

Twenty-seven

Black & White

Cookie caught up with Reenie in front of W.T. Grants on Palisade Avenue in the heart of *Ghetto Square*. The girls crossed the street, turned onto North Broadway and walked past the Donut Den. Cookie looked in through the glass store-front and saw Tommy Parrello staring back at her. He was standing at the counter with Mike Trapani, who was shoveling a slice of pizza into his mouth. The Donut Den had always been Kitty's favorite place to get pizza. Kitty called pizza *hot pie* and Cookie wondered why. She had never heard anyone other than her mother call pizza *hot pie*. Kitty's Aunt Mary O'Leary had worked at the Donut Den for years. She was a tiny woman, well under five feet who had a voice as loud as thunder. Although it was strange to think of buying pizza in a donut shop that prided itself on its éclairs and signature buttercream donuts, it was known for having some of the best pizza in Yonkers.

"Don't mind you calling me a nigger," Reenie told Cookie. "I consider it a great compliment."

Cookie rolled her eyes at Reenie. "Don't you keep talking at me like that girl. You're a flaming honky motherfucker, if I ever saw one."

Reenie shook her finger as an admonition. "You talk like you're tough, but you're really not."

Cookie felt confident and triumphant that so far she had gotten away with setting Toni Ferlinghetti straight. She didn't tell Reenie what had happened, and had no plans to tell her. Some things were best kept to one's self. She also knew that, sooner or later, she would pay for what she had done. When she least expected it, Toni would pay her back.

"You're not going to find me talking trash. Not ever," Cookie said. Not even if it's the right thing to do, to be friends with someone."

Wearing navy blue *Keds,* Cookie broke into a slow swinging dance, bending and straightening her legs, waving her arms high and extending them in the air as far as she could. Going forward and back, she started shimmying to one side, then did a glide, crisscrossing her legs in long, sweeping scissor moves. She danced to the music heard in her head. For a second she thought if she heard songs playing in her head, she was getting the same sickness Kitty had, but she changed her mind. Unlike Kitty, Cookie could always make her thoughts stop, then start up again, and stop again, on command.

"I can't keep up with you," Reenie said. "Slow down." Cookie continued to practice her moves. Her legs felt strong and limber, the way her legs used to feel when she played kickball every day on the street.

The two girls were walking north on North Broadway. Every so often a lot stood vacant in between two old brick buildings. When property taxes went unpaid, the city was known to tear down buildings. After the building was demolished, they'd put up a chain link fence around the lot and leave it vacant where it was inevitably overtaken by weeds and became a dump-off site for garbage. It was like this all around the Getty Square area: on Broadway, Main Street, Palisade Avenue, Nepperhan Avenue, Ashburton Avenue, and especially on all the small side streets and arterials; big gaps randomly appeared in the urban façade, like missing teeth in the grin of a sick old man.

"Things are getting really bad," Reenie said. "The prejudice is so bad and it's getting worse. The cops harass teenagers and even young kids. I've heard them call little kids names."

Cookie nudged Reenie's arm. She was trying to be tough and make light of a rotten situation. "What's it to you?"

"It's going to mean something to you! I'm telling you the way things go down around here!" Reenie gave her a cold glare and spoke about Herman Lynch. "The other black boys don't like him because he works at the library and doesn't talk like them. His grandmother was a schoolteacher and doesn't let him talk like a nigger. The boys in the 'hood didn't like that, and said he wasn't black enough. His grandmother stopped teaching because too many white folks didn't want her teaching their kids. She was into book reading and worked at the library. She makes Herman work at the library too. She was real hard on him and stricter than ever now that his mother died. You do know about his mother?" Reenie asked.

"I know she OD'd," Cookie said.

"Things are real bad here and getting worse. Last week there was a fight right out in the open on Ritters Lane," Reenie said. "Someone called my grandmother to come outside and she did, with her friend Helen Slocum. Cops were on the street, shouting, and it was a three-ring circus. I don't even remember who started the fight or who was fighting. I was freaked out. Helen spoke up and said something to the cops and they knocked her to the ground. She's an old woman."

Reenie looked at Cookie waiting for her reaction.

At first, Cookie didn't seem too interested. Her mind had wandered off far away from Yonkers. "She ought to bring charges," Cookie said finally. "That's not right. Somebody should stand up for her."

"The main witnesses were boys in the 'hood, niggers, and couldn't say nothing without getting themselves into trouble.

Helen Slocum did file a complaint," Reenie said. "But nothing's going to come of it."

"How do you know?" Cookie asked. Don't they have to investigate a complaint?"

Reenie shook her head. "Helen Slocum is black."

"Yonkers, Yonkers," Cookie said. "The city of dangerous living."

"My grandmother's getting old," Reenie said. "There are too many things to worry about, robberies and killings. There are drug dealers everywhere. People are getting strung out on smack. It's getting harder and harder for her to go up and down three flights of steps. We're up on the third floor, and sometimes the roof leaks and water comes in. The landlord doesn't do nothing. He says if you don't like it, then go somewhere else."

Ever since November 6, 1967, Cookie felt responsible for everything, even the reality of the pain that went part and parcel with life in the projects. Here, today, exactly three years later, she didn't know what to offer Reenie in the way of consolation. She thought of going to church and lighting a candle, the same way her grandmother used to offer up novenas to the saints, but that only worked if *they* let your saint stay on the list. Cookie smirked to herself; she couldn't explain everything that was going on in her head to Reenie.

She sincerely wanted to apologize for the things that were happening in Reenie's neighborhood. There would be raw strength and honesty in her apology if only she could assume responsibility for what was happening. If Cookie could bear the weight of this burden, then she'd offer a blanket apology to everyone. She wished she could fix it all and make it better. Sometimes the sheer enormity of it all took her breath away.

Both girls knew the hard truth about *Ghetto Square* that no one wanted to talk about. The invasion of heroin dealers, drug lords, crooked cops and crooked politicians was turning this poor urban neighborhood into the killing fields. People were so desperate, not wanting to feel the pain, turning to smack and dying the same way Herman's mother had died. Cookie was done messing around with half-truths and bold lies depicting Yonkers as *Leave it to Beaver* land.

"I want you to stay strong, no matter what," she told Reenie. "Promise me."

Reenie peered at Cookie through her long, curly fringe of black hair and nodded, *I promise.*

As the sun started to go down on this clear cold Friday night in November, Cookie and Reenie headed *Down the End* on a mission to find a guy with a car who would take them on a joy ride. The most likely driver was Arky Lovato. He'd drive anybody anywhere and anytime, night or day. On Palisade Avenue, one by one, the storefront lights flashed off, going dark at the end of the business day. The liquor store, pizza place and Donaghey's Pub stayed open for business, but hardly anyone was around. Brilliant stadium-style lighting from the Palisade parking lot illuminated most of the street. For a Friday night, traffic was slow. A jumbo balding man was propped up against the guard rail in the parking lot, eating an extra large hoagie and washing it down with a bottle of the chocolate-flavored drink, *Yoo-hoo*. He crumpled the wax sandwich paper into a ball, stuffed it into a brown deli bag and tossed it into the narrow rounded opening of a bullet-shaped metal garbage can. He seemed mightily pleased with himself that he had made a clean shot. So much for entertainment *Down the End* on a Friday night.

Reenie and Cookie hightailed it to North Broadway, with the implicit intention to head toward Untermyer Park, and walked by the concealed opening of the *Owl Hole*. It was getting cold and Cookie could see her breath curling like slow steam rising in the night air. Up ahead on North Broadway, flashing lights warned of emergency vehicles. It could have been the police or an ambulance, and she thought of something happening to Kitty or Donny. She didn't worry so much about Johnny. He could take care of himself.

Cookie heard the sound of *Psssst, Cookie* traveling in an arc, flying through the air, from everywhere and nowhere in particular. She could not tell which direction the persistent whisper was coming from. The front of the *Owl Hole* was malformed and gangly, with giant hedges and overgrowth camouflaging its hidden steps and the descent into its secret alcove. The same dense bushes that concealed it from discovery also stopped anyone who was there from being seen. The *Psssst, Cookie* sound was awfully funny, like someone had trouble forming a tight-lipped whisper. And that realization made Cookie immediately know who was there.

Herman Lynch bounded out to the sidewalk on North Broadway and told them the unthinkable. He was shaking and rocking to emphasize the urgency of the situation. A police car had swooped down on Louie Santamassino's house. Herman was more worried about the dog than Louie. He thought they were going to take Louie to jail. If he didn't do something right now, the dog he had given to Louie would go the pound and end up sitting on death row.

Cookie had her suspicions about what was going down, but nothing could be proven. The three of them raced through the back woods and cut through the private yard, where the Rosners stood in the back yard looking over at the spectacle next door, trying to shield their eyes from the red lights blaring from one police car. Cookie was anticipating the sight of Louie's Madonna. As she had expected, the Madonna was still the chief landmark in Louie's yard, and tonight she had taken on the red patina from the glow of the cop car. Cookie looked at Herman.

"The dog," he said. "This could be serious." His eyeglasses reflected colorful halos of red light.

Reenie nudged Cookie's arm, telling her that she wanted to leave, but Cookie bade her to stay. "Please, Reenie, this is important. The dog Herman found is here. He gave the dog to Louie. He's here now, somewhere. See what I'm saying?"

The *Afro Sheen* slicked on Reenie's long black hair caught shine from the siren lights. Her eyes glowed with a certain tenderness that Cookie had never seen before. "I've lost just about everything," Reenie said. "I don't want to lose no more."

The terror of noise, commotion and sirens gave the three kids an extra edge over time and space, enough to leap the back fence and land in the thickets of conifer hedges and honeysuckle bushes that had gone dormant for the winter and had thinned to woody vines. The noise from Broadway was a combination of brakes, skids and U-turns running together and jelling into a cacophony of keen alarm. There were panicked police out there, and a lot of them. There were so many lights that Cookie could hardly see.

Herman's eyes appeared huge behind his glasses. "They must have sent all the police in the station." Outside, in Louie's long drive way leading up to his house, the police lights were sort of pretty. Red and blue, blinking faster than the lights on an old jukebox. Car radios gave off static in-between the low, dull tone of controlled voices.

Louie Santamassino's backyard was flooded with light. The house lights were up, like opening night at the Biltmore. There was the sound of cursing or the repetition of foul words. The closer Cookie, Herman and Reenie came to the purported scene of the crime, it was obvious that all of the cursing was coming from Louie Santamassino. He wasn't happy.

Fran Ochiogrosso was standing there with her hands on her hips. Her hair looked freshly curled and she clutched a winter-thick woolen robe tight across her breasts as though she was trying to hold them up. Cookie didn't know if she was feigning modesty or trying to show the Yonkers cops that she had a really big package to protect. Fran acted as though she thought she was famous for her breasts, which were as unctuous as ten gallon jugs of olive oil.

Other neighbors came out to see what was going on: The Cuomos, the Rizzutos, the Zacchios, and the Lovatos. The

Rosners stayed to the sidelines, keeping their distance in their own protective bubble, away from the growing number of curious onlookers. It was a way to keep themselves safe from a crowd that could turn ugly and suddenly erupt into the Yonkers equivalent of a pogrom. Jews were everywhere in Yonkers, but outnumbered by the flanks of Italian, Irish, Polish, Portuguese Catholics who referred to Jews as the *Jewish people,* which was another way of saying Jews were *different. The Jews were different, alright, Cookie thought.* If it hadn't been for her fourth-grade teacher, Mrs. Chachkes, she might never have found her words.

Cookie saw a red beam of light crossing Bert Rosner's face and illuminate the lens of his thick, black framed eyeglasses. His eyeglasses were the same kind Herman wore, except Bert Rosner had a black elastic strap holding his glasses securely in place. Those glasses could never be knocked off of his face.

The street was turning into a huge block party. Cookie half-expected to see the things that connote Italian feast and celebration: a steel band playing calypso music; a slow procession of old people welling up behind the exalted statue of San Gennaro; sidewalk vendors pulling up curbside to sell stale pretzels, soft drinks, Torrone, sausage on a stick and rock-hard cannoli. Although there was none of this, every one here had been to Little Italy at least once, and wished it was true, even if was not. There was lots of talk. The crowd had grown in size and had become heated, clamoring for a showing. Fran Ochiogrosso was delighted to have an audience. Standing on the sidelines, she produced a pack of Kent 100s from the pocket of her robe and lit up. Cookie suspected Fran drank often and to excess behind closed doors. It was the only explanation for her leathery skin. Fran was about the same age as Kitty, but looked ten years older.

The young German shepherd had grown beyond proportions and barked furiously at the assembled crowd of friends,

neighbors, and law enforcement officials. Herman was scared
out of his wits and ran toward the dog; he just called him dog
because on the day he had given him away to Louie, he still
did not have a name. The dog must have remembered Herman,
because he seemed delighted with his soft *Hush Puppies* and
affectionately nipped at his feet. Herman was half-scared and
half-thrilled to see the dog still alive.

Louie called to him, "I've named him *Blackster!*"

Cookie looked at the circle of cops who had formed a loose
brigade around Louie, who looked besotted with grief. He was
sweating and his hair glistened under the strobe lights. He
was so sad, Cookie wanted to reach out and hug him. All of
this hoopla seemed to suggest that Louie had killed his wife
and had buried her in the yard.

Fran looked at Cookie and said. "He killed his wife. He
did. And I know she's buried there. I saw him bury her body."
Her eyes enlarged and took on a round, yellowish cast from
the flashing strobe lights. "I had to call those lazy good-for-
nothing cops every day for two months before they'd come
out here. Now I'm wondering who's going to take care of the
funeral." She moved forward, stealthily inching closer to the
cops, telling them where the body was buried. "Right there,"
she said pointing as if she had nailed her prey. She spread her
arms open wide to demonstrate the expanse of a black mound
of dirt that was covered with chrysanthemums in a bushel
of gold, orange and brown, looking as if the flowers had been
freshly planted in the earth.

"Dig," some cop commanded.

"No, don't," Louie said. "Please don't do that to me." He
looked sadder than the day Cookie and Herman had seen him
crying over Roscoe. "Don't do that, please!"

"No!" Herman called out. "That's not right to dig up his
dead dog. How would you like it if someone came to your house
and dug up your dog?"

The cops dismissed Herman as if he didn't know what he

was talking about. Two cops took heavy shovels and began to dig, flinging up frozen clods of soil from the yard.

Fran clutched her robe, seizing it up to her neck, showing a fresh burst of cleavage. "Where's the funeral going to be?"

Reenie whispered in Cookie's ear. "Let's take her out. She doesn't deserve to live. She is truly evil and *so Yonkers.*" Then she smiled at Fran and said. "Sooner or later, everybody ends up at Sinatra's Funeral Home."

Fran nodded with approval. "They do such nice work there. Especially for us Italians. Now if his wife's Irish, she's better off at Whelan's," she snorted.

Once you're dead, you're dead, Cookie thought. "I didn't think those things mattered," Cookie said.

"You always did live in a dream world," Fran told her. She stepped back and opened her robe just long enough to flash the police her large size-peach teddy. Under the robe, a companion piece cover-up was appointed on her shoulders like it was a robe on a beauty queen. Fran Ochiogrosso was no contestant, and had the thunder thighs to prove it.

"No matter what you do," Louie yelled. "Don't touch my Sumac trees." He pointed to a small grove of three trees that still bore the last vestiges of blood-red leaves. "I've got the only Sumac trees left in the neighborhood! Some lunatic cut them all down! Don't touch them!"

If the cops heard Louie's rant about the Sumac trees, they didn't let on. Under the strobe lights, the cops unearthed a tarp-covered lump. A body was there. A serious-looking dude in a suit rushed forward and looked under the tarp. He could have been a medical examiner. The man looked confused and didn't say anything. For a long time, he searched, opening the tarp, looking in. He moved all the way around the tarp, pressing down on top of it as if he was judging the size of the body. He lifted the top portion of the tarp, looked in and poked. No one knew what was going on. He finally said, "no human remains. It's a dog."

Louie didn't emote his grief audibly and looked at the cops as if they were beyond stupid. "I could have told you that if only you asked me. Did you have to go and dig him up?"

"Poor Louie," Cookie said. She saw the solemn faces of the Yonkers cops. An officer came up to Louie and told him it was against city ordinance to bury dead animals in the yard.

Louie swung his arm haphazardly into the air as if he was too exasperated to comment. "It's my dog," he proclaimed. "I can do with him what I want. That's all there is to it. If you want to give me a ticket, then give me a ticket. But that dog meant a lot to me, and he's staying right here."

Fran blessed herself with the soulful precision of the sign of the cross, hissing smoke from her mouth and nose while she clenched the last remnants of the Kent 100 between her teeth. She had a calm look on her face now. Her fidgeting came to a complete rest. The only thing worse than her non-stop prattle was her complete silence. It might mean that she was thinking, and that could be scary.

Herman knelt before Blackster, who licked his face as if he was trying to heal the sore wounds he had incurred just being here with these crazy white people and the Yonkers police.

Fran gyrated her mouth several times and cleared her throat as if she was about to say something. Cookie watched her face closely for a clue as to her next gesture. Cookie could tell Fran wasn't too embarrassed about what had happened. It was as if, *oh well,* she didn't get him this time, then she'd have to wait for another grand opportunity. Fran looked at Louie, who seemed too confused to be angry about what had happened. In her own awkward way, she was trying to figure something out and come to some sort of simple understanding.

Louie looked at Fran like he could sense what she was thinking, nodded his head and shrugged. "My wife left me a long time ago. You think I like talking about things like that! Why do you spend so much time watching me, looking at me... all the time, all the goddamn time, instead of looking at yourself?"

Fran didn't have an answer for him. Cookie wished she knew Louie's true feelings, and if he was capable of forgiveness. Most Italians are not forgiving, even though they love to say they are, and long before you can muster the courage to ask. On that chilly November night in 1970, the only thing that remained clear was the cold, practiced smile of the Madonna.

Twenty-eight

Thursday, December 17, 1970

Cookie had missed the Number 2 bus. The ground was frozen and small patches of ice crunched beneath her feet. She hopped while she walking, trying to warm up. No such luck. She didn't have a hat, scarf or gloves and blew on her hands to warm them. Her bare legs under her woolen skirt felt frigid and had turned the shade of a white ash tree. The Number 2 bus had a long route and took a half hour to travel from Tudor Woods in the North End all the way to the end of the line in the Bronx at 242nd Street, where the Broadway IRT subway began. She had walked too far or not nearly far enough, and was stuck in between two bus stops when the next scheduled bus came barreling down the street.

She knew no matter how fast she ran, she would not get to the next stop before the bus arrived. And she couldn't count on the driver to be so kind as to wait for her. This was Yonkers, and most bus drivers didn't like their jobs all that much and didn't make a big show pretending that they did. Yonkers bus drivers especially disliked Catholic schoolgirls, who had a tendency to make their jobs even more loathsome.

The bus was full of schoolgirls. Cookie recognized them by

the color of their uniforms. Any color meant the girls weren't wearing uniforms at all. The non-uniformed groups were from Gorton and Commerce—the public high schools—and looked indistinguishable. In Cookie's opinion, these kids were extremely and unequivocally dumb, but exceptionally lucky. In the public schools, girls wore regular clothes and there were no nuns. Cookie looked at the bodies crammed inside the bus to find someone who would stand out, someone familiar. For an instant she thought she saw Reenie Ruggiero, but this bus was traveling north, and Reenie lived in the south near *Ghetto Square*.

No one waved to her from the windows. No one knew her. She was a freshman girl, sadly unpopular, and doomed to another year of anonymity. Toward the back of the bus, a bunch of teal blue uniformed bodies were jammed together in a dense cloud of cigarette smoke. Cookie knew the girls were smoking *Marlboro* because that's the brand everyone smoked in 1970.

Even though New York state law said you had to be 18 to buy cigarettes, no one enforced the rule. Cookie had bought her first pack of cigarettes at Morsemere Market the week after her wicked encounter at Christ the King School. The brand was *True Blue*. Cookie saw the ad on TV and liked the jingle *America's Most Talked About Filter Cigarette*. She and Reenie headed down to Warburton Avenue and crossed over to the Kennedy Marina on the Hudson River, sat behind a dilapidated shed next to the railroad tracks and smoked one cigarette after another. The girls didn't get sick from smoking so many cigarettes because no one told them to inhale the smoke. Even back then, you could smoke cigarettes anywhere you wanted, and the Kennedy Marina was so rundown, it was as good a place as any to smoke up a storm. Smoking cigarettes with Reenie that day was the first bad girl experience the two of them had shared. For Cookie, it was more than engaging in a bad-girl activity, but it was the first outrageous act where she was driven by a desire to stick up for herself and fight back. She was tough. So was Reenie. Cookie didn't know what made Reenie so tough, but thought it had something to do with living so close to the projects in a one-bedroom apartment that she shared with her grandmother and her older brother Billy Dee. She didn't know what had happened to Reenie's parents and did not want to ask.

Thinking about the first time she had smoked made Cookie want to stop and light one up, but she was so cold, she had to keep moving. The girls in teal blue on the bus looked ethereal in the haze of smoke, almost as if they were from another world. In some ways, the other girls were strange and unearthly. Cookie went to *the Heart* and they were from Blessed Sacrament Academy, also know as BSA, or alternately as the *Bullshit Academy*. The girls from BSA were known to be sleazy and wore too much black eyeliner. Rumor had it that no one wanted to hire BSA girls to babysit their children because they would snuff out small children by placing pillows over their faces while they were sleeping. Other rumors hinted that BSA girls would clean out medicine cabinets of all pills, even laxatives, and sell them to the rich kids who lived on Riverdale Avenue and went to the Bronx High School of Science.

Although most of the BSA girls were Italian and consequently had lost their virginity by age 14, the school's glee club was leading a small backlash movement to restore an image of purity. It was the girls of the glee club who influenced the school to adopt a new uniform. BSA girls used to wear hiked skirts like everyone else, but not anymore. What appeared to be a teal blue skirt was not what it seemed to be! The skirts had secret compartments! Beneath the teal blue skirts there were culottes, big fat pants for each leg; culottes could not be hiked! Cookie was having a hard enough time surviving at *the Heart*. No matter what, she did not want to end up at BSA.

She regretted missing the bus. Most of all, she regretted having to wear a school uniform and having to drag around the impossibly huge book bag that weighed her down, despite the fact that it was mostly devoid of books except for the black & white composition book that contained some of her thoughts about the world and her book-in-progress. She had given her book a working title: *Beneath the Passion of the Angelic Mystery Rose.*

She put on her transistor radio and stuck in the earplugs. A news report droned on about President Nixon warning the North Vietnamese that there would be more bombing raids if they continued to attack the south. Other cheerful news reported that the US had performed a nuclear test in Nevada, while the Soviet Union had performed their own nuclear test in Eastern Kazakh, a place that sounded like a mashup of Cossack and *Kazam,* and magic words *Allahkahdabra* and *Allahkazam to* Cookie's sensitive ear, which heard words reverberate long after they had been spoken. She wished she could Kazam and whisk her way out of here. No matter what she did in her own fourteen-year-old life, war raged in Vietnam and a much larger spectacle threatened to erupt between the United States and the Soviet Union. *Any day now, we could all be blown up in a nuclear catastrophe*, she thought, scuffing the tips of her *Bass Weejuns* in the earth and not making a dent because the ground was frozen stiff. The weather report said it was thirty-four degrees, not terribly cold, and it wasn't windy, but she felt a chill down to her bones. There was a cold war going on and no one wanted to stop the puffing and preening while *they* put our boys out there to bleed to death and get blown up in fields far from home.

She had walked briskly enough to make it *Down the End* in fifteen minutes. She was thinking deeply for a while and did not see what was coming. In fact, in retrospect, she had not considered that Toni Ferlinghetti would try to take her on at all, but there she was, in all of her gum-cracking, wise-ass'ing, big hair, mean girl in full *Gina* glory. Toni Ferlinghetti was a glorious sight to behold. Where Cookie was lacking a hat, scarf and gloves, Toni was decked out in fur-cuffed gloves, a scarf richly detailed with small fur pom-poms and a soft cashmere-looking cap that sat tilted on the side of her head, intending to show off her lustrous mane of brown-black hair. She smiled at Cookie. Her smile was open, wide, generous and full of malevolent intent.

Toni Ferlinghetti wasn't alone. She had surrounded herself with her girlfriends: Terry Columbo, Noreen DiOreo, Debbie DiLorenzo, Mary De Luca, Diane Mancini, Angela Palumbo and Anna Maria Scarpino herded around Cookie, jostling her, getting too close for comfort, laughing, while they kept their eyes on Toni Ferlinghetti, waiting to take her cue and not do anything without her consent. That didn't stop them from laughing, and they were laughing right at her. They were more than Toni's friends. They were her acolytes, conspiratorial in nature and determined to make right what had been done wrong to Toni.

Cookie felt a strange sense of calm. Maybe because it could not get worse than this. When you hit bottom, there is nowhere to go but up. It was like Janis Joplin singing *Freedom is just another word for nothing left to lose*. And Cookie had nothing to lose. By standing up for herself and confronting them, she was going to show them that she had gumption, guts, what Kitty called a raw, crazy kind of courage.

Cookie stepped forward and looked directly into Toni's amber eyes. "What's your problem?"

"What's the problem?" Toni countered. "Are you fucking serious?"

Toni and her bevy of girlfriends moved in closer to hear exactly what was going on. Cookie could smell their gum, a combo of *Juicy Fruit*, Wrigley's *Spearmint*, *Doublemint* and *Bazooka Bubble Gum*. The cold air seemed to make the collective scent of their breath rising like steam more acute. She was outnumbered by a pack of she-wolves wearing lip gloss, smacking their lips and cracking their gum in random pops.

"You're the problem." Toni's amber eyes had dark specks in the center that flashed fire. "I can't believe you don't know that you're the fucking problem."

Cookie intentionally baited her. She knew that in a million years Toni would never admit that she had socked her in the stomach. No one had the audacity to do that to Toni Ferlinghetti, and she was too proud to admit what had happened between them.

"You don't like my ponytail, right!" Cookie took off the slender band that held her ponytail and shook her hair free. Then she snapped the rubber band between her fingers like it was a slingshot. "How's my hair? Or maybe it's my skin. I'm too white, right? Isn't that what it is? I'm too white to be Italian."

Toni glared at her with contempt. "No, it's that nigger you hang out with. Everyone's seen you walking *Down the End* with him. What's his name? Herman Lynch. His mouth is deformed. He's so ugly."

Toni walked so close to Cookie that she could feel her hot breath and the smell of her gum, which she suddenly spat out of her mouth and onto the sidewalk. "With a mouth like that, how well does he kiss?"

The girls were giggling, not knowing what to do. There were random comments, quips about Cookie: *pumpkin face* and *white*, but they hung on to every word Toni said. "I bet you haven't kissed him," Toni said. "I bet you've never kissed anyone. Have you?"

Cooke didn't show any emotion, but inside she was seething. A physical fight she could take. Even though she was vastly outnumbered, she was tough, athletic and had a take-no-prisoners attitude. She'd fight to the death. This kissing stuff, though, she could not take. What Toni Ferlinghetti had said was true. She had not kissed a boy.

Toni teased her, grinning and nodding her head as if she

was rocking to a song. "What does it feel like to kiss? How is it done? Aren't you worried that when the time comes to kiss a boy, that you will not know what to do? The boy will know you do not know what to do. As soon as he realizes that you do not know how to kiss, he will dump you just like that." Toni snapped her fingers and smiled at Cookie.

Cookie felt so besieged, she did not notice that many of the girls who had arrived with Toni were leaving. Toni didn't seem to notice either. It was very late in the afternoon and most kids had to be home before dinnertime. Since the bevy of girls had stopped moving, Cookie had no way to warm up. She was shivering and growing mad at herself, thinking Toni would think she was afraid. Her core body temperature had plummeted. Even her teeth chattered. She wanted out of here, and began to plot her escape.

"Why don't we head over to the parking lot?" she suggested to Toni. "Maybe you can help me learn how to kiss."

Toni was suddenly interested, but disgusted, one and the same. She must have figured that she had backed herself into a corner and had given Cookie the upper hand. "Have you ever kissed a boy?" she asked.

Cookie looked at her with blank eyes and a lack of expression. Even though she was shivering, she managed to sustain a poker face. There was no way she would bare her deep embarrassment to the Queen Bee of Italian girls.

"Come with me," Toni beckoned her with a smile that twisted her lips into a defiant grin, showing she was the one who had to be in charge.

The jubilant procession of Italian girls, led by Toni Ferlinghetti, took up the entire width of the sidewalk on Palisade Avenue in front of Urich's. Toni nodded toward Urich's. "Hey everybody, don't you just want to stop here and get a hot fudge sundae?" Toni was greeted by sounds of *Ewww! No, I'm freezing. It's too cold for ice cream.* "How about you, Cookie Colangelo, want some ice cream?"

The girls cracked their gum more furiously as if they were trying to raise their body temperature. Cars slowed on Palisade Avenue to check out the girls. Waving, horns beeping, some cars slowing down, others revving their engines; a group of Italian girls making the scene always got attention. Even though they were all bundled up in winter coats. Boots, galoshes, scarves and mittens, every one knew what was lurking underneath their winter finery that had been purchased at *Korvette*'s or *Lerner*'s in the Cross County Shopping Center. They were Italian girls, and some men have said when Italian girls are about fourteen, there is no more beautiful sight on the face of the earth. Gorgeous creamy skin, shiny dark hair that bounced, perfect round breasts, and hips not too wide, not too narrow, just the right size. These were Italian girls, and they were the eighth wonder of the world, only surpassed physically by great beauty of geographic scenic grandeur, like the California coastline or the Grand Canyon.

Toni grinned enthusiastically. Cookie knew she craved attention. She also knew Cookie was innately shrewd enough that she figured she had the upper hand. There was no way Cookie could prove she was an experienced kisser.

Once they made it into the Palisade Parking Lot, Toni toyed with her, "Name three boys that you've kissed," she said, slanting her eyes.

"There have been a few," Cookie said, shivering, growing even colder now that she had stopped walking again.

"What are their names?" Toni smiled. Her white teeth looked like fangs and reminded Cookie of the nun, Fangs, at Christ the King School.

"I'm not telling you their names. I don't have to."

"I've kissed seventeen boys, Toni said, "and I can tell you all of their names. I can also tell you my rating scale. I've rated them all on a scale from one to ten. Know Tommy Parrello? He's a nine. The best I've kissed so far. Most are threes or fours." Toni jutted her chin as if to say *I dare you to tell me the truth.* "There is a way I can tell how many boys you've kissed, Cookie Colangelo." Toni smiled at her mockingly. "What do you say we practice?"

Cookie closed her eyes and shuddered. The only way to get through the experience was to record it in the space in her brain where she made her words. She pushed her face forward and puckered her lips, waiting for the inevitable first touch of Toni's kiss. Toni made good on her word and pressed her lips against Cookie's lips, which trembled slightly under her impact. Then she rammed her tongue forward to push open Cookie's lips and stuck her tongue down her throat like a rotary drill, probing deeper and deeper still. Cookie was only aware that her breath tasted more like a menthol cough drop than Doublemint chewing gum, and that she seemed to be gagging on her own tongue.

Wiping off her mouth, Toni reeled away from Cookie. "You've never kissed a boy in your life, Cookie Colangelo! You don't know how to tongue. French Kiss! Know what I mean?"

Cookie wiped off her mouth with her sleeve and looked at Toni. "Overall, I'd say you're about a two! But maybe you're just having a bad day! If you want, we can try some other time, but not now, because I'm so damn cold and I want to go home."

Cookie stomped off. She didn't hear any of the girls' voices trailing behind her. She did see Arky Lovato pulling up into the lot, and other boys coming in to see why there was a sudden meet-up of Italian girls. Arky was driving a brand- new orange Ford Mercury Cougar that had black racing stripes and a spoiler. By *North End* standards, this was one helluva car. Cookie didn't care about how Arky had come into a car so fancy that it was an Italian girl babe magnet. Cookie had a stunning revelation, one that she had not anticipated. She could see it was going to be increasingly difficult to get Arky to be her driver around town. It was first come, first served; the competition from Toni was formidable. Cookie walked backward, checking out the ensuing scene. Toni had propped herself up against Arky's right bumper and kicked at his tire with a slight tap of her toe. Any time a guy showed up, Toni dropped her girlfriends like hot potatoes. The rest of the girls had disbanded and trickled onto Palisade Avenue, breaking up into groups of two and three and heading in opposite directions. She walked faster and turned the corner onto Roberts Avenue. She couldn't wait to get home to wash her mouth out with soap, take a hot bath and spray on *Ambush perfume,* or whatever it took to erase the invasion of Toni Ferlinghetti.

Twenty-nine

The Glass Owl

Cookie headed to Getty Square to go Christmas shopping. She thought of taking Donny with her, but she was nowhere to be found. Donny was missing in action a lot these days. Kitty still spent most of her time sitting on her chair in the living room, listening to instrumental music on WPAT-FM, but didn't do much of anything else. Johnny was gone all of the time now, out with his friends, playing music in the city, sometimes for pay. He had joined the local musicians' union in New York City and played on the weekends for Weddings and Bar Mitzvahs, or at least that's what he said he did when he was gone for days at a time. Cookie knew he spent most of his time at Lynn Oliver's studio on the Upper West Side jamming with real musicians, most of whom were black.

Everyone knew that if you made it in New York City, you could make it anywhere. On a clear day, from a limited vantage point on North Broadway, half way between the North End and Getty Square, after the trees had shed their leaves, she could see the Manhattan skyline. And while it was only miles away, it was a world so far removed from Yonkers it might as well be a foreign country. She believed in New York

City as much as she believed this was the place where her father had staked his heart. Not that it mattered.

Johnny Colangelo sold liquor to bars, restaurants, taverns, hotels and country clubs, or any entity that would buy hard liquor, most notably Seagram's, in bulk quantities. As far back as Cookie could remember, her father had been a liquor salesman who didn't want to be in the liquor business. He wanted to be a jazz musician. He wanted to live, eat and breathe music, which is why he spent every spare minute in the city at an obscure studio on the upper west side, playing all of the percussion instruments in the world with a hardcore jazz man named Lynn Oliver. Cookie's father said he could never be a real jazz musician because he had a wife, kids and a house to support. For this reason alone, he felt removed from the real jazz community, who didn't let anything, including women and children, stand in the way of making music.

If Johnny Colangelo couldn't be famous, then Cookie would have to do it for him. Someday she would become famous herself. She quickly walked by the Yonkers Savings and Loan Association building that housed her father's office, deliberately avoiding a chance encounter with him. She didn't want to see him now. He was so far removed from her life that he might as well not be her father at all. It wasn't his fault that she felt this way. It was as if all of the prior connections of her past, her grandmother, Johnny, his sisters, all were strangers to her now, familiar from past encounters, but no less strange. She had not seen many of them in years, not since Kitty had gotten so sick. She passed window storefronts, not taking a glance at her own reflection in the glass. She knew her looks had changed. She was growing up and no longer an exception among Italian girls. She was becoming one of them, and that feeling alone was worrisome.

It was funny to consider that boys and men never used to bother with her, and now she was fast becoming a major man magnet. Weirdos, creeps, schoolboys, grown men and perverts

of all ages, sizes, body types, races and ethnicities—the com-
bined forces of the men from Yonkers acted like they owned
her and they never stopped coming on to her. They only thing
worse than being groped at all the time is when the men and
boys ignored her. She hated it when they bothered her as much
as she hated when they ignored her. It was the chief moral
dilemma in being an Italian girl, and one from which she has
never recovered. Feeling as though she was being airlifted by
the crush of bodies, Cookie moved with the crowd crossing
Broadway against the blare of car horns coming from beat-up
old cars and commercial delivery trucks. A D'Agostino Grocery
van was trying to turn into the lane where she was walking.
The guy rolled down the window and hollered at her, "What
are you going to do stand there all day?! You're not good-
looking enough to stop traffic!"

"Asshole," Cookie yelled, giving him the finger. Getting
singled-out and yelled at by the grocery guy mortified Cookie.
In this part of town, she didn't want any attention drawn to
herself. She walked faster, tottering on white leather platform
boots, clattering on the pavement, wishing to God that she
had not switched-out her flat blue oxfords for trendy platform
shoes to give her height and show off her best asset—her legs.
It was hard having her heels hitting the ruts of broken, uneven
pavement. Every step she took threatened to twist her ankle,
and she inwardly cursed herself for not spending enough time
training to walk in high heel shoes on a city street. It was sort
of like learning how to dance. You had to train to get any good.

Before she had met Herman, her trick knee would have
gone out by now. Herman had helped her change all of that.
She pulled herself upright, tightening her abdomen, and felt
confident in her stride. She saw a slender decorative Christmas
tree growing in a large planter. The tree was too small and
delicate for the container and was topped with a small tin star
and a set of fragile red twinkle lights. She felt a sort of tenderness for the tree. It was a kindred spirit, a living, breathing

thing that had been forced to grow up before its time. She walked tentatively now, guarding herself, guarding her hurt pride, trying to understand all of the things that had happened to her, and at the same time, letting go.

She was so used to protecting herself in this strange, dirty part of the city that she didn't really embrace the fact that the chance of getting mugged, molested, hassled or killed here was slim or remote. People feared violence happening more often than it actually happened. More often than not, the only violence that happened were the words spoken from one's mouth. People talked like they were trying to start a fight, but they weren't; it was just the way they talked. *Them's fighting words*, Cookie thought to herself. She stood still for a moment, hoping and praying no one noticed her and no one knew she was not supposed to be there. She reached into the depths of her shoulder bag and felt around until she found a pack of *Juicy Fruit* gum. She pulled out a pack with three sticks of gum. Unwrapping the foil, she popped a stick in her mouth, savoring the first burst of sugar. She actively chewed on the right side of her mouth. Her molars on the left side were bothering her and were sensitive to every single thing she put into her mouth. She felt a piece of tooth splinter into a fragment or two and get stuck in the gum in her mouth. She was only fourteen, and her teeth were falling apart. She could not remember the last time she or Donny had been to the dentist.

She came to the front of the *Happy House Gift Shop* and stopped walking. She glanced at the glass storefront and looked beyond her own reflection and inside the store. From the corner of her eye, something sparkly caught her attention. Clear glass in a store front window reflected light from a slant of sun that had penetrated in between the wall of two concrete buildings. Inside the window, a glass object lit up as bright as a small beacon of sun. A small glass owl was more noticeable than the company it kept among glass dolphins, glass elephants, glass bears and too many glass bulls to count.

The sight of the owl tapped into a private little opening into Cookie's soul. Every time her knee went out on her and she hit the ground, she felt like an owl, a *Blind Owl*. She wanted to own the glass owl in the window. He would understand her in a way no one else could.

Cookie saw a small display sign in the window. She was looking at *Steuben Glass*. Known for its decorative glass and lead crystal, Steuben was an American icon that commissioned the toniest of artists, Georgia O'Keefe and Salvador Dali, to make exclusive pieces and once-in-a-lifetime limited collections. Standing outside looking in the window, she saw herself in the glass. She had forsaken the ponytail. Her long, light brown hair was parted in the middle with the same lack of style as the Mona Lisa. Her tall white boots hugged her well-formed legs just above her knees, and her thighs were smooth and athletic. She looked like an ice skater she had seen skating around Rockefeller Center on TV, advertising Christmas in the city. Her maroon plaid scarf fell around her shoulders like a loose mantilla. Her face was casting angles and curves and was no longer an unformed mass of cheeks and chin. She was becoming a woman. She was transfixed on both her own image in the storefront window and the small glass owl on display from behind the glass. She wanted to hold the owl—just once.

She remembered the *Blind Owl* Alan Wilson, and how sad she was because he had died. She read stories about how he came to be friends with old-time blues musicians like Son House, who had lost his way and stopped making music. The Owl grew close to the old blues man and helped him to remember the songs he had made, and to find his way back to making his own music again. She heard Son House's song *Death Letter Blues* playing in her head and she thought she should find a way to learn every word in this sad song about a man who had lost his woman the same way she had lost her friend *the Blind Owl*. Her Owl had a way of connecting with old-time blues men the same way her father connected with his black jazz man friends in the city. When Son House, *Father of the Delta Blues,* came back to play again, the *Blind Owl* was right there with him. Playing guitar and the harmonica, the white boy Alan Wilson was with the old black man, backing him on two cuts. Cookie heard the cuts when Johnny took her with him to Lynn Oliver's studio, where the musicians were all pressed up close together and jamming, only stopping to take smoke breaks. Johnny loved his music as much as her *Blind Owl* or Son House lived their music, and there was something sad about that. Beautiful too. As Johnny would say, *YONKERS, Yonkers!*

In the reflection of the store front window, a black face came into view beside her. "I never thought I'd catch you here." Herman gave her a smile that barely raised the corners of his mouth. He was wearing a red plaid woolen overcoat and had black *Hush Puppies* that came up to his ankles just below the flare of his too-short bell bottoms. "I'm looking for a present for my grandmother," he said. "Don't know what to get her. All she wants is books, and I'm tired of giving her books all the time. Especially when she can borrow books any time she wants at the library."

The front glass door of the *Happy House* was thrust open and startled them both. Cookie felt a burst of warm air coming from inside the store. A tall, slender man with a receding hairline looked at them with mild disdain. "Don't just stand there," he said. "You're blocking the window. Instead of just standing there, why don't you just come in." It was more of a blithe remark than a genuine invitation, and it made Cookie feel uncomfortable.

She looked at him, wondering what he wanted from them and if he was really inviting them inside. He had a pencil thin moustache and his receding hairline bordered the crown of his head like the front rim of a helmet. Like a Capuchin monk, the dome of his head was completely bald and encircled by a narrow band of wispy hair. He had more hair growing on the sides of his head than on top. The overall effect made him look strange and stern. He didn't seem to be the type of guy who would unzip his pants and show his dick to her as if it was his favorite pet. Nor did he seem like he would try to touch her in some indecent way.

Although he looked creepy, Cookie could tell he was perfectly harmless. Young Italian girls just know these things.

Herman shrugged and looked at Cookie. "Well, let's go in. The man said we could go in. Let's take a look around."

He didn't smile but continued to hold the door open. "The music boxes will only be here for another week."

Cookie didn't know what he was talking about. Neither did Herman, but he looked at her like, *Let's go and do it.* She followed him, cracking her gum in a little pocket of air pressing in her right molar. She loved the sound of her popping gum. It made up for any awkward bursts of silence when two people should be talking.

"Please don't make that sound," the man said. "It sounds like chalk scraping on a chalkboard, and it grates my nerves. Plus, it's cheap and disgusting."

Cookie felt scared enough to tuck the gum in her cheek. She didn't swallow, and she didn't say anything.

"Is that what they teach you to do in Catholic school? Crack your gum! You must be from Park Hill, or worse, Nepera Park."

No one had ever talked to Cookie quite this way. Come to think about it, she thought everyone talked to her in a condescending way. From the nuns at school to her father and the men on the street to the other kids her own age, everyone talked to Cookie Colangelo with a tone of disrespect, as if she was as unusable as broken glass, a throwaway. It made her remember the small glass owl and her reason for loitering there. Sometimes she felt as fragile as glass, about to break into pieces. Others would walk over all that was left of her in pieces and further crack her into smithereens.

"Well just don't stand there! Come inside. You're welcome to look at the music boxes."

Cookie still didn't know what he was talking about, but she walked through the door he continued to hold open for her and stepped inside. The gallery was dark, with black lacquer walls and recessed lighting. There were many pillars of different heights made from black stone holding beautiful glass objects, some huge and mounted on a single stand.

"*Reuge*," he said. The man sounded as if he had a European accent. French, German, Italian, Cookie couldn't be sure. "You should see the *Reuge* music boxes while the boxes are still here. A young lady and gentleman like you," he said acknowledging Herman, "would appreciate their delicate beauty and fine artistry."

The balding man trailed alongside of her but was careful not to get too close to her or Herman, and kept a polite distance. His walk was brisk and bristling with annoyance as if his only mission in life was to be perpetually unhappy with everything he came into contact with, including Cookie Colangelo and Herman Lynch. And not because he was truly unhappy. His disgruntlement was simply his innate style, his preferred way of coping with the world.

Cookie didn't say anything to the man. He introduced himself as "Giorgio." He announced his full name in a formal tone as if he were conducting a liturgy. "Mr. Giorgio DeSutter." He tilted his head forward and for the first time, Cookie could see he had a large thatch of hair growing on the back of his head. She felt sorry for him. If he had been a kid growing up in Yonkers, everyone would have made fun of him. Between the name and his head, he had no other choice in life but to be a monk or a guy who worked in a store selling glass objects.

"Giorgio," Cookie said softly. It was the first time she had opened her mouth and had said anything. As soon as she did, she was immediately sorry.

He closed his eyes. "Mr. DeSutter," he corrected her. "I only work here on the weekends around the holidays, but during the week, I teach music at Gorton High School. I'm a teacher of music," he said proudly, pulling himself up to his full height.

"My grandmother's a teacher too," Herman said. "Except she doesn't teach anymore."

"Did she teach at the high school level?" the man inquired. "I know many of the high school teachers in Yonkers."

Herman shook his head. Cookie thought something was troubling him and reminded herself to ask him later. Cookie didn't know any of the teachers at Gorton High School, or any of the students. After she left Public School #16, her world had changed. The public school kids and the Catholic school kids morphed into two distinctly different cultures and there was little contact between them. Except for Herman, she didn't even know any of the kids in public school. She wasn't even sure where he went to school.

"Where do you go to school? I can't believe I'm asking you that now."

"Gorton." Herman smiled at Mr. DeSutter. "Next year I'm taking your class," he beamed. "I love music."

"Do you play any instruments?" Mr. DeSutter looked at him as if he was assessing his ability to be in the school band.

"No," Herman said. "I can dance." "My body's an instrument. Just like this. Watch." He broke into a soft tap routine, shuffling steps in perfect beats of eight.

"I see." Mr. DeSutter looked incredulous. "You're pretty good."

Without meaning to do so, Cookie emitted a small pop of gum, hardly a full-blown crack. No doubt about it, she was turning into an Italian girl who could crack her gum.

"Honestly," Mr. DeSutter admonished her. "If you ever want to get anywhere in life, you must stop that annoying habit."

Cookie didn't mean to offend him. "I think he's the real thing," she whispered to Herman. "A genuine Italian, the kind from Europe. He's so <u>not</u>-Yonkers."

"How do you know?" Herman whispered back.

"Because he doesn't know why Italian girls crack their gum."

Herman wrinkled up his nose in confusion. "I've been meaning to ask you that."

"It's sort of a girl thing," Cookie laughed.

Cookie looked at Mr. DeSutter and nodded her head with singular determination. "I'm going to leave Yonkers one day and I'm going to be famous."

"Really," Mr. DeSutter said, raising his eyebrows. "And what are you doing all the way down here on a Friday? Aren't you supposed to be in school? What is your name, Miss?"

"I'm not going to tell you," Cookie said defiantly. "It's none of your business."

"I'm not going to turn you into the authorities, if that's what you're thinking," Mr. DeSutter said.

"We were dismissed early today for Christmas break," Herman said.

For the first time, she noticed the kindness in Mr. DeSutter's eyes, as if he felt for her in some way that was definitely not perverted or crazy like so many of the other men in her life she had known. "Most people just call me Cookie."

"What an interesting name. I'll wager you're one tough Cookie."

"She is," Herman chortled, catching himself mid-way into a laugh. "Cookie's the toughest girl *Down the End.*"

"Don't go saying that trash about me."

"What are you going to do about it, honky?"

Cookie looked at him and rolled her eyes. There he was, teasing her as if she was a puppy like Blackster. She folded her arms and tapped her foot.

"Very well," Mr. DeSutter said softly. "Have it your way, both of you have some inside humor going on that's way over my head. No worries. Go on and check out our display of music boxes downstairs." Looking at Cookie, he said, "If you're going to be famous, you need to see everything in the world that is magical. And you can start by getting rid of that gum."

She tucked the wad inside her cheek but she wasn't about to let go of it, not yet. "Cookie really is my name."

"There is no doubt in my mind whatsoever that Cookie is your name." He pointed to a gilded stairwell that led to the gallery downstairs. "I won't be joining you," he said. "I have other things to do, and must stay up here with the customers, but you can take as long as you like down there. It's almost Christmas and we have quite a display."

Cookie felt self-conscious in her hiked short skirt and gangly white platform boots. Now was not the time to be showing off her legs. She didn't feel artistic or in possession of a frame of mind sensitive enough to look at music boxes. She felt like a total clod, very clumsy; awkward was the best way to describe her tentative movement. As she walked through the narrow aisles in the store, she saw her reflection in the mirrored walls. She was trying so hard to be careful, not to bump into anything, and not topple the thick glass round table that held hundreds of glass animals. Refracting the rays of late afternoon sun flashing in sheets from the street, the menagerie of animals lit-up and glowed with the uncommon blend of fire and the chill of winter ice. Herman, on the other hand, was so delicate on his feet, it was as if the tips of his toes were barely touching the gleaming tile floor and he was walking on air.

She walked carefully to avoid knocking into Herman or a black onyx pillar that stood defiantly in the room as if it separated the ordinary objects from exquisitely fragile works of art. The pillar came fleetingly between Cookie and Herman, separating them for an instant, and both said: *Bread and Butter*, walking around the pillar leading to an intricate network of display cases full of etched glass shelves that were as fancy as anything Cookie had seen in a museum.

Cookie felt like she had walked around in a circle and had not gone anywhere, but when she looked around, she realized that both she and Herman had arrived at the far corner of the store that led to the beginning of a hidden staircase leading downstairs to a basement level.

Charging up the staircase, a woman wearing an overly large navy blue overcoat almost knocked them over. Instead of going around them, she was intent on barreling past them as if she did not see them. Cookie suddenly realized it was Millie Mangano, and she did not even look up. She was refusing to look at them. Millie's coat bulged in front as if she was trying to conceal stolen goods. Her hair was a shining bob of dark hair and she carried a rectangular pocketbook that was a distinct blue tone, bolder and brighter than her navy blue coat. She looked away and tilted her head sharply to the ground with the precision of a torpedo. She pretended to be preoccupied with seeing each step, and not tripping. She nudged past Cookie and Herman who was right behind her, brushing her elbow against the side of Cookie's arm, but pretending no trespass had occurred.

"Millie," Cookie called out. "What's gotten into you?"

Millie paid her no mind and looked at Cookie as though she was a familiar stranger, someone she had seen before but could not remember where. Out of all of the thousands of people in Yonkers, how could she possibly not know the identity of a fourteen-year-old girl wearing white platform boots with a black boy in tow? Cookie was too stunned to say anything, and too scared to think something like this could have happened to her. She thought for sure she had been caught playing hooky, and she braced herself for punishment. Cookie waited and held her breath expecting a yell or a slap, which would have been a normal response, but the woman looked through Cookie as if she was invisible. The golden light from the display cases shone on the crown of the woman's head, giving a softer edge to her dark hair. Millie Mangano said nothing to Cookie and walked away from her, leaving a wake of strong perfume. *Jean Naté, Evening in Paris*? Whatever Millie was wearing, the heavy floral scent clung to the air in the stairwell like an unmovable cloud.

Cookie stood in the middle of the stairwell. Herman didn't prod her to go down the steps. He knew something was wrong, and seemed to sense that the woman Cookie called Millie had intentionally shunned his friend.

On the upper landing, Millie Mangano seemed to know Giorgio DeSutter. The two of them passed a quiet glance in an intimate exchange. "How'd you like the music boxes?" He shook her hand gently, but firmly bidding her to stay longer. "Can't you stay a little longer, Millie? Marco is coming soon and I can leave. I'll take you out for some coffee."

Millie patted Giorgio on the cheek. "I have to get back to the office," she told him. "By the time I go shopping, it will be too late and Johnny will complain. Believe me, I don't want to hear the sound of his complaining." She took both of his hands into hers and patted his hand. She looked at him as if to make a promise. "Next time I'll get here early and we'll go to the Donut Den."

Cookie suddenly realized how it felt to be invisible. She had experienced the feeling before, but each time you're treated as though you're invisible, it might as well be the first time. It's a feeling you never quite get used to, and Herman must have felt the same way. "Okay, Cookie, let's go. Let's go downstairs and take a look."

Cookie wanted to leave, but felt too awkward to make a quick exit. She was feeling pressured to stay. Herman was with her, and it wouldn't be fair to make him leave. All she wanted to do was to lay claim to a small glass owl that understood her more than anyone else in the world, except for maybe Herman. She gripped onto the handrail, made of wood and coated with thick varnish that gleamed like liquid under the hot light. She made her way down the steps that led into a place that did not appear to be a basement at all. Full of burnished wood curio cabinets and interlocking display cases, the room was a separate gallery, with soft lighting and windowed showcases full of mechanical music boxes.

"Wow, "Herman said. "Look at this! I had no idea things like this even existed. Look at these boxes." His voice drifted in the cavernous below-basement level room, and his footsteps grew so soft, it was as if he was gliding across the shiny parquet floor.

The exhibition consisted entirely of *Reuge* music boxes. Cookie read the descriptions and remembered how Giorgio DeSutter pronounced the name *Reuge*. Even though she had heard Giorgio mention the name, it was so far from her realm of the familiar that she did not know if *Reuge* was the name of an artist or a company, or even possibly a type of wood, a wheel or a metal sculpture.

Each music box was a jewel and a world unto itself. A tiny cardinal mounted on a gilded gold sphere, a blue jay with green and gold wings, a bird resembling a parakeet with a black beak and gold-tinged wings. Some of the cages were animated with automatons of amazing singing birds. A small sterling silver winter forest was hidden deep in the boughs of trees and rabbits nestled everywhere in the magical underbrush. One music box had been bleached to soft white and was encircled with a trio of hummingbirds. *Precious woods and inlaid wood in colors, ranging from amber to black lacquer, with textures of inlaid flowers, leaves and trees in burnished gold and an inlay of mother of pearl and* golden-hued *burr myrtle wood*, Cookie read in the small placard mounted on the wall, were laden with swirls of ribbons and inlaid with delicate hand-painted flowers. A miniature grand piano imprinted with leaves was carved in solid silver. Another music box was hand-crafted in the shape of a violin. Cookie and Herman had entered the world of magical mechanical music boxes and even though their music could not be heard, the sight of these exquisite boxes made Cookie's heart sing with words of praise, and made Herman want to dance. He was so excited, he jumped straight up in the air like a rocket and came down in a landing as soft as dust.

Cookie had never seen anything like these boxes before, and it told her what she had always instinctively known. The world was a powerful and mysterious place filled with magical things that far exceeded what any Italian girl from Yonkers would ever dream of. She knew there was so much more out there. And as soon as she left Yonkers, one day, she would know everything. Her thoughts were interrupted by Giorgio DeSutter, who was standing beside them. He fluttered his hands as though he was yearning to wear small gloves and let them to do the talking.

Giorgio DeSutter looked at them. "Which one is your favorite?" Herman favored the grand piano and said so, pointing to the display, then clapping his hands on the sides of his cheeks. "The sight of the piano makes me want to move."

Cookie felt timid, as if she was out of her element and in another realm. She didn't know what to say. "The music boxes are all so beautiful. Each one is a work of art, in its own right." She could not believe she had said such a thing. She normally didn't talk this way. Giorgio DeSutter bought out some strange formal side of herself she had not come to know until now.

"Then you don't have a particular favorite." Giorgio DeSutter looked at her with grave concentration and shook his head to show he meant to drill down and understand what Cookie was really thinking. It wasn't an invasive move, but seemed kind, and as if he cared about something more than he was able to share with them. "You have something to say, don't you, Miss Cookie?"

"Uh huh," Herman agreed. "Man, does she ever have a lot to say."

"I do," Cookie said. "I love the music boxes, but the one thing I love more than anything else is made from glass."

"Mostly everything in this store is made from glass." Giorgio DeSutter swept his arm around the store in a swirling motion, taking inventory of what was there. "Our world is made of glass."

Herman rolled his eyes and smiled. "I think I know what she's going to say."

"No, you don't," she kidded Herman.

Mr. DeSutter looked at Cookie and smiled. If you could pick just one, what would it be?

"The Owl," she said.

"A Steuben glass owl?" he asked.

"The Owl," Herman said. "That's the one, I knew it!"

"Come with me. Come with me." Mr. DeSutter's walk was brisk, pure economy in movement and as taciturn as the expression on his face. Three rows of deeply furrowed lines were etched in his craggy forehead, and on both sides of his eyes the creases turned downward, making him look sly. He didn't act as though he was sneaky or had an ulterior motive. Instead, his every movement exuded a divine discontentment or spiritual dissatisfaction with the status quo, but as Cookie was learning, it wasn't necessarily the way he really felt about life or anything. He liked to fuss and fume because it was how he dealt with the world; nothing would ever be able to disappoint him.

The three of them moved quickly up the steps, with Herman in the lead taking two steps at a time.

"Come with me," he said again to them on the landing that led to the main floor. Far back on the floor, a long wooden banquette cabinet took up most of the length of the wall, and a podium displayed an ornate cash register that was on the small side, and meant to be understated. It was as if the *Happy House* fully intended to be a museum and not a retail operation selling bric-a-brac and *objets d' art*.

It was the owl she wanted more than anything. The banquette had many drawers. Giorgio DeSutter began opening and closing drawers, searching for something. He talked to himself a bit in a fussy tone of voice, saying, *No, that's not the one. No. No. Where could it be, I wonder*. He opened a drawer in the kiosk podium that held the cash register and found what he was looking for, "Ah hah," he announced. He took out a small cardboard box that bore the logo of Steuben glass, opened it and pulled out a small object wrapped in tissue paper, which he removed and revealed a small glass owl. "There are many glass owls that we sell. And these owls are all consistent, stamped out of the same mold, but this owl is different. Someone made a mistake." He held the glass owl up to the light and moved it around to fully show it. "This one has a defect. You see, its eye has been damaged, and it appears to be cracked."

"Wow!" Herman said. "How much is it?"

Giorgio DeSutter placed it on top of the banquette. "Normally it would be sixty dollars, plus sales tax, of course."

"That's a lot of money," Herman said.

"It's the cost of thirty ludes," Cookie snapped. She stepped from side to side. Her white platform boots were wearing out their welcome, and her feet had begun to hurt.

Herman mirrored her moves and looked at her, shaking his head disapprovingly. "Cookie."

Mr. DeSutter examined the glass more closely. "It's not really cracked, you see, but no one will buy it because it's defective. I can't do anything with it but send it back to Steuben, and maybe they'll give me a credit," he paused thoughtfully, "for the wholesale cost."

"How about a discount?" Cookie asked.

"Yeah," Herman agreed. He rapped his hands on the top of the banquette counter. Playing the drums, hearing a beat in his head, his drum-playing was gentle, deliberate strokes that communicated enthusiasm that could not be said in words or by silence.

"I think I shall just give you the owl." He began wrapping it back in the tissue paper he had discarded. "That is exactly what I shall do." He stuffed the owl into its small box and handed it to Cookie. "Consider it my gift to you for Christmas."

Cookie held the box in her hand and looked away. She did not know what to do. No one had given her a gift quite like that, and she did not trust the intentions. *What did he want from her*, she wondered? She felt a mixture of confusion and discomfort. She did not want to hand it back to him. She stood motionless. Herman was by her side. "Wow, just take it," he said. "And don't forget to say thanks."

"Thank you." Cookie was embarrassed by the gift and could only get over feeling awkward about it was if she passed on her gift to someone she cared about. "I want you to have it." She handed the small boxed owl to Herman. "I want you to give it to your grandmother." She looked at Mr. DeSutter. "I want his grandmother to have it. Don't ask me why. I just want to give it to her. Is that okay? Do you mind?"

"It's yours. You can do with it whatever you like." Mr. DeSutter smiled and nodded. "I can see that in spite of being a tough cookie, you have a generous spirit."

Cookie looked at Herman. "It's the only way to keep the owl alive between us."

Herman's eyes looked big behind his glasses, even larger than usual, and he wasn't saying anything to Cookie, just standing there.

"I look forward to having you in class next year," Mr. Giorgio DeSutter said as if he was dismissing them. Then he bowed politely. The yellow spotlight overhead cast a wavering beam close to the top of his head that made his circular fringe of hair more golden than brown, and his grey flecks had now been transformed to silver highlights.

Cookie and Herman thanked him again, not in a large way, but more as a matter of being polite, and left the store. It had grown darker. On the verge of dusk, a few flurries floated in the air. A city bus roared by and Cookie noted it was a Number 2, which she could not catch in time even if she ran to the stop, and would have to wait a while for the next one. She shivered and cinched her woolen coat closer to her chest.

She was sure the temperature had dropped below freezing. She didn't get why Giorgio DeSutter was being so generous. Surely he expected something in return. She didn't know much about him. On the other hand, he might be one of those angel people who come into your life and give you a leg up to the next place along the way on your journey. In the long run, Cookie never did find out why he had given her the owl. Not that it mattered. She and Herman had an affinity for owls, and that's all there was to it.

Thirty

A Lame Leg

Cookie left Herman in Getty Square to go to Johnny's office. Herman was close enough to home and could easily walk there. She really wanted the owl, but she had surprised even herself by giving it to Herman. Cookie had acted out of impulse. Some impulses were good; some were bad and got her into big trouble; but this impulse was truly grand and made her feel as if she had created a pocket of warmth in a cold world where there was hell, and heaven was only a place she could make for herself, the same way she made her words. She didn't understand her impulse to be generous any more than she understood the powerful shield she had built to house her feelings. It was dark by the time she pushed open the heavy brass-framed glass door, entering the building where Johnny worked. She might get lucky and he would be wrapping up his day's work and offer to drive her home. *Fat chance*, she thought to herself. Johnny was never there when she needed him. Then the funny thing is how he would show up totally out-of-the-blue, as if someone had let the genie out of the bottle and conjured a fantasy father for her.

Cookie remembered marching through Getty Square in the St. Patrick's Day Parade. She wore the full regalia of her Catholic school uniform, including immaculate white gloves she had surreptitiously borrowed from Kitty's closet. Suddenly, Johnny popped up on the sidewalk in front of St. Mary's Church. He was standing there on the street yelling his head off, *Cookie! Cookie! Cookie*! The St. Patrick's Day Parade was a big deal in Yonkers, and everybody was there. Crowds thronged both sides of the street and it was hard to see any one person. And yet there he was, waving his arms, his face the color of an old-fashioned fire hydrant; he had popped into her life like an unexpected apparition. He waited for her at the end of the parade line. He kept exclaiming, "Your lines were so even and in tempo. Your uniforms were all lined-up. Your gloves were so white. Your school band was the best in the whole parade, and really big. You were tremendous-looking!" The parade, pomp and circumstance and, of course, music, spoke to him in a way most other things in life could not, and he had tears in his eyes.

Johnny didn't have tears in his eyes now as he stood behind his desk, with one leg jacked up on top of the old radiator that ran along the wall under the entire length of the window. The window was open a crack, letting in cold air. He was smoking a cigarette, a *Tareyton*, one of many to come. He had recently changed his brand from *Lucky Strike* to *Tareyton* so he would have the benefit of its new charcoal filter. He also liked the brand's advertising image of the guy with the black eye. Cookie could tell when Johnny was really upset. As he came to the end of one cigarette, before putting it out, he'd use it to light a new one. "Millie tells me you've been going out with a black boy," he said.

Cookie didn't bother taking off her coat. She knew she would not be staying long, and she would not be riding home with him tonight. "Herman Lynch is my friend."

"Friend," Johnny said. "I don't see how he can be a friend. He's black. Tell me how he's a friend."

"We're friends," Cookie said.

"Blacks & whites don't mix! Not around here! This is Yonkers!" Johnny took his foot off the radiator and turned around to look out the window. "Tell me how far this friendship goes! What are you doing with this boy?"

"It's not what you think. It's not the way you're making it out to be. We're friends."

"You expect me to believe that! You're a girl and he's a boy, and there's hormones and all that, and you're telling me you're not doing something that you should not be doing! With a black boy, for Christ sakes. It would be bad enough with any boy. An Italian boy, for god sakes, but a Negro boy! Jesus, Mary and Joseph. How could you to such a thing to yourself! How could you do such a thing to me and your mother? Don't we have enough problems as it is!"

Cookie backed up toward the door, looking for a way out. "You're never home! You're off with your musician friends, who are mostly black, and you hide it. You hide it from me. You hide it from everybody."

Johnny crumpled up an empty pack of Tareytons and threw it on top of the desk. "Look at you! Look at you! You're wearing go-go boots, and sleeping in the gutter with a Negro boy!!"

Millie walked into the office, stood in the doorway and played with her earrings. She took them on and off, finally placing them in her hand and shaking them like she was rolling dice. She had a necklace and a bracelet to match. They were made into the shape of twisted glitter Christmas trees. She changed her jewelry like the weather. Depending on the season, she wore giant fake pearls, pink and blue rhinestones, purple lacquered knobby buttons and black oblong fobs. Each season had its own look.

"'Tis the season to be jolly," Millie said as she yanked the Christmas tree earrings from her ears. Millie often boasted that she had purchased most of her jewelry, reduced for quick sale, from Berdy's Jewelers in Getty Square. She wasn't boasting now. Clinking her earrings in her hand, she spoke as if Cookie wasn't there. "She's with the boy all the time. Everyone notices and everybody's talking about them. They think they go up to that Untermyer Park and have sex at the Eagle's Nest."

"Who's they?" Cookie snapped. "Who's they? Oh, my God. How could you... they... say those things about me!"

Millie pulled bobby pins from her hair, actually freeing them from her black fall wig. Her bouffant had fallen sharply to one side, grazing her shoulder and taking on the appearance of a shrunken head.

"He's my friend," Cookie said. "He's my good friend. My real friend."

Johnny folded his arms across his chest. His eyes blazed with red-hot rage. "Couldn't you just have an imaginary friend?"

"He's my friend," Cookie insisted. "My friend."

"You can't be friends with black people," Johnny said. "And you can't have sexual relations with anyone at your age, especially them. It's wrong. What if you got pregnant!"

Cookie tore into him. "What about you! You're such a hypocrite! You're never home. You're in the city all the time at the studio with your friends. And they're black. You have black friends, good black friends. Why can't I?"

"They're not black," Johnny said. "They're musicians."

Cookie looked at her father. He did not know the truth. He was incapable of knowing the truth, and it was very weird to explain why he could not see a simple set of facts that were undeniably true. She was beginning to understand something for the first time. There was some semblance of fairness in the world. There was a special corner where she could create her own heaven, but it was not here, not in this office with her father or Millie Mangano.

"Why'd you come down here?" Millie asked. "This is your father's place of work, and you shouldn't be here, especially not if you're going to be sleeping around with black boys."

Cookie could not tell them the truth. Johnny and Millie were not able to deal with the truth. She did not have anything more to say to either of them.

Millie looked at Cookie as if she wanted to brand her with the scarlet letter. It wasn't disgust, contempt, anger or sadness. It was as if Millie was convinced Cookie had committed the lowest, most despicable and morally reprehensible crime on the face of the earth. "I heard you were caught with a black boy. A colored boy. Negro. Too bad he has a harelip."

Cookie felt like she was in shock. Her body was moving, but she wasn't thinking about what she was doing. She left Johnny's office and walked down the steps instead of taking the creaky old elevator. On the way down, she pulled out her pack of *Marlboro*s and lit one before she even got outside. Her hands were shaking each time she took a drag from her cigarette. She was seriously shaken, not because her father was accusing her of things she had not done, but because he did not believe her. Nor could he see the flaming hypocrisy in the circumstances. He could have black friends, but she could not. If she had black friends, she was tainted, whereas his black friends gave credence to his talent as a jazz musician. *I hate him*, she said to herself. And as much as she felt that way, she felt even worse hating a parent, because if he died, she would feel terrible about hating him so much.

She walked on Broadway, heading to the bus stop to catch the Number 2 bus home. The snow had matured from a few flurries to a light patter of steady small flakes. By the time she got to the bus stop, she huddled in the doorway and clutched her coat to her chest. She didn't have a hat, a scarf or gloves, and her fingers were frozen. The snow reminded her of another time and place. Her mind wandered back to the blizzard of 1966. It was Christmas Eve, and no matter how long Johnny Colangelo had been gone, off playing his music, he always came home on Christmas Eve.

Cookie was with her father, the two of them alone in his

car. The snow was falling, tumbling down all around the iced-silver blue Cadillac that took on the otherworldly glow of a fragile crystal sled. Cookie and Johnny were queued-up in line to get gas at the last available pump at the Texaco station on Nepperhan Avenue. The windows were fogged up. Cookie remembered that distinctly. Johnny took his big arm and brushed away the icy glaze from the windshield so she could see out the window and so Johnny could keep an eye on the gas station attendant. He didn't think he'd get a full tank of gas if he didn't keep an eye on the guy and his pump. Cookie and Johnny had finished Christmas shopping.

Every year on Christmas Eve, Johnny took Cookie to H.L Green's in Getty Square so she could pick out something she wanted. That year, Cookie had picked out a child's plastic typewriter that was almost like a real typewriter; it made small and capital letters and had a blue and white carrying case. Johnny was surprised that she wanted a toy typewriter and thought she was weird and said, *"Don't you want a doll or something?"* He bought Donny a children's Electric Organ that had a three-octave keyboard. All the stores were closing. Even though it wasn't yet the end of the day, the storm had people worried and they were going home early. One by one, in sequential order, the streetlamps flickered on in a neat row down the left side of the hill. The faint glow of the streetlamps against the greying pallor of the storm filled Cookie with a sort of cozy defiance. She felt secure enough and childish enough to wish.

Oh, I wish, how I wish, Mommy wasn't crazy, she said to herself. This was a private thought, one she didn't share with her father, and kept to herself. She watched the white sky for a sign, an answer, anything, but there was nothing, not that Christmas. Kitty's sanity was one thing Santa Claus had trouble bringing. It didn't come in a package and it couldn't be wrapped. Searching through the sheets of snow thickening into white-out conditions, all Cookie saw were the missing bulbs and critical decorative parts of the city's dull seasonal display. Fake poinsettias crowned the top of every streetlamp, like collars under broken clowns.

Johnny was watching a young woman leave a store. She might have been the last clerk on shift, or the owner. Not that it mattered too much. Johnny liked to watch women, especially the prettier ones. The woman stopped to lock the store and pulled a metal grid collapsible accordion gate—the crimeproof kind—across the front of the storefront window. She struggled a bit against the force of the wind and snow and caught her stocking in the metal; it snagged into a run. She seemed to utter a soft curse under her breath. Then she looked around to see if anyone had caught her moment of petty irritation. She didn't seem to see Cookie and Johnny in the car.

A red plaid woolen scarf framed her face like a mantilla. She was very pretty and had big eyes and a pink complexion, like one of the Victorian dolls in the Knepfer's Toyland store-front in Getty Square. The young woman struggled to cross Nepperhan Avenue against the wind and snow. There was something awkward about the way she walked. She didn't have the seductive saunter of Kitty or the cocky bounce of a young girl like Cookie. Her legs seemed to drag like dead weights, one behind the other. Then Cookie noticed that it was the same leg, one leg, that kept her down and moving slow. Johnny noticed the same thing.

The look on his face turned peculiar, and he nudged his daughter. "Look at her, Cookie. Will you look... she's gotta lame leg."

"Yeah, Daddy, I can see."

"But she's so beautiful," he said, throwing his hands up in the air as if he wished to God he could not see. "She's so beautiful, and yet she's got this terrible flaw."

He started to cry. "She reminds me of your mother."

Cookie was more scared than she was embarrassed for him. She had never seen him cry before. Not even when he talked about the winter he had spent on the front lines in

Korea. Johnny cried until the gas attendant banged on the frozen window and asked for six bucks. He never did it again.

At fourteen, Cookie had already experienced it all. She was the girl who had the sensibility to take charge of her own life, because no one else could do it for her. Cookie was overwhelmed by emotion, a strange mixture of grief, sadness, despair, and anger. There was no sense of bargaining here. She didn't have anyone to count on and trust, except for Herman Lynch, and to some extent, Reenie Ruggiero. She didn't tell Reenie how she felt about things because the two of them were always trying to show who was more tough. With Herman, though, he seemed to just know things. He could sense the feelings percolating deep down inside, in a place that Cookie did not even know how to reach on her own. She loved Herman in a way she could not define. She would always love him. He spoke to her like a wise old owl, and she would never forget that. She would walk to the ends of the earth to protect Herman Lynch. Herself too.

Thirty-one

Wednesday, February 10, 1971

Cookie Colangelo was unstoppable. There was no way Johnny Colangelo could restrain his daughter. Although he had half-considered sending her to reform school, he didn't have the direct line to get Cookie sentenced. Had he thought of such a thing, Kitty, as crazy as she was, would have stopped him. Besides, he was hardly ever home, so it's not like he could ground Cookie, banish her to her bedroom and restrict her from doing whatever the hell she felt like doing. She would hang out with Herman Lynch or Reenie Ruggiero, with whomever she wanted and whenever she wanted, and no one was going to stop her.

For both Herman Lynch and Reenie Ruggiero, the week had been eventful. The day before, Satchel Paige had been the first Negro League player voted into the Baseball Hall of Fame. Herman was so proud, he had taken to wearing a Brooklyn Dodgers baseball cap and a T-shirt with Jackie Robinson's magic number 42. Many years later, Robinson's jersey number 42 was permanently retired from Major League Baseball. On this bitter cold February day, Herman admitted he felt silly wearing a baseball cap, but he was so darn proud that he wanted to make a statement.

And make a statement he did, *Down the End* where he met up with Cookie, and Reenie, who did not have good intentions. Reenie wanted Cookie to sell her ludes, but Cookie was done dealing drugs and told her so. Even though she had never amounted to being more than a small-time operator, she was worried that Reenie was going to get hurt and take too many ludes, the same way the *Blind Owl* had taken too many *downers*. Cookie fumed that she had medical-grade ludes, and not knock-offs made in the dorm room of a chemistry major going to school at the State University of New York at New Paltz. Every hippie kid and gangster wannabe in Yonkers knew all home-made drugs, acid, mescaline, speed, uppers & downers were all made at *New Paltz*. She thought Reenie would fare better to use Cookie's ludes rather than knockoffs cut with rat poison, so Cookie hatched a plan.

She grabbed Reenie by her collar, as if she was a feral cat picking up its offspring by the scruff of the neck, and shook her. "You're not doing ludes any more. You hear me? You're done."

"Get off of me." Reenie wore a fake fur-lined Cossack hat and a navy blue wool cape. She was dressed warm and shivering anyway.

Cookie grabbed her even tighter by the neck and squeezed so hard that veins were protruding. "Tell me you're done. Say it. Make me believe it."

Herman stood behind Cookie. "Cookie," he said. "Stop it. Leave her be. Let her make up her own mind. How'd you like it if someone was forcing you to do something?"

Using her indomitable will, Cookie was going to ensure that Reenie would not take a bad batch of drugs. "You mean a lot to me, and I don't want you to die."

"That's it, Cookie, show her that you care about what happens to her instead of bullying her."

"I'm not going to die," Reenie said. "I know what I'm doing."

"Cookie's right," Herman said. "It's time to stop using.

What would happen to your grandmother? Who would look out for her? She's old and can hardly climb those steps up three flights. You can't only be thinking of yourself, girl. What would she do without you?"

"Now you sound like me," Cookie smiled at him. "I thought we were supposed to let her come to terms on her own time." Cookie nodded to Herman and let go of Reenie. "I'm only saying so because I care."

Even though Cookie did care, on another level she was more concerned over the prospect of not supplying Reenie with quality ludes and having her get hurt using bad drugs. If anything bad happened to Reenie, it would be her fault. "I do care about you," Cookie said.

"I got it," Reenie said. "It's not like I'm addicted."

Herman was moving around, and not necessarily to keep himself warm. He would be moving no matter what temperature registered. It was his way; he was a *mover*. "You've got too much going on for yourself to be messing with drugs. Next thing you know, you'll be shooting up like my mother, and now she's dead. I don't want that to happen to you, Reenie. It's not worth it."

The three of them walked into the Palisade Parking Lot, flapping arms and stamping feet. Small patches of ice formed a pastiche of Rorschach-patterns on the ground and every word and breath emitted a small cloud of steam. The weather in February could grow balmy, teasing the first signs of spring, or descend into the frigid depths of winter and set the record for the coldest day of the year. Cookie plugged in the earplugs for her transistor radio and heard a news bulletin about a new military operation taking place in one more episode of the Vietnam War, Operation Lam Son 719. She didn't know what the number meant, and it was not explained by the radio announcer. In other news stories, aftershocks were being reported from Los Angeles, where the day before the Sylmar earthquake had struck the San

Fernando Valley. And the third manned spacecraft Apollo 14 had returned to earth.

Cookie screwed up her face and tried to understand how we were putting people on the moon while back down on earth we had unleashed a killing machine in the jungles of Vietnam. Instead of Neil Armstrong's line, *one small step for man; one giant leap for mankind*, which much to her chagrin, was grammatically incorrect and should have been *one step for a man* to be a parallel construction with *giant leap for mankind*. Cookie knew her words! In her estimation, he should have said: *one step forward, ten steps backwards*. Cookie laughed to herself. It would have been funny to hear the first man on the moon, Neil Armstrong, speak the truth.

Cookie was so deep in thought that she did not see what was happening. Herman was trying to get her attention, but she had paid him no mind, not because she didn't like him, but because she could be that way—shut out the world and become lost in her own thoughts. Herman had walked to the front of the Barber Shop and stood on the sidewalk that marked the entrance to the Palisade Parking Lot. He was talking to Mike Trapani and Tommy Parrello. Cookie saw they were laughing at Herman. She was sure they were making fun of him. Cookie yanked out her earplugs. Reenie was talking back at them and she looked angry.

The Barber Shop was located next to the entrance to an apartment building, and next to that there was Hedy's Luncheonette. Hedy and her waitress Oonah had come out to see what the ruckus was about, but they did not intervene. Reenie and Herman looked like they were having a face-off with Tommy Parrello and Mike Trapani. Cookie didn't know why Tommy hung out with Mike, who was nearly three years younger and not popular. She speculated they might be birds of a feather flocking together, bully birds.

"All I want is her notebook," Herman was saying. His arms were crossed and he was moving in place, with hops so soft that his feet slid on thin patches of ice, randomly thatched panes covering the sidewalk. He was so agile, there was no danger he would slip and fall.

Tommy looked at Reenie with contempt and spat out, "What are you, a nigger lover?"

"Don't you talk about my friend like that," Reenie shot back. "Only friends can call each other *nigger*."

"Nigger," Mike said. "And I ain't no friend."

"You're not allowed to call me that," Herman said.

Tommy shoved Herman, not too hard, just enough to show him he was boss.

"Hey," Herman protested. "It's not like you can get away with pushing me around."

Mike Trapani shoved Reenie hard enough to cause her to wobble and fall. She picked herself up quickly from the concrete and tried to steady herself.

Herman blocked Mike's arm to keep him away from Reenie. "Hey, man, don't you touch a girl like that. What's the matter with you? Show some respect."

"Respect. A nigger's going to tell me about respect!" Mike's face turned red and he yelled, "Did you touch me, nigger? Am I imagining things! You touched me, nigger!"

Tommy Parrello grabbed Herman and pinned his arms behind his back while Mike Trapani zeroed in and punched him square in the face. Blood immediately spurted from his nose and mouth. His black-framed eyeglasses flew off his head and landed on the pavement in front of the red, white and blue Barber Shop kiosk. The force sent Herman reeling back into Tommy's arms, almost knocking him over. Mike Trapani lunged forward to hit Herman again. Cookie didn't have time to think. She didn't know what bothered her more, the sight of blood spurting from Herman's mouth or his owlish eyeglasses that had been flung to the ground. She didn't know what she was doing; it wasn't a conscious decision, but she leapt up in the air and delivered a high kick right into the side of Mike

Trapani's head. He instantly looked dazed, but still had the strength to deliver one more blow to Herman's face, wounding him and splashing his blood like rain from a chaotic red cloud into the cold night air.

"Look, the nigger's got red blood," Tommy yelled, laughing. "Red blood, damn! Who would believe it!"

Reenie jumped up on Tommy's back and began punching his head. He swerved and hurled her backwards, knocking her to the ground. Cookie jumped up in the air and delivered another blow to Mike Trapani's head, jostling him, fueling his rage. Turning into a mammoth red-faced monster, furiously hitting, punching, swinging blows at both Herman and Reenie, who tried to cover their heads, using their hands and arms as shields from the intensity of his repeated blows.

Tommy Parrello grabbed Cookie and held her head under the crook of his arm, dragging her forward and closer to Mike Trapani, while she kicked and struggled to free herself from his hold. Mike Trapani turned away from Herman and Cookie and flung back his arm to punch Cookie. A car squealed, almost running them over, and skidded to a stop at the entrance to the parking lot right in front of them. Whoever was in the car slammed down hard on the horn. A haze of smoking exhaust and fumes rose in the freezing air. Tommy's grip loosened on Cookie while he looked to see who it was. Mike was breathing heavy, trying to see who was in the car. Onlookers had gathered and at the head of the crowd Fran Ochiogrosso had opened her mouth wide, exuding breath like smoke, but not saying anything.

Tommy let go of Cookie, who turned around with vigorous movement and kicked him hard right under his knee cap. Tommy buckled over, clutching his knee, screaming in pain. The car was a smoking spectacle, and for the first time both Reenie and Cookie exclaimed *Mercedes Benz*; it was the first time the girls had ever seen one up close. Steam coated the windows and exhaust from the car rose in the air, temporarily concealing the driver. Even in the heat of the battle, the girls were in awe of the car. Their only reference to *Mercedes Benz* was in the song sung by Janis Joplin. The crowd murmured a low ripple of excitement when the owner of the Mercedes began to surface. Louie Santamassino got out of the car, slammed the door shut and came over to the group where he had a sizable audience that was growing larger by the second.

Herman was bleeding from his mouth and nose. He used the sleeve from his baseball jersey to wipe away some of the blood from his face.

Fran Ochiogrosso ran forward and produced a wad of tissues from her oversized red pocketbook and gave them to Herman to stop his bleeding. "I saw the whole thing," she said to Louie, but he ignored her.

"I was just down here getting Blackster some food, and I have to see stuff like this. And it makes me sick." He turned to the girls and Herman. "What led these boys to do these things to you?"

Herman stepped forward and nodded to Mike Trapani. "He took Cookie's notebook and I asked him to give it back to her."

"And he hit you?"

"Yes, sir."

"He hit me first," Mike said. He was still breathing hard. His huge, fleshy face puffed up, rounder and red with embarrassment.

"He did not," Fran yelled. "I saw the whole thing, from beginning to end."

"Did I ask you for your two cents?" Louie shot back.

"I didn't hit you," Herman said. "I moved your arm away from Reenie after you hit her. You have no business hitting my friend."

Louie Santamassino committed assault with his eyes. He looked at Mike Trapani and Tommy Parrello in such a way that they both knew they were dead meat.

"If you ever do anything again, even the smallest, slightest thing, you will have to answer to me. It won't be fun. I promise you."

Louie started with Tommy Parrello. "I don't like what I'm seeing. So maybe you want to explain and tell me what I'm seeing, so maybe I can think this thing isn't happening."

Tommy shrugged as if he was trying to rise to the occasion enough to be tough. "It's nobody's business. This nigger was bothering my friend."

Louie pressed his lips together and shook his head like he understood. He kept shaking his head and closed his eyes. No one from the crowd said anything; they just waited. Not even the hiss of a soft whisper seeped into the cold air. Louie's eyes were closed. He could have been praying. No one could tell what he was thinking, or if he was thinking at all. Across the street, young guys were tumbling out of the Palisade Pizza Place and watching the commotion. Tony, the owner and chief pizza-maker, wearing his tomato-splashed whites, came to the doorway. New to the scene, Tony remained quiet and watched. No one asked what was going on. Louie Santamassino had a reputation. No one knew for sure what it was. No one knew if he was violent, and no one, it seemed, wanted to find out.

Louie was actually downright small and wiry. The deep craggy lines in his face were devoid of expression or emotion, and he never smiled. He looked blank, yet malevolent, and this combination alone made him seem utterly terrifying.

He said to Tommy: "Look at me." Tommy looked at him, trying to avoid making eye contact. Louie slapped him in the face. "Look at me again," Louie said quietly. This time, Tommy didn't raise his face. Louie slapped the other side of his face harder than the first blow.

He turned to Mike Trapani. "Want to know what it feels like to have a bloody nose?" He smashed his fist into the center of Mike's face and instantly produced a gush of blood. Tommy

Parrello was backing up, limping and holding his wounded knee, trying to slink off. Louie lunged forward and took him by the collar and butted his head right into Mike Trapani's head, producing a bang and a yelp of pain so loud, Blackster popped up in the passenger seat of Louie's car and began barking. The dog's ears stood up straight with the proud points of a pure German Shepherd.

"Quiet, Blackster," Louie said, but the dog did not cooperate. He had tripled in size since Herman had given the dog to Louie, but he was still a high-strung puppy needing Louie's full attention.

Louie looked at the two beaten boys and said, "God, I love that dog." He shifted his head from side to side almost as if he was in a wondrous child-like state and innocent. "See that dog there. That dog's my only friend."

Fran clapped her hands as if she was emotionally overwhelmed. "Oh my God, that's so sweet. That's the sweetest thing I've ever heard you say, Louie."

Louie looked at her as if to say, *What the fuck?*

Mike Trapani's battered face had already begun to swell, with red bruising that had not yet turned colors. No one else spoke, no one left the crowd and everyone was listening. Toni Ferlinghetti and her entourage of girls had descended on the scene like a swarm of killer bees and for the first time in her life, Cookie observed the impossible. The entire bevy of Italian girls stood quiet and still, nary a stray sound, not even a single crack of gum.

Louie spoke so softly to the two boys that Cookie had to listen real hard to hear every word. "I'm not going to kill you here, because there are too many witnesses, but if you ever, and I mean ever, lay your hands on these kids again, there's going to be trouble."

Both boys nodded, red with embarrassment and stained with a potent combination of both dried and wet blood. They didn't say anything. Mike Trapani was still bleeding from his nose and sniffling to stop the blood from running down his face and into his mouth.

Fran lit a cigarette and cackled through her smoke, murmuring endearment. "You did good, Louie. I appreciate what you did, Louie. Everybody should be as brave as you."

Toni Ferlinghetti asked, "What happened?"

Louie looked at her and tried to smile, but the best he could show was a gentle grimace, a knowing smirk. Even the great Louie Santamassino didn't know what to do with such amazing *Italian girl beauty*. Toni knew he was powerless. Every red-blooded man in the world was weakened by her beauty. And Louie Santamassino was no exception. She smiled at him, tossing her full head of sexy big hair, flashing a full *Gina Lollobrigida* siren call, and cracked her gum in a repeated succession of pops that sounded like an automatic weapon.

"Mike Trapani took her notebook," Reenie said.

"So what's the big deal? "Toni rolled her eyes at her. "I don't get what all the fighting's about."

"You leave them alone, and that goes for the rest of you too," Louie said, looking at Toni. She didn't say anything but the expression on her face spoke for her. She looked like she was taken aback and confused that anyone would talk to her that way.

"You leave them alone. All of you," Louie told the crowd. "These kids are my friends. You leave them alone."

Louie looked at Reenie, Herman and Cookie. "If anyone ever bothers you, you tell me." Then he turned to Mike Trapani, "You give her that notebook back by tonight. You go up to her house, you go up the steps. Quietly. And you put the notebook in the mailbox, and you do not disturb her family. The Colangelos are disturbed enough as it is."

He looked at Cookie as if he was trying to force a smile. "You let me know when you have your notebook back."

Louie Santamassino walked to the front of the barber shop and looked in the window, but steam had frosted the glass and he could not see in. He picked up Herman's glasses and quietly handed them to him. Giving Louie that dog had touched him a way that he had never been touched before. Everyone was so used to being scared of Louie that they forgot he was a person, a real human being. Louie turned around, walked away, and got into his Mercedes, where Blackster jumped on him, licked his face and barked. Louie drove off in a plume of steam and smoke, squealing his tires and skidding on the icy road. The only sound came from Blackster barking, then growing faint, until the Mercedes Benz turned the corner and traveled on toward North Broadway.

Arky Lovato drove up in his very first set of wheels, the old army jeep that had a big plastic clock affixed to the front bumper. The hands on the clock were still set to six o' clock. The radio from the jeep blared *Gimme Shelter* by the Rolling Stones. He stopped the jeep in the front entrance to the parking lot, the same place where Louie had screeched his car to a halt. Arky rolled down the window, turned down his radio and called to Toni Ferlinghetti. Her eyes looked big, luminous and round, and she rolled them dramatically, turning her head away to purposefully snub him. He gunned his engine and offered to give her a ride home.

No one could crack gum as well as Toni Ferlinghetti. She could do ten pops in a minute. Her one amber eye was sloped down. She had a half-smile on her face. No one could do coy better than Toni. Arky called to her, again asking if she wanted a ride. Toni moved her head, alternating sides, as if she was considering getting into the jeep with him. Jekyll and Hyde-like, she smiled at him to his face and sneered at him behind his back, while making cutting little remarks about him to her girlfriends, who laughed along with her, looking over to the poor besotted creature, a lowly guy too stupid and too smitten to know he was being played.

Arky had no clue. He sincerely tried to court the favors of Toni and called to her, saying he had tickets to see Grand Funk Railroad play in a concert down at the RKO Theatre in south Yonkers. Yet, Toni had arrived at a more sophisticated phase of torment. She looked disgusted when she saw him, but her perfect white teeth were chattering and her face was the deep color of red that skin gets when exposed to extreme cold. She left her girlfriends to freeze to death on the sidewalk, walked over to his jeep and got in. The least she could have done was jam a few girls into the jeep with her, but had she shown generosity or kindness, she stood to lose her status as Queen Bee. Yonkers was a cruel urban jungle, and all Italian girls recognized at an early age that showing any sign of compassion was a weakness and a sure sign of death.

Fran Ochiogrosso insisted on taking Herman Lynch to her house to clean him up before he brought his mashed-up face home and horrified his grandmother. She brought him into her kitchen and instructed him to wash off his wounds with soap, water and then peroxide to kill any germs. She couldn't bring herself to take a washcloth to his face, and not because she did not want to touch a black person. Not wanting to tend to his wounds had nothing to do with Herman being black. Fran was so squeamish at the sight of blood that she threatened to faint. She had a lifelong aversion to the sight of blood. Once, when Fran's youngest daughter fell in the back yard and split open her lip, she had to tell the kid what to do and gave blow by blow instructions on how to clean her wound and ice her lip, but the whole time she could not look at her. She could not bring herself to see the blood.

It upset Fran that those boys had beaten Herman and roughed-up her girls, but she was thrilled at the sudden valor of Louie Santamassino, and it became clear that she had become smitten with him. Overnight, hate had begun to grow into love, and that was sure better than having love turn into hate. Although it was a well-known Yonkers precept that in order to hate anyone really well, you had to first love the person. Why waste great rage, anger and hate on someone you did not know? To hate really well, you had to invest in someone. Anonymous hate was all talk, venting, sheer noise, and it didn't mean anything.

Fran hit the tip of her long *Kent 100* against a plain, amber-colored, square glass ashtray with the accuracy of a baton twirler. Aside from ridding herself of some ash, she admired her own jerky movement. The ritual ash-flicking made her feel good about herself. It was something she could always count on during times of great stress, and it made her feel alive. Everyone was smoking except for Herman, who was standing over the sink, a package of *Birds Eye* frozen peas pressed against his face. The girls passed a *Marlboro* back and forth between them like it was a joint.

The smoke flowed from Fran's mouth and nose in a single stream as she tossed her head and said, "Cookie, there is something I've always been meaning to tell you."

Cookie wasn't interested in hearing what Fran had to say, and told her so. In a funny way, she knew what was going down. "I don't want to talk about it," She stubbed out the last of her *Marlboro* in Fran's massive ashtray, stood up and put her hands in the pockets of her jeans.

"I saw what happened to you that day," Fran said. "I walked to school early." She looked at Reenie and Herman. "I was the school crossing guard at Cookie's school. I heard what Fangs did to her and saw her standing in the school yard."

"Stop." Cookie shook her head. "Please don't."

Herman took the *Birds Eye* brick of frozen peas off of his face for an instant. "If Cookie doesn't want to talk about something, you shouldn't make her."

"Thanks," she said softly. She was mortified that Fran knew what had happened, and felt trapped. She needed to get out of here but there was no graceful way to leave Reenie and Herman in Fran's kitchen.

"Well, I'd like to know what you're all talking about," Reenie said. "Why am I always the last to know? It's like I'm the third wheel or something. And I'm getting sick of it."

"I'm sorry." Summoning her courage, Cookie said, "All I can say is, I know how it feels to get beat-up when you didn't do nothing wrong." She looked at Herman, "I'm sorry about what they did to you, and thanks for trying to get my notebook back. It means a lot to me. What you did."

Fran picked up a new pack of cigarettes and tapped them against her palm, packing them to make sure the tobacco didn't have trapped pockets of air. "If you don't pack your cigarettes," Fran said, "they don't burn smooth." Then she looked at Cookie, "You didn't do nothing wrong, Cookie. That nun was nuts. Everyone knew she was nuts, and that's why they finally got rid of her." Fran lowered her eyes as if it was the only way she knew how to be sincere. "It's why I always worried about you, because that nun did that to you and you hadn't done anything wrong."

Cookie meant to tell herself *Stop*, but this time she didn't. What was the point? She went inward, deep down inside, trying to find a well of water to drown in. She stood there for a while, not saying anything, just thinking about things, what had happened to Herman and what had happened to her.

She remembered that day because after school, her face felt too hot to touch and her head ached enough to remind her of the day she fell and got a concussion. She felt queasy in her stomach, and her hair hung forward in her face in a tangle of knots. She might have suffered from a concussion and should have said something to someone, but she couldn't bring herself to talk. Cookie was in shock.

"I saw you that day," Cookie said to Fran. "You were getting kids to cross the street. You wore the same brown uniform that you wear now. You have the same job now that you did back then. You asked me where my mother was, and I wouldn't tell you. I didn't want her to know what happened. It would have hurt her too much."

The look of sadness that crossed Fran's face was unmistakable and sincere. She put her hands up to her mouth as if she would cry. "Why didn't you tell your mother? She's your mother. She needs to know those things."

"It would have hurt her too much," Cookie said. "And she's been hurt enough as it is. Imagine being smart, but having a brain that doesn't work."

And my brain did work, Cookie thought. Full of blue sky and sun, November 6, 1967, was the first clear, cold, crisp day of the fall. In the morning, on the way to school, Cookie's feet scuffed up piles of red leaves that had fallen to the ground from the Sumac trees. She had misjudged the chilly temperature, didn't think to take a winter coat, and wore a small white sweater over her plaid jumper.

Cookie remembered that the day started out with someone making fun of her. Smirks, laughter, keening coming from Toni Ferlinghetti; it all cut her to the quick. After morning prayer and the pledge of allegiance, the class was still standing and had not yet been summoned by Fangs to return to their seats. Cookie was standing by her desk at loose attention. She could feel eyes on her back and hear giggling and whispering. She turned briefly to the side and caught them pointing and talking excitedly to one another. The girls were pointing, alright, and they were pointing at her back. She did not know why. She thought it might be her hair. She had not worn her usual ponytail and her hair fell long and wavy clear down to the middle of her back.

She took her hands and smoothed down the back of her hair. Then she smoothed down the back of her jumper. She thought maybe the wool of her skirt had risen in the air, got stuck and showed her underpants. Or maybe she sat on something. Then the fire bell rang, and everyone was lining up in rows. There were seven rows, nearly eight desks to a row. Row by row, a procession formed, lining up and moving out of the classroom, into the hallway and down the steps to go outside. The girls did not stop laughing. Cookie giggled about being cold. *I'm going to be so cold.*

Fangs was coming up the steps and her face was redder than usual. Cookie did not understand how the nun had gotten ahead of the entire class, over fifty kids, only to turn around and come back up the steps. That's when the nun struck her. She struck her once, then twice more. She pulled her out of the line and pushed her up against the green cinder block wall. Banging her head against the wall, not once, several times, more than once, maybe three times, it was hard to remember exactly how many times. Cookie felt as if she would pass out. She saw an instant of blackness. She could have blacked out for a moment. The nun kept slapping her. Her face was in a state of blood lust, and her eyes bulged from her head. She could not stop hitting Cookie.

Cookie told the story of what happened with Fangs in a flat, monotone voice. "The worst part came afterward," Cookie said. "Fangs made me stand in the parking lot behind school while everyone in the building streamed out of the school on two sides."

"That's when I saw you," Fran said.

Cookie stopped talking and could only think. *I couldn't look up. I kept my head down. My face was on fire. I felt like I had been mistaken for poison like a Sumac tree, and cut down.*

Reenie came up to her side. "Are you okay?"

Cookie nodded. "The weird thing is, no one ever said anything about it to me. Everyone pretended like the whole thing never happened."

Herman had put his glasses on. His face looked bruised and swollen, but the bleeding had stopped. "It didn't break you, Cookie. It made you stronger."

Reenie hugged Cookie. "Why didn't you tell anyone what happened with Fangs?"

Cookie shrugged. "I didn't think anyone would believe me."

"Just like Helen Slocum," Reenie said. "No one believed her because she's black."

"I believe you," Herman said.

"Me too." Reenie sat down at the kitchen table across from Fran. "What happened to Cookie is just like what happened to Jimmy Turner. He was in the fifth grade and talking out of turn. Fangs took his head and bashed it against the blackboard ledge. Blood streamed from his head, and he had to get five stitches."

Fran winced. "That's god-awful. It's god-awful. Oh my God, I'm going to be sick."

"Oh man," Herman says. "My face hurts so bad. Nobody never did anything like this to me before. I mean, my mother slapped me a couple of times, but nothing like this."

In a funny way, Cookie thought of Mick Jagger, and the song *Gimme Shelter* popped into her head like it was a vinyl record with an old phonograph needle stuck, skipping on a broken track. Her face felt white-hot and pinched tight, like she was going to faint. Remembering what had happened now was in some ways worse than when it had actually happened. Until now, she had never told anyone. It didn't feel any better talking about it than if she had kept it to herself. She would always see the face of the nun, red and full of rage.

The memory of her sixth-grade classroom swirled around in her head, and was soon overtaken by layers of new imagery. She saw the American flag, crowds thronging in the mud-swamped farmland at Woodstock, newscasts of footage showing caskets coming home from Vietnam and anti-war protesters marching, activists marching to secure their civil liberties; some getting gunned down in the streets, the images of her heartthrob *Blind Owl* Alan Wilson, Jimi Hendrix, Janis Joplin, all dead now; Johnny murdering the Sumac trees because he couldn't be a black musician, and Kitty wanting to be much more than crazy; Donny being abandoned like an orphan; Herman's bloodied and battered face, with his owlish glasses laying splat on the ground; somehow all of these things came together in the image of a tall statue of the Virgin Mary—just like the one in Louie Santamassino's backyard—dressed in blue and wearing a large halo dotted with yellow stars, symbolizing life on earth and beyond in a place called heaven.

Fran's voice had grown raspy from her smoker's cough. "It's like Mae West said: There are no good girls gone wrong - just bad girls found out."

"Do you really think she meant it that way, or she was just stupid?" Cookie asked.

Herman broke into a loud guffaw that caused him to howl out in pain from the wounds on his face. "Oh man, that's cold, Cookie, don't make me laugh."

"It makes no difference being good," Reenie said. "There's no point in doing things they say you should be doing. They're all a bunch of liars."

Cookie remembered life before *Fangs*. She was polite, soft-spoken, a good girl; with her hair wrapped in a neat ponytail, she prayed to God to make Kitty well and aspired to become Saint Bernadette. She liked some pretty weird things. Rocks were her among her friends; so was Lizzie Lovato. The two of them were rock hounds, picking up rocks from the street, in neighboring yards and in their own back yards. There was a steady supply of milky white quartz and sparkling granite. Sometimes, Lizzie found fossils and shouted out in a babble of geek-girl glee, getting excited at the spidery lines of a dead bug imprinted like an etch-a-sketch on a flat grey rock.

Cookie spent a lot of time at Lizzie's house; the two of them ignoring Arky, who was such a doofus that his goal was to one day become a New York state trooper just so he could drive fast legally, chasing people who were speeding. Cookie and Lizzie were inseparable New York working-class kids, street-wise, a little tough, playing street games, kickball, basketball and touch football in the woods behind Untermyer Park. It was Lizzie who encouraged Cookie to read, the same way her fourth-grade teacher, Mrs. Chachkes, encouraged her to write, and Mrs. Kerry had put her in charge of kindergarten books. Cookie and Lizzie were psychic twins, good girls to the quick,

until the day Cookie dumped her because Lizzie was still innocent and she was not. Cookie had lost much more than Lizzie
Lovato. She had lost who she had been.

In the aftermath, everyone had let her down. Her teachers,
her parents, the Italian girls, the boys she knew she would
never love, and *Blind Owl* Alan Wilson, who had flown the coop
far too soon. She thought one day even Herman and Reenie
could let her down and leave her life. Even after the three of
them stood up at Fran Ochiogrosso's kitchen table, and placed
their hands, one on top of the other, covering each other in a
small ceremony that meant, *I've got your back.* Cookie would
have to think hard about the prospect of losing them and wait
to see what would happen. There was no one to rely on but
herself, and that wasn't an awful thing. She knew she could
always count on herself.

That night, Mike Trapani left her black & white notebook
in her mailbox. In the middle of the night, wearing only her
nightgown and socks in the freezing cold, she trundled down
the steps and pulled it out of the mail box. When she came in
from outside, Johnny was waiting for her at the front door; he
looked at her oddly. Clutching her notebook, she told him what
had happened; only the bare minimum of what she thought
he needed to know—that was the best way to deal with him.
Johnny thought she was strange, and told her so. *What's the
big deal! You wrote the pages. Just remember what you said
and write those words again.* All of the pages in the notebook
were intact. She scanned some of the poems and stories she
had written months ago. On every page, some words were
struck out and new words were written in the margins. She
realized that many poems needed to be tweaked and rewritten.
She had her work cut out for her. No matter what, she always
had her words.

Thirty-two

Italian Girls

Why do Italian girls crack their gum? Herman wanted to know the answer to one of the world's greatest natural mysteries. Cookie had found her poem *Why Italian Girls Crack their Gum* in her notebook, but even after she read it to him, he still didn't get it. This was an indication to Cookie that she needed to rewrite her poem or tweak it in a way that captured the powerful message of Italian girls as a force of nature. In the meantime, though, she owed it to Herman to graphically explain the finer details.

Personally speaking, Cookie thought cracking her gum was cute and sexy; it showed extra sassiness. Everyone's saying it's cheap and trashy for a girl to crack her gum, but it all boils down to is having the right attitude. Polite society might say cracking gum is cheap or rude or childish, but when you come right down to it, Italian girls cracking gum is the same as crows crowing and owls hooting. It's a form of protest, from being gifted with one of nature's double-edged swords.

When Italian girls hit fourteen, something happens to them almost overnight. They embody a powerful and contradictory force by becoming both prey and predators. Girls go from being mommy's little helper, to becoming a raging sex goddess. The transformation of an Italian girl cannot be described as a phenomenon resembling the first bloom of maidenhood. Like a chrysalis emerging spud-like from a cocoon and bursting into the world as a magnificent monarch butterfly, the adolescent Italian girl is a sexual force of nature to behold. If you believe in God, there is something perverse about a God who would allow a fourteen-year-old girl to look like she was twenty-five and have no vested interest in wanting to remain a virgin for very long.

Of course, they have all of the right attributes: perfectly formed large breasts, shapely smooth legs that look best bare and without stockings, wider than average hips, slender waists, thick, luscious hair, clear eyes, white teeth and smooth olive skin. Their lashes are so abundant that they do not need to wear mascara, but they do so anyway for dramatic effect. Young Italian girls don't suffer from acne, obesity, thin hair, or irregular menstrual cycles. They do not suffer from depression or other forms of mental illness. They are too busy making everyone around them, and especially men, stark raving crazy. Why be depressed when you torment hordes of men?

The one thing the Italian girl prides herself in, above and beyond all other things, is her mastery over creating drama. They are all of this and more, sustaining an erotic mystique so breathtaking, it will stop your heart; the sight of them will stop your clock. Having good looks is one thing, but what separates Italian girls from gobs of other teenage girls is that they have a certain attitude. The Italian girl attitude is based on the deeply held belief that the function and purpose of everyone in this world—and especially that of men—is to completely and utterly devote their lives toward pleasing them.

This attitude should be a red flag, a flashing neon warning light that stops grown men in their tracks from getting swept away, but it doesn't. Quite the contrary, Italian girls use drama, tantrums or heightened emotional tirades as a cyclonic force, bringing men to their knees and forcing them to submit to their every slightest whim. Being a man-magnet is not solely due to their physical appearance. Italian girls have a haughtiness, arrogance, and natural sense of entitlement. It's not about being beautiful. Plenty of women are beautiful, but rarely are there creatures who truly believe they are meant to not only ensnare men, but to enslave them. Italian girls are confident that the whole world should repay them for the burden of having to bear such extreme beauty and charisma. Italian girls were not molded in the image of God, Eve, The Virgin Mary, or any other female saint, living or dead. The object of Italian girls is to make men pay for original sin. And in this way, the Italian girl prototype was modeled after Adam's evil first wife Lilith, goddess of the night, who feels no compassion for mortals, has no conscience to speak of, and has the allure to charm wild beasts and snakes. This God, the God who created Italian girls, is no friend of mankind.

"I've never heard anything like that before," Herman said. The wounds on his face had completely healed and it no longer hurt Cookie to look at him. "Are you going to turn into a total Italian girl?" Herman asked.

"I don't have a choice," Cookie said wryly. "I was born this way."

"Aren't you kind of exaggerating?" Herman asked.

"This is a bit of an exaggeration," she told Herman and winked. "I just want to show you how I've got the dramatic bit down cold."

"I'll say," Herman laughed.

Circa 1971, in Cookie's estimation, Italian girls were hit on—on the average—of thirty-six times an hour, or more than once in a minute. It's not easy having to constantly fend off unwanted advances. As much as women want to fall in love and mate, they are cursed with having to suffer a constant barrage of crude language, poorly designed *come-ons* and clumsy groping. The men come in droves, and in every type, shape and form under the sun, bald, fat, short, muscular, tall, lean, young, old, middle-aged, decrepit, sickly, hideously ugly, dangerously diseased or scarred, prepubescent, gangly and adolescent. They hover, stalk, loom, lurch, press against you, rub against you, hump you, dry hump, zip up their fly, zip down, rub their pricks inside or outside their pants, or they will wave to you in a way that indicates the are trying to get you to give them, at the very least, a hand job outside their pants.

Since Cookie turned fourteen, she could not keep count of how many times guys tried to paw her backside, begged her for her phone number, yelled undisguised catcalls in broad daylight from across the street, threatened to give her a babysitting job, asked her if she had a boyfriend, masturbated in front of her, from a car, bus, subway or the inner doorway in front of a store or apartment building, asked her for a blow job, offered to be the father of her children, grabbed her around her waist and accidentally touched her blooming breasts, outright grabbed her breasts, cried in love-struck anguish, threatened suicide and followed her home, on foot, by car, on bike, motorbike, motorcycle and skateboard.

Nothing will stop men from chasing after Italian girls. And what is the response of the Italian girl? She laughs in the face of the man who has been made weak in his knees and groin. Either that, or she will marry him, which is really the same thing as laughing at him right in his face. All the more reason why she explained to Herman that he was the most special man in her life and he explained he already knew that. She and Herman were star-crossed lovers, except they were never going to be lovers in the physical sense, and ruin what they had, but would stay together and grow tighter than any two people could be.

Down the End, Cookie avoided going to Morsemere's Market because the manager, Leo DeMarco, had become bewitched by her presence. Leo DeMarco had fingers that were thick, pink and shriveled like Nathan's hot dogs. So out of shape from living on cheese, sausage and the market's signature vanilla frosted crullers and jelly donuts, he wheezed when he breathed. Cookie could hear him coming down the aisle because he lumbered from side to side as if he was trying to hold up his pants. While Cookie was on the aisle plucking cans of *Campbell's Chicken Soup* into her shopping cart, Leo came up beside her to give her an affectionate, generic side hug. Soon his fingers surreptitiously inched up her waist in a rapid spider crawl that squeezed the flesh under her breasts. As she yanked away from him, he pretended that he did not know what he was doing and that his hand had found its way there accidentally.

Cookie went out of her way to avoid being alone with Mr. DeMarco. It was bad enough that he sneakily groped her breasts in public. She could not imagine what he would do to her if he caught her alone in the back room, or in some place where no one else was around. Every time she came to check out at the register, he would dismiss the clerk that was on duty so he could ring out Cookie's basket of groceries. He always gave her back the wrong amount of change. Too much or too little; he was laying the bait for future engagement. He was just dying to get her alone in the back room.

Even the neighborhood vagrant, Frankie Curtin, had the hots for Cookie. Calling Frankie Curtin a *vagrant* is not accurate. It was 1971, and everyone called him a *retard* and treated him as if he was a village idiot. Frankie Curtin was an old man who roamed the streets of the North End holding out his grubby weathered hand, begging for money. Some of the North End Italian boys tossed pennies at him and made him pick them up off the street. The meaner boys threw rocks at him and chased him down the street. No one knew for sure where Frankie Curtin lived or what was wrong with his brain, but one thing Cookie knew for sure, the minute he spotted her walking on Palisade Avenue alone or with someone else, he'd come running up to her and say, *Got anything for me, girlie?*

His smile was more lascivious and horny-looking than the loose, lopsided grin of a simple *retard.*

And one day in the spring of 1971, Crazy Dave the hippie guy from Untermyer Park who looked like David Crosby of Crosby, Stills and Nash, came up to her and said, *Look, it's little Cookie Colangelo, all grown up.* Swarthy-faced, with hulking ears, a huge moustache and a fixed stare, wearing the working-class uniform of a denim blue shirt and stone-washed blue jeans, he just put his arm around Cookie. He looked at her like he understood her, which was purely laughable. *Will you look at those cookies!* And before she knew it, he had thrust his tongue into Cookie's mouth. As savvy as she was, she hadn't seen it coming.

Cookie knew that in the long run, she couldn't be anything she wanted to be—that was a bullshit lie they tell kids to make them think they could do anything. Being anything you want to be could be true for rich kids, but it wasn't true for working-class kids. Her life was like playing a game of poker. She had been dealt a hand. She had no control over the cards that she had been dealt. She could only choose how well to play her hand, or not play at all. She believed she was destined to do something. She might have been an Italian girl, but fortunately, she also had her words.

She thought one day she would become famous as a writer. She had started to write a book. It was called *Beneath the Passion of the Angelic Mystery Rose.* The main character was a lot like Cookie, except her name, despite countless revisions made to the first page of the book, was still Andrea Verrone. She went to the Summerhill School in London, where the students made their own rules, unlike *the Heart,* where Cookie was expelled at the end of her ninth grade.

One day, unexpectedly, Mr. DC summoned Cookie to his office, which was adjacent to the big, fat oval office that belonged to the principal, Sister Hilda Marie. He sat behind his desk and smiled at her. Over the course of the school year, he had gotten rid of his pom and now sported a crewcut that was as slick with *Brylcreem* as his prior hairdo. Cookie examined his legs that sprawled out sideways from his desk as if he thought the slouched look made him appear to be sexy and relaxed. His grey pants were short, *high water pants,* to be precise, and exposed his fraying, white athletic socks. She spied his white shins that were bare of hair and she wondered if he shaved his legs. She had always been attracted to men with hair on their legs. Maybe it was an Italian thing, and one more sign that she was, indeed, turning into a full-fledged Italian girl. "Do you know why you're here, Colangelo?" he asked.

Cookie didn't feel nervous. She viewed him as a lowly life form. Someone she had to put up with in the immediate future but who one day would be gone forever.

"Would you like to explain to me what happened *Down the End?*"

Cookie looked at him. She was confused and didn't know what he was getting at. She was *Down the End* all the time; one day melded into the next with little reason to cite one day as more important than another.

"With the black boy," Mr. DC said. He leaned further back in his chair, tipping it as if he was on a rocking chair. "I heard about a fight with you involving Michael Trapani, Thomas Parrello, and Regina Maria Ruggerio."

"It's Reenie Ruggiero," Cookie said. "She goes by Reenie. Everybody knows that."

"You've always been a big clown, Colangelo. Big clown." Then he looked at her in a way that told her he had it out for her and there was nothing she could do. "I'd like to save Regina from the kind of trouble she's been getting into lately. I don't care much about Tommy Parrello. He's a thug. But Mike Trapani's a good kid."

"No, he's not. He's a bully. Everyone knows he's a bully. Give me a break."

Mr. DC sat upright in his chair and straightened his back into a stiff posture. He placed his knees together and his hands firmly on the desk. "Colangelo, you make so much trouble for yourself. Why can't you be respectful like the other girls in the school? You show disrespect to everyone. You're a bad influence on the other students. You don't live up to our standards here. You are too much of a non-conformist, and a threat to the ideals of the Sacred Heart. I'm going to have to ask you to leave the school."

Cookie didn't know how to respond to him. She thought the reason was obvious. She felt her ears burning, but knew her face had drained of blood. Mr. DC was a creep, and she hated him.

Without warning, Sister Hilda Marie popped her scary black & white nun head into the office, where the door had been left open. "I'm sorry about the loss of your brother," she said, poking in. "I want you to know that we pray for his dearly departed soul every day."

Cookie meant to tell her that she didn't have a brother, but there was no use expending the energy to travel down that rat hole. Cookie lifted her hand and gave her the peace sign.

Mr. DC flinched at Cookie's audacious behavior. "It's really a shame," he said. "For a girl, you're smart. You're a good-looking enough girl. You could have made a great future for yourself in this school. You can do the work if you want to, but it's clear you don't want to do the work, and you've got nothing but trouble on your mind. You're never going to amount to anything."

Cookie understood what he was saying, but she felt confused. "What am I being expelled for? What's the reason? I haven't broken the law."

"Oh, come on, Colangelo. You know the reason. You're a troublemaker. I want you to agree with me. This way I know we're on the same page."

Cookie wanted to protest. She felt she had not been that bad. She knew Johnny would kill her. "But," she stammered, "you still haven't given me a reason. What should I tell my father?"

Mr. DC smiled, sat there and didn't say anything. It was as if he had her exactly where he wanted her. He wanted her to squirm. Glancing down at his paperwork, he read notes from his files as if he was weighing and deliberating an alternative. He shifted in his chair a few times, leaning backward, then he looked around the room. He looked thoughtful, as if he wanted to appear to be fair to her. "Do you have anything to say?"

"Yes," she said and leaned forward, a gesture of sincerity. She knew no matter what she did, he was through with her.

"Well, what is it, Colangelo, I haven't got all day."

"Your pants are too short." Cookie rose from the chair. She felt the backs of her bare legs un-sticking from the seal that had been made with the Naugahyde seat. She pressed her skirt down, in case it was rising up. She thought of all the girls at *the Heart* who loved the school so much that they dyed their hair with streaks of gold and green, the same as the school colors, and here she was, being expelled for being a non-conformist, a virgin non-conformist, no less, by a guy who wore high waters. He was a fascist. She walked out of his office and quietly closed the door.

Thirty-three

Boom Boom

Johnny and Kitty sat at the dining room table. Cookie had yet to face the home front with news of her expulsion from *the Heart*. Her parents never read the notices that were sent home from school, but in this instance, expulsion warranted a special phone call from Sister Hilda Marie, who expressed sincere regret to Kitty over the loss of her son in Vietnam. Kitty told the nun that she didn't have a son, but it made no difference. Everyone knew Kitty was schizophrenic, so it was entirely possible after numerous shock therapy treatments and doses of psychotropic medication, she might have forgotten she had a son. After Kitty hung up the phone, she complained. *Imagine that,* Johnny*! The nun was trying to tell me I had a son, a dead son, no less. How rude is that! What a whack job!*

Johnny had a squat glass pot of Martinson's coffee going and Kitty drank a glass of water. She was a purist who never drank caffeine or alcohol because they ran interference with her delicate brain chemistry. For a couple who had lived apart for years, each in his or her own world, Johnny and Kitty had now come together to face a common challenge—their daughter had been expelled from school, and it was a public disgrace.

The easy listening station WPAT-FM was set on low on the Hi-Fi in the living room and could barely be heard. Kitty looked like a movie star. She was that good-looking. Wearing coral knit pants and a low-cut melon-colored peasant blouse, she wore complementary coral lipstick, and her big sexy hair was teased high and tucked into an extra wide white headband for this special occasion; she was dolled-up to help Johnny sort through what should be done with Cookie, who was now school-less. Kitty's eyes were shining. She looked happy, as if she was expecting good news. There was something extraordinary about Kitty and the way she could stop being insane and occasionally become calm and rational, a fortress in the midst of a storm.

Donny burst into the room, tucked her legs under a cushion and sat in front of a new miniature TV that had a screen only twenty inches wide. She was sucking her thumb, even though she wasn't supposed to. Cookie went over to her and gave her a kiss. She smelled like a warm blanket and clean, lightweight summer cotton. She smiled softly and had a trace of sadness in her eyes that were as blue as Johnny's. No one allowed Donny to revel in being the baby of the family, and she had been forced by circumstances to grow up far too soon. The real baby of the family was Kitty, who gave Johnny a cute smile and squeezed up her shoulders and pressed her hands together in a way that showed a surge of cleavage rising in her peasant blouse. Cookie groaned inwardly to herself. Her mother oozed as much sexual prowess as Jim Morrison, the sexy snakish lead singer for the Doors, who had just released *Riders on the Storm*. The song later became the informal anthem for the Vietnam War, but for the time being, it played in Cookie's mind, reverberating like ocean waves in anticipation of the tsunami that was about to occur.

Johnny blew up like he had endured an explosive mortar round, and clutched his hands to his chest as if he had taken a direct hit. "What are you doing, Cookie! Explain yourself to me! You're out there day and night with the colored boy, roaming all over Yonkers in the black neighborhoods and now this! You got yourself expelled from the best Catholic school in the city!! How could you do this to yourself! How could you do this to me!"

Cookie sat at the table and didn't say a word. She had no idea what to expect now, or where she would go to school. She decided to let Johnny proceed until he came to the end of his rant, which always came to a natural conclusion when it became clear that nothing was going to be resolved. Soon he would be gone, off playing music and jamming at his true home—the studios and clubs in the city.

"I've seen you hanging out with that black boy. Let me tell you something, you're headed for trouble. Really big trouble."

Cookie glared at him defiantly. "Two people can like each other a lot and not be having sex, if that's what you're worried about."

"That's disgusting," Donny called across the room. She had grown long legs, a long torso and although she was five years younger than Cookie, she was almost the same height as Kitty.

"Go somewhere else while I'm talking to your sister," Johnny yelled.

"Where?" Donny cried out.

"Anywhere. I don't care. Anywhere but here." Johnny broke open a pink packet of *Sweet 'n' Lo*, dumped it into his coffee cup and over-stirred the coffee far beyond what it took to dissolve the artificial sweetener. Johnny could not stop moving. Stirring the coffee was pure percussion, and the same as playing an instrument. "Yeah, sure. Don't give me that bullshit. If you're with this boy all the time, then you're doing something you shouldn't be doing!"

Cookie told him off. "You have a dirty mind!

"He's Italian," Kitty suddenly piped up. "He was born like that!"

Johnny made a clicking noise with his mouth and looked away as if he was ashamed over what Kitty was saying. He grimaced, throwing his head back, shaking his shaggy hair to the side and looking back as if he was in a state of disbelief. "Jesus," he said. "Give me a break."

"Honestly, Johnny," Kitty said. "She loves that boy, but she's not having relations with him."

"Sure she is," Johnny insisted. "What do you think the two of them are doing together all the time?"

"I know my daughter," Kitty said, smiling and looking slightly google-eyed. "There's no way Cookie's going to be kissing some boy that doesn't even have a lip."

"What do you do with him?" Johnny asked her. "As if it's any of my business. I would just like to know for my own information." Johnny tapped the side of his head like he had put his thinking cap on. "I just like to know what a boy and a girl can do together if they're not having sex."

"We laugh, we talk, we share stories and we dance." Cookie glared at him. "I help him. He helps me."

Kitty leaned forward and looked at Johnny. She was saner and more real than any other time Cookie had seen her mother during her entire life. "She loves him, Johnny, can't you see that? Best friends, that's what you call it. They're not like us, Johnny. Look at us. We've had a lot of red-hot sex together. But you don't really like me. And I don't like you."

"Jesus, do you have to talk that way in front of the kid!"

"She's seen enough of us to know the truth," Kitty said. "Leave Cookie alone."

Johnny feigned choking back his coffee, but it was just an act to make a point. "I'm not going to be taking instruction from some crazy broad."

"I'm doing alright, Johnny." Kitty fluffed the headband that pushed back her big hair away from her face. "I'm better than most, and not as bad as some. Whenever I go to the nuthouse, they only keep me there for three weeks. Just three weeks. Some of them are in the nuthouse for years, years, Johnny. Me, three weeks." She held up three fingers in a salute. "I'm not *that* crazy, Johnny."

"Three weeks," Johnny said. "You're right." He looked at Cookie sheepishly and whispered. "That's all my insurance will cover. Three weeks in the nuthouse. Anything extra and I have to pay out of pocket."

The awkwardness that could have happened as a result of Johnny revealing why Kitty only did three-week stints at the nuthouse was interrupted by Marvin Gaye's *I Heard It Through The Grapevine,* growing closer and closer until it came in through the front door. Attracted to the sound of any music, Johnny was up on his feet and heading to see where it was coming from. Cookie knew who had come looking for her.

Donny had brought Herman into the living room, where he took his boom box off his shoulder, turned it off and set it on the floor. "Hey, Cookie," he said. "I thought you might need some music to cheer you up."

"What's he doing here? For crissakes," Johnny stared at him as if he had dropped in from another planet." He put his hands on his hips and looked at him. "Where'd you get that thing?"

"They call them boom boxes now," Herman said. "I had one of the first you could get. Want to see how it works?"

Herman knelt down on the floor beside his Radiorecorder, while Johnny leaned over him, staring at the giant radio as if it was something he had never seen before. He didn't ask any questions, he didn't comment, he listened intently, hanging on to every word Herman said in case he missed something. It was clear that Johnny recognized how this Radiorecorder *née* boom box would be a tremendous boon to him in the studio. Herman rotated the circular dial, going from station to station, easy listening, hard rock, country western, classical, instrumental, up and down the AM and FM bands. He opened a panel door on his boom box, popped in a small tape cassette into the open compartment, and cranked the volume to John Lee Hooker playing the guitar to his song *Boom Boom.*

Without seeming to realize it, Johnny was swaying with the music, nodding his head, and a trance-like calm spread across his face. He was totally mesmerized by *Boom Boom* and mouthed the lyrics, *that baby talk, why don't you talk like that. Well, baby.* Johnny started stamping his foot on the floor and tapping the wall with his hand like he was doing a brush-beat on a snare drum. John Lee Hooker struck the right chord with Johnny. To him, John Lee Hooker, along with Bukka White and Muddy Waters, was more than music or entertainment, it was high religion.

Herman launched into a dance, doing triangle-shape hops and jumps, with his knees collapsing and arching in deep bends, rapidly shifting the precision of his weight from one foot to the other. His movements were uniform, seamless and totally hitting every beat in *Boom Boom*. Donny swayed back and forth the way kids do when music touches a primordial chord and makes them move; she could not help but dance. Cookie joined Herman, rocking and taking turns doing the same steps, until the two of them ran their own version of a soul jig to the natural end of the song, stopped dancing, looked at each other and broke into laughter.

As much as Johnny had been swept away by the music, he recognized the gravity of the situation. A black boy had come calling for Cookie. To put it more precisely, a boy had come looking for his daughter and he was so damn cocksure of himself that he thought that maybe Johnny would not notice one small detail—he was black!

"Look, Johnny," Kitty said. "He has such nice white teeth. They're so even," she smiled.

Cookie looked at Herman and shrugged. "That's my mother," she told Herman. "Everyone calls her Kitty."

Johnny put his hands into his pockets like he was a tough guy and gave Herman the once over. Then he looked at Cookie. "Is this *You*?" he asked. "*You?*"

Cookie was confused by what Johnny was saying. "What are you talking about?"

"The poem," Johnny said. "The poem about the boy *You*.

You know what I'm talking about. You wrote the thing." He scratched his head. "*When I see you my heart bursts into a tremendous fire, You are the fulfilling dream of my every desire.* You see I remembered it," Johnny said. *"You."*

"Are you *You?* What's your name?"

"I'm Herman Lynch." He extended his hand, but Johnny was having none of it.

Johnny took a step back, then forward. He dropped his hand awkwardly to his side, then reached out to offer his own hand to Herman as if he did not know what else to do. "Are you, *You?"*

"No sir," Herman said. "I'm me."

"The poem *You* was about the *Blind Owl* Alan Wilson," Cookie said.

"Well then, who's this boy?" Johnny asked.

Cookie looked at Herman and smiled. An unspoken sentiment passed between them. The timing was right to let Johnny have it between the eyes. She turned to Johnny and assumed a knowing air, one of maturity, as if she was far wiser than her years, and gave it to Johnny in a verbal one-two knockout punch.

"He's my nigger."

Johnny was beside himself; the expressions on his face alternated between grief and despair; there was a touch of outrage too. He could not believe his daughter had used the "N" word. He railed and cried out. At one point, he put his face into his hands as if he meant to cry. She had hurt him. She had disrespected him. She had hurt the very core of his deep abiding passion for his music. Kitty looked at him as if she thought he was the crazy one, and he was. He called out to his mother and his father, to God and to his country that in no way had he ever raised his daughter to say such a filthy, blasphemous word. It just wasn't okay.

"That's not okay! I'm sorry," he said to Herman. "I apologize for my daughter. I didn't raise her to talk that way."

"It's alright," Herman smiled. "She's talking straight. I'm her nigger."

"And I'm his honky." Cookie smiled.

Donny screamed with glee and began laughing uncontrollably, holding onto her stomach. She was laughing so hard that she fell to the floor and rolled on the ground like a happy-go-lucky puppy.

Herman put his boom box on and the three of them began to dance and sing to the high falsetto voice of the *Blind Owl* Alan Wilson singing *On the road again*. Cookie knew the lyrics by heart and in her head, heard each line coming well before it was sung. Knowing the lyrics and the rhythm gave her an extra edge to her moves. Kitty quietly left the room without saying a word. She didn't really like having people in the house, and preferred the calm of sitting in her living room, staring at her window full of color and glass to watch the light shining through the day during different phases of the sun, taking each small object to a different hue, color and translucency, transporting her to a safe and sacred place that quieted the more raucous voices in her head. With the exception of Johnny, everyone was having such a good time that no one responded to him when he said, *What is this, own a Negro day*? Johnny liked the music, but he didn't seem to like or understand what was happening to his daughter. Cookie knew he didn't understand who she was or who she was becoming, but maybe in the long run that was okay.

Thirty-four

Mabel Kerry

I want you to meet my Grandmother, Herman had told Cookie.
She wasn't too keen on spending a hot summer afternoon close
enough to the projects to hear the incessant scream of police
sirens, dogs barking and street thugs talking too loudly in the
streets, and she told that to Herman, but he was being real
stubborn and insisted it was time to meet the most important
person in his life, his only next of kin. Too hot to walk, Herman
and Cookie boarded the Number 2 bus bound for Ashburton
Avenue. School was out for summer and kids took to hanging
out on the street because there was nowhere else to go. Plenty
of guys were hanging around outside of Herman's building. All
black. No one said much to Herman or paid mind to the fact
that he was with a white girl. It might not have been much of
a surprise. According to Reenie, the guys thought Herman was
not black enough, too white, an *Oreo*, but no one hassled him.
It was sign of respect on account of Herman's grandmother.

Herman told Cookie that his grandmother's name was
Mabel and that she used to be a school teacher. He didn't know
why she had stopped teaching school, but she loved books,
learning and helping kids, so she took a job as a circulation

desk clerk at the Carnegie Library in Getty Square. She had
not gone to library school and saw no reason to become a full-
fledged librarian, so long as they let her work with books and
gave some extra part-time work to Herman too.

Herman and his Grandmother Mabel lived on the first
floor of the same brick tenement building where Reenie
Ruggiero lived. Cookie was half-expecting to see Reenie and
sure enough, she was bounding down the steps from the third
floor just as Herman and Cookie were walking in the door.
Reenie gave them a big smile and the *high-five;* the three
of them stopped and talked. Reenie was real surprised that
Cookie had not yet met Mabel, and told her how much she
would like her. She was full of sass, *piss and vinegar,* Reenie
described her, and said no one messed with her in a bad way,
or messed with her in any way. "Kind of like us," Reenie said,
punching Herman lightly in the shoulder before she bounded
out the front door, saying she would stop by later, *lude-free
and not totally clueless,* a sarcastic comment aimed directly
toward Cookie.

Herman's apartment had a tiny entranceway for a foyer
that led into a larger living room. Cookie had been here before,
but she had not remembered the large fan set to high in the
middle of the room, its rotator blades moving fast in a whirring
blur. The fan was set close to the same spot on the floor where
the puppy had accidentally piddled. The linoleum tiles looked
like they had once been stark blue and white, but now, due to
age and wear, the tiles had faded to light grey-blue.

Mabel wasn't in the living room, but given the sight of
the fan being on, Cookie felt for sure she was there. In a
funny way that Cookie had yet to fully define, she felt Mabel's
presence was some kind of reckoning for her; something she
had to come to terms with after a long struggle. The two of
them made quite a bit of noise traipsing through the small
apartment and right into the kitchen, where Herman immediately opened the refrigerator door and chugged from an open

carton of milk. Grandmother Mabel sat at a grey Formica-top kitchen table and helped herself to another cup of tea. She was drinking from a dainty porcelain teacup, which was painted with faded delicate pink flowers and had the faintest trace of green stems.

"Offer your friend, Cookie, something cool to drink," she said. "There's some lemonade in the refrigerator."

Mabel looked up at Cookie, and when their eyes fastened on one another there was a flicker of recognition that took Cookie's breath away. Her heart skipped a beat. She felt like she had encountered a ghost. Her reaction was excessive and noticed by Herman, who didn't know what to make of it. Not so much with Mabel. She wasn't necessarily seeing what Cookie had recognized.

"Mrs. Kerry?"

"You know her?" Herman look confused. "You mean you know each other?"

Cookie nodded slowly. "She was my kindergarten teacher."

Herman pulled out a chair from the kitchen table and Cookie sank into the seat across from Mabel. It had been ten years since Cookie was in kindergarten. She had grown from being a tiny kid and had become a young woman. Things come and go and people change, but ten years for Mabel Kerry was not nearly as radical a passage in time as it was for Cookie. Mabel wore her hair the same way, in an old-fashioned permanent wave with a long sweeping brown bang that was pushed to one side. Only now her hair had greyed, and she wore the same black-framed eyeglasses as Herman.

"Mrs. Kerry, you were my teacher in Kindergarten." Cookie was hardly aware that Herman had set down a glass of lemonade on the table in front of her. She noticed Mrs. Kerry had taken off her eyeglasses and held them in her hands. "School #14. Do you remember me?"

"Lord have mercy," Mabel Kerry said. "I'd like to say I remember you, but you're all grown up now, and back then if you were in my class, you were just this high." She held her hand up below the height of the kitchen table, which was about three feet tall. "I'd like to say that I recognize you, but the truth of it is, I had so many students and when they grow up they become different people. Most of the time," she smiled.

"You look exactly the same," Cookie said.

"Black don't crack," Mabel laughed. "Come here, child, sit down, and let me take a good look at you."

She asked Cookie her full name and Mabel seemed to recall *Concetta Colangelo*.

"You used to make me put the books away. Every day," Cookie said. "I was the keeper of the books."

"Ah, Yes," Mabel's eyes flickered with a trace of recognition. "I do remember you. You were so afraid of me," she said. "You were always keeping your distance. I worried about you."

Cookie shrugged and looked away. She didn't know what to say. She was so stunned by the revelation that *Mabel*, Herman's grandmother, was actually Mrs. Kerry, that Herman's presence receded into the background. In a move toward self-protection, she went inward, in her own mind. Her first teacher winds up being black in a school full of white kids. She didn't know how to reconcile this small fact by willing it out of her mind as a contradiction. *A mere contradiction*, she said to herself and smiled because she had thought of the word *mere*. It made her feel so knowledgeable and grown-up. She was in a daze and looked around the kitchen. A relic from the past during the time when the apartment building was first built, the kitchen had a large cast iron double-sink, chipped and scratched on its corners from years of use. The single large white gas stove and an old *Ironside* dingy-white refrigerator dominated the room.

There was a stillness in the room that was the same as a moment of stillness in a dance. Even though Cookie and Mabel had taken a pause, there was movement taking place between them. This moment of silence wasn't uncomfortable or the least bit awkward, and only a bridge to the next leap of faith that both women would take and share between them.

"I do remember you now, Cookie. I gave you the job of putting books away. I figured if you came to love books, your fear of me would go away."

"My fear did go away." Cookie looked up at Mabel Kerry. She had been left alone with her. Herman was no longer in the kitchen, but he was still around. She could see him in the living room, flipping through the albums in his record collection that were stored in a weather-beaten wooden *Dellwood Dairy* milk crate.

"You're a brave young woman," Mabel told her. "Thank you for being friends with my Herman. He's not an ordinary boy," she said. "Herman is a special person and he's going to make a difference in this world. He's more sensitive than most." She looked at Cookie and spoke softly. "That's why I protect him so."

Herman put on an album by Richie Havens singing *Freedom*, the same song he had sung at Woodstock. In retrospect, Cookie came to think of Woodstock as being not a good place for gangsters like her and Herman and Reenie to hang out and learn the ropes. The only black people at Woodstock were a few musicians. Jimi Hendrix for one. And Richie Havens for another.

"Just for the record," Cookie said out loud, "Woodstock was overwhelmingly young, privileged and white."

Cookie realized Mabel had no idea what she was talking about. She wasn't tracking Richie Havens' song *Freedom* with what Cookie was recollecting about Woodstock. "It was also very muddy and gross."

Mabel laughed and told Cookie she was a funny girl, but funny in a good way, who reminded her of Herman's mother, *Annie Cole*, who had worked as a clerk in the *Rite Aid Drugstore* in Getty Square. She had *high ambitions,* Mabel told her. Annie Cole wanted to go to college to make something of her life, but she got mixed up with the wrong crowd and got pregnant by a boy who left her to have the baby on her own. She quit working, and when the baby got to be too much for her, she started using drugs. Mabel felt that Annie Cole would have turned around. She wasn't in too deep. She would have come back, but she got her hands on some bad stuff, and that's that.

Mabel's face was full of joy and her eyes welled a slight touch of tears. "I wanted Herman to bring you here so I could talk to you so you can see what you're up against," Mabel told her. "Being with Herman means you're going to have to fight your whole life through, and I want to be here for you as long as I can. God willing."

Mabel explained how life was hard for black kids like Herman, even for kids who have people who care about them. "You have to fight for everything and if you're not willing to fight, well then, it's not that you'll lose a job or a friend. You could end up losing your life. Look at what they did to poor Emmet Till for just looking at a white woman. They took that poor boy and beat him to a pulp so that his own mother could not recognize him. Richard and Mildred Loving were put into jail for loving one another, and the state of Virginia had them arrested for getting married. Even after they moved to another state, the Lovings were not allowed to be married. It went all the way to the Supreme Court, who ruled that it was unconstitutional to declare a mixed race marriage as illegal. That was only four years ago. There's still a Ku Klux Klan active and afoot with their burning crosses, nooses and nasty talk, only no one wants to know about it, and no one puts a stop to them. They don't want black & white to mix."

Like a prayerful song, Mabel's voice took on a softer cadence. Cookie could see pain in her face, but she saw great wisdom too. There was something infinitely tender about the way Mabel looked, full of compassion and love. Cookie had never seen a person take on the countenance of a wise old Sumac tree, silent, strong, so full of fire and brimming with hope. "People are people, and there is no stopping people from getting together. Black & white isn't so important. People will get together no matter what. It's part of what makes us human."

Cookie nodded and listened intently, but she didn't talk about Herman. She didn't mention that their relationship wasn't that way, like the Lovings. And she thought telling Mabel the truth about the nature of their relationship would have betrayed her pact with Herman. She and Herman had exchanged secrets. She knew something was different about him, and even if she couldn't give it definition, and Herman couldn't give it definition, it was something he owned and no one else had a right to it. Herman's eyes were green, like her eyes. He knew about her darkness inside, why it was there and why over time, her darkness could deepen and would always be offset by the way she felt about people, good and kind people. She knew Herman's secret, that he thought women were beautiful, and especially men. What he said was sacred between them. Cookie and Herman had vowed, without saying as much, to keep each other's secrets. It was a secret pact that would endure a lifetime. He had touched her. He had touched her in ways she could not explain. He had touched her heart. She felt small tears in her eyes, like a newfound well had been sprung. It was a start, and sort of hopeful to feel again. "Mrs. Kerry," Cookie began to say. "There is something you should know." She told Mabel how when she was four years old, grown-ups had told her if Mrs. Kerry touched her, she would turn black too. *Oh Lord, did they really tell you that*, she laughed. "I think you touched me," Cookie said. "You touched my heart."

Thirty-five

Angels and Owls

Sometimes having an angel come into your life does no good at all. There are consequences to everything. Doing good for someone doesn't always produce a good outcome, and the worst circumstances in the world can help to shape a good person, or encourage someone to grow stronger. And in the long run, no one ever knows the true outcome. For better or worse, we are all stuck in this world together, and when the day comes and we are no longer together, it usually means someone is gone for good. More than anything, Cookie did not want to lose Herman Lynch or Reenie Ruggiero. She wanted to go down the road with them. *On the Road Again.* Being with them was like being with the *Blind Owl* Alan Wilson. There was something about growing up in Yonkers that made her feel like she had a genuine 'hood, *Down the End*, and she and Reenie and Herman were real friends, *we took care of one another.*

There was always a feeling that Louie Santamassino was looking out for them. Whether the three of them could see Louie or not, he was giving them protection. People might be prejudiced against Herman for being black, but if anyone messed with him, they'd have to deal with Louie, and no one wanted to do that.

Herman came to get Cookie at her house because he was beside himself with excitement. *You're never going to believe what I found.* He wanted to take Cookie. He wanted to take Reenie. *Take your sister too. She's got to see this!* Herman was so excited that he took to moving around so much that it redefined the notion of high energy. He wanted to take everyone to show them what he had discovered down in the deepest thickets of Untermyer Park in an area so hidden and so unexplored that it was located in a place darker and denser than the Devil's Cave.

Cookie found Donny hanging out on the street in front of their house with Lizzie Lovato. On this day, the first moment Cookie set her eyes on Lizzie, she looked at her in a different light. The girl was still living in a naïve dream world full of fossils and rocks, but Cookie owed it to her to teach her a thing or two about living with people instead of rocks. When you come right down to it, you find an old fossil, pick it up and look at it, you really can't tell what color the creature had for skin when it was alive and kicking. There was something to be said for thinking about what we had in common underneath the skin we wore around our bodies like old but familiar coats, some thin like cotton, and some as thick as armor. Any way you look at it, skin was just nature's way of protecting the heart.

It was a motley crew that descended into the lower wooded and gnarled labyrinth of Untermyer Park. Donny was constantly posturing and trying to be as tough as her older sister. Reenie Ruggiero and Lizzie Lovato found a mutual affinity for collecting potato bugs. Both girls liked to pick up bugs and see how they curled into a ball to protect themselves, and said something about feeling the same way about themselves. It was a motley crew alright, who had no business being together, except Herman had made it happen. After all the time that Cookie had spent away from Donny, more than anything, the girl loved spending time with her older sister. She giggled too much and didn't talk, but she was so excited that she almost seemed to be crying out, *I love you, I love you, I want to be like you. I want to go wherever you go. When I grow up I want to be just like you.*

The thing Cookie loved most about Donatella Colangelo was the fact that she was her sister. Her little sister, to be precise. It was Cookie who had given her the nickname *Donny* and it stuck with her until the end of time. Other than that, she hated everything else about her. She was young, goofy and a tagalong. She was blue-eyed and blonde, blonder than Cookie would ever be. Cookie was held captive by her own long brown ponytail. Cookie's own eyes were green and no one in the entire world had green eyes except for Martians on the TV show *My Favorite Martian*, and of course, Herman Lynch, but he didn't factor in to this particular equation.

The group had crossed far below the thousand steps of Untermyer Park that led down to an intricate network of paved trails and narrow, dirt-covered pathways. Old stone stanchion posts, decaying obelisks and falling-down blocks of greystone sat like signposts, leading the way into previously uncharted territory. With the exception of Herman, none of the others had been here before. In the woods, adjacent to the Aqueduct, there was an old stone footbridge crossing what appeared to be part of a stream, but as Herman pointed out, it was runoff from the old Aqueduct. Everyone seemed reluctant to walk across the bridge, fearing it might collapse under their weight. Herman led them around the bridge. He acted as their guide, reassuring them it was okay to be here. He was like a saint in a world that did not welcome the mystery, truth and reverence for a life larger than any one person. Right past the bridge, an opening to the tunnel showed an inner cavern. Large sewer pipes had broken away from the water-carrying arterial and sat on the floor of the forest in cylindrical shapes and shaved shards of concrete. All of the concrete bore the signs of decay. Coated with orange and green stains deposited by rusty water and moss, whatever function it served in the past was no more. The former aqueduct now lay in ruins.

"This place is creepy," Cookie said.

Herman put his hands to his mouth to shush her. He pointed to a grove of Sumac trees and signaled for everyone to follow him up the footpath. Three ancient trees stood in the small clearing. Herman kept his fingers to his mouth. *Quietly. Keep it down*, he whispered. He moved so slowly toward the trees, setting the tone for everyone else to follow, almost creeping and pausing, one small footstep at a time. For someone as quick on his feet as Herman was, slowing down seemed to be a drag on his effortless lightness and took extra effort to be still. Herman put up both his hands and turned around to face everyone. He indicated everyone should stay still and move no further. Then he pointed to one tree trunk that had an opening, its own roughhewn cave. Herman pointed to the wooden cave within the innards of the tree and continued pointing until everyone could see what he was seeing. What was in the opening appeared to be inner layers and rings of its own wood; the innards of a tree trunk, but on closer inspection, it soon became apparent that the opening was occupied by a bird, and not an ordinary bird. Without a doubt, the bird in the trunk cave was an owl, who had made a nest there. His yellow eyes were wide open and he was completely alert.

"He's awake and he can see us," Herman said. "This is how owls act during the day. He's almost in a trance. He can see us and hear us, but he's sort of asleep, it's almost like he's sleepwalking."

"Wow," Donny said. "He was born that way!"

"That owl is on ludes," Reenie said.

"And it's natural." Cookie elbowed Reenie in the rib.

"He's a great horned owl," Lizzie said. You don't see them too often in Yonkers, but the owls are here. He's also called a hoot owl, and even though his eyes look so big, his ears are just slightly smaller than our eyes. Look at his ears," Lizzie pointed and whispered. "Those tufts of feathers aren't really ears. His real ears are down on the side of his large owl head. Great Horned Owls are also known as the tiger of the sky because these owls hunt prey much larger than themselves. His wingspan can be up to five feet," she said, spreading her arms open wide. "He likes being down here, close to the river! There are lots of good things to catch down here, like squirrels and rats!"

Herman grinned and turned to Cookie. "It's the *Blind Owl*, Cookie. He came back to see you."

Cookie had no reason to think that what he was saying wasn't true. Staring at the owl in this tree trunk took some time getting used to. An owl was in the woods of Untermyer Park! But it wasn't entirely far-fetched; there were all kind of owls in Yonkers. It's just that most of the time, no one was looking for them and if you weren't looking for them, you'd never see them, because owls are so still, in camouflage during the day and stealthily unseen by night.

All five of them stood there and stared at the owl. No one moved or said much of anything. Mesmerized by the owl, Cookie felt instantly attached to the bird, as if he was part of her and she had become part of the owl. She didn't feel as though she was invading the owl's space, nor did she think the owl minded being stared at for so long. The owl was a brilliant force of nature, a sight to behold, and no one wanted to change the dynamic of this fleeting instant that everyone wanted to hold onto, because it would never come exactly the same way again. No one wore a watch, and no one had a way to tell how much time had elapsed. And in all of that time, there was a long-lasting and lingering sense of awe for the owl.

After a time, in what seemed to be an eternity and a minute, one and the same, everyone moved together toward the path up out of the woods and toward home. No one said a word. No one had to say anything. On the way out of the woods, Herman told Cookie that just because Alan Wilson was named the *Blind Owl*, that didn't mean he could not see. He could see. He could see too well. He saw too much. Seeing so much made him sad about life. Sometimes getting so sad can take your breath away, and it hurts so bad that a person will do anything to stop the pain. The *Blind Owl* should not have died. Someone should have been looking in on him. *Should have, could have.* Cookie knew Herman might have been thinking the same thing about his mother and told him so. Cookie had experience looking in on her mother, and no matter what you do or how much you love someone, it doesn't mean you can save someone from dying too soon. *I hope you're not blaming yourself for your mother*, Cookie told Herman. He didn't answer her directly and mumbled he understood what she was getting at, but she knew him well enough to know he was thinking about what she had said. *You've got to let yourself off the hook*, she told him. There was more than one way to die. And dying young and foolishly didn't make it any more romantic than dying old and alone.

That summer, Jim Morrison had been found dead in a hotel room in Paris. He was one more casualty among the rock stars Cookie loved and practically worshipped. Cookie and her tribe still believed becoming famous was a way to get out of Yonkers. Now it was as if becoming famous could be a short-lived fling with tragedy, instead of suffering from the long and drawn-out death by living in a place that would not allow you to become who you were meant to be. Jim Morrison was only twenty-seven when he died, the same age as Janis Joplin, Jimi Hendrix and the *Blind Owl* Alan Wilson. And while it wasn't clear that Jim Morrison had overdosed on drugs, and the official cause of death was described as heart failure, one thing was for certain: the '27 club' had been born. Cookie didn't want to love another rock star, or even like one. Every one she liked died young, foolishly and alone.

Ludes became a passing fancy that both Reenie and Cookie had given up. Cookie quit selling them, and Reenie quit taking them. One day in August, the girls made pot brownies in the basement kitchen of Toni Ferlinghetti's house. Cookie and Reenie baited Toni to invite them over and brought a nickel bag of reedy, low-quality pot, full of stems and seeds. The girls took the entire bag and mixed it into a *Duncan Hines Brownie Mix* and baked the batch in an old white porcelain gas stove that was in Toni's basement. Cookie had to light a match to ignite gas. She didn't know gas stoves too well and thought they were unpredictable. She was wary of them. Everyone in Yonkers knew of someone who had died by leaving the gas on for heat at night through the long, cold winter. Keeping a gas stove on all night was a cheap way to heat a home, especially if home was a rundown tenement flat with a walkup, no elevators, no front yard and a back stoop.

Even though it was Toni's house and her oven, she claimed she didn't know how to work it. Cookie twisted the black knob, but it seemed to be stuck. She prodded it to the right with all of her might, and finally it clicked on and everyone could instantly smell the gas. Cookie flicked the match and it went out. Then she struck another and another. The flint patch on the side of the matchbox was worn to shreds. She tried to find a place to strike. Finally, success and a small flame sparked. She held it down to the pilot light in the oven. Immediately there was a loud explosion and a huge fire blew up inside the oven. Flames leapt out of the open door and singed the wispy ends of Cookie's ponytail, which had fallen to the front and across her chest. That was how the girls got their first and only batch of pot brownies into the oven. Full of stems and seeds, the brownies tasted so bad that Reenie and Cookie spat out the first bite and left the whole batch with Toni to do whatever she wanted to do with the worst pot brownies in the world.

In those days, no one called pot *weed*. It was always called *pot* or *grass;* sometimes it was called *dope*. Cookie and Reenie smoked it four times a day: in the morning before school, during lunch break, right after school, then late at night after dinner, Cookie and Reenie would go to Untermyer Park or *Down the End* and smoke again.

Eventually, Cookie stopped smoking pot. She felt like it messed with her memory, and the words she scribbled in her black & white notebooks lost crisp precision and took on a scattered, halting, barely discernible meaning. Soon Cookie and Reenie stopped getting into trouble and headed home early in time for dinner. Everyone in the North End had supper before 6 p.m.

Cookie did go to another school. Mabel Kerry knew Sister Mary Claire, who was the principal of Blessed Sacrament Academy, and made a formal introduction. At first Cookie was resistant to the prospect of going to another Catholic school, especially an all-girl school, where the Sacramentine nuns were cloistered and needed to get permission from the Pope just to leave the convent. Johnny gave her a choice- BSA, also known as Bullshit Academy, or a truancy school for juvenile delinquents in Tuxedo Park. By this time, Cookie had become smitten with the radical activist group, the Weathermen, and threatened to blow up the boarding school. BSA became the only recourse. Sister Mary Claire surprised Cookie by kneeling before her, and saying, *I'm your servant. I'm here on this earth to serve you.* Cookie was impressed that the nun seemed to know her place in the world, and this one act alone quelled Cookie's natural tendency to be overly rebellious. Despite her trauma with Fangs, not all nuns were bad.

Mr. Giorgio DeSutter became Herman's music teacher and took him under his wing as his mentor. He thought Herman would benefit by taking dance lessons in the city, and soon Herman was honing his talent. It was as if Mr. DeSutter had taken a hammer and a chisel to a hunk of stone to create a genuine work of art. Yonkers could be that way. Cookie thought, there were angels along the way, who came into our lives for a short burst of time. You never know for sure who these people are or where their journey began, and where it will end, but when you least expect it, these people magically show up and touch your life in a way you had never imagined.

Everywhere Cookie went with Herman or Reenie, she felt a presence. There would be a car parked on the side of the road with the driver checking the rearview mirror and automatically, they knew who it was. They had the protection of Louie Santamassino. It was kind of like having a weird uncle as a guardian angel.

Cookie began hatching her escape plan to get out of Yonkers and took Reenie with her. She was so excited and proud of herself for finding a way out of a place with the funny-sounding name of Yonkers. She started by frequently traveling to Manhattan and the two of them thought nothing of skipping school for the day to get there. Taking the Broadway IRT, now renamed the Number One train, which traveled from the Bronx and coursed through Harlem, it dropped them off on the west side of Manhattan. While she was on the subway, Cookie tried to write in her black & white composition book. In the morning, the subway car was full of the incredibly smart Jewish kids wearing yarmulkes, ear locks as soft and as tender as tendrils on young plants and somber black cassocks. They were getting off at the stop for the Bronx High School of Science. And then there were the gangsta boys who were drinking from liquor bottles that were hardly camouflaged in small brown paper sacks. The gangsta boys were not going to school.

She thought of the Rosners, with numbers from Auschwitz stamped on their arms, and the image of the dirty yellow brick Yonkers projects popped into her mind. There was no difference between Nazi concentration camps and *Slow Bomb*; one guaranteed quick extermination, and the other promised slow death.

Riding the subway kept Cookie and Reenie on edge. Sometimes Herman rode along with them. During those days, it was dangerous to ride the subway. It was long before the politicians cleaned up the city, and even longer before Manhattan was turned into a theme park, a *Disneyland* for rich people. Gangs patrolled the subways day and night looking for *honky motherfuckers* wearing jewelry and snatched gold chains from their necks.

There was an unspoken ballet of the ghetto, and it meant making all the right moves to show you were tough. Posturing, there were lots of things to track, moving parts to control. Cookie coached Reenie. Herman too. You had to project an attitude of *don't mess with me*, and wear a vicious sneer, a tight cocky grimace, and at the same time, never make eye contact. *Make eye contact out there and you're dead,* Cookie told Reenie and Herman. *You have to look straight ahead,* Reenie said. Look neither right nor left, as if you're looking right through people and seeing what was behind them. And all of this time, you never slow down. *You keep moving. No matter what, you have to keep moving,* Herman added.

Cookie thought she had learned something about the heart of prejudice, but she wasn't sure yet. She had to take time and wait over the long term to look at the big picture. You might be scared of someone who didn't look like you, but if you made friends with someone who was different, came to like them or even love them, all of the differences melted away. She thought back to her kindergarten class. Mrs. Kerry had touched her, and Cookie had indeed turned black. *That's my story, and I'm sticking to it,* Cookie thought. Trying to write in her notebook took effort. Cookie's hand bounced and her cartridge pen skipped across the page and left tear-shaped blobs of ink, some oblong, others as round as black pearls. Cookie always found it hard to write in her notebook while she was jostled around on the subway, but she didn't quit.

Allow me to introduce myself. My name is Concetta Mary Colangelo, but everyone calls me 'Cookie.' I dropped the 'Bernadette' because I'm not ever going to be a saint. I'm bad, I'm really bad and I like it that way. I've got gumption and I'm full of courage. I'm going to stand up for myself, no matter what. If I could do just one thing in this world, I would do something that touches another human being. I have no choice, but to be who I am.

End Notes

Cookie Colangelo left Yonkers at seventeen and never looked back.

Herman Lynch won a full scholarship with the Alvin Ailey Dance Theater and became a professional dancer.

Arky Lovato is a gypsy cab driver who picks up passengers from the Metro North train station at Larkin Plaza in Yonkers.

Reenie Ruggiero became an attorney with the ACLU.

Lizzie Lovato became a Paleontologist on staff at the American Museum of Natural History in New York City.

Mike Trapani is a local politician in New Jersey.

Tommy Parrello became a teamster.

Toni Ferlinghetti married a New York City cop.

Fran Ochiogrosso retired and moved to Florida.

Mr. DC was fired from his post as principal at a public school in Rockland County for impregnating a sixteen-year-old girl. At the time, he was married and had three children.

Johnny Colangelo died in the 1990s. It wasn't until many years later at Johnny Colangelo's funeral that Cookie had an understanding for the depth of her father's courage. A man came to the funeral to pay his respects and to express gratitude. In the winter of 1950 on the battlefield of Korea, Johnny Colangelo had saved his life.

Kitty Colangelo became a floral designer and worked in a florist shop for ten years. She and Johnny never divorced.

Donny Colangelo became a research physician specializing in infectious diseases.

Mabel Kerry worked at the Yonkers Carnegie Library until she retired in 1978.

In 1982, the city of Yonkers razed the **Yonkers Carnegie Library** and terminated the bookmobile service.

Christ the King Elementary School was closed in 2010, and the building is currently being leased as an annex by Yonkers Public School #16.

Around 2005, Untermyer Park underwent a revitalization and renovation effort, restoring its architecture and gardens to their original grandeur.

About the Author

Patricia Vaccarino is originally from Yonkers, New York. After college, she traveled across the country in a battered Chevy Impala on I-40 and up the California coast on Pacific Highway 101 to "see America" and landed in Seattle, where she worked as a paralegal in antitrust law, and later went to law school. She began writing professionally—articles, copy, scripts, and press releases and was asked by a film production company, Kaye Smith Productions (founded by Seattle businessman Lester Smith and Hollywood celebrity Danny Kaye), to do their Public Relations outreach—that was her start in P.R. Patricia Vaccarino owns Xanthus Communications, a national P.R. firm, and the media company, PR for People®, where people share their news with the world. Patricia Vaccarino has written award-winning film scripts, press materials, content, books, essays and articles.